A Personal History of Thirst

JOHN

BURDETT

WILLIAM MORROW AND
COMPANY, INC. NEW YORK

A PERSONAL

HISTORY OF

THIRST

It is the policy of William Morrow and Company, Inc., and its imprints and affiliates, recognizing the importance of preserving what has been written, to print the books we publish on acid-free paper, and we exert our best efforts to that end.

Library of Congress Cataloging-in-Publication Data
Burdett, John
   A personal history of thirst / John Burdett—1st ed.
   p.cm
   ISBN 0-688-14399-7
   I. Title
PR6052.U617P47   1996
823'.914—dc20   95-38113
                                                             CIP

Printed in the United States of America

First Edition

1 2 3 4 5 6 7 8 9 10

BOOK DESIGN BY CAROLINE CUNNINGHAM

For Laura

Author's Note

The bar of England and Wales being a relatively small profession, it is important to emphasize that this is a work of fiction and that every character portrayed herein is fictional. For the record, in fourteen years of busy legal practice I did not knowingly come across a dishonest barrister, solicitor or policeman.

ACKNOWLEDGMENTS

Without the great patience and resourcefulness of Sam Vaughan this book would never have seen the light of day. Without the friendship and persistence of Alison Whyte it would never have reached Sam Vaughan. My eternal thanks to both of them.

Ruled by no laws of logic, indifferent to the demands of expediency, unconstrained by the existence of external reality, the id is ruled by what Freud called the primary process directly expressing somatically generated instincts.

THE NEW ENCYCLOPAEDIA BRITANNICA

A Personal

History of

Thirst

PROLOGUE

The thief liked to walk around the back streets of Knightsbridge late at night. It gave him a vicarious feeling of wealth and security. Other places and other people aspired; here, ever since anyone could remember, dwelt the people who had arrived or had been born, so to speak, in a state of arrival. He had nothing against them, no political ax to grind, having long since passed through that stage. These days his sense of social order was almost Hindu: they belonged to the wealth-owning caste just as he belonged, when the whole story of his life was told, to the caste of thieves. If it was a system without salvation, it was also a system of fixed identities: No one was obliged to be upwardly mobile, with all the agony that entailed.

He loved big windows, high ceilings, the wealth of generous spaces. It untied a knot in his guts to walk around Montpelier Gardens, or Beauchamp Place, or Egerton Terrace, at one or two o'clock on a Saturday morning, looking up into flats still lit, glimpsing the luxury within, speculating on the relationships that required illumination at such an hour. Somehow he doubted that anyone was solitary in that area at that time; he knew those parts of London where solitude and misery were endemic, which was one reason why he came to Knightsbridge, where he was sure they were not.

He was a professional. He stood in an ancient perpetual relationship to those who put up bars and set alarms against him. He was part of them. Though they might disown him by day, by night he was an archetype of their dreams, a staple of their conversation, a provision in their annual budgets. He added the light, chill brush of risk to their walks around the block at night. His was the shadow that forced them to walk faster, his the footsteps in the alley, the eyes gazing from a dark corner. Though they would never admit it and were hardly aware of it, he was their last hold on poetry, the last segment of the unknown that was not susceptible to control, the last factor that saved them from the fate of the bland.

He was a specialist—a curiously modern phenomenon: a connoisseur of the art of the joyride, who had studied his subject in depth. He read manuals for the latest cars and, though not of a scientific inclination, studied the circuits of alarm systems. And he was cool. Despite the bad nerves that tormented him at other times, on a job he possessed a glacial control. He needed it, for he never picked the kind of nondescript vehicle that cannot be distinguished from the ten thousand others of its kind. His forte was the elegant, the luxurious, the exotic car most other thieves dared not touch because they would be recognized by police within minutes of the calls going out to radio cars and motorcycles. He stalked a chosen car, kept records sometimes for weeks of the comings and goings of its owner. It was a time-consuming system, but it worked. So far he had never been caught.

Outside Grosvenor Mansions, for example, a Porsche 944S2 the color of a chile pepper appeared at about midnight on a Friday. The owner looked to be a professional in his early forties, a doctor or a dentist. Not a lawyer. The thief knew lawyers and doubted that a lawyer of that age could still be so eager, naive almost. A doctor perhaps, who had spent his youth struggling and studying, had married the wrong woman too early and now felt cheated. Probably it was the feeling of being cheated that made him believe he was justified in deceiving his wife. Did he still live with her? Did he tell her he was out on a call every Friday night? The Porsche, too, would be something the doctor felt life owed him. The thief could understand that. And the girl? Younger, certainly, but not very much younger. The look on the doctor's face was intelligent as well as passionate, discerning as well as eager. Not a man to fall for just a child or a terrific body. The thief envied him the freshness of his passion and decided to steal the Porsche.

He waited under an archway while a light went on, on the third floor. In the gloom of the London evening the couple were illuminated for a moment, she standing motionless, he walking toward her, hands aimed at her waist. Then the woman remembered and released a blind. Cut off from their intimacy, the thief smiled. Theirs was not the kind of tryst that has drinks first. Perhaps five minutes for "How was your day?," another five to undress, ten to fifteen for foreplay; the doctor looked like a man who would take pride in his foreplay.

The thief looked at his watch. The doctor was surely a romantic. Even if the car alarm did go off, what could he do about it—dash downstairs in his underwear? She would never forgive him—for she must be a romantic, too, waiting up until twelve every Friday night when she could have been at a party, or with an unattached man. She must never be allowed to say, "Your Porsche is more important to you than I am." He crossed the road to the low fast car. There was something wrong with him, he knew, that he felt more a part of the lives of those two people, for whom he was less than a shadow, than of his own life. But he was too busy now to think about that.

He expected the Porsche to be a challenge: perhaps a sophisticated alarm trigger using microwave and ultraviolet, with a central locking system. But there's not much room under the hood of the Porsche 944 for the alarm unit, only one place, in fact, to put it, and the thief knew where that would be. A simple task to open the hood, gently so as not to activate the sensors, then cut the lead to the battery. There was an optional backup battery system, but most people didn't bother to have it installed. If the doctor had bothered and the alarm went off, the thief would run.

But the thief was lucky. As he passed by the door on the driver's side, he noticed that the doctor in his haste had only half locked it. It was caught on the first catch but not the second. The alarm could not have been armed.

From his pocket he took a skeleton key, moved it expertly in the door, and, forty-five seconds later, opened it. The same key would work for the ignition. The thief was excited now, excited yet cool. The cool side of his brain clamped over the hot excited side, giving him a feeling of intense controlled energy such as athletes and addicts know. He held his breath, counted to five, slipped the key into the ignition, jiggled it so that its imperfect shape caught the levers and the engine fired. Seconds later he put the car in gear, eased slowly out of the parking spot, slipped into second gear at the corner, and sped off.

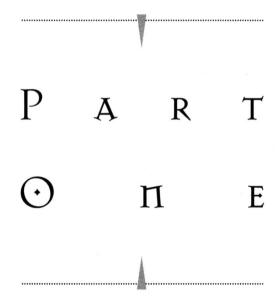

PART

ONE

I

The Sunday after Oliver Thirst died, two policemen came to see me at my house in Hampstead. I knew them both well. They were too senior to be making routine calls, and theirs could not be a social visit. I concluded that they intended to charge me with murder and made arrangements accordingly.

George Holmes, the older of the two, had telephoned earlier in the morning to ask in his most diffident voice if it would be convenient to come by. He sounded tired; I remembered that he was due to retire that year. I had known him in his younger days, when he seemed to have the energy of ten men; now, evidently, the burden of countless crimes had exhausted even his great strength. The other, Vincent Purves, I didn't know so well, but I'd spent a decade in more or less the same line of business, so that he, too, had become familiar to me. I knew their quirks, their weaknesses, the nature of the talent that had propelled them ever forward in their careers.

I knew, for example, how sly George could be and was a little nervous in consequence.

Through a window I watched them drive up and down my street a couple of times looking for a place to park, although they seemed to keep missing one in front of the building immediately opposite. Eventually George found a spot to the liking of his dented and dirty old Rover. Vincent, still slim and wiry at fifty, was the first out. George took his time, dipping his head back in to reach for his trilby and tobacco. I remembered that he was equally deliberate and unhurried in the witness box. His brown leather brogues crunched up the short yard to my house, and I was there to open the door as he rang the bell.

"Told you, no chance with this bloke." George pushed the trilby back on his head. "He's always ten steps ahead."

"That right?" Vincent said.

"Not half. The number of times he cut me up in the witness box in the old days, after ten minutes I didn't know if I was the co-accused or the tea lady. How are you, James, my lad—can I still call you that? It's good to see you."

We exchanged handshakes and smiles as I showed them into the study that I had made grand by knocking down a wall between two rooms. George whistled.

"Well, well, you have come a long way since Billericay Magistrates Court."

There was an expensive van Gogh copy by an ex-convict who had become famous, some leather furniture, an antique desk I was proud of . . . but I doubted that these items had the power to impress George, any more than the litter of documents and open books. As usual, it was a working Sunday for me. I turned off the desktop computer, watched the screen die.

"Drink, chaps? Scotch, beer, cognac, sherry?"

George nudged Vincent. "Clever, eh? Very subtle. He wants to find out if we're on duty or not." George winked at me. "I'd say that in the circumstances, Vincent, you're more or less bound to have a drink—otherwise you'll give the game away."

"No, no, I won't, thanks all the same."

George settled for a stiff Scotch and water. I poured myself a large Armagnac and watched them over the rim of the glass. Suddenly the words were out.

"Actually, I'm glad you chaps showed up. I want to confess to the murder of Oliver Thirst."

Vincent blinked, and a face George normally kept hidden was suddenly glaring at me. It was an ugly face. He recovered himself in seconds and started fumbling in his pocket.

"What's up, George?" I asked.

"Bugger."

He fumbled some more. "Forgot to bring any handcuffs—you bring any handcuffs, Vincent?"

Vincent looked sickened and refused to play.

"That's it, then. Can't arrest you, old son, no handcuffs. But tell us, how did you kill Oliver Thirst?"

"Slowly, every day for the past eleven years."

George's body sagged with relief.

I said: "I'm sorry, I shouldn't have done that. I know you're here to ask me about Thirst, you're only doing your jobs—I do appreciate that it's you chaps I have to deal with and not some smart-arsed kid trying to score points—but the memory is still painful to me. Very painful. Anyway, after George rang me this morning I prepared a short written statement. I calculated the approximate time of death from the newspaper reports, and you'll find appended to the statement the full names, addresses, telephone numbers, of all the people I was with during the relevant period. There's one name I haven't written down, because it's confidential. During the latter part of the evening I was with an ex-client who wanted to complain about a lifelong relationship of manipulation and corruption with a senior police officer. Naturally I advised him to go to the Complaints Against Police unit. I've had a copy of my statement sent by post to my solicitor."

I took two copies of typed script from the desk, slipped them into clear plastic folders, and gave them one each.

George avoided my eyes as I handed it over. "Mind if I read it now?"

I shrugged. He carefully took out a pair of spectacles and started to read. Concentration and the spectacles made him look grim.

"'First met Thirst fifteenth June 1976 at Tower Bridge Magistrates Court,'" he read out, then fell into silence.

To me the dry data contained in that single sentence was as evocative as incense; from it expanded an overpowering perfume as if my thin script had been one of those trick greeting cards you rub until they release some fragrant odor. There floated past me a hot morning when I crossed the Thames from north to south on that famous bridge, my heart singing because I was off to my fifth court appearance in one week.

Tower Bridge is an ancient tribunal, the underground cells genuine dungeons carved out of rock and enclosed with steel bars. He was sitting reading *The Guinness Book of Records* and didn't bother to look up when the sergeant on duty unlocked the gaol door to let me in.

"Your barrister's here, Oliver," said the sergeant, who seemed to know him.

Still he did not look up. "'The largest object stolen by a single person was the SS *Orient Trader,* a 10,640-ton ship. Stolen by N. William Kennedy armed with only a sharp ax. On fifth June 1966,'" he read. His accent was a gruff, unadulterated cockney. Finally he raised his head, stared into my eyes for a long contemplative moment.

His was an unforgettable face: beautiful, naive, crooked, electric with anger. A criminal's face: the innocence and the guile remained quarantined from each other, either one likely to take over from one minute to the next.

"That's what I call taking and driving away. Can't compete with that," he said at last.

"I thought you were pleading 'not guilty,'" I said.

He pretended to think about it. "Oh yeah, I forgot." His features distorted for a moment, for some unfathomable reason. Then he smiled.

My account was exactly two pages long, but George took seven minutes to read it. He must have memorized every word. Vincent had long finished by the time he looked up.

He took off his glasses, folded them carefully, put them back in their sheath.

"Looks watertight, James. Very professional."

"You realize I couldn't afford . . ."

"Course not, old son. Man in your position, you've got to take preemptive action when the likes of us come visiting. Everyone will understand—everyone."

"It's just that I'm taking silk this year, if all goes well."

George let his mouth hang open. "You hear that, Vince? We're practically in the presence of royalty."

"Don't, George," Vincent said.

George ignored him. "D'you know what 'taking silk' means, Vince?"

"Course I know. Means he'll be a Q.C. and get to wear a silk gown."

"No, but do you *really* know?" George narrowed his eyes. "Queen's Counsel are barristers so masterful and of such unimpeachable integrity that they're qualified to advise Her Majesty herself on all matters pertaining to the laws of Great Britain." He looked at me, eyebrows raised.

"That was true a hundred and fifty years ago," I said. "Nowadays Her Majesty tends to prefer slick solicitors and two-hundred-pound-an-hour public relations consultants. Q.C.'s take whatever work they can get, just like everyone else."

George shook his head. "The top of the greasy pole, king of the heap, eh? Well, well! Now I understand. It's not just a question of being clean—you've got to smell of roses, old son."

He handed back the transparent cover, folded the statement carefully into quarters, and slid it into a pocket. He fumbled for his pipe, asked me with his eyes if I objected, proceeded to scrape and stuff.

"No missus, I take it?"

I shook my head.

"Long time to be carrying a torch, isn't it?"

"I've been busy, George—you know that. It's difficult to go courting when you work till eleven every night and all day Sunday."

"Must be. I wouldn't know. I married two weeks after I finished training at the old police cadet school in Hendon. It was a different city then, of course. I lived on my own beat and had all the time in the world—went home for lunch and tea breaks. Kept an eye on my two girls in the school playground."

He paused in his musings, as if suddenly catching on to something.

"I remember the day you changed sides, James. The best example of poacher turned gamekeeper I ever saw. I flatter myself that I had something to do with it during our little chat on a train to Sheffield—remember? Within weeks, it seems to me, you were gaoling the same hard cases you'd spent your career defending. Very understandable in the circumstances. Every detective inspector with a weak case wanted to have you instructed. There was a notice up in the D.P.P.'s office: James Knight bites legs. You had quite a following in the force after you adopted the lonely life of a prosecutor. The very blokes who'd been after your guts fell head over heels in love with you. And there were all those cases you did for me. I daresay you did get busy."

I nodded. "It's still there—the note, I mean. I had to see the director the other day, and she showed it to me."

George jerked his chin at Vincent. "See, every time he speaks he reveals how far he's come. Nowadays he just walks straight into the office of the Director of Public Prosecutions and she grovels." His smile was tobacco-stained. "You must be right proud, James."

"No, George—that's what I was about to say. Only madmen are proud of putting people in jail—even though it has to be done."

He lit his pipe with a solid-gold lighter I remembered because it seemed so out of character, then began delving in his pocket. "Well, back to the case in hand and just to make sure we're talking about the same bloke..."

A clumsy cue from a subtle man. Was George losing his touch? I took the slim pack of color photographs he handed to me. How could we not be talking about the same bloke?

His eyes studied me while I examined the pictures. If he entertained the old-fashioned notion that the sight of the victim would unnerve the culprit, I must have passed the test with distinction. After the first corpse, nothing is more ordinary than death.

In the pictures, a man no longer young, with features no longer capable of expressing anger, lay with a small neat hole in his forehead. If I was surprised at all, it was at how harmless he looked. The pictures showed the same scene from different angles. Some revealed that the body lay in a London street. A wide-angled version took in a shocked passerby and one quarter of a Ford Cortina. After a quick glance, I placed each one at the back of the pack.

Only the last was of a living person. The sound I uttered—I think something between a sob and a gasp—seemed to me to have come from someone else. I handed the pictures back and took a long swallow of brandy.

"Sorry, old son," George murmured.

I turned to see Vincent scribbling something in his notebook.

"Sit down," George said. I found myself obeying. "You're a sensitive man. Highly strung, brilliant even. A spell inside that would just be a drag for the likes of the late Oliver Thirst, for James Knight would be torture. I want to be kind, but I need some answers. And if it wasn't us it would be someone else—you know that."

"What do you want to know?"

He relit his pipe with the gold lighter, eyed it fondly for a second before replacing it in his pocket.

"It's a funny thing with your high achievers. I once knew a boxer—amateur flyweight champion—could hardly say boo to a goose out of the ring. Everything he had went into his boxing. Inside the ring he was a wicked machine. Could have turned pro, but his wife wouldn't let him. Then the minute he gave up boxing, she went off with another bloke. Great men have great weaknesses, James. Tell me about the Yank."

"There's nothing to tell, I've not seen her for over a decade. You must know that—I'm sure you've spoken to her."

"But never an hour passes . . . ?"

"I haven't thought of her in years."

He looked relieved.

"I'm not going to say any more, George. You'll have to do it properly, or not at all."

"It's my guess that you must hate her guts—when you think about her, I mean."

"No comment."

Vincent, whose bladder had always been conveniently weak, asked where the bathroom was. George took the pipe out of his mouth and stared at me long and hard. I felt awkward, and I suppose he did, too, as if our power to speak had been inexplicably cut off.

"Want to see the garden?"

"Good idea," he said.

Vincent was diplomatically long in the bathroom. I led George out of the study and down the hall to the kitchen, past the pile of dirty plates and mugs waiting to be washed, a couple of empty wine bottles.

The back garden was the length Edwardians thought necessary for privacy and the proper exercise of children: about seventy feet. Too many when you had no interest in gardening. I had put in a rock pool with goldfish near the house, and left the rest to run wild.

"Never figured you for a goldfish man," George said.

"Actually, I'm not. I'm a wildcat man. A big tom that runs wild on the Heath comes along every now and then and eats them. Sometimes I watch. I think of the pond as his larder. I replenish it once a month."

It was one of my standard gambits, intended to amuse or shock, depending on the guest. George simply nodded absently. Once again we found ourselves staring at each other as if struck dumb.

Vincent reappeared.

"Ready to go, George?"

A somber nod. "Ready when you are."

George paused at the front door to put on his trilby. In the parking place that he could have taken was a battered van of the commercial, windowless variety. I suppose my eyes rested on it for a moment longer than was natural.

"You haven't changed, James. You know, there's something I've always admired about you blokes, and it's not your cleverness. Prisons are full of clever people who weren't clever enough when it came down to it. It's detail. Your amazing capacity for detail. I'd hate to see that wasted. If there's anything I can do, anything at all . . ."

"Actually—yes. I seem to have lo-lo-lo-" A childhood stammer, the very defect I had cured by choice of profession and unrelenting will, had suddenly returned. I tried again. "I seem to have lo-lo-lost all the photographs of her." I looked away, avoiding his eyes.

He fished out the thin pack of photographs and took the last one off the back.

"If you promise not to kill her, I'll give you her phone number."

"I promise."

He scribbled a number on the back of the picture and handed it to me.

"I'd be interested in anything she has to say."

"You don't think I'm going to . . . ?"

He raised a finger. "You need time to think it over. You've spent half your life building a career, you're taking silk this year. We don't want anything to interfere with that."

I took the photograph and watched George crunch back down my little path. There was no skip of victory in him. He seemed suddenly tired again.

Vincent carefully closed the gate behind them.

2

I had not, of course, lost any photographs. I had destroyed them, for what I considered at the time to be reasons of mental health. And now, like an addict, I had sold my pride for the chance once more to be sick.

It was not a good photograph, although it was a startling one. I guessed that it had been taken with a powerful telephoto lens from some invisible hideout. Photographers sensitive to the finer points of portraiture tend not to find themselves on the payroll of the Metropolitan Police. But it was enough. As I gazed greedily at it, I felt the resolution of years start to crumble. The gray barricade of files, documents, feverish hard work, cynical humor, melted as if the sun itself had turned a corner and was marching relentlessly back toward me. I poured myself another Armagnac, lifted the phone, dialed the number George Holmes had given me.

Over the telephone lines, that voice tantalized like a song from a distant shore. I knew it so well I could place the origin of every vowel and consonant as if I had been responsible for teaching her the language, which in a way I had. It took an expert—or a lover— to recognize the washed-out tones of New England.

"The police came," I said. "I suppose they've already spoken to you?"

"Mm. Yesterday. It's been a long time, James."

"Eleven years, five months, and a few days."

"You shouldn't have phoned—they'll be expecting us to talk. They could hurt you. You're a big man now."

"I'm also a suspect."

She laughed at such absurdity. And when I asked her if she wouldn't like to come round and talk about it, she agreed in her friendly American way, forgetting immediately that I was a big man who could be hurt. We talked around his death for a few minutes; the last thing she said was, "I keep remembering that night you came home and told me about him. It all started then."

My training in pedantry protested into the silence that this was not quite accurate. It had all started a number of hours earlier, when, after I had won his case for him, he invited me for a drink. This was theoretically against the rules: a barrister did not, in those days, meet with a criminal client unless in the presence of a solicitor. But there was even then a compulsion about him that would not be denied, and a weakness in me that had to do with that beautiful summer's morning and what was left of my youth. It had to do with her, too, in an oblique way. Then, as now, conventional success in my profession generated zero sex appeal. The fight for love and glory required a little cheating and a little protesting, or so it seemed to me.

We happened to be in an historic area crowded with pubs boasting unique views over the Thames and American professors searching for the site of the bench where Shakespeare last sat, but it would not have occurred to him to take me to one of them. "Having a drink" to him meant standing at the bar in some grim hole south of the river where the ashtrays are not heavy enough to be turned into weapons and there are few tables and chairs and the windows are dim with crime. I accepted a pint of flat beer, knowing that I should not have been there and waiting for the moment to break. He avoided my eyes, which enabled me to study his face: a strong jaw, an aquiline nose, and pale skin on which the grayness of incarceration still hung.

He took a long draught of beer and began his summation of the morning's events, as he began most sentences, with "Yeah."

"Yeah, you did me grand, James. I ain't saying you didn't. Gave the Old Bill some real stick—went white when you asked all that about his notebook."

"Old Bill?"

He stared at me. "You know what that means. Cops. Fuzz. Rozers. Old Bill."

"Yes," I said, "I know what it means. It's been a while since I last heard it." I smiled.

"But while I was watching you and listening, do you know what I was thinking? I was thinking I could have done that—I could have been up there where you are—if I'd only had the chance."

It was a version of the I'm-as-good-as-you-are mind-set, except that in his case he seemed convinced that by some grotesque accident he was living the wrong life. As if he was, in his own way, like those people who claim to have been born into the wrong sex and eventually undergo drastic surgery.

It was on the point of leaving him that I took the step, like a blind man walking along a cliff edge, which secured my fate. In an absurd moment of weakness I said, "We must meet again," and immediately averted my eyes from the terrifying gratitude that filled his face.

After George and Vincent had driven away, and I had watched the commercial vehicle slink off a quarter of an hour later, I climbed the stairs to my bedroom, holding the lumbar region of my back with the palms of both hands. It was an old injury, which always made me think of Thirst. When I was nervous or exhausted, it ached most.

In the bedroom, I kept my private library. It had started off with the *Golden Treasury of English Verse* that my mother won as a school prize at her orphanage, and a small glass-and-walnut bookcase of obscure eighteenth-century origin. Now there were three walls of books that I'm proud to say had nothing to do with law. My mother died when I was in my early teens, and the collection began as a kind of guilt reflex. Having had a boy's contempt for her books of poetry, after she died I started by forcing myself to read it, and by the time I was twenty I had become addicted. My lawyer's mind, when it failed to create a compelling phrase of its own, would call one up from a past master. On the whole, judges and juries enjoyed this quirk, although friends sometimes found it pretentious. It marked me out as an eccentric, a cross I bore cheerfully for the sake of a mother who had not lived long enough to disillusion me.

I stroked the bookcase. "Daisy," I said.

Ever since my mother died there have been only two kinds of women for me: those worthy of undying faithfulness—and the rest. It's a poor thing, I can report, to be a living cliché out of Freud and Jung.

When the doorbell sounded for the second time on that eventful Sunday, it was as if a clock that had stopped eleven years earlier had restarted. I ran to the door, overjoyed that one man had died and I was a fool again.

3

Her entrance was all grace and irony.

It would not be true to say that she looked as young as ever (she was at an age when women's bodies and faces change), but she stepped as lightly as ever, as if she intended to proceed through life with no more baggage than she was born with. Her hair was the same unmanageable blond, her wit as wicked. The ponderous edifice of wealth, eminence, and ego I trundled about with me lasted no longer than half an hour in her presence. She delved into her selection of New York voices to make some joke—hilarious at the time, impossible to recall—about my van Gogh reproduction, which I caught in a delayed way because I was opening a bottle of wine. When its meaning hit me, I had to lean against the fridge to avoid spilling the wine while my poor thin body shook with laughter and relief. By the time she saw what she had done, tears were streaming down my face and she had to brush them away, just as softly as I remembered.

I said: "I'd forgotten how good you are with accents."

"I used to have an American one, darling—surely you remember?"

"Never Bronx, though. Say tomato."

"T'maydoe der you, bud."

There's nothing like an old joke to test for vital signs in an equally old relationship. I laughed, she smiled warmly.

It was my best wine, a Chassagne-Montrachet I knew she would love, for all her principles. We got through it nibbling cheese and talking about everything except what had brought us together again. She still taught English at a polytechnic, still believed passionately in unilateral nuclear disarmament. Still kept up with the latest trends in feminism and hated the police.

"Were they hard on you?"

"Harder than they were on you, I bet. They managed to make me feel like a whore, a murder suspect, and a gangster's groupie in the space of about ten minutes. They make you feel dirty, don't they? As if you have no privacy, after all."

With her eyes she challenged me to agree.

"They're only doing their job—I know, I know, like Eichmann. Let's not get into that."

Old programming had made me steel myself for a fight, but she let it go with a shrug and a smile.

"Do you still have all those Hitchcock videos?"

The second Montrachet disappeared while we watched *Rear Window*. By the time it finished, an evening chill had forced us to snuggle up close.

"Are we going to talk about it?"

"Not yet, James—let's not."

I coughed. "You haven't seen the rest of the house."

I held my breath. She smiled wryly but allowed me to take her hand and lead her to the stairs. It seemed the most natural thing in the world to take her into my bedroom as if eleven years had been telescoped into five minutes. She stood by the window looking out on the street, her back to me. I buried my lips in her neck.

"I'm in shock, James—you know?"

"Yes, I know. That's why you came round, and that's why we drank so much, and that's why we're doing this now. It's natural."

"*Are* we doing this now?"

"You mean, is this really happening? You feel realer than anything else in my world."

"Do I? Realer than law?"

"Much."

"Realer than God?"

"I'd trade him for you anytime."

"Realer than your career?"

I sighed. "I'm actually rather tired of my career."

She held my wrists. "Oh, James! This isn't right. Not tonight."

"You want me to stop?"

For a moment her body froze, then she relaxed backward into my arms.

"Your neighbors will see."

I said: "So draw the curtains."

She did so, then turned, her shirt gaping where I had opened it. She put her arms around my neck.

"I'll stop if you tell me to," I whispered.

"Stop."

"I can't."

She smiled, closed her eyes, leaned her head back. "Your hands are shaking."

"It's been so long. Touching you there makes me tremble."

"You don't have to explain."

"Do you really want me to stop?"

She groaned. "Not now."

Afterward, as I played with her ear, I said, "You know, I did the strangest thing when they were here—I confessed."

Her body tautened, as if she was thinking fast.

"What did you say?"

"I told them I murdered him."

She raised her head until the cords in her neck strained. "You what?"

"I couldn't resist. I was sure they weren't serious about suspecting me, but I wanted to provoke them."

"They didn't take you seriously?"

"No. I turned it into a joke—said I'd murdered him in my imagination every day for the past eleven years. They seemed relieved. But they were wired, I'm sure. When George Holmes drove up, he was careful to leave a space for an unmarked radio van, which means a couple of operators recording my interview. I don't really know what they were up to."

"But why on earth did you say that? Why?"

I licked a nipple casually. "I really don't know. Bravado. It doesn't matter; they're not about to charge me."

"You're sure?"

"Oh yes, quite sure."

"How are you sure?"

"I know George Holmes. He's not going to charge me."

She let her head fall back to the pillow. She lay thinking for a moment, then turned to lay her cheek on my chest.

"When I was coming here I did think about—you know—if we would be lovers again."

"And?"

She sniggered. "I decided I wouldn't let you. Unless you could make me want you as intensely as before."

She fell asleep in my arms, and I must have dozed off soon afterward. Hours later I was awakened by a shuddering, it seemed, in the middle of the night. Her hands were over my eyes, and I thought she was trying to blind me until I realized she was trying to wake me in some desperate way. She clung to me and gave huge, loud, inelegant sobs on my chest. As if the nightmare had jolted her back to some earlier personality, her accent was suddenly Connecticut again, with a dash of New York.

"Oh Jesus, James. Oh fuck. He's dead. He can't do any of this—he can't breathe, drink wine, screw. *He's a fucking dead man.*"

I wrestled with her until she was quiet. She looked at me with a kind of cowed resentment.

"You don't give a shit. Do you?"

4

It was class rage that propelled me to meet him the next time.

I had lost my first jury trial because Benjamin Franklin, my client, was black and the judge was a bigot. I was furious and frightened that in 1976 there were still men in positions of power in England whose humanity did not extend beyond the magic circle of white male public school Oxbridge graduates—my credentials would only get me past the first two hurdles. My political views had stuck somewhere in radical chic, and I professed a kind of sex-appeal socialism. I had also boasted to Daisy that I expected to get my client off.

He was all dreadlocks and marijuana, a compulsive burglar of limited skill who studied the Bible when he was not coveting other people's stereo systems. The only reason he accepted me as his counsel was the Rastafarian significance he found in my name: I was, he said, his White Knight. When Daisy heard that he was black, she thought of the black activist writers imprisoned in San Quentin and packed me off to work with a black power salute. Explaining my failure to her would entail a degree of outraged posturing, which I rehearsed to myself in a cab on the way back to chambers from court. For half an hour I was a world leader of indeterminate race, hailed by millions, tubercular with righteous indignation, adored by Daisy.

From this late-twentieth-century fantasy I emerged into the equally fantastic time warp that was headquarters for London's trial lawyers, or barristers. A few unique acres of seventeenth-century Thameside tenements, it was called the Temple for having once been the meeting place of the Knights Templar, a mysterious chivalric order of crusaders of which modern barristers are attenuated descendants, though it suited our style to retain the mystery, even to the point of being arcane. We called our offices "chambers," our office managers (who were mostly male) "clerks," our colleagues "members of chambers," and all members of chambers were "tenants," because we paid rent to the "Head of Chambers," who was usually a "silk" or Queen's Counsel, so called for his right to wear silk robes with elaborate cutaway sleeves about a yard long. When we worked in teams, the most senior was a "leader" and the other team members were "juniors." Work (which came to us only through solicitors) we called "instructions," and the formal request to appear in court was called a "brief." Quaint upon quaint, we maintained the gentlemanly fiction that we were not in it for the money. "Solicitors" were originally named by barristers for their contemptible trade of procuring clients on our behalf and arranging fees; not a task we would have contemplated undertaking for ourselves, our duty being to argue before the court for the fun of it, all the time wearing horsehair wigs that went out of vogue with Charles II.

Disdain for the criminal client was still *de rigueur* in 1976, and our self-imposed rules required that we never met with him unless his solicitor was also present, to prevent contamination. There was even a kind of ethics pornography: stories wherein the barrister hero escaped by the skin of his teeth from overfamiliar overtures from his gangster clients.

In the clerks' room I found a meeting of eighteenth-century gentlemen whose plump backsides had, so to speak, privilege branded all over them. They fell silent in the middle of a discussion as I entered, because I was not one of them. Roland Denson, a music hall aristocrat, lounged against the marble mantelpiece, fingering a gold chain that looped across the belly of his black cutaway waistcoat. A scene in the prefects room from *Tom Brown's School-days.* I glared at Denson, who glared back while resuming the debate in the teeth of my presence.

"But look here, when all's said and done, do we really want another outsider as a tenant—another of those chaps with a massive complex about having clawed his way up from the gutter?"

Denson had continued loudly while I edged into the room. In the silence that followed, most of my colleagues had the decency to avoid my eyes. The room waited for me to say something, but I was paralyzed with rage. The ability to deal with calculated rudeness was one of the many social skills I had never acquired.

"An outsider like me ..." I could not finish the sentence. The telephone rang, and our quick-witted clerk called out that it was for me. Normally he would have checked to make sure it was not a client telephoning a barrister directly.

"It is, sir, it is for you," the clerk said as I crossed the room to take the call. For a moment I thought the caller was speaking in a foreign language. Someone in the room said, "You pompous prick, Denson," and these words, delivered in an upper-middle-class accent, split my attention. Only a second later did I realize that the voice in my ear was speaking in cockney.

"Yes, Oliver, yes, of course I'll meet you," I said, as much to the room as to the telephone.

Half an hour later I left chambers with intent to commit a far graver sin against professionalism than having a drink with a client after a case. I had allowed a known criminal to telephone me at my chambers and agreed to meet him close by the hallowed precincts of the Temple, with no solicitor in sight.

I carried over my shoulder a purple bag containing my wig and gown, on which my initials had been embroidered in gold. I walked down Middle Temple Lane, past names of barristers that sprang from a tribe grown powerful, so the story ran, by colonizing my own—Pearson-Rhys, Sir Cecil Maffeking-Gray, Lord Cranthorpe, Mr. & Mrs. Oliver Coldstream-Hill—through cloistered walks and tended gardens, fountains and dahlias. Why, I wondered, had I chosen for myself a path down which unhappiness was guaranteed? However much I succeeded, I would never belong. The bar was still a club for the protection of aging public school boys fixed at the emotional age of thirteen and a half.

I turned right out of the Temple into Temple Place, where a dozen or so homeless men and women were waiting for the afternoon soup vans. In the summer heat the stench from their bodies was overpowering. It permeated the whole park, at the other end of which Thirst was sitting on a bench. My anger over the scene in chambers had abated during my short walk, and now that I had escaped from that room I no longer had any motive for meeting him.

"You must never again telephone me at chambers; it's against the rules," I said. "Nor can you ever again be my client—is that clear?"

He wore an ill-fitting suit of thick gray woolen material, a woolen tie badly knotted. The top button of his shirt was left undone, but he had combed his hair.

He stood up, and I saw that his right hand was bandaged.

"Had a bit of a knuckle," he said. "Some bloke in a pub accused me of being a grass, so I had to wallop him."

"Bit of a knuckle," "grass," "wallop"—it was a foreign language spoken by a different race who lived south of the river. If he'd simply said that he'd had a fight because someone had accused him of being a police informant, he would have disappointed me. With crime, as with so many things, the charm is in the packaging.

The bandage looked fresh. I could see the scene, a group of desperadoes in a pub, sour with alcohol, spitting insults. Thirst deciding, for the hell of it, to take umbrage. How hard had he hit him? Hospital?

"Did you? Grass?"

The bloody and oddly poetic world in which he lived, or perhaps the bad fit he seemed to make in it, intrigued me. I had read his probation officer's report and a short note from a psychiatrist:

Exceptional intelligence. IQ of 140. Disturbed childhood. Makes intermittent efforts at adjustment. The

next few years will be crucial. Criminal psychosis likely if no creative channel is found for his energy and talent.

The report from the probation officer was equally divided between awe at my ex-client's potential and fear of the consequences if he failed to adjust.

Thirst answered my question with a sidelong glance as I led him past the bag people, whom he called "dossers," and along the Victoria Embankment to Waterloo Bridge.

"I suppose you've been seeing your latest lawyer in the Temple?"

He grunted. "Just a silly little thing. I'm pleading guilty. Need someone to say I'm a good boy really—what d'you call it?"

"A plea in mitigation."

"Yeah. Mickey Mouse stuff. Not big enough for you."

"I wasn't touting for work, for God's sake, I was simply wondering how you came to be around the Temple and why you telephoned."

I scanned the street ahead. Why was I doing this? Someone from my chambers might see me at any minute; many barristers commuted from Waterloo Station and walked across the bridge. Nobody would say anything to me, but the beginning of a question mark would form—a small piece of dirt, seeding more. How to get rid of him?

Midway across the bridge, I paused automatically at the spot I usually chose. It may be that you can tell something about a Londoner depending on which way he looks when he crosses the Thames. I always looked east, where the open sea waited fifty miles downstream, the traditional route for generations of Englishmen seeking ways of escape. Thirst leaned against the balustrade, facing me and looking inland. I'm shortsighted, and it was only at that moment that I was again close enough to observe the perpetual flow of energy across his facial muscles, the discriminating alertness in those bright brown eyes. My irritation diminished a degree. Was there not a right under the law to freedom of association? How dehumanizing did upward mobility have to be?

"Well, what can I do for you?"

"Just wanted a bit of advice, that's all. You being from the same neighborhood, like, maybe you could help."

"With what?"

"See, I never had your chances—"

"Please, not that sob story; save it for your social worker. We come from the same neighborhood. I'm four years older than you, in other words the same generation. You had my chances. Exactly the same ones."

"So how come you're up there and I'm in shit? Because you're better than me?"

"The difference is that I never allowed myself the luxury of self-pity, and you do."

I had not intended to say so much. I looked down at the flow of water around the pier beneath us and at the antics of some debris caught in a whirlpool. When I looked up again he was staring at me. I sensed that in a way he could never articulate, he was shrewder and longer-suffering than I. From what depths had he *already* climbed? He blinked, twitched, his face changed again.

"Yeah—maybe. But see, I'm in trouble. I don't mean with the Old Bill—I mean with my own head. When I was a teenager I thought I could take anything, but I can't, James. I've got to get out or I'll go nuts. Sometimes I think I'll kill someone, I get so tense. And I don't know why, that's the weird thing. Everything I done, I was in control, I knew what I was up to. Until recently. I don't do drugs, I'm not a boozer, I keep fit, see? Ever been out of control, James?"

"No, never." Was that true? True enough for him.

"I'm scared. Last time I was inside, there was an old bloke about sixty—been in and out all his life—what do you call them?"

"Recidivists."

"Yeah. One of them. Loved the nick. Safest place, he said, boasted about all the convicts he'd sucked off—no teeth, see. Gums Gillespie his nickname. I don't want to end up like that."

He was still young enough to hold an echo of the girlish good looks he must have possessed as a teenager. Large eyes, long lashes, high cheekbones, a mouth that must have been fine before crime set it hard.

"How much form have you got?" I asked.

"Previous convictions? Quite a lot."

"Anything coming up?"

"One or two little things. I can handle them, find a good barrister like you to get me off. It's afterward I'm talking about."

"Afterward?"

"Yeah, the future. I never thought about it before; the future was always, you know, half an hour's time. I don't regret nothing. But you change, don't you?"

"What do you want to do?"

"Dunno. Maybe music, a rock band. Maybe travel. I've never been out of England. Never been out of London hardly—except, you know, in a prison van. I could do something, I could be up there. I'd be good. There's nothing I can't do. Anyway, I got to get out."

I had no need to ask what it was he had to get out of. It was everything: the grime, the crime, the favors, the vendettas, the police, the pressure. But his plea was for an instant solution, a magic carpet. If I had made it, why not him? How hard could it be, compared to the path that led to Gums Gillespie?

"I can't tell you if it's worth it or not," I said quietly, "but money and education are the only ways out of the swamp, and you haven't got any money. You're smart, everyone says so. But you can't talk. Why not go to a college? A polytech."

"Back to school? Who would take me—with my record?"

"They won't ask about your record, and it's not the same as school. My girlfriend is training in a poly—they're for blokes like you trying to better themselves."

He sighed, then turned and spat into the water.

"Got the address?"

I scribbled down on a card the name and address of the educational institute where Daisy was doing a term of hands-on teaching practice.

"Yeah, ta."

He turned and walked away. I watched him go with the comfortable certainty that he would neither use the card nor contact me again.

I heard a short time later that he had been sentenced to twelve months in Wormwood Scrubs for the offense of causing grievous bodily harm.

I cannot say that I thought about him very much as the glorious summer of '76 continued, incredibly, into September and October and finally dwindled in fires of gold and russet throughout London's parklands. His name came up from time to time because his solicitors, who had been pleased with the way I had won his case at Tower Bridge Magistrates Court, were sending more and more work. From them I learned that he did, indeed, suffer from that most ancient human need: the need to betray.

He was known among his predator peers as a grass, and for that reason could not expect a comfortable sojourn in the Scrubs. Perhaps they would let him out early, before his statutory parole date. The solicitors had heard that he was having a particularly rough ride.

The thoughts I spared him were few. The sunless misery of his summer inside could hardly cast a shadow over the brilliance of mine outside. At the time, I "put my hand up," as crooks say on the rare occasions when they make a confession, to two ferocious passions. One was ambition, the other was Daisy, and in flagrant violation of all the laws of life, I seemed to be allowed to indulge them equally and in parallel.

5

The Monday after his death I awoke with Daisy still hanging on to me in her sleep in a fetal position. He had died on a cold windy night at the end of March, but now it was early April, with all the agonizing promise of spring. Light flooded my bedroom, trapping her discarded clothes and underwear in a golden pool on the floor. Her blond hair spilled chaotically over my pillow and chest, leaving uncovered an elegant shoulder and the dimple her collarbone made where it joined her neck.

I lay breathing shallowly, so as not to disturb the moment, while something at the top of my head was exploding with happiness. Her eyelids fluttered; she opened them and closed them, raised her head slowly to look at me, smiled.

"That's the best sleep I've had in years," she said.

"How many years?"

She stroked my cheek.

Later, I made coffee and phoned my clerk to tell him that I would be working at home that day. By the time I returned to her with the coffee, the smile had given way to a frown.

"What is it?"

"I don't know if I should be here."

"Aren't you happy?"

"That's the trouble. I don't deserve it. What kind of woman am I?"

"A beautiful, generous, witty, sexy woman."

She allowed her blue eyes to dwell on my face for a moment. "Have you really forgiven me?"

"I've really forgiven you."

"And you love me again?"

"You know very well I never really stopped."

"And that justifies everything?"

"Everything."

"Supposing everyone was like that?"

"Then the earth would shine like the sun."

She puckered her brow. "What's that a quote from?"

"*Les Enfants du Paradis*—you remember?"

"I remember it all. That's the trouble."

A moment fourteen years before in which Jean-Louis Barrault had begged Arletty to stay and Daisy and I had loved each other in a cinema in Camden Town inspired me to eloquence. "Well, where else would you go?"

In the event, the case was easier to win than I had expected. I had supposed that she would fend me off with the inevitable "Let's wait, James," but like me she seemed to be aware that when you're hurtling toward forty there is no longer that much time. By mid-morning I had persuaded her to live with me again. It was to be a temporary arrangement, of course. Like life. She dressed and paused, waiting for a cue.

"There's no point in delaying. Let's take my car and load it up with your things this morning."

"This is the first day of the rest of your life," she quoted in a New York accent. "What about the police? I'm sure they're watching my apartment. Won't you be compromised?"

"Not by collecting your things. Any compromising was done yesterday when Holmes and his sidekick came calling. Don't worry, I won't suffer because of you."

I led her the short distance down the street to the lock-up garage I rented. Hampstead is all double parking, herbal remedies and stone-ground bread, cute lanes with secondhand bookshops and a pub on every corner, a temple of mellow quaintness. It is also a ghetto for misfits. When all was said and done, she was, like me, a born outsider, and as her fine hair caught the sun and she smiled at me, I fancied that she had come home.

Then I opened the garage door and she saw the car, a brand-new black Jaguar, with a space-age dashboard. A desperately expensive toy for a man desperately trapped in bachelorhood. It was exactly the kind of car *he* would have bought.

"Jesus, Jimmy."

"I know."

I remembered not to open the passenger door for her, but when she was seated showed her how to adjust the position electronically. Reversing into the street, I flicked the stub gearstick around with defiant panache.

She sat with her seat belt across her dead center in the passenger seat—as if afraid to touch the sides of this engine of evil—and began to giggle.

"What?"

"Thousands of horsepower, dozens of fuel injectors, holds the road like a racing car, and you still drive like an old lady in a Morris Minor."

I was pained, then amused. It was quite true. I'd developed the bookworm's ineptitude when it came to physical objects, combined with the coward's fear of them. Electric drills, screwdrivers, staplers, motorcars—they all turned clumsy and rebellious in my hands. And yet I'd been a practical lad, before I turned scholar.

"It's so dumb, the police even putting you on the bottom of a list of suspects," she said, "if that's what they've done. Imagine you with a gun." She leaned over and kissed my cheek. "Any man who drives a Jag this slowly wouldn't hurt a fly."

We stopped outside her house, which was in a turning off that end of Elgin Avenue where the grand mansion flats of Maida Vale give way to the sad terraced houses of eastern Ladbroke Grove. Hers belonged to a housing association that had converted it into three flats. She had the middle one. Below lived a woman with four children and a confusing stream of lovers.

"You know, before I moved here I wouldn't have believed that such people exist; I thought they were a figment of the right-wing imagination. She's got pregnant again just to get a bigger place," Daisy said.

Above her a West Indian couple held relentlessly noisy parties that began Fridays and went on until Sunday mornings.

"Make sure you lock your car," she said.

"Have you lived here since you left?"

"Yes."

"Four years?"

"Nearly five."

I allowed myself to look glum.

"I didn't want to be rescued," she said. "I wanted to be left alone. I became paranoid about people knowing my address. If I'd received just one more threat of violence, I'm sure I would have ended up in a straitjacket."

"I could have kept a secret."

She squeezed my hand as we negotiated a barricade of dirty toys. From the top flat, reggae with megabass flooded the little house. Daisy turned the key in her door, and the music seemed to get louder as we went in.

"I don't exist; for them I just don't exist; it's me who's the black in this house," she said when someone walked heavily overhead.

While she opened drawers and threw things into a bag, I wandered fascinated between the two rooms of the little flat, contemplating the meanness in which she had to live. If wealth means having enough money to buy what you want rather than what you need, then I had been wealthy for some time. It had crept up on me. Daisy's standard pinewood table and chairs had become my oak antiques, her posters of Haywood gallery exhibitions, my expensive copies and one original, her blankets my duck-down quilt. As she marched about, angry and embarrassed at the deafening music, I looked on her flat with the eyes of a snob and at the same time was conscious of a certain unlovableness about my own house.

I was thankful that she had kept no visible memento of her life with him.

"Didn't he give you any money at all when you split up?"

"We didn't split up; I left him. And how could I accept *that* money, even if he'd offered?"

When she'd finished packing, she took me aside to show me something in a piece of aluminum foil. It was a small lump of hashish.

"Better chuck it, I suppose. I'll have to give it up soon anyway, won't I?"

"No, bring it. I want you complete, all vices and virtues intact."

I received a grateful kiss, but she threw away the little piece of foil.

We hauled two cheap suitcases and a backpack down the narrow stairs and over the toys. Outside, I was only half surprised to find George Holmes waiting on the other side of the street, his hands thrust deep into his Burberry, trilby pushed back on his head.

I had detected no police presence while driving up to the house. He'd always known how to run an efficient operation. His old Rover, not in evidence when we arrived, was parked down the road, so he must have given instructions to be contacted when we showed up. I could always demand to know what he was doing there, but that would have been demeaning for both of us. I endured his stare while we put Daisy's luggage in the boot of the Jag and drove off.

"He's the cop who came to see me last week," Daisy said.

"George Holmes. I mentioned his name to you once years ago."

"So what was that all about?"

"It was a warning. He thinks one or both of us are making a fool of him, and he's angry. George Holmes angry is a dangerous man."

"Why would he be angry?"

"Because he used to like me, and admire me, and because he feels cheated by Oliver's death, and because he's a man with a mission."

"What mission?"

"Oh, the usual 'clean up the city' sort of thing. I've often heard him rage about drugs destroying the minds of innocent children."

Daisy colored. "I told you I never accepted any of Oliver's money after I left."

"I don't think that would impress George." Even to myself I sounded like a moralist in a soap opera.

"I'm not sure this is such a good idea," she said, but she didn't tell me to turn around. Then she said, "George Holmes—isn't he the one who gave you my phone number?"

"Yes."

"Then why would he be angry about us meeting?"

"I think he expected me to do it all over the phone."

"All what?"

"All our talking."

She buried her fingers in her hair, pushed back until her hands were over her ears. "He's tapped my phone, and I am a suspect?"

"Oh, yes."

"And he wanted you to trick me into saying something?"

"He's a sly man. Who knows what he really wants?"

We had turned a corner, but she looked back anyway. "He looks so straight." Her hands were shaking, her cheeks were suddenly blotchy.

I intended, as soon as she unpacked, to tackle her about the photograph George Holmes had given me the day before: Daisy in plastic earmuffs taking aim at a firing range with a small pistol. But before I could bring it up, she raised a question of her own.

"Jimmy, don't be angry about this, but there's something I need to know. It's ridiculous, I'm sure, but that policeman seemed to be looking at you, not me. I can't pretend that part of me isn't relieved that Oliver's dead, but if you had anything to do with it I couldn't live with you, I couldn't be your lover."

I stared at her. In view of the photograph, it was a strange thing to say.

"You read the newspaper report," I said. "The killing had all the signs of a professional assassination. A single shot between the eyes with a small-bore handgun taped in all the right places to avoid fingerprints and left at the scene of the crime. As you used to point out, I can hardly wield a hammer. Whoever did it has had plenty of target practice."

Daisy Smith blushed deeply and changed the subject.

6

We had a long moment of conjugal bliss, Daisy and I, before George Holmes came back. Although I said nothing to Daisy, I guessed that time was short for one of us and canceled all my appointments. For two weeks we hung suspended between crime and punishment, and I found that the wild strawberries tasted all the sweeter for that. Despite the knowledge that her telephone had been tapped, Daisy seemed blissfully ignorant of the legal machine that, I was sure, had been cranked up and was even now making its slow, relentless progress from somewhere in Scotland Yard, across London, and up the hill to Hampstead.

It amused me, how quickly Daisy grew used to living in my house and driving my Jaguar. She continued to complain about the car's ostentation but confessed to reluctantly falling in love with its comfort and power. She was more of a natural driver than I. She would drive around in it for hours to soothe her nerves.

She had changed. Did I say that she had not? It's true that
when she first came through the door of my house that Sunday
after he died her observations seemed like an echo from the past.
But like most good entrances, it was largely bluff. Eleven years is
a long time in sexual politics.

The passionate convictions of her youth had formed, in the end,
a set of off-the-shelf opinions to be handed out to strangers: this is
who I am so far as you're concerned. In fact I noticed after the first
day or two of awkwardness that her own opinions bored her. She
would stop in midsentence and sigh. More than once she said, "I
don't really know anymore."

"Neither do I."

"I spent a huge part of my life feeling resentful. I've broken
with all my friends, my affairs with men have all been a disaster.
At the time I always blamed the others. Now I wonder. If this is
a chance, a real chance to get something right, then for God's sake
let's please do it."

My back gave me trouble from time to time during the day, especially now that I was indulging again in sexual athletics. I caught
Daisy staring as I put my palms to my lumbar region to ease the
ache. This and other evidence of Thirst's impact on our lives were
all around us, like unexploded bombs. By unspoken agreement we
never mentioned any of them. Daisy carefully massaged the muscles
of my lower back without murmuring, as she might have done, "So
it's still giving you trouble after all these years?"

By the fourth day of her staying with me we had both made
the discovery that we were neither the people we had been more
than a decade before nor the people each of us had presumed that
the other would become. With some glee I revealed that I had a
small but active circle of friends who had helped me survive the
last decade.

"You're not such a loner anymore, then?"

She, on the other hand, had become a loner.

"I went through a period—maybe three years—when I didn't
trust anyone. Neither women nor men."

"Fancy you being the antisocial one. You used to make me feel
like a social defective."

*   *   *

That she had been damaged was painfully clear. She took innocent questions as a challenge, something she had never done before. She had no objection to being alone in the house, even
welcomed it when I went for walks on the Heath by myself. But
she disliked going out into the street on her own. She reminded
me in an odd way of ex-convicts—hyperalert to threats both real
and imagined, eyes that darted at innocent words. Although it
was not obvious at first sight, intimacy revealed a history of physical damage too. Fingers were crooked that had been straight,
there were strange scars under her chin. Had I not known the
answer, I should have said something like, "What monster did
this to you?"

On the fifth day she burst into tears again in my arms.

"He's dead, Daisy, it's over."

"That's why I can let myself cry. Oh, James, I can't believe
this—it's too good; life isn't supposed to be like this. It's making
me paranoid that something will go wrong. Tell me nothing's going
to go wrong."

I swallowed. "Nothing's going to go wrong."

"But it's so hard to take—that our happiness should follow
from someone's death. It's like some American cops-and-robbers
show—a bullet in the right place solves everything. I was expecting
to feel wretched and guilty for the rest of my life."

Sex became a frequent and indispensable retreat, a warm safe
cave into which we would crawl to recover from the unaccustomed
discipline of sharing another's state of mind. When we made love,
at least, we were both in the same mood.

"We're doing this more often than we did as kids."

"I've got a lot of time to make up for," I said.

"I can't believe you haven't had a woman for all those years.
It's downright—"

"Morbid?"

"Darling, don't give me your lecture on the loss of integrity in
modern life, please. I haven't had a man for years, actually."

There was something about the way she said it. "Does this

mean I'm going to have to hear about your *de rigueur* lesbian affair?"

She smiled. "Poor Jimmy, you really are a lone warrior fighting against the twentieth century. It's not all bad, you know. Yes, I did have my *de rigueur* lesbian affair, as you put it. I needed love, was incapable of trusting a man, so I tried a woman. Which was dumb of me—I mean to suppose that woman as a species is genetically more reliable than man. I discovered that people who feel incomplete will betray you sooner or later—they have no choice. And since most of us are incomplete, most of us are also treacherous. I also discovered that I'm incurably heterosexual. That magic stick of yours is indispensable to my well-being, so please don't start a sulk—it always used to shrivel when you sulked."

"I'm not sulking. Really."

"If it makes you feel better, there's one thing I do agree with you about."

"What's that?"

She smirked in the old way. "Tastes awful."

The implication that I had completely deprived myself of that voyage of self-discovery that usually involves some combination of promiscuity, mysticism, drugs, and a visit to California finally prompted a confession.

"Of course there have been other women—I said I'd never loved another, not that I'd never had another."

"Tell me. I'm interested."

I told her, and in the telling made it sound more glamorous than it had been. Almost exactly once a year for three months I would find myself having an affair with a woman who saw my emotional frigidity as a challenge. The number of times I was called a brick wall or its equivalent was painfully telling.

"They all fell into a mold—hot chicks on the surface, desperate for love and babies underneath."

"I feel sorry for every one of them. Fancy falling for you in your implacable phase. I know what it feels like: it feels like being a ripe peach flung against a—"

"Don't say it."

"But tell me—wasn't there one, just one, who grabbed you by these just a little bit more firmly than the others?"

"Yes, I suppose there was. It was quite early on, actually, only a year or so after we split up, you and I. She went to live in Australia. She was more perceptive than the others; when she left, she said, 'I love you, but not enough to spend the next ten years trying to heal you.' Horribly accurate in the circumstances."

"Do you want to hear about my adventures?"

"No, thank you."

In the only sense that matters, I knew exactly what she had done and the kind of people with whom she had done it.

I had changed more than I had realized, as became clear after the first few steamy days of bed and breakfast. For one thing, our bodies were not capable of carrying quite the same mythical charge they had carried a decade before. I could still adore her soft breasts and silken thighs, but they were no longer indistinguishable from God. Her breasts and backside, though still pretty, had sagged slightly. And her thighs, though still soft and yielding, were, despite a fascist regime of cottage cheese and diet biscuits, amusingly chubby. She feared the onset of varicose veins in both calves.

My own body had not fared much better. I had kept my hair, but it was graying around the temples, shockingly white on my chest. My arms and legs were as wiry as ever, but too many business lunches and beers after work had swollen my gut, and a career spent on my bum had flattened it.

Yet these recent defects were openings, invitations to tenderness rather than disappointments. Despite her nerve-racked state, Daisy's body loved love, and it was in the security of warm flesh to warm flesh that she was best able to relax. Orgasms were no longer torn from her amidst exaggerated moaning. They seemed to bubble up to the surface in multiple ripples that sometimes went on so long that she apologized for being greedy. My own virility was so flattered by such appreciation that it surpassed, in stamina at least, the heroic feats of my youth. My body liked her body and was inclined to burrow inside it for animal warmth.

Daisy had made it a condition of the deal I had negotiated with her on that Sunday that we would not use contraceptives. I continued to find the prospect of fatherhood daunting, but my reasons were different than they had been a decade earlier. I had the money now but was not at all sure that I had the energy. Even Daisy was not wholly without reservations.

"What about adolescence?" I said. "We were bad enough, but at least there was still some respect left. Kids today leave school barely numerate, obsessed with sex, drugs, and shoplifting."

Her eyes darted. I bit my tongue, embraced her.

"I'm sorry—that was a stupid thing to say."

"No, too close for comfort, that's all." She held my hand for a moment, patted it. "I suppose I ought to tell you that I got caught in the end—shoplifting. It was a pair of tights. Fined twenty pounds at Tottenham Magistrates Court. It was awful." She gave a quick smile. "But you're right, I am numerate at least—modern education is appalling. I suppose that's another contribution—teaching, I mean—that I made rather a mess of." She looked at me. "I want to have done something, James—something real, even if it kills me."

After the initial excitement of the first few days, I wondered what to do about this new awareness that I was not alone. I began to go for long walks over the Heath. When I returned, Daisy would make a pot of tea. I found the idea that someone would remember how many sugars I took quaint and disarming. I answered questions about what kind of bread I liked, what did I eat in the evenings, where was the nearest bakery.

"Look, you don't have to do all that, you know."

She put up her hands. "Don't deprive me of a chance to grow up. I've spent a long time thinking that the only salvation is to be useful to at least one other person. I want to be useful, I even want to be used."

"But aren't we getting into traditional sexual role play—all that?"

"Don't gloat. Yes, I admit that in the end there's nothing you can't politicize if you really want to. Let's start with fulfilling my need to feel useful and see what happens."

I do believe that for a while both of us forgot that our idyll was made possible because somebody had murdered Oliver Thirst. Until, of course, George Holmes returned to remind us.

7

We were in my study, which was large enough to serve as a sitting room. Daisy sat on a new sofa under the van Gogh that had never been quite the same for me since she had made fun of it. An old cardigan over a thin cotton dress kept her warm against the slight spring chill.

She was sewing a button back on one of the collarless shirts I used for court. She wore spectacles for reading and close work now. Every so often she peered over them to look at me. I was rereading *Anna Karenina*. I knew whenever she looked at me and made a point of returning her ironic smile. We had examined times and dates and decided that if she was ever going to conceive, she would have done so the night before. I had never taken seriously until then women's claims that one can "just know."

"Done. Would you like a cup of tea?" She put the shirt on the sofa beside her.

"You're being exceptionally kind," I said.

"I know—well, you lost a lot of protein last night. I expect you're still weak."

"That's true. Nonetheless, I'd like to stand behind and fondle you while you're making the tea."

"At your age? I'm beginning to think you've had some kind of operation you haven't told me about—isn't there something they do with monkey glands? Last night was like being impaled by a scaffold pole."

"You say the nicest things."

She leaned over to kiss me on my forehead. "Toast?"

"Wonderful."

Just then the doorbell rang.

"I'll get it," Daisy said.

"No, I will. You make the tea."

Hoping that the caller was not one of the stuffier solicitors who instructed me—I was wearing jeans and a sweater, no shirt—I opened the door. George Holmes was standing on the steps holding his trilby in his hands and twisting it. Two young uniformed policemen stood uncertainly beside him.

"I've come to arrest your American friend," he said, "on a charge of murdering her husband." He sounded nervous, even a little frightened.

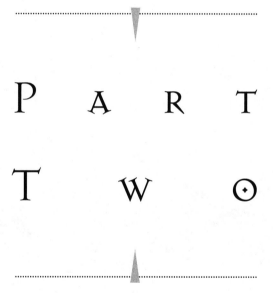

PART
TWO ☉

8

"W-w-w-would you like to watch a Hit-Hitchcock film at the film soc?" was the first thing I said to her after "hello." I could hardly believe that I'd had the guts to walk up to her in the students' bar and ask her, much less that she'd said yes.

We were both undergraduates at Warwick, a hip new university with a reputation for academic brilliance and radical views: left was good, right was bad; rock was better than Mozart; cinema was better than theater; drugs were better than alcohol. Che Guevara, Bertrand Russell, and Mick Jagger were heroes in more or less the same league, perhaps because they all had long hair and made attractive wall posters. Capitalism worldwide was sure to collapse the day after tomorrow. Criminals were victims of an unfair political system. Anything was better than growing old. She was twenty, I was twenty-one. I had watched her for a week in increasing anguish before I'd screwed my courage to the sticking point.

The film was *Vertigo,* in which there is a poignant scene where

Kim Novak says to James Stewart: "Oh, Scottie, I'm not mad—
and I don't want to die!" I remember the line because that was the
moment when Daisy put her hand on my thigh. I thought it was
in appreciation of Hitchcock's stagecraft, but I wasn't sure. After
the film I managed a very hurried kiss on her cheek and said good
night with a nervousness the swift brush of her hand across my
face did nothing to alleviate.

I did not sleep that night, and the next day fell into depression.
It was obvious to me that I must plod doggedly on with a courtship
that would quickly expose me—if it had not done so already—as
manifestly unworthy of her. She was a sort of upper-class American
(from New Haven, Connecticut, wherever that was) and, I feared,
out of reach, despite her name. Nevertheless, I would not give up
lightly, for she intrigued as well as attracted me. Even her accent
was an enigma. I knew enough about her culture to realize that
she came from money, but there were times when her accent
sounded, to my ear, more like something from the streets of Har-
lem. She swore a lot (we all did in those days), but when she said
a word like "shit," it had a special authenticity: you could almost
taste it.

She telephoned me in the men's block at about eight that night
and asked if I wanted to eat with her in the dining area of her
dormitory. I made no mention of the sausage, egg, beans, and chips
I had eaten an hour before and stammered an affirmative.

The dining area was at the end of a corridor of private rooms
where the women undergraduates lived, two women to each room.
The Women's Student Officer had selected as Daisy's roommate
someone called Brenda. It was she who came down to meet me.

"Daisy and I are just about to eat."

I followed Brenda's authoritative buttocks up the stairs. Daisy
looked up from a chopping board at which she was attacking some
garlic and caught me staring at Brenda's vast chest, which I negotiated on entering the room. In the split second that it takes to
exchange glances, Daisy colluded with me in wonderment at the
size of Brenda's free-ranging breasts. In my opinion there is nothing
in nature quite so compelling as a beautiful woman with a sense
of humor.

The three of us sat down in the brittle neon-lit Formica-based decor of the dining area to a saucepan of spaghetti and a frying pan of bolognese. The spaghetti was thinner and more resilient than the ones I was accustomed to eating out of a can, but I wasn't hungry and would have eaten anything.

"There's plenty, so anyone who's hungry can just help themselves," Brenda said.

Daisy fixed me with her eyes. "Go ahead, James, help yourself."

"Here." Brenda stood up. With a huge ladle she plunged into the depths and drew up a great tangle of gray spaghetti.

"I've got a brother, so I know all about the way men eat," Brenda said. Daisy looked away.

"Please, you have some more, Brenda," I said.

"All right." She stood up again—better leverage—and this time came up with a great coagulated knot, which she dumped on her plate.

"There's drama society tonight, if anyone's interested," Brenda said.

"Are you interested in going?" I asked Daisy.

"Are you?" she replied sweetly.

I was about to concoct some excuse, when I saw her barely suppressed grin and stopped.

"I'm not really the acting type," I said.

"Not really a thespian," Brenda said.

"A what?"

"A thespian—it's a better way of saying 'acting type.' "

I blushed. "I thought . . ."

"We know what you thought," Daisy said.

"What?" Brenda demanded. "What did he think?"

"He thought a thespian was a lesbian with a lisp—didn't you?"

"Something like that."

This time Brenda blushed. "Well, I fail to see any reason for confusion."

"Just my ignorance," I said, catching Daisy's eye.

"What about you, Daisy?" Brenda asked.

"I'm not really the acting type." Daisy winked at me. "But don't let us stop you."

"Oh, no! I wouldn't go without you," Brenda said.

"We're very close, you see," Daisy said.

"It's amazing, isn't it?" Brenda's face lit up. "We're only one month into our first term. I was nervous about sharing with an American, but now I feel as if Daisy and I have known each other all our lives. It was a kind of instant bonding. Couldn't believe my luck."

"That was a wonderful movie you took me to last night, James," Daisy said.

"One of his best, I think—it's that point in his career where he becomes an artist rather than just a craftsman."

"Who?" Brenda said.

"Alfred Hitchcock," Daisy said.

"Oh, I've never liked him. All that *Psycho* stuff. Did you say he was an artist? I've never heard that said before. Surely all he does is make films? Frankly I think it's silly to call a filmmaker an artist."

"What a wonderfully basic conversation," Daisy said. "Well, if he's had enough to eat, I'll walk James back to his dorm."

"Whatever for?"

"In case someone tries to mug him."

"Don't be silly—mugging is an American problem."

"That's why I have to protect him." She pulled up her sleeve and crooked an arm to show practically no biceps. "Yep, honed my survival skills on the streets of the Big Apple."

"I'll come with you," Brenda said.

"No you won't, darlin'," Daisy said, exaggerating her accent.

Brenda sagged. "Oh well, you're the boss."

"Better believe it."

As we left the overlit area of her dormitory I experienced a jolt. Daisy had taken my hand.

"What the fuck do I do, tell me what do I do?" she said.

"About Brenda?"

"Who else?"

"She obviously—"

"Thinks I walk on water and hasn't even begun to come to terms with the fact that she's a goddamn dyke to the fingertips. I've never felt so claustrophobic in my life."

"You'd better be careful," I said. Only the week before I had seen a film about a psychopathic lesbian who killed her best friend. "Can you change rooms?"

"If I do she'll be suicidal."

"That's better than getting so involved she harms you."

Daisy grinned. "Harms me? What I'm afraid of is that if it goes on much longer I'll wring her neck. Ever loathed someone's *smell*, Jimmy? I don't mean their bad smells, I mean just their basic *who they are* odor."

"Nobody called me 'Jimmy' before."

"Sorry—it's an American reflex."

"I like it—a lot."

We'd reached a wall that ended in the entrance to my dormitory. Not exactly a secluded area, but I had made a vow to myself that I would kiss her properly that night, and there didn't seem to be any other opportunities. I drew her to me.

As I put my arms around her waist, her hands grasped my bum in a kind of lascivious bonhomie.

"Do you know you have a great ass?"

"I c-c-can't believe you said that."

"Why not? Never dated an American before? You want to bonk me, don't you?"

"Bonk you?"

"Yes, sweetheart—isn't that what you call it over here? How about fuck, then? I'm sure *that's* Anglo-Saxon."

"For G-G-God's sake, of course I want to b-b-bonk you. I've thought of it every second for the past thirty-six hours."

She giggled. "Better take me for a walk in the woods, then, Englishman, or it'll be wet dreams for you again all night."

I learned more about her during hurried lunches on the way to our different lectures, on walks in the forest near the college campus, at dinners from which Brenda was ruthlessly excluded, after moviegoing, in bed. Daisy talked a lot about her parents. Her father was "a shit, I mean world class, a psychopath."

"Psychopath? I thought he was a professor of psychology."

"Mm-hm, he is. At Yale. The syndrome of the sadistic psychologist hasn't reached these shores yet?"

"I don't know anything about psychologists."

"Which earns you ten points right off. Here's all you need to know. Psychology majors are of two kinds. Those who start off caring about people and those who see it as the ultimate power play—mind control. But when they qualify, there's really only one kind, that I've met anyway, and I've met dozens."

"The power freaks?"

"You got it. He works a lot in industry. It's the psychological equivalent of those Nazi doctors in the concentration camps: how will performance be altered if I cut out that bit, graft on this . . . see?"

"Not really. I didn't know that psychologists worked in industry."

We were walking across the campus. She stopped short under a horse chestnut tree. "You didn't?" She grabbed my jacket, pulled me to her. "Wonderful. It's like landing on some desert island and finding a perfect example of Natural Man. Unpolluted, pure, and free."

"I've never been called that before. I've always thought of myself as a fairly typical example of urban neurosis."

She shook her head. "You're talking mild influenza. You ain't got nothing I can't fix with a sustained diet of sex and self-indulgence."

We walked on. "I'll take the cure."

"Sure. Just wish I was in the same happy state."

It was my turn to stop. I held her at arm's length. "You've talked like that before. What exactly do you mean?"

She gazed at me for a moment. It was one of those May days when the English spring retreats back into winter. The cold pinched her features, her nose was red from catarrh, tears formed in her eyes from the wind.

"I mean I watched that bastard destroy my mother. He picked her up here in this country—she's British. A pretty little specimen to experiment on, unlikely to kick him in the balls the way an American woman would have when he played his games."

"Games?"

"He destroyed her. I think he wanted to see how long the human female can last without love, affection, attention, under a regime of sustained contempt. He got his answer—not very long. She had her first breakdown soon after I was born. She's in a mental hospital here in England now. Oh, she's not, like, sick. He just destroyed her self-esteem to the point where she can't summon the audacity to get up in the morning." An inner storm twisted her mouth. "She's on welfare over here. Can you believe that? The asshole just cut her off."

"So that's why you're in England—to be with her?"

"And to get away from him. He phones me, tries out some clever little game on me that he's dreamed up, some way of getting me back to the States. He doesn't like it that I'm as smart as him. Smarter. I know all he knows, and my conclusion has been to reject him all the way, including his name."

"Smith is your mother's name?"

"Right. I changed it legally when I came here. I'm no longer the daughter of Sebastian J. F. Hawkley, psychology professor, obsessive social climber, and sadist."

"I expect he wouldn't approve of me."

"I wouldn't touch a man he would approve of."

9

Little by little I began to see my appeal. After all, I was hardly the catch of the campus. There were plenty of guys wondering openly why I was so lucky, when she could have had next year's Young Businessman of the Year or this year's president of the Student Union. But they would not have evoked the kind of disapproval I was likely to enjoy if I ever met the upwardly mobile professor. I stammered, my accent was unreconstructed cockney, the chips on both my shoulders frequently made me brusque and arrogant. It was obvious by looking at me that my access to tertiary education was due to various Education Acts and other socialist legislation that provided, now I think of it, a fairly generous package of maintenance and other grants for the poor and bright. I was, as one of my colleagues in the law faculty once remarked, an almost perfect example of the kind of kid the reformist legislation had all been for: my father was a carpenter who frequently fell unemployed, and my mother really did take in washing to make ends meet. Better: we really did live in a council flat in Southeast London, five minutes from the docks. There's nothing quite as unique as a living stereotype. As far as Daisy was concerned, only an illiterate black man with a criminal record could have been more eligible. I was unprepared, though, for the proposition she put to me one night a week or so after we became lovers.

We were naked in bed, a frequent state of affairs, and she was fondling me after lovemaking.

"Jimmy, d'you really love me?"

"You can see as well as the rest of the world that I'm totally, hopelessly, insanely nuts about you."

"Then if I asked you real nice, you'd do something that's important to me?"

"Of course. Anything."

"I want you to help me kill my father."

Her hand left my penis to hold my jaw and turn my face to her. My laugh, I suspect, was hollow.

"Of course, I don't mean it like that. I may be fucked up, but I'm not stupid." She turned in the bed, knelt to face me, her breasts hanging loose. She was fired by enthusiasm, causing them to wobble. "See, I intend to do exactly what he and every other shrink would advise against doing. I intend to suppress him, cut out every bit of him, the half of me that is him—amputate, make out he was never there. Psychologists would see that as surrogate murder. They'd be right."

"What'll you put in the void?"

"You. Not just your heart and your cock, but your whole culture. Because he's American I want you to help me be English. I want to be the woman I would have been if I was brought up here with Mom, if he'd never existed."

I scratched my head. "Where would I start?"

"With the accent. It's so important to you people. I want to talk like you."

"Like me?"

"What's so funny?"

"Haven't you noticed I'm trying to stop talking like me? Every word I utter betrays my class, my background."

"Damn it, I like your class, I like your background." She hit me with her fists. "Do it, Jimmy, it's what I want."

I thought for a moment. "Say tomato."

"Say tomato?"

"Not ter-may-doe; tom-ah-toe."

"Tom-ah-toe?"

"Well, it'll need work, but you have a good ear."

She lay back on the bed. "Toe-mah-toe? Sounds faggy, but I can live with it. So, are we doing the Queen's English or cockney?"

"We'll start off with the Queen. Cockney's for the advanced course."

It was my last year and Daisy's first, though no one seeing us together would have guessed that I was her senior. She had taken two years off between school and university and possessed the exotic quality of undergraduates who had done a spell as real people. As for me, being neither sporty nor sexy, and suffering from a mind-numbing class complex, I had devoted my first two years to study intensive enough to retard my development in other areas.

Not that I was entirely without my charms, within the special context of that distant epoch. The other day Daisy took out some rare photographs of me as a student: jeans, thick sweater, long hair, and a wispy brown beard; gaunt cheeks with eyes haunted by ambition; a long possessive arm around Daisy. I was and am fairly tall: slightly under six foot, with a stoop more of the gorilla than the scholar. But my God, we were so young! In the picture Daisy is as innocent as a doll, and in my case the facial hair and primate posturing are all too obviously reflexes of a vulnerable child within.

"People say you're brilliant," Daisy said without approval.

"I work at it."

I had worked at it so much that my final year was not quite the endurance test it was for everyone else. I'd set myself a heavy but achievable schedule of work and devoted every spare minute to Daisy. I had moved back onto campus that year to be near the library, but Daisy soon changed my mind. The obvious strategy to escape Brenda was to move into a student house in one of the towns within a ten-mile radius of the campus. We took a huge room with a shared kitchen in a large Victorian mansion. We had known each other by then for three months and were making love as often as most couples who have just met.

Sometimes when she was clowning Daisy would get onto the bed, roll down her panties, pull her skirt up, and twiddle her thumbs. If I took too long to join her she would start whistling. I was a fastidious fellow in those days and a bit of a prig. I don't think I would have found such behavior amusing in anyone else, but the truly beautiful have a superior magic. Their jokes can break your heart.

There were moments, though, when I had to suppress what I supposed was my innate British squeamishness. I had a working-class weakness for big breakfasts: fried eggs, beans, sausage, fried white bread, large mug of tea. Daisy liked to eat her cornflakes wearing a T-shirt and nothing else, sitting on a bench in the kitchen with her legs apart.

"I think it's important that we demystify cunts—you agree? Most of the time it's a pretty unattractive organ. We should never have romanticized it. Disillusionment is what causes misunderstanding, hatred of women. We program men to think of women as pure mythic creatures. Then you see a cunt menstruating or a baby and afterbirth popping out of one, and the illusion's shattered. The poor guy's switched from doting sucker to misogynist. Know what I mean?"

I looked down at my fried eggs, which I preferred underdone. Nodded.

I had plenty of work to do—at least five legal topics called "heads of law" by June—and Daisy did not. She had opted to study English and American Literature, a subject generally regarded as a cop-out. While the rest of us wrestled with disciplines that were never intended to entertain, Daisy and her colleagues in the English Department sat around absorbed by the chronicles of Jay Gatsby or Mr. Pickwick. Daisy believed she had acquired enough of labor's honor by spending nearly two years selling advertising space in New York, before her flight to England. She'd earned enough to pay for her first year at Warwick, after which her connection with the English welfare system, through her mother, enabled her to obtain a grant.

"Are you going to be studying tonight?" was a question bursting with charm. She meant that if I was not studying she would, of course, stay to make love with me. On the other hand, if I needed to work she would amuse herself. She possessed, indeed, a social talent I would have found intimidating had she not been so attentive to me. She had the capacity to pick up friends and make a party apparently out of the air. She quickly won over the other students in the house, a rather lugubrious group of literature scholars who supplied her with hashish and LSD—free of charge, as far as I could gather. When I was studying she would disappear into the rooms downstairs for a few hours, then reappear with a smirk on her face. In addition, there was a rather more select group, with perfect vowels and golden futures, who rode horses, drove around the countryside in MGs with the tops down, went to London for weekend parties in Knightsbridge, and lived relentlessly extrovert lives. This group loved Daisy and believed her to be the right sort of American (I doubt that she shared with them her mission to demystify the human vagina). They seemed to revel in the capriciousness with which she treated them. If she was bored with her dope-smoking friends downstairs, she could pick up the phone and within minutes be driven along country lanes by some young gentleman out of the thirties, complete with cravat and sports jacket and a group of jolly song-singing types in the back. She knew very well how threatening to me such jaunts could be and handled me perfectly. I don't believe I have ever seen a woman deflect jealousy in her lover with such grace. She did it by letting me feel the strength of her commitment below the belt, where it counts.

Little by little she picked up English idioms and her accent changed. She was a good mimic; by the end of the year I was envying her ability to slide up and down the social scale simply by modifying vowels. Better, she developed the persona of a demure English girl, like a second skin to be adopted as it suited her. When expressing intimacies, though, she reverted to American mode. Even this seemed to have a number of facets.

I said: "Sometimes even your American accent changes. It can sound like New York to me, then like something else."

"Yeah? You notice that? I'm New England, but that time I spent selling advertising in Manhattan kind of molded me. New York, for me, is a mood. So is England, come to think of it."

"I envy your fluidity. I'm straining every nerve to move up a couple of strata in British society."

"Don't strain, babe. Let it flow."

Despite this good advice, a deeply lodged insecurity caused me to brace myself against the moment when she would fully realize what a lowlife I was in the context of the British class system.

I 0

But the shock, when it came, was not at all what I might have expected.

It was in early June of that year, dangerously close to my finals. All lectures and seminars had ceased, and all of us in our last year were cramming our skulls to capacity with the kind of knowledge that is used only to pass exams. I heard Daisy's voice outside the room say "It's here," followed by a heavy knocking. A man in his early forties with a clipped mustache and a light check suit was standing there. Daisy, trying to look nonchalant, succeeded only in looking sullen.

"You'd better let him in."

"Do you want to tell him, Miss Smith, or shall I?" he said when he'd entered the room.

"He caught me stealing a box of tampons, he's the manager of the supermarket, his name is Mr. Brown. He's involving you to make a point and to humiliate me and to show how weak and inferior women are."

He looked away from her as from a delinquent child. "I wonder if you and I could have a little talk."

"Can I go, then?" Daisy asked him.

"Yes, you can go."

I'd never before seen a man address Daisy with contempt. He sat down on a sofa we mostly used to make love on.

"What are you going to do?" I asked him.

"That sort of depends on you. I want you to keep her out of my shop, I don't want her anywhere near it; I don't even want her looking through the window. I especially don't want her walking in drugged up to the eyeballs, pinching things."

"You're making a big meal out of a box of tampons, aren't you? She clearly isn't drugged."

"No, not today. And today it was only a box of tampons. She didn't know, but the time before was her last chance." He took out a piece of paper. "I'm fed up with her. Okay, let's face it, half of you students have got sticky fingers, but she's different, a bit twisted. I know, I can always tell. You want the list? This is it."

He read from his piece of paper. It was an unexceptional list of household items, sweets, groceries. It was also disturbingly long, with dates and times against each item. Many of them were things Daisy usually bought out of our common fund.

He took out another piece of paper and handed it to me. It was a confession to theft not merely of the tampons but to the whole list, signed by Daisy. Brown had taken the statement himself. It was meticulous and professional—a man, clearly, who had made a study of shoplifting.

"I'm surprised you let it go on for so long," I said.

"I have my methods. And now I would like to know how you propose to pay."

"For the tampons?"

"Not just the tampons, the lot. I'll give you an itemized receipt."

So that was the method. "Fair enough, but I want that statement."

He shook his head. "Oh no, I keep the statement as security, to make sure she never sets foot in my shop again."

I went to the bedroom, where we kept a biscuit tin for the kitty. Brown's price tag just about cleaned us out for that month.

He stood up to go. "If you want my advice—"

"I don't."

"If you want my advice, I'd be careful. I know she's stunning, but she's got a problem. Maybe it's drugs, maybe it's something else, I've watched her. It's like watching two different people, bright and gay one day, utterly depressed the next—and usually alone."

"Alone? Ridiculous; she has dozens of friends."

Brown shook his head. "She's a performer. That's my impression. Puts on an act. Underneath, there's a problem. And a lot of loneliness. Well, you won't take any notice of anything I say, so I'll be going. Just keep her out of the shop, that's all."

As soon as he left I began composing a lecture to give Daisy. Something about the difference between crimes of flamboyant self-indulgence like drug taking and crimes of dishonesty, which always have a squalid dimension. Unlike her, I was brought up on mean streets. I knew what happened to thieves in the end. It wasn't pretty.

I had to go look for her. I found her in our local pub, sitting alone with a pint of beer. She was staring sullenly straight ahead and seemed not to have noticed my arrival. I pulled up a chair.

"Don't."

"Don't what?"

"Don't give me the lecture you've been preparing. If you do, I'm out of here. You'll never see me again. I'm sorry about two things. I'm sorry I got caught, and I'm sorry you were dragged into it. That's all."

I ordered a beer and sat with her in silence for a while. I tried touching her on her arms and neck several times, but she seemed almost insensate. Her flesh was devoid of its usual electric glow, as if her spirit had fled. Then, after another pint, she nodded without smiling.

"Let's go, James."

In bed that night she said, "Do you know who he reminded me of?"

"Your father?"

"Correct."

"But why? Your father is a sophisticated American professor. Brown's just a manager of a small supermarket."

She sighed. "The fanaticism. Didn't you see the look in his eye? He didn't care about the money. He cared that I was wrong and he was right."

"Your father's like that?"

"Oh, sure. He's a thousand times more sophisticated than Brown, but see, ultimately psychologists have to believe in the rules of society. They're our priests. Society's rules shape our minds, and the shrinks are a big part of the shaping process. According to them, if you're at war with society, you're at war with yourself. A sociopath, a psycho."

"To a lawyer, that doesn't sound all wrong."

She turned to face me. "Did I ever tell you my Montezuma story?"

"I don't think so."

"When Cortés first conquered Mexico, he kept Montezuma under house arrest. One night Montezuma heard one of Cortés's soldiers urinating near his bedroom. The next day he complained strongly to Cortés, who was very sympathetic and had the man reprimanded and removed."

I waited. "So?"

"Montezuma was a cannibal. Every morning he ate the flesh of children who had been freshly slaughtered. See, in his kingdom there was a rule against pissing within the hearing of the king, but no rule against eating children."

"So there's a difference between law and morality?"

"You got it."

"In a different time and place, Brown and your father would have been cannibals?"

"Or Gestapo."

I scratched my head. "But does theft become right, just because you don't approve of the society in which you live?"

She lay on her back again, stared at the ceiling. She seemed to be quoting from a book. "In some Hindu cults, deliberately breaking sacred laws was a magical act that liberated the soul and opened the mind to a greater reality. Never wanted to escape, Jimmy? I mean from all of it, even the body itself? Just fucking take off and fly without looking back, forever?"

I waited until the next evening to probe further.

"Don't psychologists believe that one's relationship with society is determined by the relationship with the stronger parent?"

"Sure."

"So your view of society is really your view of your father?"

She yawned. "Don't get polluted too soon, Natural Man; I might go off you." She glanced at me. "Okay, you really want to get into this? Look at it from the macro point of view. American society produced my father, right? He's just a microcosm of those values. It's not irrational to treat America with the contempt he deserves."

"But this is England."

"You really think there's such a big difference? Far as I can see, this is the States in a kind of grub state. You know, the full metamorphosis into the air-conditioned nightmare hasn't happened yet, but it's just a matter of time."

I felt like an amateur who'd stepped into the ring with a world heavyweight.

"So tell me, what was so very bad about your father? Did he beat you?"

"Ah! Natural Man! What I wouldn't have given for an old-fashioned thrashing, followed by a cathartic hug. A good beating would have been charmingly naive compared to what my mother and I had to go through."

"Like what?"

She thought for a moment. "It's not easy to explain, it works on such a subtle level. See, psychologists are known to be extremely controlling parents. They have a paranoia about their kids' developing deviant behavior. So parental control goes right down to the wire. Nothing escapes examination, every gesture is charged with symbolic value. Peeing in your pants, picking your nose, blinking—"

"Blinking?"

"Sure. There's a whole body of learning devoted to blinking.

'Daisy, what's going on? Your blink frequency is off the scale, honey.' "

"A little claustrophobic maybe, but surely not—"

"Let me tell you one thing about my father. He was asked to take charge of a mental hospital in Vermont one semester, thanks to some academic paper he'd published about catatonics. His theory was that it's mostly a defense mechanism that can be broken. The hospital was full of extreme cases—criminal psychos—and of course catatonics. He saw it as a challenge—how to beat catatonia the American way. So he took six of the milder cases, told them that they weren't going to get anything to drink until they spoke. Catatonics, as a rule, just don't talk, right? Then he had them injected with saline solution that contained a massive concentration of salt. They were literally dying of thirst within an hour."

"So what happened?"

"Five of them started screaming for water. The sixth held out until irreversible brain damage. She traded catatonia for a coma. Died within the year. My father saw the experiment as a personal triumph. Course, the five survivors stopped talking again as soon as they drank the water, but Dad used it to score points with the APA—the American Psychological Association. That's the man who reared me."

"Didn't he get in trouble?"

"Nah. The whole hospital board was behind him. They hushed it up. Who's gonna fight for the rights of a dead catatonic anyway? Atrocities happen every day in American nuthouses."

"Did he do anything like that to you?" I asked, my blood beginning to boil.

She held up her left arm to show me a long transparent line of scar tissue about a quarter inch thick on the back of the forearm. I'd mentioned it once, but she'd refused to talk about it.

"He did that?"

"No, I did. His favorite punishment was solitary confinement— in the boiler room. I'm not talking hours, but days, sometimes a week. Imposed with maximum cruelty, so that he'd let you out in the sunshine to make you think it was all over, but he was only giving you a taste of what you were missing. An hour later, you were back alone in the dark. One time—I was about thirteen—I realized I was starting to lose my mind. I knew I had to scare him out of it. So I pressed my arm against one of the hot pipes until the skin started to burn. I kept it there until it was a real mess. I knew he'd be scared of any implication of physical brutality. It worked. He never locked me up alone after that, but he had other methods. I was right, though, about nearly going out of my mind. If it hadn't been for Mom, I'd be a basket case by now. She never judged or punished. She was just there with a lot of healing love." She smiled. "Like you, Jimmy. I'm sorry if I got in a pissy mood over what happened with Brown. See, you never judged me before, unlike any American man I ever knew. I couldn't stand it if you started now. That has to be the deal, darling. You want me to go, I'll go. But if I stay, it's on a nonjudgmental basis. Agreed?"

"Sure." I rubbed my jaw. "But I'm a little out of my depth here. How long does it take a person to get over a childhood like that?"

She stared at me, blinked, smiled slowly. "Oh, baby, you're so cute. I know what you believe. You believe there's a moment in everyone's life when they finally grow up and everything's all right with them forevermore. Don't you? C'mon, admit it."

Since there were no serious repercussions, the incident soon faded from view, melted down and purified in the heat of our passion. But to the rest of the world, Daisy was subdued for a while and went out less, even when I was working. Quite often she sat and stared. And of course the supermarket was a constant and unpleasant reminder, especially if Brown was standing near the door, with his legs planted apart, watching us.

As far as I was concerned, I don't believe it would have made much difference in the long run if she'd been caught robbing a bank. The fact is that my heart was full of gratitude. Her capacity for love and friendship, if anything softened and increased by the incident, was overwhelming to one who had assumed the environment to be unremittingly hostile. My nerves unraveled in her company, and she gave me what must be the greatest gift a young woman can give to a tormented young man. She taught me that I was neither unlovable nor unsexy, and as a result I became, I trust, a little less of both. I know that it is a desperately unfashionable thing to say, but in return I do not believe I have ever seriously loved another woman.

Social conditioning is a curious phenomenon. There is a passage from Dickens I would sometimes take out and read when she was not there:

> Cast in so slight and exquisite a mold; so pure and beautiful; . . . the changing expression of sweetness and good humor, the thousand lights that played about the face and left no shadow there; above all, the smile, the cheerful, happy smile . . .

This inner image of Daisy existed in parallel with the knowledge that she was a thief, by some definitions a drug addict, and harbored dreams of patricide. I had a client once, a delightful West Indian lady embezzler in her sixties, of Punjabi extraction, who had been one of the last indentured servants in Jamaica. She told me that the remarkable thing about Christianity in the West Indies in her youth was that the blacks really believed that the whites obeyed the Ten Commandments, despite daily proof to the contrary.

I I

By the middle of 1976, my undergraduate worldview had crumbled. I had spent a year of hard graft studying in London for my bar exams and then served my required twelve months apprenticeship as a barrister, called "pupillage," while Daisy had finished her degree. The need for one of us to commute, weekends, between London and Warwick had made not a dent in the intensity of our relationship, but now I found myself plunged into what as students we had referred to as The Future. None of the descriptions of reality provided by Mick, Che, or Bertrand quite prepared one for the gritty taste of the thing itself.

I had given up my beard, long hair, jeans, sweater, and two thirds of my stoop, cynically discarded a whole identity, in fact, in exchange for a place at the bottom of a long and crowded ladder. A ladder, moreover, that seemed to be planted somewhere near the center of the pit. What my clerk meant when he described my cases as "good quality" was that I was spending more and more of my working day with increasingly vicious criminals. Gradually the incompetent burglars, the clumsy shoplifters, the sad addicts of indecent exposure, gave way to men (they were usually men) who did not care at all if they permanently damaged the bodies or ruined the lives of innocent people. To meet the victim of a violent crime can be a harrowing experience when you are representing the man who did it. No doubt I began to talk about crime, the law, and the police in a way that as a student would have got me lynched.

My final defection came one night at the beginning of winter when I summoned the courage to walk into El Vino's Wine Bar in Fleet Street, where the other barristers from my chambers congregated after work. A debate was in progress about the morality of prosecution work.

"Pure prostitution," one young idealist said. "What do you think, Knight?"

I managed to stammer and confess that my attitudes had begun to alter radically. I gave the example of a pretty girl of eighteen whose face had been smashed and sinuses permanently ruined by my brute of a client, whom I had successfully defended because of a technical flaw in the prosecution's case. I had told a furious judge why he could not allow the case to proceed, but was not particularly proud of the result.

"Don't get overinvolved, for God's sake," an older barrister advised. "You'll spend the rest of your career oscillating between loathing the police and loathing the criminal. Just remember, neither of them eat at our mess or belong to our club."

"Hear, hear."

It was the most seductive phrase anyone had ever spoken to me, and I found that its warmth, like the wine, instantly began to worm its way into my heart. It meant, quite simply, that for those of us in the club, the war was elsewhere.

I took to going to El Vino's regularly after that. Within a week it seemed that I was an old hand myself, with a regular seat and a certain welcome.

Like an Islington slum, my gentrification took place almost overnight. Scrub a cockney clean, throw some money at him, change the angle from which he views himself, and you will invariably find a would-be aristocrat all ready to rise at ten-thirty and swagger down the Strand. I exchanged my barber for a hair stylist and my Burton's suit for something by Yves Saint Laurent, albeit still off the peg. To Daisy's alarm, I found that I enjoyed French cuffs and bought some gold cuff links with a set of new shirts. As for my breast-pocket silk handkerchief, Daisy fished it out on the first day and claimed, afterward, to have done something obscene with it so that I could never bring myself to wear it again.

Unlike Daisy, my colleagues approved of my newfound sartorial awareness. Within a month, gibes, camaraderie, and red wine at El Vino's had become what Daisy called my "male support system." In revenge, she went to assertiveness training classes and refused to do the dishes.

Living in one room, there wasn't a lot to wash. I had bought extra cups and tea plates, which collected on the coffee table during the week until Saturday morning, when we had a division-of-labor day. Daisy devoted some of her raised consciousness to the issue of whether it was more traditionally female to wash than to wipe and decided that it was, with the consequence that she wiped while I washed.

12

One night after El Vino's, I returned to our tiny bed-sit in Belsize Park, to the familiar acrid smell of Daisy's joint and a dope-inspired smirk.

"It's all over, Jimmy. The inquisition's caught up with you."

"What are you talking about, junkie?"

It was cold outside, and I was numb after the walk from the underground. For once I was glad Daisy kept our little room at a tropical temperature. She liked to smoke her marijuana naked in a semi-lotus position, one heel pressed into her vagina. This was more or less all that remained of her yoga phase, although sometimes she closed her eyes, put her hands on her knees, and chanted a mantra. Her full breasts, only slightly pendulous, pointed at me as I crossed the room toward her. There she sat, an angel smoking a joint.

Her perfect body made a perfect contrast to the chaos in which she lived. The bed was a mess, open books were strewn over the

floor, clothes left wherever she had taken them off. Loathing un-
tidiness, I could never bear to be in the room alone.

Her flesh felt like hot silk under my frozen hands.

"Don't. You're freezing."

She shivered but did not try to stop me. I made goose pimples
ruffle the skin of one arm; a nipple puckered under my cold touch.
I knelt down so that I could continue to trace her unresisting flesh
as far as her thighs. She obliged by moving her heel. I stood up
again, started to undress, looked for a spare chair on which to hang
my suit—there were none. I laid the jacket carefully on the end of
the bed. It was a daily concern of mine, how to live with Daisy
and have smart clothes to wear for court.

"I'll soon warm up. You know the statutory penalty for risking
my career by smoking cannabis at home."

"Now?"

I stood on one foot to take off a sock.

"Immediately."

I took off the other sock.

"Which way, sir?"

"That was pretty good. Are you warmer now?" she said later.

I reached under my left thigh to remove a new feminist pa-
perback. "Part of me is."

"Which part?"

"Not sure, you'd better check."

"This part?"

"Yes, that part's quite warm."

"This part?"

"Ditto."

"Now, what about *this* part?"

"Could do with some warming up."

"You mean you want some more?"

"Yes, I believe I do."

"Can you, straight away?"

"I think I can tonight."

"My God, you must have been eating oysters at one of those
swanky bars in the City." She yawned. "You can use me if you

like, you wicked man; I want to turn around. Hey, by the way. . . ."
She reached for a piece of paper, one breast dangling off the bed,
the other crushed under her. On the paper she had scribbled "Reverend James Hogg" and a telephone number. I took the paper,
tossed it on the floor. She lay dreamily on her side with her back
to me, and only grunted when I entered her.

Eventually I remembered to ask about the Reverend James
Hogg.

"I didn't quite understand what he was saying—I was stoned.
Something to do with Wormwood Scrubs and ring him when you
get home, no matter how late." She mimicked a fey male voice.

She relit her joint as we lay tangled and naked. I listened to
the catch of her breath as she sucked in.

"Like a puff?"

She handed it to me. For once I took a long draw. The drug
seemed to gather together the soft glow of red wine that lingered
from El Vino's, my satisfaction at the progress of my career, my
apparently inexhaustible appetite for Daisy, and postcoital contentment. For a full ten minutes it seemed to me that nothing could
ever hurt me again. I expanded to take in the room, the city, the
world. Then Daisy's voice punctured the moment.

"Are you going to call him?"

"Who?"

"Our man from God."

"What?"

"The Reverend James, junkie!"

"Oh, I forgot."

"You're stoned." Daisy giggled while I sleepily dragged on a
pair of trousers and a sweater to go downstairs to the phone in the
freezing hall. The contrast with my contentment of seconds earlier
made me irritable. The receiver was cold against my ear. A tense
high-pitched voice said something about Oliver Harry Thirst and
parole and suggested that we meet somewhere at my convenience
as soon as possible, perhaps after work the next day.

"What's it about, exactly?"

"I'd much prefer to explain face-to-face. May I put it like this—
that it may be an opportunity to contribute in a slightly different
way to the legal process? Do bring your wife."

"She's not my wife, Reverend; we just live together."

"Do please call me James," he said as we hung up.

When I returned to our room, Daisy was sitting up in bed, wearing a huge dirty white sweater that I found very sexy. Once she'd gone out to post a letter wearing it and nothing else, and I had been angry and very aroused. Ever since then the sweater had served as our equivalent of black stockings and French lingerie.

"What was it all about?"

"Oliver Thirst."

"Hey! That good-looking crook you take for walks?"

"If you make that kind of insinuation, I'll have to demonstrate my virility."

"Again?"

"Afraid so—that sweater drives me crazy. Look!"

Later, she said, "What did the padre say about Thirst?"

"He wants me to help rehabilitate him."

She raised her head from my chest. "And you will, of course?"

I tried to press her head back down. "We're meeting the reverend tomorrow. We'll see."

"We'll see," she said into my breastbone.

13

The next evening we walked up the hill to Hampstead, to a pub where real ale was sold and the Reverend James Hogg waited. I had come from a conference with an armed robber (he had destroyed the face of a middle-aged man at a petrol station by firing a shotgun at him) and his equally dishonest solicitor; Daisy had come from another unnecessary assertiveness training session with her women's group.

She tended to emerge from such meetings with the dangerous eye of a zealot and an unfocused fury in search of a cause. Her moods were not improved by what was, for her, an unusually busy timetable. When not honing her personal assertion skills, she was training to be an English teacher at a further-education college. Eight hours or more per day of focused attention left her either exhausted or hyper, depending on how she had slept the night before. We walked in silence. I was careful to make sure that she led the way.

He was already there, standing at the bar, and despite the number of people around, I knew him instantly. He looked uncomfortable, but then his was the kind of presence that would have looked uncomfortable anywhere. What one noticed immediately was a powerful physique that filled the Harris tweed jacket and open-necked checkered shirt and ill-fitting denims.

It was a body built for rugby or wrestling. An impeccable musculature moved effortlessly under his clothes. But out of it emerged a thin neck and a small chinless head. In any other mold this would have amounted to ordinary plainness, but on top of such a body there was the strangeness of incongruity, like a bodybuilder with a withered limb.

His turtle face was the opposite of his body: weak and inchoate, ready to assume the shape of whatever personality it was close to.

"Two Jameses," he offered apologetically when we introduced ourselves.

"Not as good as two Dicks," Daisy said, and he blushed. It was the most vicar-like thing he did all evening. We watched him gesture weakly to the barman for drinks.

The drinks came, two and a half pints of dark beer, the two pints for Daisy and me and the half for himself.

"I telephoned you last night because—"

"Because Thirst wants early parole and he's in some other kind of trouble that would cause problems with the parole board—am I right?" I had worked it out when I woke that morning and remembered the phone call. Now my armed robber had put me in a hostile mood toward villains.

"Well, yes." He blushed again. "Oliver did say you would need talking round."

"Old Jimmy's a flogging, hanging, let-'em-rot type these days," Daisy said. "You should have called three months ago, Reverend, when he was a civil-rights, amnesty-for-all, break-down-the-walls-which-divide-us type. He's been remarketed. The humble workingman's cottage that was his soul is now a 'bijou residence within twenty minutes of the city,' as your British estate agents like to say."

I held my hands up helplessly. "It's a no-win situation. If I tell her to shut up, it's a classic case of male dominance."

"You bet," Daisy said.

"I would not suggest that Daisy shut up," Hogg said. "I thought that what she said was very . . ."

"Very?"

"Very witty."

"Thank you, Padre." She bared her teeth at me. There was an awkward silence before I stood up to go to the toilet.

The men's toilet at this particular pub was famous for its graffiti. I searched the walls for something new and witty to cheer me up but found only the same old jokes. The one I liked best was a diagram of two cubes bearing the legend "Balls by Picasso." Another scrawl said, "Life on earth is a cure for all those diseases you caught in space." I wondered if women would think up some good jokes for their walls now that they were liberated.

When I forced my way back through the throng, they'd bought more drinks.

"Guess what, the reverend's father was a power freak just like mine, and he hates his too."

"I didn't say I hated him." His blushes were as predictable as a church bell by now. "He was a colonel. The British officer mold is a good two hundred years out of date." He looked at me earnestly. "It's so uncompromising, you see—black or white, good or bad, accept or reject. It's essentially . . . well, un-Christian."

"So did you accept or reject?"

"His father wanted him to be a chaplain in the army, but he told him where to shove it." She sounded excited.

Another blush. "I . . . well, if you want to know, I went through something of a crisis. I was being trained to be a kind of apologist to God for the officer class and a father figure to the troops. But except in Belfast, it seemed to me . . . well, even the sergeants had new cars, semidetached houses. I wasn't there to relieve suffering; I was there to relieve guilt. I wondered if guilt wasn't the only Christian thing we had left. I asked myself where Christ would have worked if he'd been born in modern England."

"And the answer was Southeast London?"

He frowned. "Sorry, it's very self-indulgent of me to talk about myself. I came to talk about Oliver."

"How well did he say he knew me?"

"He said you were his only friend."

"I met with him socially twice—once after I got him off a criminal offense of which he was clearly guilty, and once when he telephoned me in chambers and we went for a walk over Waterloo Bridge. We only got halfway. He stormed off in a huff because he didn't like the advice I gave him."

"What advice was that?" Daisy said. "Pull your socks up, Carruthers, and remember you're British?"

Just as I was about to lose my temper, Hogg intervened. "He didn't say he knew you well; he said you were his only friend. Look, I'm obviously not handling this very well. He's not ... well, it doesn't seem to me that he's asking very much. You don't have to put him up or guarantee his overdraft or anything of that sort. A lot has happened to him in Wormwood Scrubs; he's had a rough time. He was raped, he got syphilis, the other inmates think he's a grass, and you know what that means—I'm sure I don't need to tell you. People of his background get trapped. The only people they know are other criminals. To walk across the no-man's-land between their world and ours, they need at least one hand reaching out from the other side."

"Grass?" Daisy said. "I learned that once. It's a verb, too, right? I grass, you grass, etc.?"

"Police informant," Hogg said.

"I love crookspeak," Daisy told Hogg.

"So what does he want?" I said.

"Well, there's this other silly offense hanging over his head—he used a phony check to buy a pair of trousers. Of course it's not the sort of thing he would ever go to jail for, but if his conviction stands he'll never get parole."

"So what can I do?"

"He wants someone clever to think up an argument for an appeal. He says all the other criminal barristers he knows are just hacks. They only go through the motions; with you he might have a chance."

I felt Daisy's eyes on me. Angry that she thought she had the right to regard this as a test, I found myself saying the things she was most likely to loathe in exactly the kind of voice she was likely to detest.

"I'm afraid it's quite out of the question—I have my career to think of. A barrister can't be seen befriending convicted criminals and then representing them as a favor. Our reputation is everything. How could I have any credibility in front of a judge if I started making friends with crooks?"

"But you did, didn't you?" he asked, seething with compassion. "When you went for a drink with him the first time, then when you agreed to meet him at the temple? Was that not motivated by sympathy, kindness?" His eyes gleamed.

"No, it wasn't. Neither of you understand, and you never will. Guilt is a middle-class vice and do-goodery exists to relieve you of the discomfort of guilt. Not to help anyone. I don't have class guilt. We're practical people, us working-class lads, and guilt has no practical value. If you weren't both living in some guilt-ridden fairy tale, you would realize the enormity of what Thirst needs. He doesn't need to get out of jail one month early; he needs to be relieved of twenty years of programming. To be convinced that the description of the world he's been learning since birth is fundamentally wrong, and that your white-collar toy town is the real thing. Don't you see? His whole problem is that he sees the world more accurately than you. He knows it's rotten and hostile and corrupt. One little drop of sugar-coated kindness isn't going to change that. Prove to me that he's got it in him to amputate his past—like I did. Can you do that? And if he does, will the result be all that much of an improvement?"

"If you think that, why did you meet with him?" Daisy demanded.

I turned to her. "The same reason What's-his-name looked back at Hades—the fascination the one that got away feels for the others still squirming in the pit."

The rest of that evening is a blur to me. Hogg left soon after my harangue, saying he was not as clever as me, just a humble clergyman. He was sorry to have upset me.

Daisy demanded another pint of beer, which she drank very quickly before telling me what a disappointment I was to her. Male insecurity made all men sell their souls for power and status. She had thought I was different. What had happened to me? Didn't I care anymore? I had a real chance to help a fellow human being, and all I could do was worry about what some pompous geriatric judge would say.

By the end of the pint she was comparing me with her father. I was turning into an English replica of him. If I thought she was going to slave and kowtow for the rest of her life like her mother, I needed to have my head examined.

The momentum of her mood forced her to end on a high note.

"You've blown it, baby. I hope your goddamn career is enough for you, because there isn't room for me and it both."

I was upset and drunk and yelled back. "Look at you. You think it's a showdown at the O.K. Corral. Grow up, Yank, for God's sake."

The only scene left to her in the theater of tantrums was to storm out of the pub, which she did. I finished my beer slowly and followed, ignoring amused stares from the other drinkers.

I found her a hundred yards down the road, sobbing against a lamppost. I put my arm around her. She pulled me against her and covered my face with tears and kisses.

"Oh God, Jimmy, what's happening to me—us? I don't want us to lose it, Jimmy. I really don't."

I held her tight. I wanted to say that I loved her for her madness as well as her wisdom, that I loved every inch of her. As it was, I said something quite different.

"I don't know, Daisy. Every time you come back from that women's group, you want to pick a fight. Don't you think you might stop going?"

"If you stop going to El Vino's."

We walked home in a state of exhaustion. I insisted on making love, which she did obediently and passionlessly.

"Anyway, What's-his-name didn't look back to see the others still squirming in hell; he looked back to make sure What's-*her*-name was okay. They weren't too hot on the classics at your wonderful British concrete comprehensive, were they?" she said before turning over and falling asleep, apparently instantly.

I also fell into an alcoholic doze, until the buzzer in our room woke me, a signal that I was wanted on the phone in the hall. I pulled on a sweater and jeans and stood shivering while Hogg, tense and apologetic as ever, tried again.

"I telephoned to apologize. It wasn't very clever of me, just putting it to you like that in front of your girlfriend without any thought for your career. I've been thinking about it. What's so special about Oliver Thirst is the obvious question you must be asking. Why stick our necks out for him and not somebody else?"

"I know, I know, an IQ of 140 and a terrible childhood—"

"No, no, that's just it, the point I so stupidly failed to make is this: you said can I prove that he will change? Well, of course I can't prove it, but I've spent a lot of time with prisoners, and I've never seen anyone so determined to get out and stay out in all my life."

"Reverend—"

"No, please. I think I realize where I went wrong. The last thing you want in this situation is the personal connection, am I right? A prison chaplain contacting you on behalf of a prisoner without going through a solicitor is a breach of your rules of etiquette?"

"Well . . ."

"So suppose Oliver's solicitors formally asked for you to conduct the appeal, and our little conversation tonight is totally forgotten—wouldn't that be acceptable?"

"Well . . ." I tried to think. It was against the rules to represent a friend, but Thirst wasn't that. Hogg sensed victory and kept talking.

"I mean, I expect it would enhance your career, wouldn't it—at your stage, to have solicitors asking for you to do an appeal? It would be a bit odd, wouldn't it, if you refused? In those circumstances, I mean?"

He had a point. Much as barristers affected to look down on solicitors, we depended on them entirely for work. If one was asking for me personally to do something difficult and challenging like an appeal, it could help my marketing.

"Possibly . . ."

"Then you'll do it?"

"If the brief is properly delivered, I'll consider it, if I have no other engagements. I'll have to get a leader, of course. I'm too junior to do it all on my own."

"Whatever," Hogg said. "I'll tell Oliver. It'll all be on legal aid, of course."

"Of course."

14

Within days a clerk from a firm of solicitors I had never worked for arrived with the brief for Thirst's appeal. I happened to be in chambers, and my own clerk rang me in my room.

"It's from a firm we don't normally work with, sir, and it's an appeal. The brief has your name on it."

I walked down the creaking old corridor to the clerks' room. Michael, my clerk, wore a queer look on his face.

"This is Mr. Drew from Southall, Baines and Low."

The solicitor's clerk wore no tie or suit. He was unshaven. His eyes darted.

"I was told you'd agreed to take the brief," he said.

"Impossible—surely you know it all has to be arranged through my clerk?"

"Oh—yeah." He gave a long wink to Michael, who looked away.

I beckoned Michael out of the room. "What's wrong?"

"It's rather odd, sir—we've refused work from that firm in the past."

"Why?"

"They're a bit notorious, sir. That clerk's done time, and the senior partner only just escaped being struck off the roll last year—a suggestion of fraud. Some chambers have banned them altogether, though they're quite popular with heavy villains."

"Shall I refuse the brief?"

"It's up to you, sir. I suppose just once wouldn't hurt—it would be good for you to have your first appeal under your belt, get you into a bigger league."

"I'd better have a look at the brief. Will you fetch it for me?"

Michael brought the small bundle of papers. It was properly done up in red tape, but most of the documents were not typed at all. They were written in black ballpoint in a childish hand and full of misspelled words. There being no logical order to the narrative, I had to spend ten minutes working through them before I was clear about what had happened. Thirst had bought a book of stolen checks from his co-accused, a young man named Spoke, for thirty pounds. Both had been staying in a dormitory in a Salvation Army hostel at the time. Doubtless Thirst had used a number of the checks for his fraudulent purposes, but he had been convicted on only one count. He had written a check for fifty pounds to buy a new pair of Levi's and some other articles of clothing. I noticed, with a little twitch of excitement, that the shop assistant had been an accomplice, although the shop had not pressed charges against its employee—out of fear perhaps. Shop windows are easily smashed.

I took the papers to my room. A winnable appeal was considerably more tempting than one which simply went through the motions. When Hogg spoke to me that night, it had not occurred to me that Thirst might actually have a chance, albeit on a technicality. People remembered junior barristers who won cases in the Court of Criminal Appeal. A good Queen's Counsel could build an argument out of that shop assistant. So could I. I picked up the phone.

"Michael, tell that clerk to go. I'll think about doing the appeal and let him know by four this afternoon."

I looked at my watch. It was lunchtime. Daisy, who had Wednesday afternoons free, came into town to have lunch with me when I wasn't in court. I put on my jacket, looked into the clerks' room, told Michael I would be a couple of hours.

"I know, sir—Wednesday." He smiled. The last time Daisy had been in chambers, she had made an outrageous joke that Michael and the other clerks laughed about for days. "Terrific tits *and* a sense of humor," I overheard one of them say.

"These Yanks have fantastic appetites, too, they say."

"No wonder he's so skinny."

"That's enough, you lot," Michael had said.

I always looked forward to these lunches, even when I knew we were going to argue. Law can be a monochrome pursuit. Daisy, with her moods of many colors, chased away the feeling of mental arthritis that came from too much law.

I walked across the open quadrangle with its large flagstones, around Temple Church, where crusading knights were buried, past the news vendor on the corner of Fleet Street, and up Chancery Lane. The whole area was teeming with lawyers in search of lunch, mostly barristers in smart three-piece suits, some with wing collars. The women barristers, sensitive to any accusation of professional coquetry, wore severe suits, white blouses buttoned up to the neck. I often marveled at the way even beautiful women could extinguish their sex appeal when it suited their purposes. I admired them, too, for competing in a very male profession where the odds were stacked against them. It would have been so easy to manipulate through sex, but so far as I knew, they usually resisted the temptation.

Daisy was already waiting in our favorite Italian restaurant, saving our usual table by the window, since no reservations were accepted at lunchtime. She wore a bright-yellow silk scarf loosely knotted around her neck. Soft cotton dresses with large floral patterns were part of the latest neo-Victorian phase. Daisy's dress was one she'd been talking about for weeks and must have bought earlier that morning. It fitted closely around her torso like a bodice, was white with enormous crimson roses that clashed, I supposed deliberately, with the scarf. As she twisted around in her seat to kiss me, it was obvious that she was not wearing a bra.

"Thank God you've arrived—they've been hassling me about keeping the table."

"Italian waiters hassling you? Dressed like that, I'm surprised they didn't offer to clear the whole place."

"D'you like it?"

"Actually—yes, very much."

"You don't think it's too over the top?"

"Of course it is. That's why you've chosen to wear it in a restaurant you knew would be filled with members of the world's most conservative profession."

She leaned forward. "Well, a touch of color won't do them any harm."

People—the women as much as the men—stared at her as they entered, passersby in the street did a double take through the windows. It was impossible to avoid her, like a candle in an otherwise dark room. I felt immensely proud and faintly mischievous.

"I shouldn't tell you this, but I doubt that there are ten other women in England who could wear that dress and get away with it. Especially with that scarf."

She fluttered her eyelashes. "Well, maybe the scarf is a bit much." She unknotted it, tossed it carelessly on a seat beside her. More roses bloomed.

"What shall we order—the usual?"

"I think so. And first things first."

I ordered a bottle of Chianti Classico. Daisy ordered insalata caprese followed by lasagna, I wanted prosciutto with melon and then spaghetti.

"You always order spaghetti."

"Reminds me of the first meal we had together."

"Brenda."

"I wonder what happened to her."

"I saw her in the street a while back—she pretended not to recognize me. Very short hair, back and sides, very fierce-looking."

"Political lesbian?"

"Probably—but I doubt that it's purely political. Remember

that sort of breakdown she had when I moved in with you?"

We sipped our wine, remembering.

"You've got something to tell me, haven't you?" Daisy said.

"How did you know?"

"I've lived with you on and off for four years, I've broken all your codes, pal. There was an I've-got-a-bit-of-news-for-her smirk on your face when you came in."

"My God, don't you find intimacy scary sometimes?"

"Sure. That's why I'm glad you're not as intuitive as me. So let's have it."

"The brief for Thirst's appeal arrived this morning. Delivered by an ex-convict."

"And you're going to do the appeal?"

"A brief for a gangster who's claiming to be my friend, delivered by an ex-convict working for one of the most disreputable solicitors' firms in London? Out of the question."

"More than your job's worth, I suppose?"

"Exactly."

"You're lying." She picked at her salad. "You've decided to do it."

"No."

"Well, it's up to you—it's your career after all. I'm not going to interfere, any more than you would with mine."

"Why on earth should I do that? I've always encouraged you. I happen to think you'll make a great teacher."

"I wasn't referring to teaching. As you know, my real talent lies in shoplifting."

"I see."

"And maybe burglary. I was reading the other day about a dramatic increase in women burglars. I think I'll go to a gym, get fit, and become a cat burglar."

"Don't expect me to represent you when you get caught."

"Don't worry—I know I'm expected to die rather than damage your career."

The waiter brought Daisy's lasagna and my spaghetti, poured us some more Chianti. His eyes dilated over Daisy. He asked with special care if everything was all right.

"Terrific." Daisy gave him a dazzling smile.

"You are the luckiest man in London," he said to me, "if you don't mind my saying so. Another bottle?"

"If you're going to say things like that, how can I refuse?"

He nodded. "One bottle is never enough when you're in love."

Daisy and I looked at each other and laughed.

"Sometimes, Daisy, you have this disgusting way of giving the whole world a hard-on."

"On the contrary, dear boy, as you people say. I have to tell you it's our ultra-hot passion which has that effect. Now, are you going to come clean about that appeal, or do I describe in a loud voice how I recently robbed Boots of five packets of Tylenol, a family-size box of Kleenex, and a packet of condoms?"

"Don't believe you. We don't use condoms, you're on the pill, and Tylenol is an American brand name—you hardly see it over here. But if it will keep your voice down, I'll admit that I'm inclining toward accepting instructions to represent Oliver Harry Thirst in his appeal against conviction. Subject, of course, to further consideration."

"Inclining toward, are we? And what would tip the balance, d'you think? A blow job under the table maybe?"

"Daisy—not so loud. Please."

"Okay, you asked for it." She fished in her handbag for a pen, started to write on a paper napkin. When she had finished, she passed the napkin over to me:

> Between Daisy Smith of the one part (hereafter "the Fellator") and James Knight of the other part (hereafter "the Fellatee"):
>
> In return for the Fellatee accepting instructions to represent Oliver Harry Thirst in his appeal, the Fellator hereby undertakes at a time and place of the Fellatee's choice to perform oral sex on the Fellatee for seven minutes or until orgasm, whichever is the sooner.

"Did I get the legalese right? Just sign at the bottom, please." Daisy handed me the pen. I signed the napkin. She sighed. "I presume you want to defer payment till after lunch?"

*   *   *

We managed to finish both bottles of Chianti, which was unusual for us. The waiter waved happily when we left, holding hands. The fresh air only made me realize how drunk I was.

"I'll walk with you back to chambers," Daisy said.

We crossed Holborn and proceeded a little unsteadily down Chancery Lane. Near Lincoln's Inn we both stopped on a common impulse. The napkin was now in my pocket.

"Oh Christ," I said. A massive erection made walking uncomfortable.

Daisy, staring at my crotch, put a hand on it. "Take me somewhere, Jimmy—please. I'm gonna die if you don't fuck me in the next five minutes."

The walk down Chancery Lane, across Fleet Street, and down Middle Temple Lane to my chambers had never seemed so long. My mind was reluctant to focus on practical issues like how to cross the road safely. The imminent merging of our flesh had become an obsession. I felt unusually violent. I wanted revenge on her for making me want her so much.

I experienced no shame as we passed Michael on the stairs, although I knew, vaguely, that I would do so later. I thought that he looked faintly disappointed. My intentions, despite the polite smile fixed on my face, must have been all too obvious.

Once inside my room, I closed the door, pushed her roughly against it, locked it, and drew my hand up her dress, all in one premeditated movement.

"D'you want me to do what it says in the contract?" Daisy said.

"No. I want you much too badly for that."

There are moments, unchronicled usually, when a man feels the whole of his stock of seed pass, along with half his soul, into the body of his beloved. On the floor now, we gazed, drunk and exhausted, into each other's eyes.

"Wow," Daisy said.

15

My preparation for Thirst's appeal obliged me to visit him in the Scrubs, one of London's half-dozen jails of medium security for male offenders that date back to the Victorian era and suffer from serious overcrowding problems. I had visited clients in prison many times by then, but this was different. There was a connection between us. I felt him drawing me.

As each successive steel gate opened and then shut behind me, I felt like a nervous diver dropping into a black lake. I had my equivalent of an air supply, which is to say my right to leave at will, but the further I descended, the greater the risk that I would be somehow trapped.

"Prisoner?"

"Oliver Harry Thirst."

"Visitor for prisoner 732 Thirst."

"Thirst—732!" His name and number were sent bouncing off

the steel and concrete until they reached his cell, while I was walked to the interview room.

I was unable to shut out, as I usually did on prison visits, the thousand symptoms of a brutal and stunted masculinity—prisoners and screws alike. Viscous lechery, a black network of petty jealousies that bound them fast, infantile fixations that lived on twisted and thwarted in grown men, all were expressed through sustained glares, grotesque grins, childish graffiti. I had the impression that Thirst dwelt at the heart of this darkness. Despite—or perhaps because of—his penchant for betrayal, he was in many ways the recidivist's idea of royalty: good-looking, muscular, ever ready for violence, an unerring command of the dialect, an indifference to solitude. And he often implied through encoded words and gestures that only this extreme test of incarceration was worthy of his manhood.

"How are you, Oliver?"

"Fine, excellent, never been better. Always feel healthy in the nick—no booze, lots of exercise, no tarts to break your balls."

At the same time he was more desperate to get out than any prisoner I had ever seen. Without warning his narrowed eyes would dilate with anguish. I felt his envy of my freedom like a physical force pulling at my solar plexus. By turns he was hopeful and despairing.

"We gonna win, then?"

"You know I can't answer that."

His quick mind had seen from the start the importance of the appeal. Although the crime was minor, it came at a critical point in his accumulation of convictions. If he won, he might be let out early and have strings pulled for his rehabilitation. If not, he would be classified as a lost cause and left to rot.

I took him through his statement carefully, matched it to the evidence he had given at trial. The world that lay behind the documents was by now exceedingly familiar to me—a world where checks were stolen and traded like an alternative currency, where dishonesty guided the mind as it foraged in the high street, in shops, at night in quiet turnings. Where familiar English words carried subtle, cryptic meanings and almost every deliberate act had, as its objective, a victim. Sitting with him across the cheap prison table, the screw in profile on the other side of the reinforced glass, I felt as if I had stepped through a curtain. The distance any criminal practitioner needs in dealing with his clients, the conscious clipping of normal human intercourse in order to avoid overfamiliarity, was difficult to maintain with Thirst. It was as the social worker had said—he was intelligent. He knew what I was thinking, saw where I was going in my strategy for his appeal, was ready with the kind of answers I needed for my ideas to work.

"I like it. Yeah, that's just the way they think in the appeal court. More technical."

We are all most easily seduced by understanding. As a kind of trade-off for his effortless penetration of my mind, I was drawn reluctantly into his.

But I had only to step out again, into the light, for his influence to collapse. His world ended where mine began—the frantic thrust of daily affairs absorbed me totally. For him the great day no doubt arrived with agonizing slowness, while for me the time passed in a flash.

16

I slept little the night before. Old hands, even the toughest of them, confessed without shame to attacks of nerves before appearing before the Lord Chief Justice in the Court of Criminal Appeal. It made no difference that I was being "led" by a Queen's Counsel, which meant that I would probably not have to say anything.

I had prepared the case and done the research, and Harry Beaufort, Q.C., was dependent upon me for his lines. The case was in the ten-thirty list, and at about nine he was looking at the papers for the first time.

Beaufort was short, aggressive, and fifty, with a red face and an intimidating temper. I had chosen him because he often prosecuted and was therefore likely to gain the respect of a conservative court. He was unused to concepts borrowed, in part, from the law relating to bills of exchange and said "fuck" and "shit" a lot as I tried to explain the case to him. Then, at about nine-thirty, he said, "Got it," and I could see his mind close around the case like a steel trap.

"I suppose we'll have to see the illustrious client."

We put on our wing collars and gowns and walked across the Strand to the huge palace-like building that houses the Royal Courts of Justice. A lift took us down to some underground cells.

Thirst was classified as dangerous, which meant that there were a lot of burly warders standing around his cell. They knew Beaufort and called him "sir" with tangible respect. He used his angry voice to make them open the door quickly, without the usual standoff.

He and Thirst stared at each other from opposite ends of a social scale. Thirst was sitting in the corner of his cell and did not seem nervous. I knew enough about criminals by then to realize that he expected to lose the case. It's hope that causes tension.

"What's the story?" Beaufort said.

"No story. Mr. Knight had some good ideas, so I appealed."

"I know that—why the fuck do you think I'm here?"

Thirst smiled, almost shyly. I could see he liked Beaufort.

"So I ask again, what's the story?"

Thirst looked flustered for a moment under Beaufort's stare. I had no idea what was going on until Thirst lowered his eyes.

"I'm going to go straight this time, Mr. Beaufort, if you and Mr. Knight get me off."

"If we get you off it'll be thanks to this wizard." He jerked a thumb at me. "I don't give a damn if you go straight or not—have you any idea how many Jack the Lads I've seen in this very cell over the years? You know what? You all look the same to me, every one of you. That's what I've come to tell you—every little Jack the Lad who ever thought he was getting away with something looks about as interesting to me as a week-old dog turd. Because that's what you've made of your life, you've turned it into a stale piece of shit. If you remember that, it'll do you more good than a thousand probation officers. As for the appeal, you've got no chance, none at all."

He waited for this depressing advice to sink in. Then:

"Unless the Chief's in the right mood."

Thirst's face lit up again with that awful beam of gratitude. Beaufort could play him like a cheap whistle if there really was a chance.

"So—" Thirst began.

"So start praying. We're going up to court."

The Chief's Court in the Royal Courts of Justice may be the most intimidating piece of theater to be produced by a theatrical nation. Oaken terraces slope down to a well where humbled advocates plead heavenward.

As we entered, three empty red thrones waited on a dais so lofty it could have been part of another floor, quite separate from the one where we sat—and dedicated to other, more important business.

On a level with the dais but clinging shamefully to another wall was an iron cage with an inner door that led through labyrinths measureless to lawyers down to the sunless cells from which we had just emerged. It was part of the Victorian intention that when the court was sitting, the eye would move from the resplendent ones in ermine to the occupant of the cage and back again.

Beaufort sat in the row in front of me and below, reserved for Queen's Counsel. He put on his old gray wig carelessly and lounged against the bench with the silks whose cases were before ours.

A loud noise like the crack of a whip sent everyone, including Beaufort, to his feet. The Chief and his two assistant judges, in their Gilbert and Sullivan robes and wigs, walked briskly along the dais. We all bowed and sat down.

"Yes?" the Chief snapped.

"The Queen against . . ." the clerk shouted. One of the silks stood up and started to present his case. The Chief waited irritably for about a minute before interrupting.

"You mean to say, Mr. Cruikshank . . ." In an incredulous tone, the Chief restated the barrister's argument in terms that made it sound absurd.

"He's in a hell of a mood today," Beaufort said.

While the other silks argued their cases, Beaufort studied the books that we had brought with us and which I had carefully tagged at the relevant cases. His concentration was furious for about forty minutes, then he relaxed and listened to the other arguments.

About halfway through the morning, I happened to look up to the public gallery, to see Daisy sitting there. We'd had a dreadful argument the night before, identical in many ways to the one we'd had after meeting Hogg, but this time I had commanded the moral high ground: wasn't I representing Thirst in his appeal the very next day? Daisy had been more than usually contrite that morning. Now her chaotic blond hair tumbled over that huge dirty white sweater, and she waved gaily. America had at least left her unintimidated by British pomp. I wrote a hurried note: *Sorry we can't meet for lunch.* I was sure Beaufort would want to talk about the case if it was not over by then. My solicitors' clerk delivered the note and came back with another, written in her large generous hand and relying, for security, on some paper-folding trick:

> Jimmy darling, I just had to come and see you on your big day. I'm so sorry about last night, don't know what got into me, it must have been the time of the month because I've just started.... I do understand about your career and everything and I just love you to death. Good luck with your case, I know you'll win. Love, your adoring Daisy. P.S. You're a terrific fuck, too.

I hurriedly folded the note and was slipping it into an inside pocket when the head usher yelled out: "The Queen against Thirst."

The inside door of the hanging cage snapped open, and Thirst strode forward between two heavy warders.

From the moment he entered the cage I knew that Daisy's eyes were fixed upon him. I could feel her fascination, I knew her so well. For a moment I felt that I had our three fates in my hands. If I lost the appeal the animal would be caged indefinitely. But it was too late; the machine that was Beaufort's mind had already taken over—and anyway, I didn't believe in premonitions.

"M'Lud...," Beaufort began. As I listened, I had to admire the sophistication with which he had packaged my complicated argument. In turn he lolled casually against the bench behind him or turned sideways to put his foot up on his own bench, talking to the Chief as if on equal terms. The way he put it, you would almost believe there was no room for doubt. The Chief seemed amused.

"But if I understand you aright, Mr. Beaufort, you don't attempt to say that your client did not intend the fraud?"

"I submit that there was no fraud, M'Lud. This check, uniquely in my experience of cases like this, never could have had any validity, and the shop had actual or constructive knowledge when they accepted the check. There was no charge of attempt or conspiracy on the indictment."

"Was this put to the Court at first instance?"

"I'll let m'learned junior answer that." He sat abruptly down and started fiddling with some papers, quite as if he no longer had any part in the case. I stood up, with a huge hole where my stomach had been.

"Yes, it was, My Lord."

"Well, where in the transcript do we find it?" The Chief was suddenly furious again. For an awful minute I fumbled and found the passage. The three old gods peered suspiciously at their copies. I could feel Thirst and Daisy boring into my mind.

"But it wasn't put to the jury in the judge's summing up?"

"No, My Lord."

The Chief conferred in whispers, first with the judge on his left, then with the one on his right.

"Yes, very well, Mr.—er—Knight."

Beaufort immediately stood up and continued to develop his argument, while I sat down with relief. I sneaked a look at the gallery. Daisy, grinning, had both thumbs up. In the cage, Thirst sat on his bench, hands on both knees, elbows out, legs open, leaning forward.

Beaufort sat down shortly before one o'clock. The Chief said they would consider the matter over luncheon, and we all shot to our feet as the old men walked out in a row. The warders took Thirst away to his lunch in the cells.

"There are a few points I want to discuss," Beaufort said. I followed him down the long marble corridor. I was half afraid that Daisy would pop out from somewhere and tell Beaufort what a terrific fuck I was, but we managed to cross Fleet Street without ambush.

"Appeal allowed," the Chief told us after lunch.

I was still young enough to look for my approval not to Beaufort or to Thirst but to the gallery. Daisy beamed at me and with huge gestures the whole court could follow signaled that she would see me at home in an hour or so.

Beaufort sent me to see Thirst while he slipped off to El Vino's for a glass of wine before they shut at 3:00 P.M.

I felt terrific. There is no experience in the world quite like winning for the appellant in your first criminal appeal. It was a feeling, I discovered, that existed independently of the moral reservations I had begun to develop. To have snatched one vulnerable human life from the steel jaws of the System precipitated a thrill of boundless power such as David must have known. I knew, too, exactly what David had done with his favorite girlfriend while Goliath was still warm. I had quite forgotten my earlier premonition.

I spent the minimum amount of time with Thirst, who told me I was a genius, then treated myself to a taxi back to Daisy.

I thought there was a chance I would get there first, but when I reached home I found her naked with a bottle of champagne, all aglow. She was very moved by my victory. It meant a lot to her that Thirst would probably now go free a month or so earlier.

"You've done something incredible today, Jimmy. Think how awful it must be to be young and in prison. I think I'd die."

It was one of those occasions when the mysterious processes of her sexuality determined that our lovemaking would possess a holy dimension. Like any good artist, she needed only a minimum of props. Champagne lay with ice in the washbasin in the corner of the room, two sparkling clean tulip-shaped glasses waited on a table, she had combed her hair and swept it back. Her eyes were deeply vulnerable, her belly quivered when I touched it. I didn't need to be told to be gentle. She came with a great cry, her face twisted in disbelief.

"My God, that was amazing." She put her head on my shoulder, took a deep breath. "Wow." I felt her place a hand between her thighs. "I think you might have broken something."

"You're hurt?" I started to get up.

"Joking. Relax. You went so deep, though. I didn't know either of us had that kind of length." She whispered: "Stay still. I might not be able to walk for a while. If ever."

I squeezed her closer. She swallowed hard; some tears made my chest wet.

"Can I tell you something very personal?"

"Of course," I said.

"You're not to use it against me, ever—if you do, I'll just deny I ever said it."

"It's a deal."

"When I saw you in court, doing your job, saving that Oliver Thirst from more misery and strife—being so effective in the world, I mean—and then I thought of how you are with me, so gentle most of the time and such a vigorous lover, I thought you were a very complete man. I mean, I don't think I'll ever be as complete as a woman as you are as a man, not till I have a baby anyway."

To my astonishment I began to sob.

"Why are you crying?"

"Because you don't seem to realize that you make me complete, if that's what I am. Sometimes I don't think I could even stand up straight if you weren't in my life." I dragged a forearm across my face. "Let's have some champagne, for Christ's sake. This is ridiculous—I win my first appeal and spend the rest of the day in tears."

She sniggered. "It's just catharsis—you were very tense this morning."

While my cheeks were still wet, she bobbed out of bed, buoyant again, and untwisted the wire cage around the neck of the bottle. It went off like a gun, and the cork hit the lampshade. We were still poor enough to be urgent about not wasting the champagne. We managed to save most of it by pouring some into a mug. The emergency changed both our moods.

"Crybaby."

"Same to you."

I swallowed my champagne in a great gulp so that I would have an excuse for my light-headedness.

"I suppose young Mr. Thirst was pleased when you went to see him?"

"More than pleased. For once that great crust of braggadocio seemed to fall away. It was a little embarrassing—he kept calling me a genius."

"So you are."

"Don't you start; I need to keep my feet on the ground—I'm back in the Magistrates Court tomorrow, with a drunken driver. It was weird, though, Thirst's humility. He even said he agreed with Beaufort. Said it several times, in fact."

"Why, what did Beaufort say?"

"He told Thirst that his life was just a stale turd."

"In those words?"

"More or less."

"That was very direct."

"You haven't met Beaufort. If you think I'm getting hard, you should meet him."

"No, thanks. One heavy-duty, hyper-macho, case-winning lawyer is enough for me. What else did Thirst say?"

"Well, he's pretty sure Hogg can convince the parole board to give him early parole now. Hogg is close to the chairperson, apparently, a woman. He says he'll really change his life. He kept saying he'd rather die than go back inside."

"D'you believe him?"

"While he was saying it, certainly. That's the odd thing about some crooks: they're totally sincere; it's just that their minds change from moment to moment."

"So for you he's still a crook?"

"You mean he might have stopped being one the minute his appeal was allowed?"

"Don't play dumb; you know what I mean." Her voice had sharp edges. "I mean, if he really has decided to go straight, do you classify him as a crook still? At what point does redemption come into it in your system, if ever?"

I swallowed some more champagne. "It's not a matter of redemption, it's a matter of resisting the next bent opportunity and the next and the next, consistently, for the rest of his life, like an alcoholic resisting a drink."

"He needs a woman."

"That's what women always think."

"But you said something in the pub that night with Hogg—you said even if he succeeds, would it be worth it? What does that mean?"

"Take a reformed alcoholic. Okay, he's stopped drinking, but the despair that made him drink is still there, expressing itself in some other form. Now he lives according to all the rules, like a machine, nobody can fault him, but does it bring any satisfaction? In the final analysis, does it make any difference that he's stopped drinking?"

"That's pretty bleak," Daisy said.

"It would be bleak if there weren't any Daisy Smiths in the world. Daisy Smiths are the only real redemption."

"So he needs a Daisy Smith?"

"Exactly."

"That's what I said—he needs a woman."

"You win."

"Let's make love again," Daisy said. "It's ages since we last made love."

Afterward, she lay on her back, staring at the ceiling.

"You know, your client has an extraordinary face."

"Yes. I thought you'd notice."

"Reminded me of someone I once knew."

"Not your father this time, I'm sure."

She smiled. "No, not him. Jay Katzo. Don't get jealous—he wasn't a lover. Not in the way you're thinking."

"In what way, then?"

"In my last year of high school I was still very much under the influence of my father. I thought maybe I'd be a psychologist like him. I asked him for some practical experience of what it was like as a profession, hands on. He pulled strings to get me time at that same hospital in Vermont I told you about. I would go weekends for maybe three months. The place fascinated me. I helped prepare the medications, chatted with the shrinks, got to know some of the patients. Not the catatonics, of course, but the others. Jay Katzo was in for life. A psycho. He'd been convicted of, oh, say a hundred counts of rape. He was considered safe by that time—I guess he was in his late thirties—and he kind of made friends with me. Of course the nurses watched him with me like a hawk, but he was always very respectful, made a point of calling me 'Miss Hawkley' and never looking at my tits or my ass the way most of the male shrinks did. I guess he lulled them into a false sense of security, and they had a lot of faith in the medication they were giving him. One day he suddenly pushed me into one of the padded cells and slammed the door and leaned against it. This guy is big, maybe six five, two twenty pounds. I'm scared shitless. He takes all his clothes off and stands there with the biggest erection I've ever seen. Something you'd expect on a donkey, you know?"

"Not really."

"Hang in there—it's not the ending you're expecting. So there I am seventeen years old, literally dribbling with terror, not even capable of screaming for help. All I can think of is that huge thing of his will tear me apart any second now. Then he starts to speak. He has this extra-deep voice, eerie. 'This is the message you came here to receive,' he says. 'You wanted to know what a man is because your father's misled you. He's not a man, I am. Look.' So I look, and he says, 'No, not at my cock, sweetheart. Look into my eyes.' So I raise my eyes slowly, and I can't help noticing his body, what good shape he's in. And his eyes are deep brown and on fire, that's the only way I can describe it, and there's this electric energy flowing all over his face, as if he's plugged into some power line. This naked man is extra alive, his whole body kind of glows. And I nod, 'cause my father's eyes are dead. Blue and dead. And Jay Katzo just laughed while the male nurses started ramming open the door. I had to hear his screams while they beat him, and his long groan when they got the hypodermic into him." She reached behind her for her cigarettes, hashish, and papers, prepared to roll a joint. "I don't know, ever since that day I've wondered if he spent the next twelve months in solitary just to tell me something I needed to know. There was, like, a spiritual connection between us. He never even touched me."

"And he had a face like Thirst's?"

"Almost exactly. And the same physical presence. You know, like he had an extra male chromosome or something? And brown eyes like him, too."

"My eyes are blue," I said.

17

Hogg sent us a Christmas card—emphatically modern, the Christian theme underplayed—and then, early in the new year, an invitation. He had the use, he wrote, of a vicarage in Essex during February, the incumbent, whom he referred to as "dear Percy," being away at a conference in America debating hidden racist attitudes in the church. He was inviting friends down on each of the four weekends. Would we like to come? Which weekend would suit? He added a footnote: *So peaceful, the stress and anger simply melt away and everyone rediscovers the art of gentleness.*

I was in favor of being rude. I hoped Daisy would feel the same way, but she wanted to go. She felt no instinctual loathing for the convivial world; for her such a weekend in the country could never be, as it would be for me, a chore. And she was fed up with the city in winter, the perpetual fug in our tiny room, the filth of the underground, the damp city cold that was impossible to keep out no matter how many sweaters you wore. *Her* childhood (winters skiing in Colorado, summers on private beaches or yachts in Maine or Massachusetts, belonging to her father's friends) had not prepared her for the claustrophobia of the inner city in January. We were having arguments that had as much to do with getting in each other's way as with our political differences. And then, she had liked Hogg.

"Let's go, Jimmy, please."

"What will you do for it?"

"Anything."

And she did.

Disagreements were often settled in this way.

And so one fine Saturday in February we took the underground to Tower Bridge and walked with our overnight bags to Fenchurch Street railway station. Fenchurch, the Tower, Eastcheap, Elephant and Castle—these names were as much a part of the territory of my childhood as Belsize Park and the Temple belonged to the present.

"I remember when the whole of the East End went for holidays to Southend-on-Sea," I told Daisy. "Fenchurch Street station used to be teeming with cockneys, men with suits but no ties, women in long-waisted dresses with huge polka dots, kids like me sharing boiled sweets mouth-to-mouth, all of us hoping to get burned in one day by the sea. My mum always bought me rock candy that said 'Southend' whichever way you bit it, and there was a little train that took you out to the end of the longest pier in the world— or so they said."

"Sometimes I just don't get it with you," Daisy said.

"Don't start, darling. Please."

We were alone in the railway carriage. I slipped my hand under her sweater and caressed her breasts through the unusually firm bra she was wearing. She made no protest but waited until I withdrew my hand.

"You can't get out of it with smooth talk and a grope. I want to know why you've betrayed your roots."

I fought my instant anger. What right did she have to judge me? What noble feat had she ever performed? She'd graduated with a degree far below her potential and was working as a fill-in teacher in her usual half-baked fashion. She took sick leave so that she could walk over Hampstead Heath, smoke a joint, and drift off into some reality-proof world of her own.

"You don't know anything about my roots, Daisy, apart from what I've told you. You don't know what it's like coming from the wrong side of the tracks."

She was standing up and looking out the window. I stood up behind her to put my arms around her waist, careful not to do anything that could be construed as a grope.

"Wrong side of the tracks? Nineteen seventy-seven, and he's talking about wrong side of the tracks! The tracks are in your head! After the revolution they'll send you to work on a pig farm in the Hebrides for ten years until you develop right thinking."

"What revolution are we talking about?"

A pout. "The women's revolution."

"Ah! That one."

"Yes, that one."

"When everyone's kind and supportive and nonthreatening and vegetarian, and we all drink Nicaraguan coffee?"

She jerked her elbow back into my solar plexus, turned around to face me.

She hit me with the heel of her hand. "You're so fucking smart—it's impossible arguing with you. The problem is you don't believe in any of the stuff I believe in. We're politically incompatible."

"Maybe, but I'd probably work on a pig farm in the Hebrides if I could be with you. After the revolution."

"Would you?"

She picked at something in the fabric of her jeans, then suddenly looked me full in the face. "Am I really dumb, James? Or is it that you have a knack for making me feel that way?"

"Let's go to the restaurant car," I said. "I need a coffee."

"You're only allowed Nicaraguan."

I looked out the window of the restaurant car as the train rattled down the old bent track: East India Docks, Bow, Stratford, Barking—places to my mind as ancient, rotten, and somehow eternal as the first suburbs of Rome or Athens. A few stations after

Romford, we got out and caught a bus to the little village where Hogg was staying.

We were no more than sixty miles out of London, yet I felt the onset of agoraphobia. The people we saw seemed to be stranded in a kind of lobotomized inertia. The bus was empty except for Daisy and me and an old lady, who glared at us. The bus driver called the old lady "love" but turned away sourly when Daisy said goodbye to him with her sweet smile. Why did she need to be liked by a surly bus driver?

Hogg was waiting at the bus stop. He was wearing a polo shirt under a thick tweed jacket.

"Just in time for lunch." He beamed.

The old square tower of the church was the tallest thing in the village and clearly visible from the bus stop. We walked past expensive new cars and old stone cottages whose juxtaposition reminded me of adverts in *Country Life*.

Everyone we passed seemed to be doing exactly what people in the country are supposed to do: a middle-aged housewife was cleaning a beehive, a man in corduroys was building a bonfire, a teenage girl in jodhpurs and riding boots was walking toward a gate across a field. We even saw two women gossiping over a fence.

I thought that a vicar would know everyone, but nobody spoke to us. Apart from the two women, people did not seem to be speaking to each other, either. There was a lifeless quiet despite the careful attention to chores.

"They're mostly weekenders," Hogg said. "Bankers, stockbrokers, solicitors, and their families, who live in flats and town houses in the city. Most of those houses are empty during the week."

He led us into the main church drive and down a small path to the vicarage.

Which looked, oddly enough, exactly as I had imagined an English country vicarage might look. A neo-Gothic arch of molded stone was the entrance to a cloister-like alcove where you could shake off your Wellingtons. Rooms with high ceilings and bay windows all looked, on one side, up the little hill (tended lawn with cypress and oak) to the square Saxon tower. The church had been added to, bit by bit, so that it was a record of ecclesiastical architecture through the centuries. The latest addition, not attached to the building but still tastelessly close, was a garage for the incumbent's old Morris.

The rooms on the other side of the house looked out on a tiny graveyard, where you could weep over little Nell who was laid to rest in 1889, aged five, or wonder at the devastation of a cholera epidemic in 1903 that carried off Jack Hord, aged eighteen, and twelve others in a week.

Daisy was instantly at home. She offered to help with lunch, but Hogg said that someone was preparing it.

"A maid?"

"Not quite."

As for Hogg, I looked more carefully this time. He was older than I had thought (lines around the eyes and mouth I hadn't noticed in the pub, more gray than I had registered, a greater canniness behind the need to apologize and agree).

I thought him somehow dangerous, as chameleons can be, but a common denominator linked Daisy and him: an expensive education half rejected, an uncanny instinct for role playing.

It was not often that I had the chance to see her in a social context. I stood aside, feeling a mixture of pride and envy as she chatted excitedly.

"What a charming house!"

"Yes, he's quite comfortable, old Percy." By the way he said it, we understood that "old Percy" was not in the clerical avant-garde.

He excused himself to go to the kitchen. Daisy poked her tongue out at me. Hogg reappeared.

"Daisy, James, I want you to meet my secret guest."

My first thought was that this could not be the person he resembled, for no more logical reason than that he was wearing an apron and carrying a tray piled with sandwiches.

"James Knight of course you already know," Hogg was saying. "Ollie, meet Daisy Smith."

Daisy's fascination was palpable, as was her need for him to like her, but he nodded woodenly at both of us and proceeded to place the tray on a table.

"I'll just get the tea." He spoke directly to Hogg, in a voice crushed to a whisper.

"Oh yes, Ollie, that would be terrific if you would."

As he disappeared again into the kitchen, Hogg broke into a triumphant grin, like a very young boy who has played a trick for adults to applaud.

"I thought that if I didn't tell you you couldn't be compromised. This way if you get in trouble with your judges, you can blame it all on wicked old James Hogg."

I was stunned into silence. I felt an elemental rage, as if it were my own spirit that had been broken. And at the same time a deep shame, because like it or not, I served the same system as Hogg. I felt a kind of paralysis of the personality, as if the two sides of my mind held each other in an unbreakable wrestling hold. Daisy looked embarrassed.

"Yes, that's right, isn't it, Jimmy? This way you're not compromised?"

I opened my mouth, shut it, finally muttered, "No, not at all."

"Splendid," Hogg said. "Then I've achieved my purpose. I've brought Ollie and his friend together. But he's not your only friend anymore, is he, Ollie?"

"No," Thirst said. He crossed the room again with the tea, then left. Hogg beamed. He motioned us to sit down at the table— mahogany, with heavy legs.

"I'm sorry it's only sandwiches. Mrs. Alan from the village will come to cook us dinner tonight."

"Isn't Oliver having lunch?" Daisy said.

"He ate earlier."

"You got him out, then?" I said.

"Mm. Didn't I tell you in my letter? Your winning the appeal did the trick. I'd been campaigning for his release for months, but they don't take much notice of me, I'm afraid. 'That James Hogg would let them all out if he had his way' is, I suspect, what they say to each other. You see, I know this sounds dreadfully silly to a man of your calling, but when I get to know these great hairy brutes, I find them quite docile and lovable."

"Well, there's nothing like a shot of Librium to take the zap out of a man."

Daisy, who had suspended her social conscience now that we were in company, scowled at me.

"Oh, you don't want to believe all those stories you read about,"

Hogg said. "I admit it does go on, forcing the prisoners to take tranquilizers—the 'liquid nightstick,' one of the tabloids calls it— but not much in the Scrubs. In those high-security places like Dartmoor and at bins like Broadmoor, of course, but the Scrubs is a quiet place; no one really dangerous goes there."

"Nevertheless, aren't you taking a risk bringing him here? Isn't he still on parole?"

Hogg clapped his hands. "Ah, now you've seen Hogg's devilish cunning! This is the real reason why I was so keen to have this vicarage for a month. The terms of his parole permit him to stay here so long as I am also resident, or in that dreadful hostel in Islington."

"The one run by the Prisoner's Friends Society?"

"Mm! That shower!"

"And he'd rather be here?"

His features went flat. Daisy glared at me.

"Well, who wouldn't?"

"Quite," Daisy said.

I looked at them in silence. When we stopped talking, the tick of the inevitable grandfather clock cut the time up in manageable Victorian segments. Chimes on the quarter hour told you how much closer you were to the end of another eventless day.

"He was consulted, of course?"

"Ollie!" Hogg called out. Daisy was angry. Thirst appeared at the kitchen door, still wearing the apron.

"Where would you rather be, here or in that dreadful hostel in Islington?"

Thirst looked at me. "The reverend has been very kind to me."

"That doesn't answer the question. Ollie, where would you rather be?"

"Here," he said, and disappeared.

"There!" Hogg said. I looked at Daisy, who looked away.

Hogg offered the sandwiches around. Apparently he had taught Thirst to cut them up into quarters, so that each one was no more than a mouthful. I took a couple and ate them, but I wasn't hungry.

"Why don't you let me show you over the church? Ollie will take your bags up to your room. I've assumed you'll have a double room?"

"If that's not against the rules," Daisy said.

"Oh no, so long as you don't tell old Percy. He's rather old-fashioned. And perhaps," he said, fussing over a sandwich, "just perhaps it's not a good idea to let the members of the parole board know. I'm sure James will understand, a matter of credibility. You're not married after all."

He looked at me for agreement.

"What curious anachronisms we both are," I said. "I have to pretend that I don't socialize with criminals, and you have to pretend that you don't socialize with fornicators."

Hogg winced. I think the word "fornicators" distressed him.

We went out of the house by way of the kitchen. Thirst had disappeared. There was a green waterproof raincoat, of the type sold in the hunting and fishing shops in Piccadilly, hanging on the back door, a pair of green Wellingtons, and a Harris tweed jacket with leather elbow patches, which Hogg put on. There were signs (a spare lead, a large wicker basket with blanket, teeth marks on furniture) of an absent dog. Outside, there was a soft country dampness. The earth squidged underfoot.

"Shit," Daisy said, then clapped a hand over her mouth. "Sorry, Reverend."

I thought he must find it hard to believe that this was the same American feminist militant he had met in the pub that night (she was using mostly her English accent at the vicarage), but they seemed to understand each other perfectly. He stiffened and said, "Blast—it's a problem, I know. Oliver must have taken him for a walk. Perhaps a stick or something?"

"Oh, I'll be okay. It's just that it was right outside the door."

"Where is he? Or she," I asked.

All three of us looked around.

"He, an Alsatian named Cranmer, is the reason Percy let me have the place. Old Percy wouldn't move an inch unless he was sure Cranmer was properly taken care of. Funny thing is, I'm hopeless with dogs; don't know why Percy trusts me with him. I'm sure he'd never do *that* when Percy's here. I think Cranmer hates my guts, actually."

Daisy nodded vigorously. "I know what you mean. Alsatians scare the sh—the life out of me. There was one at our beach house in Martha's Vineyard when I was a kid. . . ." She told us all about it as we walked up the hill to the church. Her obvious determination to make it an enjoyable weekend for Hogg and me made me regret my provocative remarks. Why should I care about what went on between Hogg and Thirst? But what was it about Thirst that made me protective?

The fresh country air seemed to be clearing my head. I decided on a benevolent posture and put an arm around Daisy's waist.

She pressed my hand and smiled gratefully. "Look, there they are!"

We were standing on top of the hill near one side of the church. It was clear now that the grounds were encircled by a horseshoe-shaped wall, the open part of the horseshoe being the drive up to the church entrance, with a narrow separate drive to the vicarage that squatted below us. From the vicarage, a footpath led to a woodshed, from which another path led to a door in the wall. On the other side of the wall, a stretch of wasteland led to some mud-flats that merged in dull liquefaction with the Thames Estuary in the distance. I had expected "old Percy" to have an old dog, but the Alsatian racing along the mudflats with Thirst had the bound-less energy of one recently emerged from puppyhood. It ran ahead of him, then gamboled while he caught up, only to race off again.

"Cranmer's taking Oliver for a run," Daisy said.

"Yes," Hogg said. "They seem to get on famously, those two."

The dog allowed Thirst to catch up with him. Thirst grabbed it by the tail, then dived away as it turned to bite. They tumbled together over the wasteland, Thirst's forearm—protected by an overcoat—in the dog's mouth. At one moment Thirst lay across the writhing dog. We could hear its growls on top of the hill.

"Oh my God!" Daisy looked at Hogg.

With furious energy the dog wriggled up from under Thirst and clamped its jaws onto the edge of his coat, pulling back. Thirst dived with his arms around its neck, and they were tumbling again, over and over.

"I hope he doesn't break Cranmer's back doing that," Daisy said. "Isn't he afraid that Cranmer will lose his temper and bite his hand?"

"Oh my God, yes," I said. Daisy poked her tongue out at me.

"When I first saw that, I thought of calling for help, but they always manage to come out of these fights best of friends. Ollie really does have a way with that animal."

Thirst was on his feet again, running. The dog scrambled up and raced after him, barking. Thirst found a stick and threw it in a long arc toward the mudflats. The dog started after it, then changed its mind and darted back to Thirst, who knelt down to pat it, exhausted.

"You're no cunt, Crans—are you?" His breathless voice carried up to us, small but clear. "No one's going to shove their prick up your arse, are they?"

The animal barked, wagging its tail.

"Well," Hogg said, "shall we press on?"

We admired the empty church from inside and out. Hogg was proud of a window which had survived Henry VIII, and of the original Saxon tower, one of the oldest in England. After half an hour even Daisy ran out of intelligent questions. Her eyes wandered back to the wasteland outside the church wall.

"Look, Oliver's coming back."

Thirst trudged toward the door in the wall, the dog by his side.

"Suppose you're starving now? You want grub, don't you?" Cranmer wagged his tail. "Wish I was a dog. In the old days they used to cut off an animal's balls—d'you know that? Now they do it to men instead, cut them off with a hacksaw and put them in a mincer, Crans, that's what the bastards do. No anesthetic, Crans. Now don't go and drop one near the house again. No stale turds for us, Crans—okay?"

Hogg was looking over the drive, his neck craning away from the mudflats.

"Here come the Merril-Prices."

A navy-blue Range Rover was turning into the drive, its large tires crunching on the gravel. Hogg looked anxious.

"Parole board?" I said.

"She's the chairperson; he's a banker. Very influential, great supporters of the church, close friends of our bishop. A truly Christian couple. They've driven all the way down from North London to see how Oliver's getting on."

Daisy avoided my eyes.

"Let me introduce you," Hogg said without conviction.

Eleanor Merril-Price emerged from the Range Rover holding a large green apple in her hand, half chewed. She wore a long fur coat, slacks, scarf, and sweater. Elegant, tall with a long face, in her mid-forties. She watched her husband walk to the front offside wing of the car to inspect something, then shrugged and turned toward us.

"Eleanor Merril-Price, James Knight, barrister at law."

Eleanor finished chewing, threw the remains of her apple into a bush. "Biodegradable," she said, and smiled. It was a patrician's smile, full of authority and money. She allowed me to hold out my hand just long enough for me to feel foolish before shaking it, then turned to Daisy. "How beautiful you look," she said.

Her husband was shorter, stocky, with hard eyes that turned doggy when he looked at his wife.

"Isn't she fantastic?" Daisy whispered to me.

As we were about to enter the vicarage, Cranmer appeared, an inexhaustible bundle of energy.

"Oh, what a gorgeous Alsatian! Tom, doesn't he remind you of—"

"Yes, darling."

She knelt down by Cranmer and held him behind his ears, while he wagged his tail furiously.

"You'll soil your fur, darling."

"Then we'll clean it."

Cranmer woofed. Thirst appeared silently from behind the house and stood still. Eleanor got to her feet, searching his face.

"Hello, Oliver."

"Hello, Mrs. Merril-Price."

"You can call me Eleanor—you're a free man now."

"Almost." His eyes shifted.

"How are things?"

"Good. The reverend has been very kind."

She gave a short laugh that made Thirst redden. "The reverend? You don't make him call you *that*, do you, James?"

"I don't make him call me anything."

"Call him James, or Vic—it's good for him." She winked at me.

"Eleanor thinks I take my vocation too seriously," Hogg said. His blush frequency had increased. He had started wringing his hands behind his back.

"Anyone who thinks he's got a vocation is definitely taking it too seriously." She turned to me. "Have you got a vocation?"

"Sometimes, ma'am, I don't even have a job."

A poor joke, but the first of the weekend. Everyone laughed. Daisy looked proud.

"He did a good job for Oliver," Hogg said.

"Yes," Oliver said. "Got me off a driving-and-taking-away charge first and won my appeal second."

"Well, I hope the driving and taking away wasn't a Range Rover," Eleanor said.

Thirst hung his head, grinning. Hogg said, "Why don't we all go inside," and looked at Eleanor. She said, "Yes, let's," and there was a short embarrassed standoff while we all waited for someone else to go first. I noticed that Eleanor's husband, Tom, had shut down most of his functions. He had examined my face for a second to see if I was the kind of barrister of whom he could approve, and decided I was not.

When we were inside, I realized that the room's natural light had begun to fade. Already the short country day was coming to an end.

"It's cold," Eleanor said as we sat around the mahogany table.

Thirst knelt by the fireplace, lit a corner of the crushed newspaper with a match. I watched the flames grow until they curled up the chimney.

Eleanor sat at the end of the table, her long dramatic face illuminated in the half-light by the fire. "Well, let's not have an evening full of undercurrents. First I want to know if Oliver's forgiven me. If he hasn't, I shall go straight home."

"Nothing to forgive," Thirst said. "You know I don't hold nothing against you; I told you that before."

"I was against giving Oliver early parole, you see." She studied me for a moment. "Your victory in the Court of Appeal tipped the balance. I was outvoted."

I laughed. "So it's my responsibility?"

"No, it's mine."

We all looked at Thirst, who stood up. "You don't have to worry," he told Eleanor. "I'm not going back. They can kill me first."

It would have been an impressive exit had he not stumbled over a mat at the door. Everybody laughed. He found the grace to bow comically before he left.

18

At dinner Thirst watched me carefully. He was following my actions: small plate for bread on the left; tip bowl outward when finishing soup; gravy on the roast potatoes, mint sauce for the lamb; only a small helping of apple crumble. His concentration was absolute. He kept all movements to a minimum, seemed to breathe shallowly, like a fugitive waiting for the dogs to pass by. Eleanor stole a glance at him from time to time, while she kept up a discussion with Hogg about the parole board.

Eleanor had been sitting next to me, talking to Hogg. Now she turned, and I knew she was waiting for me to say something.

"How long have you been chairperson of the parole board?"

"Ah! the harmless questions: how long and do you like . . . I think there's more to you than harmless questions, James Knight. Why don't you ask me something more daring? I'm sure you'd like to."

"*Why* are you chairperson of the parole board?"

"Better, much better. Shall we say that I became interested in criminals when my son became one?"

"That doesn't disqualify you?"

"Not anymore. He's dead. Drugs, alcohol, and fast cars don't go so well together. It made me want to know why. I've read more books on criminology than you have."

"That wouldn't be difficult; it's not a compulsory subject for lawyers."

"But from your experience you know which social groups most criminals come from?"

"Violent crime is mostly committed by young men between the ages of fifteen and thirty from what sociologists call the lower-income groups. Nonviolent crime is slightly different. Women and middle-class kids feature more frequently."

"Well, so says one expert. What about our other expert?"

Thirst was listening.

"Why does a nice boy like you turn to crime?"

Her voice carried no hint of sarcasm.

We all waited for his answer. I expected him to shrug or mumble, but when he spoke, his voice was unexpectedly strong.

"I didn't; that's where you all get it wrong. We don't turn to it, it starts when you're born, only after a while they lock you up for it. Then you start running into people like you lot, telling you there's another way of living, only you've got to wipe out your past, haven't you? To stay out of prison, I have to act like I was born yesterday, start again, a twenty-year-old baby. Don't ask why we start—ask why we carry on. Because changing is so hard, that's why."

"But you're an expert, too," I said to Eleanor. "Why do you think people become criminals?"

"For boys like Oliver it may be social programming, at least in some measure. For my son it was, I suppose, our fault, Tom's and mine."

"Our fault be damned." Tom suddenly woke up.

Eleanor rose from her chair, walked over to Tom, and put her arms around him. He held her hands. We all waited for her to speak.

"I'll tell you what I would like to do, if Oliver agrees. It goes like this. With the exception of one person here, we can all more or less guess what makes each other tick. I bet I know without being told, for example, what made James Knight become a barrister, what James Hogg gets out of being a vicar. Daisy, despite the fact that she's American, I feel as if I've known all my life, though I've only been with her a couple of hours. Tom I *have* known almost all my life. One person, although I know what he's done, I haven't the faintest idea why he's done it. I don't know what makes you tick, Oliver, not at all. I've read all the theories, but I'm not an inch closer, really. One reads about sociopaths, one knows of the damage they do, the misery they cause, but one never really understands the reasons why they do it. I wondered if you would like to tell us."

Thirst's face was the color of an eggplant. He stared at her.

Eleanor walked over to him to put her hand on his shoulder. "You misunderstand, Oliver, that's why you're getting so upset. I don't want a long sob story about your social programming; I want to get some sense of the thrill of it that makes you keep doing it. Do you agree, James, that it would be interesting if Oliver would explain? We must all swear secrecy, of course."

"Certainly it may have a sublimating function if he shares it with us." Hogg sounded doubtful.

"Will you, Oliver? You have a perfect right to refuse, of course."

Thirst stood up. He wasn't blushing anymore. He was quite pale.

"You're all sworn to secrecy, right?" He turned to Eleanor. "I'll show you," he said. He walked toward the door, then turned. "I would like you to come outside," he said to Eleanor. Then to me: "You, too."

"We shall all come," Tom said.

"Yes, you can all come," Thirst said.

Eleanor and I were the first out of the door, after Thirst. He was already at the Range Rover, twisting something in the lock on the driver's side. Within seconds the door was open and he was inside the car, unlocking the door on the passenger side.

He motioned to Eleanor and me to come forward. Sure that

Eleanor was waiting for a signal from me, I walked resolutely forward. She followed. As we approached, Thirst bent down by the steering column. The engine burst into life while we were climbing into the car. I sat in the front, next to him; Eleanor sat behind me. He turned on the headlights. I saw Tom's red face and Daisy behind him, looking startled.

"Seat belts on." He did not fasten his.

He made the engine scream before letting out the clutch so that we flew forward. I could hear gravel shooting out behind us.

"We're stealing my car!" Eleanor's voice was girlish with excitement.

Thirst used the four-wheel-drive function to climb up the hill over the grass, under the cypress and oak. There would be black tracks in the morning. We emerged by a side entrance to the church. For a moment I thought he was going to drive through the heavy wooden door.

He lurched to the left, disengaged the four-wheel drive, raced the engine again. We made a screaming circuit of the church. Centrifugal force pushed me against my door. The headlights picked out patches of old stone, medieval tracery, the molding on a Gothic arch.

The car was not really built for speed. Thirst made it feel fast by using low gears, racing the engine, and double-clutching. When we came around by the main entrance, I thought he would perhaps make another circuit, then take us around the driveway, back to the vicarage. Instead he flew down the hill to the street, not pausing at the exit, turned right into the road on two wheels, roared through the village in seconds. Eleanor made a strange sound—a moan of pleasure or misery.

On the outskirts of the village the headlights picked out an animal form for a split second: long vertical ears, large startled eyes, pear-drop body. There was a thud.

"What was that?" Eleanor asked in a quick, nervous gasp.

"Hare," I said.

"Dead one," Thirst said.

We were in the unlit narrow country road now, the headlights picking off the broken white lines, which passed in a blur. I saw that we were doing eighty.

I glanced back at Eleanor, who was gripping the back of my seat.

Thirst switched off the lights and accelerated. "I'll turn them on again when one of you begs me to," he said.

I expected Eleanor to tell him, or beg him, to switch them on again. I looked back at her. Her mouth was slightly open, but she said nothing.

Thirst looked confident and alert—driving, I supposed, by a residual light still in the sky. I felt a wonderful excitement. For a second I loved Thirst.

There was a bad moment at a bend in the road. We were going so fast I was sure we were about to crash. Thirst would not brake, although he slowed, came out of an ugly front-wheel skid, accelerated again. Still Eleanor said nothing.

The needle was at ninety-five before she screamed: "Stop! This is stupid!"

"Beg."

"I beg you, Oliver, for God's sake."

He ran down expertly through the gears, executed a hand-brake spin that set us pointing in the opposite direction, switched on the lights, and drove us back through the village at a sedate twenty-five miles per hour. He stopped just before the driveway and turned to face me.

"I hope nobody felt threatened and that you'll be supportive of the way I handled the task Eleanor set me."

We both looked back at Eleanor. She shifted seats to be behind him, then put both hands around his neck. I could see by the way his veins bulged—and her cheeks puffed out—that she was squeezing as hard as she could in the effort to strangle him. He did not resist. Suddenly she let go.

"Well, I suppose I asked for it, but that doesn't mean that I wouldn't like to kill you."

"You understand, then?" I said. "Oliver's point, that is."

"It was very thrilling and insanely dangerous."

We sat, the three of us, in the stationary car. Thirst seemed to be waiting patiently for something to happen.

Eleanor burst into a peal of laughter. She put a hand across her mouth. "Tom's probably had six heart attacks." She giggled.

Thirst put the car in gear again, drove up the drive a short way, stopped.

"Do you happen to have the keys?" he said over his shoulder.

Eleanor found them in her pocket, gave them to him. He bent down to do something at the base of the steering column. The engine stopped. He put the key in the ignition.

"You'd better drive the rest of the way," he said to me. "If anybody wants me, I'll be in the woodshed."

He got out, gave Eleanor a long look, walked away.

"Haven't felt this good since I pinched an XJ6," I heard him say into the night.

I drove only a short distance up the drive, stopped the car, turned off the engine and the lights.

"I think it best if we surprise them," I said. "Let's walk the rest of the way."

I felt protective of Thirst, who had been provoked by Eleanor. I knew everything would depend on how she handled the situation when we got back, and I wanted her recovered from the hysteria by then. I glanced at the car as we passed. I thought I saw a dark patch near the offside fender.

We walked slowly. When we came within sight of the lights and the vicarage, she stopped.

"Hug me a moment, please."

I assumed that what was required was the sort of thing recommended for shock in first-aid courses. Dutifully I put my arms around her. She snuggled, then I felt her knee insert itself between my legs. She wriggled sensuously, made me kiss her full on the mouth, then pushed me away.

"That's better. Fast cars and beautiful young men can quite turn a girl's head." She touched her hair. "I was young in the sixties, you know."

She reentered the vicarage with her customary nonchalance, humming a tune.

"Thank God!" Tom rushed up to her.

I glanced at Daisy, whose features were clenched like a fist. Hogg looked miserable.

"What on earth happened? Are you all right?" Tom said.

"Of course I'm all right, darling. Oliver just wanted to make a point, that's all."

"Point be damned. He stole my car."

"Our car, darling, and it can hardly be called theft with all of us looking on, an eminent barrister in one seat, and the co-owner in the back."

"Cunning blighter!"

I stood next to Daisy on the other side of the room from Tom and Eleanor. "Tom was going to call the police," she told me in a savage whisper, "and James Hogg wouldn't do anything. I had to stop him. We had one hell of a fight. That would have been the end of the line for Oliver, wouldn't it, if the police had been called?"

"It would have been very awkward."

"I had to say some hard things about Eleanor," Daisy said. "I hope she forgives me. She's rather magnificent, isn't she?"

"Oh, yes. I think she enjoyed herself. So did Thirst."

"Where is he?"

"In the woodshed, lying low."

"Let's go and see him." Her eyes were shining.

On the path to the shed, I held Daisy's hand. I could feel her excitement, her eagerness to make him notice her, perhaps even to have him see her as a co-revolutionary and colleague in crime. She wanted credit, too, for saving him from the police.

The door to the woodshed was ajar, spilling a soft glow of light from a kerosene lamp he had placed on the floor. His shadow, which we saw first on opening the door, occupied the whole of one wall and loomed over us from the roof. He stood over an ax that had been driven into a chopping block. His giant black hand grasping the giant black ax handle dwarfed the frail human at the center of the drama. Wood splinters and the dismembered parts of trees were strewn all over the shed. Without comment he grasped the handle of the ax as we entered.

He found a chunk of wood, a cross-cut from a chain saw, placed it on the block. He looked at Daisy shrewdly. "This is what villains

do after a job, to relax." He lifted the ax, split the cross-cut effortlessly with one blow. He arranged the pieces on the block, brought
the ax down again. He repeated the performance several times.

Finally, with terrific violence, he drove the ax into the block.

"I'm really pissed off." He looked at me. "With myself—you
know?"

"Yes."

"Why?" Daisy said.

He ignored the question for a moment, then said, "Ask him—
he understands."

Daisy looked hurt.

"They were going to call the police. Daisy stopped them." I
said it for her, because she wanted me to.

"I told them it was Eleanor's fault, for provoking you."

"Eleanor!" On the wall, the black giant shook his head. A
wicked grin twisted Thirst's features for a moment. "How did Tom
take it?"

"Badly. Very badly. He'd have your balls if Eleanor would let
him," I said.

"He'd have his own balls if Eleanor would let him." He chuckled. "Want a beer?"

He fetched a six-pack from the other side of the shed, pulled
three out of the plastic rings, gave one to Daisy and one to me.

"Sorry I haven't got a glass," he said to Daisy.

"It's all right," she said shyly.

He threw his head back, poured some beer down his throat,
gazed at Daisy contemplatively.

"You know what I would give this for?" He held his right arm
with his left hand and shook it.

"What?"

"His control." He pointed at me, took another swig of beer.
"You don't know how lucky you are," he told her. "Most men are
either bastards or cunts—'scuse the language."

"Or faggots," I said, slipping unthinkingly into his conversation.

"Or faggots. So how did he take it?"

"Ask Daisy. I wasn't there, remember?"

"Who? Oh, you mean James Hogg. He was pissed off but
couldn't decide who with. Mostly with Eleanor, I think. And then

Tom and I had a fight, which upset him even more."

"It can't hurt your parole," I said, "not with the chairperson of the parole board joyriding with you, and it was her car. You took care of everything."

"Not the point."

"I know."

"Why? I don't get it," Daisy complained. Thirst, who seemed to find Daisy irritating, shot a glance at me. I had the impression that he wanted to talk to me alone.

"Daisy thinks you've struck a blow for freedom with your escapade. She can't understand why you regret it so much."

"Didn't it feel great?" she said.

"Course it did."

"So what's the problem?"

He brushed a hand over the top of his head, looked at me. Is she really that stupid? his eyes asked.

"Daisy believes in liberation, you see. Free spirits like you will knock down the walls that imprison us, burst the chains that bind us—at the same time you'll be respectful of women, kind to children, vegetarian, anti-apartheid, and concerned about the third world."

"I've had it," Daisy said. Her face was flushed. She stared at me. "You can make fun of me as much as you like behind my back." She flounced past.

"I should have sat there and took it," Thirst said as she slammed the door. He was as oblivious to Daisy's anger as he was to her. Her exit might have been a puff of air.

Sitting in the woodshed, I was unrepentant about having mocked Daisy. She struck me as a ridiculous figure. I liked his powerful presence, his daring, his wildness, his contempt for white-collar values. I liked the smell of the wood and the kerosene lamp, too. In the back of my mind was the knowledge that the weekend had been engineered by Hogg and was out of my control. I had the perfect excuse, as Hogg had intended. I could afford the luxury of relaxing with Thirst because I would never agree to see him again.

"Eleanor should have known what she was doing. It was her fault."

"Yeah, but I mean for the future, see? If I can't sit there and eat shit without doing my nut and pinching a motor, what chance have I got? All that time in the Scrubs I promised myself I wouldn't do that. I know now that it's weakness, not strength."

"Can I have another beer?" He handed me a can. "What will you do?"

"See my time out with that silly faggot—what else?"

I swallowed some more beer. His last phrase hung in my mind. Perhaps some of the exhilaration of the joyride was still in my blood. I started to laugh.

"Silly faggot," I repeated. "He probably dreams about you every night."

"Yeah, dressed up like a choirboy."

"No. On a cross!"

"Yeah!" He let out a yelp. "That would be it, on a cross! He thinks I'm going to have a religious conversion any day now—or get myself crucified. He doesn't know how determined I am."

"To do what?"

"Not to go back, of course. When I told you I'd rather die, I meant it." He took a swig of beer. "It's good talking to you, James, a kid from the neighborhood. Here, was old Glenda Feswick around when you lived in Camberwell?"

"Big tits but cross-eyed?"

"Yeah, I met her just before I went in the Scrubs. On the game, of course; she's been working the Arabs up in the Haymarket. Made so much she got her eyes fixed. Bit of a stunner now. We had a great laugh down the Elephant one night, her and me."

"I groped her once," I said.

"You and the rest of South London. Here, I'll tell you what— your missus is called Daisy Smith?"

"Right."

"Do you remember the other Daisy Smith, used to live in Gladstone Buildings?"

"Good looker. On the game at thirteen."

"Still is. Uses the prostitution to support her smack habit nowadays. Glenda told me; they keep in touch. Six kids. Two are supposed to be by her cousin; they're a bit soft in the head."

He found another six-pack, which we finished slowly, reliving our memories of the neighborhood.

"I remember the first job I did," he said. "I suppose everyone does. Real job, I mean. A vicarage, as it happened; I can still smell my own fear. Had so much adrenaline I more or less flew back over the wall. Felt let down when there was no sign of the Old Bill, so I pinched my first motor that same night. First one on my own, I mean. Did a ton down the M1, dumped it in Finchley on the way home, and had to walk because the buses had stopped. Never made that mistake again." He gulped some more beer. "You remember your first job, James?"

I decided that he was drunker than he looked. I stood up. "I'd better go. Daisy . . ."

He stood up, too, held my arm in his powerful hand, looked me in the eye. "Do you remember your first job?"

"Of course I do, Oliver. About five months before I met you, I represented a shoplifter in Bow Street Magistrate's Court. Plea in mitigation."

By the time I left the woodshed, Eleanor and Tom had gone. I found Daisy in bed under a huge eiderdown, with a reading light on. She lay on the side nearest the window, which she had opened to let out the fumes from her joint. The look on her face was quite different from the one she had worn most of the day. The cool deliberation with which she was betraying Hogg's hospitality made her look ten years older. The girlish wish to please was nowhere in evidence.

I had nerved myself for a row. "Are you still angry?"

She looked at me coolly. "Come to bed."

I undressed and slid in beside her, relieved that her hand sought out mine and held it.

"Sorry," I said.

"Oh, I wasn't that mad. I didn't want to be the fall guy for you two streetwise cynics, that's all."

Her voice was steady, calm, very womanly. Sometimes the dope took her that way.

"I wasn't making you a fall guy. I—"

"Shhh! Don't worry, be happy."

"Really?"

"Really."

"You're marvelous sometimes. Generous—"

"No. I'm just a dumb American woman. I think in embarrassing clichés, I don't make any effort to grapple with the real, dirty world, therefore I'm not qualified to talk. When I do talk it makes you cringe. I'm also a hypocrite, because I suck up to people like Hogg. Right?"

"Don't, Daisy."

She continued, ignoring me. "But supposing you're right, my ideas are clumsy, naive, I use the wrong words, there's no precision in my thinking, I'm not streetwise, but supposing the words and the ideas aren't that important because, hey, I'm not in a murder trial, I'm only trying to communicate with you. Suppose it's the feeling behind the words—the perception, if you like—that counts. I guess I feel strangled because you use your intellect all the time to put me down when I simply want to share my vision, my feelings, with you."

I tried to answer, then realized that I could do so only by using my intellect in exactly the way she described.

"Okay, suppose that."

"Then wouldn't that make you the fool?" Her hand was playing carelessly with my flaccid penis. She tugged it on the word "fool."

"Yes."

"So d'you understand a little what it's like most of the time to be a woman?"

"If you tug any harder, you'll turn me into one."

The laugh caught her as she was inhaling. She started on a long dope-smoker's cough that made her double up. I hit her with my open hand.

How frail her back, naked, while she coughed her heart out.

"It's no good; I'll have to get a water pipe," she said when she had recovered. "So what did you two boys talk about after I left?"

"What do two working-class boys talk about?"

"Women and football."

"We left out the football."

"Well, did you find out if he's having an affair with Hogg?"

"No, he's not. If Hogg had the courage he'd make a pass, but he hasn't, so there's nothing left but middle-class innuendo, a lot of untapped libido, and some mildly sadistic power games."

"Oliver said all that? Doesn't sound like him."

"Not in so many words. He said Hogg's a cunt. Cockney is a very economical dialect. And then the apron sort of said it all, didn't it?"

"It could have been innocent. French chefs wear aprons."

"Thirst will be thrilled to know that."

Daisy drew on her joint and leaned round to blow the smoke out of the window, both breasts resting against the cold ledge for a moment. She got back under the covers.

"Brrr, it's cold. So tell me something, wise one."

"Shoot."

"Why do you and Oliver dislike Hogg so much? It seems so cruel. *He* at least really believes that he's helping Oliver. And he quite likes you. He was really mad when you connived at the joy-ride—he thought you'd lost your mind."

"Exactly, that's your answer. He hasn't got any balls."

"But that's just working-class machismo."

"Not quite. Beaufort has plenty of balls, but he's hardly working-class. I bet Beaufort, Q.C., would have enjoyed that ride."

She turned around to lie facing me in a fetal position, a reliable signal for a change of persona.

"So Hogg hasn't any of these, you think?"

"Right."

"But you have."

"Unless that's Scotch mist you're playing with."

"Don't feel like Scotch mist to me, big guy. D'you want to talk dirty for a while? This dope is starting to make me horny."

I 9

Thirst sank to the bottom of my mind like a brick in a pond. Daisy did not mention him or the weekend at the vicarage for a long time, either. When memories were unpleasant or even mildly disturbing, she had a way of deleting them en bloc, like someone who shreds awkward files. We talked less, sought out activities that required companionship rather than intimacy.

Walking, for example. Daisy and I were not great ones for exercise, but we liked to stroll. One of our favorite destinations was to Hampstead Garden Suburb, where a Society for Impecunious Gentle Women had let Daisy's mother a flat at a low rent after her discharge from hospital.

There was a solemn ritualistic aspect to our visits as a couple. We'd make a point of walking over Hampstead Heath and through Kenwood, across the Spaniards Lane, then down Wildwood Road to the Suburb—a leafy London stroll full of health, freshness, and false innocence (a book called *The Sex Life of Plants* was still a favorite with alternative types like Daisy).

We often discussed moving to a larger, unfurnished flat as soon as we could afford it.

"You know what I would really like, Jimmy? A deep-blue ceiling with clouds! Have you noticed how ceilings are always so white and boring? That's because they're designed by men, who don't have to spend so much time on their backs. I bet there's a statistic that shows women have to stare at ceilings fifty percent more than men do. Hey, Jimmy, daffodils!"

I stared myopically at the yellow trumpets half buried in foliage and quoted from a poem my father had loved to listen to my mother reciting:

> *"For a breeze of morning moves*
> *And the Planet of Love is on high,*
> *Beginning to faint in the light that she loves*
> *On a bed of daffodil sky."*

Daisy embraced me. Perhaps it was the sharp breeze that made her eyes fill with tears.

"I know I'm difficult, but I love you, Jimmy. Don't let me go, will you, whatever happens?"

As we took a path that emerged at the top of a hill where Kenwood began, I can't say that I paid much attention to the evidence of an awakening earth. Spring always hits me from the inside. What I felt was an agonizing yearning and a recurring premonition that I would lose her. This thought alone had the awful capacity to drain me of energy, as if the surface tension of my ego had been punctured. Sometimes I thought she did it on purpose, as if she was able to drain my vitality. It had the effect, sometimes, of making me want to get away from her.

We sat down by automatic reflex on a bench under a horse chestnut tree. It was still early enough in the year for it to have huge blossoms that stood upright like pyramids and changed the aspect of the tree. In some lights it looked as if it were on fire.

"Isn't it funny the way we've never made a decision about it but we always sit here?"

"Daisy, what did you mean just now when you said, 'Don't let me go, will you'?"

"Oh God! You're not going to read something sinister into that, are you? It's a beautiful day, James. Don't let's spoil it."

"Well, you did say it. Doesn't it have a sinister ring? As if you're tempted to get up and leave?"

"No, it doesn't."

"What did you mean, then?"

She sat with her back straight, hands together in her lap. In her long flowered skirt and a light woolen sweater, she resembled an English country schoolteacher. Thanks to her British mother, the Home Office was processing her naturalization application without too many hiccups. With an accent nowadays that only intermittently reflected her roots, she had blended into the landscape better than most immigrants. And over the past few months she had finally been taking an interest in her students. She was teaching literature to sixteen-year-olds at a polytechnic. She liked the exuberance of the boys, with whom she had a bantering relationship, and was good at playing older sister to the girls. She was surprised by her success. The polytechnic had its problems, and many teachers who were supposed to be good did not survive there. Daisy, who took up assignments on the assumption that sooner or later she would be sacked, probably for absenteeism, found herself respected and admired.

I took her hand, half knelt beside her.

"Daisy, I wish I could stop this gnawing at my guts, but I can't."

"Gnawing at your guts? That's an odd expression! Very dramatic."

"I just don't know where I am with you, who you are anymore."

"You're not going to start with that cliché again, are you? Nobody knows who they are."

"And you can live with that?"

"Look, James, I put up with a lot from you and I sacrifice a lot. I do it for what we've had, and—and what we've got. But what

I can't have is you worming yourself into my soul for reassurance all the time. It's so suffocating."

In my pocket I twisted a handkerchief around my index finger until it hurt. "I don't know what it is you sacrifice. You're not the sacrificing type. I work three times as hard as you, pay twice as much rent, and still do my half of the household chores. What is it that you sacrifice?"

She looked away. "You couldn't handle it if I told you."

"Don't get superior; tell me."

She spoke a word softly that I could not make out.

"Pardon?"

"Polygamy. Women are basically polygamous—it's only child-birth and male paranoia that have kept us cooped up for five thousand years. The revolution is here, I'm afraid—you can't stop it, James. But I sacrifice my polygamous nature for you. I castrate myself, I suppose."

I stood up, feeling as if my stomach were collapsing. "You're selfish," was all I could find to say. She set her mouth grimly.

"I want to go now. My mom's expecting us. Are you coming?"

I was fond of Mrs. Hawkley (she had refused to change her name after the divorce, despite pressure from Daisy). I found our visits to her flat soothing. She liked me, too, and let me know that she thought I was a good influence on Daisy. I knew that she worried about her and that the worry had increased lately, just as Daisy had become more attentive. Her mother was Daisy's project of the moment.

She'd been disturbed by Daisy's new fad for narrating her sexual fantasies, although little by little Mrs. Hawkley seemed to confuse them with her own. I had an idea that on her good nights Daisy's mother rode to sleep clad in a silver spacesuit on a pink elephant, while in the middle distance Martians raped Belle Époque courtesans who looked like her daughter.

I think she was relieved that I had no delusions about her. I spent too much of my working life with the so-called underclass not to be able to read the signs. On every visit there was a new dent in her old red mini. In her flat the wallpaper was stained by splash marks from bouts with the nightly demons. Wire coat hangers on every doorknob held panties and old sweaters. The cupboard under the sink was full of empty red-wine bottles. As we sat on her mother's sofa sipping department store red wine (Daisy smoked a joint, her mother smoked a fag), Daisy would bring up that good old staple of civilized conversation, her clitoris.

"Was yours like this, Mum, at my age—I mean, really. It's like some hot little animal down there."

Mrs. Hawkley, the fag in her mouth pointing down at the avalanche of ash which had stained her old red sweater, smiled in fond and sozzled remembrance of the bush fires of her youth.

"I think so, dear. It's a while since I've seen mine. I think it's gone into hibernation."

The shock of having made a joke (I broke into surprised laughter; Daisy made a face) precipitated a coughing fit. The tobacco tar of decades churned with a sound like an old bus going up a hill. Her lived-in face, which medication, red wine, and nicotine had restructured over the years, imploded in the fight for breath. Daisy put a pretty young arm around her, patted her back.

"Isn't she fantastic? Isn't she just the best mom? Aren't women just great to survive at all—to carry on in spite of everything?"

"Gone into hibernation." Mrs. Hawkley repeated her joke as she surfaced from her battle with the monsters of the deep, winked at me in a way that always infuriated Daisy ("She still sees men as the source of authority").

"Mother Courage, that's what she is. You have to have guts to survive seventeen years with a psychopath."

"Don't talk about your father like that." Mrs. Hawkley turned to me. "Her father is a good man, brilliant. It was my fault it all went wrong. I misled him." She leaned forward conspiratorially. "I knew how to play the lady, you see. And him being American, he didn't understand that I was really just an ordinary English lass. Until after we were married, that is. I was young and stupid. All I wanted was to visit America. I would have given anything to get there. I was that generation: America was the answer to every problem, the promised land. We had one of those whirlwind romances. I was surprised he stuck with me as long as he did. I was no good at all for his career. I'm hopeless at dinner parties. He deserved better than me." She took a long draw on her cigarette. "Daisy always sees everything upside down. I'm not strong, I'm weak. Anyone can see that."

"No, no, that's just male programming." Daisy's face hardened with zeal. "That's what they make you think, that's what they've done to us—*they've colonized us.*"

"Oh, is that what it is? And all the time we used to think we were colonizing them, taming them and bringing them to heel. That's what I thought when your father went down on his knees and asked me to marry him. But I wasn't good enough, I know that."

"No, no, you're wrong." Daisy wrung her hands.

"But I don't think we were as horny as you, dear—is that the right word? I don't think we ate as much meat. Our fantasies were all different, too. We didn't have any Martians then, we had formal dances and romantic walks by ornamental lakes, and we would never dream of talking to a gentleman about our private parts, not even after we were married. We would never have called that liberation. For us, liberation was what Mahatma Gandhi wanted for India."

"Exactly," Daisy said. "It's the same thing."

Mrs. Hawkley looked perplexed. "They talk like Daisy at therapy. Everybody tells me to come out of my closet. I suppose they mean sex, but I only think about sex when I'm drunk, so I tell them some of your stories. Samantha, the therapist, was very pleased with me, she said I was definitely getting more in touch with myself. They all liked the Martian in the silver spacesuit. They said I should write it down and sell it to the BBC. They said I may have genius." She snorted and coughed. "So you'd better tell me a few more, or they'll think I'm having a relapse."

Daisy shook her head. "What am I going to do with you?"

She held her mother by the shoulders and rested her forehead on hers. The sudden touch of love made Mrs. Hawkley tearful.

"I don't know, dear—sometimes I'm that lonely I could die."

"How can you be lonely? You've got us."

"I'm lonely because I want a man, Daisy; can't you understand?"

*   *   *

Daisy would come away from such visits full of concern for her mother's spiritual welfare. She had an evangelist's certainty that her mother would be saved if only she would accept Daisy's worldview.

"Do you think she understands what I tell her?" she would ask me.

2 0

He reentered our world by one of those coincidences that, on reflection, seem to have been precipitated by an unconscious act of will in some coven of the mind.

The walk back through Kenwood from Daisy's mother's house was a ritual. Our route led down the grove of rhododendrons, past the turning that led to Dr. Johnson's Summer House, out into the open in front of the great manor house, down the carefully land-scaped hill to the ornamental pond, into the dense little wood of holly and oak, out onto Hampstead Heath and across to Roslyn Hill.

When I replay the old videotapes of memory, it seems to me that it was not only the route but also we ourselves who were fixed in a state of suspended animation, two blindfolded lovers standing still while the moving scenery (the rhododendron grove, flowering or wilting, the ornamental pond with lilies or without, the trees with leaves or bare) rolled by us.

Hindsight can provide a magical clarification to states of mind that were deeply perplexing at the time: although we didn't know it, we were waiting for him.

Then one day in late autumn of 1977 we came across Eleanor Merril-Price standing outside the manor house in high leather boots and loose sweater, as if she were the mistress of it. As we approached her, she gazed upon us with a bemused expression.

"How very odd! Do you know that you've just missed Oliver? He came for a walk with me and we had lunch. Now he's gone back to his studies. We were talking about you two, the beautiful Daisy and her mysterious dark knight."

"His black clients call him a white knight," Daisy said, smiling up at her like a flower.

"I knew you lived somewhere in Belsize Park, not far from us," Eleanor said. "I kept meaning to get your address from James Hogg."

She fell into step with us.

"Did you say that Thirst was studying?" I asked.

"James always calls Oliver 'Thirst,' " Daisy said.

"Yes. Did you notice at the vicarage that his vocabulary had improved a bit? He's a dark horse. He never told us until afterward that he sat for six O levels in Wormwood Scrubs. He passed them all with first grades in math and sociology. Now he's swotting for A levels and taking it terribly seriously. Perhaps too seriously. He lives like a monk with his books in a small room in Camden Town. I think I'm the only person he sees. We go for walks every Sunday at exactly the same time. He's become very controlled."

"O levels and A levels?" Daisy said. "What guts! He must feel like a twenty-odd-year-old high school kid. Does he want to use the exams to get into a university?"

"He wouldn't admit it, but I think so."

"Does he see Hogg?" I asked.

"I'm afraid they fell out." She hesitated. "Well, I'm sure you're both streetwise enough to understand. James Hogg grew rather too fond of Oliver, and Oliver reckoned he had enough problems. I'm afraid James Hogg came out of it rather badly and suffered some kind of breakdown. Frankly, he's the type who's always having a crisis of faith. It may not be a bad thing; even vicars need to grow up sooner or later."

"Thirst bit him," I said, "as soon as his parole was up."

Eleanor glanced sharply at me. "Well, yes, it did happen quite soon after his parole ended. Tom made the same observation. But he's terribly sincere, you know, about getting on."

"And Hogg?" I said.

Eleanor shuddered. "There was a scene. I wasn't there, but I've pieced it together. Not very pleasant. You must have noticed how strong James Hogg is? He got drunk one night—very drunk, according to Oliver. When Oliver rejected him, he became violent. I believe Oliver when he says he tried to avoid a fight."

"But they did fight?" Daisy said.

Eleanor hesitated. "I suppose there's a skill even in brawling, isn't there? No one could accuse Oliver of beating someone weaker than him, in this case." Eleanor bit her lip, then grinned. "They smashed up the whole vicarage between them. Practically every room." She looked at me and giggled. "Hogg did most of the smashing, interestingly enough. Eventually Oliver finished him off, but it was touch and go. Oliver admits as much."

"Any serious damage?" I said.

"Apart from the vicarage, you mean? Hogg's nose and one arm were broken."

"Wow," Daisy said.

We walked on.

"They enjoyed it, didn't they?" I said.

Eleanor gave another side glance. "As a matter of fact, they both came away with positive things to say about that night." She laughed. "Hogg said it was deeply cathartic and a kind of long-overdue initiation into manhood for him."

"And Oliver?"

"That it was one of the best knuckles he's ever had. But he won't see Hogg again. Best to leave on a high note, he says."

"Is he very lonely?" Daisy said.

"I think so. He has a massive complex about not knowing how to behave—not knowing the rules. He clams up totally when Tom's around. Perhaps he would be different with you two; you're more his age. He really needs a nucleus of new friends. He has no friends at all from the old days, except for someone called Chaz, who he did time with. He needs a family. Would you like to come in for tea?"

It was a house we had always admired when passing it, a very Hampstead house, eccentric and full of character, with a stained-glass conservatory at the front full of cacti and orchids.

"Hey, is this really yours?" Daisy said.

"Yes. Do you like it?"

"Like it! Do you know, we always stop just here when we take this walk and fantasize about owing it."

Eleanor beamed. "We waited for years for it to come on the market. Tom had our name down with every estate agent in Hampstead and even contacted the owners."

"It must have cost a million."

"We don't talk about that. Let me show you around; I've just finished renovating."

The walls of the hall were chockablock with eighteenth-century prints—mostly Hogarth. In rooms off the hall there was antique furniture, including at least a couple of Chippendales, a harpsichord in the front room that looked priceless even to me, an ultramodern stereo system, a television set discreetly housed in a polished wood cabinet, some Persian rugs. It was the English Dream more fully realized than I had ever seen it: discreet, old-fashioned, understated, and prohibitively expensive. In the kitchen we sat around a genuine old oak farm table that had a colorful Florentine bowl with fruit in the center.

Eleanor poured the tea. "That was a very interesting conversation we almost had, James, that evening chez Hogg."

"Before we conspired to steal your car?"

"Yes. We started to talk about criminals—their rehabilitation. I was disappointed because you didn't seem very interested."

"He's not," Daisy said. "He doesn't believe in it."

"Is that so?"

"For him life is like a Greek tragedy—you know, Oedipus and all that. The remorseless implacable Machine of Fate against which all human effort is futile."

"So there's no hope for Oliver?"

"I work with four different groups," I said. "The criminals, the people who catch them, the people who judge them, and the people who try to change them. Of the four, the latter are the most pathetic."

"And the most heroic?"

"If you like. And I should have said that it's usually the do-gooders who end up hating the villains. The police don't hate them, neither do the lawyers. But show me a probation officer or social worker who's been at it for more than ten years, and I'll show you a person who hates the people he deals with."

"Why's that, do you think?"

"Why did Hogg have a breakdown?"

"He loved Oliver and tried to change him."

"Exactly. Anyone who tries to change people is in love with failure." An image flashed up in my mind—Thirst's confident hand on the gearstick that night, the life in his eye: "What was that?" "Hare." "Dead one." "Beg."

"Nonsense!" Daisy said.

"No," Eleanor said, "I agree. I agree totally. But what about someone who wants to change? In his own proud way he is asking for help—clumsily, grotesquely even, but still asking."

"If you must give it, give it at arm's length. But you know that, Eleanor."

She gave me her shrewd, matriarchal glance. "It's an amazing coincidence, meeting you both today, because I'd half made up my mind to phone you."

"To see if we would help Oliver?" Daisy asked.

"Yes."

"Of course we'll help if we can. Won't we?"

I refused to reply.

"He's a queer fish," Eleanor said, "not totally unknown but very unusual—the criminal who really does have a brilliant mind. I'd quite forgotten what a powerful intellect is in the young. Neither Michael, who's dead now, nor my daughter, Lizzie, are—were—especially gifted; just average. A very bright young person who's escaped higher education is a frightening creature. His mind works at lightning speed, and because he's never been trained, he picks up on things that no one else notices. He told me I'd never been in love with Tom. Not a stunning observation, you might think—but for a crook, a convict with no social programming at all that I can see? Isn't that a kind of evidence of a very hungry mind?"

"What a strange thing for him to say," Daisy said.

"He says many strange things. It's weird. It's almost like being with an animal with a human intelligence—as if he works by smell. And his eyes are everywhere. When he forgets his machismo, he can be quite charming, and at first I wanted him to cultivate that. But now I don't know. The hungry animal is fascinating, too."

Daisy listened attentively.

"Perhaps you're frightened of him, James?" Eleanor said.

"Yes," Daisy said.

"What do you find to fear in him?"

"Not his intellect, though it's impressive, I agree," I said. "What I find frightening is the lies he's been told, and the rage he will surely feel when he discovers the deception."

"Lies?"

"Yes. He's very shrewd, but he wants to believe in the opportunities people are telling him about. The message he's getting from everyone he talks to is that he must educate himself if he wants to get on. I told him the same thing myself. The subliminal message is that through education he will wipe out his past, live on an equal footing with the rest of us. In a house like this, perhaps."

"Why not?" Eleanor and Daisy both asked.

"It's happened, after all," Eleanor said. "Some of the biggest tycoons are street urchins made good."

"Yes, but you've already said Thirst is a queer fish. He isn't a managing director manqué, a wise guy who will one day tumble to the fact that he's better off being dishonest legally."

"So what is he?"

"Something not at all unusual in the criminal class. He's a romantic. Have you picked up the subliminal message he's really getting? That if he's a good boy and passes his exams, he'll have a life that's as satisfying and exciting as pinching a car and joyriding late at night with the lights off. That, in one form or another, is exactly what an awful lot of people, not all of them young, really expect to get out of life these days. Offering Thirst the middle-class option is like offering sherry to a heroin addict. The addict's problem is his joy—it's too intense. But a comparable joy is the only true incentive. Thirst is convincing himself that it's there somewhere down the line. And when he finds out it's not, he'll explode. That's what I'm frightened of."

"It's fascinating to me to hear you talk, James," Eleanor said. "Very intelligent and very bleak. One could almost conclude that the underlying drive of our society is to be like Oliver."

"But that's exactly what I think," I said.

"So we just leave that brilliant mind to rot?" Eleanor said. "We're discussing a real human being after all."

The telephone rang. Eleanor answered it.

"But, darling, we discussed this and we decided that you wouldn't go to the Riviera with that crowd. . . . They are *not* nice people, Lizzie; we talked about it and you agreed with me that they were decadent. . . . Lizzie, how can you do this to me after all that's happened. . . . How could I stand to just sit here while you're up to God knows what in Saint-Tropez with those drug addicts?"

"My daughter," she explained after she'd replaced the receiver. "Seventeen is a difficult age for a girl."

"Have you introduced her to Oliver?" I asked. Eleanor blushed.

As we were leaving, Daisy said, "Of course I'll help Oliver with his A levels. James will help, too. We'll be his friends."

21

I was developing an Old Bailey practice, the highest ambition of a criminal lawyer. The Bailey, as its users call it, is a temple of crime, its stones held together by a mortar of murder, rape, and armed robbery. Every morning the most extreme of criminal defendants are delivered—live meat in ugly prison vans—and taken in shackles to the cells below. The place intoxicated me, filled me drum-hard with confidence. Part of the glamour was knowing what was behind the banner headlines in the evening papers, which always covered the most sensational trials at the Bailey. I was grateful to the Bailey for providing a sure counterpoint to the insecurity I was feeling about Daisy.

During the trial of a gang of armed robbers (a bank plundered, a policeman shot in the chest, a security guard coshed, nearly a million pounds stolen), I left the building one afternoon with my red bag over my shoulder. Beaufort had given it to me after Thirst's appeal, a tradition when a junior has pleased a silk.

I was wearing a new suit with waistcoat. It was the first I'd had made. Perfect white cuffs with gold links protruded two inches past the dark-blue cloth of the suit. These days I was sporting more flamboyant ties, vivid red with large white spots, around a detachable cutaway collar of military stiffness. Daisy has talked me out of a fob watch with gold chain: "Name one person under sixty other than a barrister who's wearing a fob watch in this day and age."

I skipped down the steps—ignoring Thirst, who was waiting at the bottom. He fell into step, also saying nothing. He wore running shoes and jeans, a sweater with sleeves pushed up to the elbow, showing the tattoos on his forearms.

"I told you not to do this," I said out of the corner of my mouth. "You're almost as well known here as I am."

I walked quickly to Ludgate Circus, often stepping in the gutter to overtake pedestrians, then down Carpenter Street toward the Embankment. I was unable to shake him. He kept up effortlessly, seeming to enjoy the element of competition. Whenever I dodged around someone, he was there beside me again immediately afterward, as if attached to me by an invisible beam.

"Where are we going?" he asked.

"We? *I'm* going home! What the hell do you want, Oliver?" I stepped around a newspaper vendor, pleased to see that the trial was in the headlines again: MASTERMIND STILL AT LARGE. I would buy the paper later. My name had appeared two days running. The defense counsel generally had been described as "expensive legal talent."

He dodged around a couple who had stopped to have an argument.

"Someone to talk to," he said. "Know how long it's been? Two weeks; spoken to no one in that time."

"You must have spoken to Eleanor; that's why you're here." I was slightly breathless. The exertion seemed to have no effect on him. I shifted the bag to the other shoulder.

He sniffed. "She said it was all right to contact you."

"I suspect she simply said that Daisy would help with your A levels." Had she simply said that? Or had she repeated Daisy's offer of friendship on behalf of both of us? Eleanor could be indiscreet, witness one night at the vicarage.

"Daisy." He spoke the name as if it were of no consequence.

When we reached the river I felt safer. At five in the afternoon, the city was teeming; anonymity was a hundred yards in any direction. Even so, I leaned forward so that my gut was braced against the Embankment wall and I faced the river. Thirst had to crane his neck to see my face. I put the bag in front of me on the wall. It was a beautiful afternoon; I could see every detail of the oppposite embankment. I was still excited by the trial and not really averse to company, even Thirst's, although I felt obliged to be short with him.

"I'll go if you like," he said.

"You checked up on me, didn't you?" I was still facing the river. "You found out I was at the Bailey today."

"You're always at the Bailey these days. Doing yourself grand, James. Hear you're in the Crook Street trial."

The tabloids had pounced with glee on the name of the street where the robbery had occurred.

"What if I am?"

"Want to know who did it?"

"Of course not; what do I care? I'm not a detective; I'm representing a defendant."

"Not even curious? Biggest gossips in the world, barristers. You're Paddy Burke's brief, aren't you? Rank amateur, couldn't rob a sweet shop in Penzance. Did you know I was in the nick with Paddy one time? He was two cells down, running a coke scam, paying off the screws. Reckon that's how he got involved with this outfit. Word is they needed to make a payment on a shipment if they didn't want the Amsterdam triads on their backs—they're basically smack and coke, see, not bank robbers, and this smack came from Thailand on the Amsterdam route—"

"I don't want to know. Anyway, I thought you were going straight."

"I am. Just wandered down the pub the other night; had to talk to somebody. Few blokes in there discussing it."

"Not in Camden Town they weren't. You must have gone all the way to Camberwell."

He grinned. "Just doing a little research for my sociology paper."

A river bus went by on the way to Greenwich. The possibility that he had obtained information about the robbery in order to impress me made me feel faintly ill.

"Have you any idea how dangerous this is for me?"

"Don't get excited. I'm straight, honest—clean as a virgin. Just happened to pick up some gossip, that's all."

"I'd better go."

"Here: Two nuns in a jungle, and one of them screws a gorilla—"

"Don't."

He told it anyway. It was funnier than I'd expected; I decided to remember it to tell to Daisy. He seemed relieved that he'd made me smile.

"Let's do something."

"You mean like rob a bank, steal a car?"

"No, that's against the law, James. Let's have a drink."

"I can't, Oliver, you know that. Anyway, they're shut."

"Not round here. I know one that's not shut—over there." He pointed across the river.

A short drink was exactly what I needed to relax and shift gears. And I was secretly intrigued by his hint that he had heard something about the robbery. Everyone knew the defendants were guilty but the mastermind had not been caught. It was obvious that I was being paid out of the proceeds of the crime, as were all the other defense counsel. How else could Paddy Burke afford me without legal aid? It gave me a mild frisson to think about the chief gangster signing a check for my brief fee, or paying it to the solicitors in new hot notes. If I spent a few minutes with him, Thirst would tell me who this paymaster was. I was also attracted to the idea of slumming it for ten minutes in some illegal drinking den south of the river—a harmless escapade to tell Daisy about. Perhaps over a drink I could explain to Thirst in a more civilized way why we could not be friends. My reputation was not so fragile these days.

"Look at it this way—where I'm taking you, if you do see anyone you know, they'll want to keep quiet about it as well."

At a bus stop, he said, "Who's the D.I. running that prosecution, then?"

"Detective Inspector George Holmes. Why?"

"Thought it was. Just wondered."

"You know him?"

"Everybody in the business knows him. A fanatic."

"You could be right."

As it happened, I had been impressed by George Holmes's fanaticism that afternoon. Some papers, crucial to the prosecution, had disappeared, and George clearly blamed the negligence of prosecuting counsel. He'd not hesitated to lecture his Q.C. on security and the need to be efficient about putting gangsters behind bars. Although a naturally conservative man, he'd been almost spitting with fury. But none of us were entirely surprised he'd reacted in that way. We'd overheard some of his radically right-wing views over the past few days.

On top of the bus, crossing London Bridge, Thirst told me who had masterminded the robbery, throwing in a few details for verisimilitude. The name he gave was the person whom others with in-depth knowledge were also naming, usually in whispers.

"I suppose he told you himself?"

"Cop told me, actually."

"Bent one?"

"You could say that. Twisted, crooked, corrupt, sociopathic— see how my vocab's improved? Am I impressing you yet? But yeah, bent says it. They don't come no benter than this one. Don't ask me who, but you'd be surprised."

The top deck of the bus was full. I was sitting next to the window on the right, looking east. Below, the river was swollen with a spring tide; a small dinghy with outboard was bouncing down toward Docklands. I could see Tower Bridge downstream and the pack of cars crawling across it. Mellow light hit the spires from the west, turning the upper white parts pink.

"How many times do I have to tell you, I'm not interested."

"Course not. Look, it's good to see you, that's all. I was beginning to weaken. As long as I can see you now and then, I can keep away from the villains."

I stared at him. "You don't think I'm going to fall for that, do you?"

He shrugged. "Worked on Eleanor." A faint grin.

"I'm not Eleanor."

Just before Deptford, everyone except us started to get off to

make connections for Docklands and Kent. While the other pas-
sengers were descending the stairs in a tired file, four punks forced
their way up against the flow.

"Oi—" The conductor started to object, then thought better of
it. A middle-aged woman said something about rudeness, and a
man said, "That was deliberate—he trod on my foot."

The complaints were muffled, however. The four punks were
all large, with complexions like potatoes, orange hair cut Mohawk
style, and tattoos on their necks that read "Cut here." The biggest—
he was over six feet—slouched past with a peculiar primate gait,
arms hanging loose from sloping shoulders. Like the other passen-
gers, I found that I was unwilling to engage his eyes, though it was
hard to avoid staring at him. His colleague immediately behind
carried a huge cassette player, which had to be held vertically to
avoid banging it on the seats.

I was curious about how Thirst would react, but he seemed
hardly aware of them. Then, as the last was passing us, he said,
"Fucking amateurs," loud enough for them to hear. The leader
turned slowly, with the same peculiar nodding motion which char-
acterized his walk. He looked up from under a low brow. The
affectation of subhuman brutality was exceptionally convincing. He
engaged Thirst's eyes for a moment before nodding his way onward
to the seats at the front. I felt a strong inclination to tell Thirst not
to antagonize them. Residual male ego prevented me.

"All these punks are just a bunch of painted fairies," Thirst
said in the same loud, even tone. "Dunno why people are so scared
of them."

The nodding, half-shaved anthropoid head froze for a second
at the top of its short arc, then continued to nod, though less convincingly. I fancied I could see a bristling on the back of its neck.

"Take that fat ponce," Thirst continued. "Bet he wears wom-
en's knickers and suspender belts."

The youngest of the punks was unable to restrain a smirk, but
the one with the cassette player turned to look at Thirst in surprise, as
if he pitied him for the mayhem he was about to suffer. The big one
changed the nod to a shake, as if he'd made a decision, and seemed
about to stand up, but Thirst was already on his feet, blocking the
aisle. It was only then that his reckless provocation made sense. He

was squaring up, like a boxer, turned sideways to the aisle, hands raised in half-fists. He was alert and eager like an athlete. You knew how fast and dirty he would be, how much he would enjoy it.

The punks suddenly seemed clownish amateurs in comparison. The big punk made a poor show of adjusting his slouch, as if he'd not intended to stand up at all, and lolled against the wall of the bus. Thirst sat down.

"Turn it on," the chief punk told his music department.

Immediately a deafening, punk-like noise filled the bus.

"Turn it off," Thirst yelled.

"Get stuffed." It was not the large punk who spoke, but the other with the cassette player.

"You what?" Thirst was on his feet again. The punk with the player looked hopefully toward the big punk, but the latter was suddenly apostate, nodding at a window. The punk with the player scowled and turned the music down.

"I said off."

The music stopped. Still Thirst was not satisfied. He walked up the row of empty seats to where the punks were sitting. I could not hear what he said, merely caught a tone of quiet homicidal menace. "I turned it off, didn't I?" The punk sounded frightened. Thirst came back and sat down.

"Punks."

At Deptford we got off and walked a short distance to a street that had been affluent in Victorian times. Its airiness was in dramatic contrast to the amorphous conglomeration of high-rise blocks, mean terraces, and ugly sixties shops in the area. Very large detached houses with neoclassic porches stood at the end of long front gardens. About half of them were in decay, crumbling, one or two done up, and the rest converted into flats. He took me to the side entrance of one that had recently been painted a stark white, the only house with a high iron gate. I noticed a Guard Dog warning. There were marigolds and chrysanthemums in the front garden; the back of a sky-blue Rolls-Royce protruded from a carport. The windows of the house were of mirrored glass, so that it was impossible to see inside.

"Thought it was going to be a hole in a wall, didn't you?"

"Yes," I said. My imagination had painted a small dark basement with Formica chairs and cheap whisky.

He executed an elaborate tap on the side door and waited until a woman of about fifty with platinum-blond hair and wearing a dressing gown came to let us in. She took a cigarette out of her mouth, coughed.

"Well, if it isn't young Oliver. Mildred? Ollie's here, with a visitor. Haven't seen you for ages, my darling!"

"'Lo, Aunt Maude," Thirst said.

"You're looking well. Give us a kiss."

He kissed her gingerly on her mask-like cheek.

"Ah! He's shy. You want to see him give us a kiss, mister, when there's no company. Well, who's this, then? Looks like a real toff."

"This is James Knight, friend of mine."

"Looks like a brief to me. I've seen those bags often enough in my time."

"That's right. I'm a barrister," I said.

"Oh-la-la, we are honored. What was it, just a drink?" she asked Thirst.

"Yeah, we won't be long."

"Better not be; you know what'll happen if he finds you here. He still hasn't forgotten that five grand."

"Figured he'd be at the shop till at least seven."

"Yes, well, make sure you leave before then."

In the hallway another woman appeared, also in a dressing gown, also about fifty. Her hair was jet black.

"Hello, Oliver."

"Milly."

Aunt Maude took us up a staircase with a thick red carpet and gold-painted handrails. Mirrors were inset in panels in the wall. A small bar with Queen Anne chairs in red upholstery waited off the upstairs hall. Maude put out her cigarette, stepped behind the bar.

"What'll it be? You name it."

The bar was stocked with the best makes of whisky and brandy, gin, vodka, every kind of liqueur. I noticed a whole row of single malts and a vintage Napoleon.

"Cold beer will do me," I said.

"I'll have a Glenfiddich," Thirst said.

Maude brought us the drinks. "Help yourselves if you want more. I'm carrying on with the housework downstairs."

We sipped our drinks.

"Been to a knocking shop before?"

"No, never," I said.

"Brought up in one, me. They're not all like this, of course. Maude got lucky after she retired from active service. This Kenyan Asian pimp needed an experienced Mama-san to run the place. I'm not too popular with him at the moment. Small matter of a few thousand pounds."

"Maude brought you up?"

"Off and on. When she had the time and the money. She's not really my aunt—that's a kind of joke; I always used to call her Aunt Maude in front of the punters. You know how whores are— sometimes they go soft over a kid. Maude was like that with me. Guilt reflex, I s'pose the books would call it. My mum's best friend before she fucked off."

"You don't know where your mother is?"

"Haven't seen her since I was four, James. One of her punters offered to marry her so long as she didn't bring her little bastard with her. South Africa, the story goes, but it could be anywhere. I don't blame her, would have done the same myself. She even sent money for the first year."

What had she been like, his mother? Hard and attractive, a brittle beauty? His father—could a prostitute even guess whose seed? Was there a part of him that cared?

"Where are the girls?" I said.

"Too early for them. Never see a whore before night as a rule, unless the punter puts in a request." He chuckled. "That's why old Maude and Mildred are still in dressing gowns. Old habits die hard. They probably only got up an hour ago."

We ran abruptly out of conversation.

"I'd better phone Daisy, if you don't mind; she was expecting me about now."

"Under the bar."

I stepped behind the bar. The phone was next to a police night-stick in one corner.

"Daisy, I'm with Oliver. . . . Yes, him. . . . We're in a brothel in South London. . . . Of course not. . . . Yes, I did say a brothel, as in bordello, whorehouse, knocking shop. . . . We're just having a drink. . . . Eleanor told him we would help. . . . I will."

I walked back to the table, sat down, and finished my beer. Thirst's mood had darkened.

"Daisy sends her regards," I said.

"You didn't have to tell her it was a brothel." His voice was thick like treacle.

"Sorry, I didn't realize. . . ."

"No, course not. Bit of a giggle, I s'pose, for you."

I shrugged. "You brought me here."

"Because this is all I've got."

I looked around the room again. A second door, made to look like a panel in the wall, led off to another part of the upper floor.

"You should have said if it was top secret."

"It's not top secret. Just no need to blab, that's all."

I put the empty beer glass down on the beer mat on the little polished oak table. The bar was polished oak, too; so were the trimmings. Discreet wealth in neon lights. The carpet was red, like so much else in the place.

"Maybe I'll be going," I said. He remained with his legs stretched out, looking down.

"This is the trouble, isn't it? I can't do this—the social bit. I'm good in a fight—if those punks on the bus had bothered you, I could have flattened the lot of them, you wouldn't have needed to raise a finger. But I can't do this."

"I'm not much good at it myself."

"Don't bullshit me. You're a toff, like Maude said. You're having a lark, slumming it."

"I *was* having a lark. Tell me another joke before I go."

He was silent for a moment. He sighed. "Not in the mood. Christ, why does it have to be this hard always? No wonder blokes go back inside."

I moved my legs, ran a hand through my hair. "Tell me about Maude, then."

"Nothing to tell; you can see it all by looking at her. That's the thing with riffraff—we're transparent."

I stood up, walked across to an elegant window that reached down to about two feet above the floor. It looked over the back garden. There were three small cottage-like structures, an ornamental pond, and a hammock. I wondered about the cottages. Leather? Rubber? Chains? What were the limits? How much decadence could money buy? A syndicate I had learned about guaranteed its jet-set clients a chance to murder a South American Indian on a tour. And then there were snuff movies. But this seemed like a comfortable English business, almost respectable. In France it would have been part of the establishment. The target was the white-middle-class over-fifty male market—doctors, politicians, respectable businessmen, lawyers, anyone with money and a mildly thwarted libido. Blackmail?

"I can tell you one thing—self-pity won't help," I said, not really thinking about him.

"You said that before, but it passes the time in the nick. Becomes a way of life, feeling sorry for yourself."

My eye finally registered a high-perimeter fence, electronic surveillance cameras set in the wall of the garage that jutted into the garden. The house was not exactly discreet. Every policeman in the area must know what it was. Someone was paying his dues.

"It must be pretty boring. What do you do all day in the nick?"

"Stare at the wall, watch telly. Sometimes there's a bit of a fight. Sometimes someone smashes a screw. Always plenty of drugs if you're into that. Sex, of course."

"Sex?"

"You knew that." He scowled. "Everybody does it. Doesn't mean you're queer if you have it off with another bloke in the nick—it's either that or do it yourself. What's the difference?"

I watched Maude and Mildred in their dressing gowns take a Persian rug out into the garden, shake it, laugh about something, take it back inside. I liked them; they put me in mind of aging monks who have come to see God in small things.

I had no reservations about being there. Despite Thirst's mood, I was enjoying it. It was pleasant, sometimes, to be in an environment without standards. Daisy would have loved it.

"Did you never get close to anyone?"

"Bloke, you mean? You want to know if I'm a homo? I was seduced by a copper when I was twelve, if that helps. Couldn't sit down for a week." He was trying to sound indignant, but the way he said it made me laugh. He looked up.

"I'm not queer. Know Marlborough Street Magistrates Court?"

"Of course."

"In one of the cells someone's carved something: 'I thought sex was a pain in the arse till I discovered girls.' That's me."

I smiled.

"Like that one, did you?"

"I was smiling because you defy all the categories."

"Me? Leave off. I only have to walk into a room, everyone sees where I'm coming from."

How did someone like him walk into a room? It could be a difficult psychological maneuver, even for me, to walk into a room full of people who understood each other so much better than they understood me. Suppose you were violent, angry, tattooed—how did you walk into a room and make a success of it?

"They see the caricature, that's all."

"Look," he said, "I'm sorry I came to the Bailey today. I was getting a bit desperate. See, things are better for me in one way, worse in another. I know what I want, for once in my life—but I'm on my own. I go down the pub these days, like the other night in Camberwell, I look at the blokes I used to hang out with, and I think: Suckers. Like old Beaufort said, they all think they're Jack the Lad, when they're really being screwed by the system. But I'm not exactly a middle-class teenager learning his Shakespeare, either, am I? You're about the only one I know who sees both sides—like me. But I shouldn't have just turned up like that—makes it awkward for you, I expect."

"Oh, never mind. I suppose I'm being overfastidious after all; it happens all the time—"

I stopped myself, but he had caught the meaning. "You mean ex-cons trying to make friends with briefs?"

"It can't be done, Oliver."

"But I'm straight now. How long does it take?"

"I don't know; I didn't make the rules."

The severity of what I was saying made his mouth twitch. But he recovered surprisingly quickly and stood up. "Quick, let's go—while you're still smiling. That way maybe you'll see me again."

It took a good two hours to reach home; most of London was paralyzed in the rush hour. I bought the evening paper at a news vendor in the underground to read about the trial. I was not mentioned, but my client was described as "cunning and ruthless."

Daisy was waiting for me in her old white sweater.

"What was it like?" she said before I'd had time to greet her properly. I knew how much the idea of brothels and prostitutes aroused her.

"I'll tell you later," I said. "I'm tired. I think I'll read the paper for half an hour."

"Don't tease."

She lifted the bottom of her sweater to show me that she was naked underneath. I changed into a dressing gown, lay on the bed. She put her head on my chest.

"It was amazing," I said. "You wouldn't believe it."

"Get on with it."

"Every room is different and dedicated to a different girl. The punter gets to choose which color he wants—black, yellow, red, white—and each room is made up to match. Thirst took me into three of them. In two of them a girl was naked, spread-eagled on the bed, tied up with silk ropes. You're allowed to whip her if you pay extra, but you're not allowed to draw blood. If you do, you have to pay a thousand pounds' fine and they kick you out."

"Can you ask for fantasies?"

"Of course. They already know most of them—all *your* fantasies are on their books. When you get to know the place, you just phone up and say, 'Fantasy twelve, please,' and the girl will be ready for you when you arrive, wearing whatever is part of the fantasy."

"Were there any punters when you were there?"

"Dozens; eminent men, too. I saw three High Court judges."

"Hey! Really? What were they up to?"

"One was wearing a nappy, another was being whipped. I forget what the third was doing."

"And you were able to see all this?"

"They have spyholes in all the rooms. Thirst showed me."

"Wow! A High Court judge in a nappy. Which one was it?"

"Um . . . Lord Justice Tomlin."

"Tomlin? The one you hate?"

"Yes, him."

"That's a coincidence."

"Yes, a terrific coincidence."

"And the other two wouldn't happen to be Peabody and Crawthorne, would they?"

"Yes, those exactly."

She hit me with her small fist, hard on the chest. "You jerk! Now tell me what it was like really."

I started to speak, but she hit me again.

"No bullshit this time."

"Oh, just a big Victorian South London house with brand-new over-the-top furnishings, mirrors everywhere, two old tarts cleaning up, getting ready for tonight."

"No girls or punters anywhere, I s'pose?"

"Of course not; it was five-thirty in the afternoon."

"And Oliver?"

"The usual combination—intermittently charming, with frightening mood swings. He was terribly offended that I told you it was a brothel."

"Probably the way you said it made it sound like you were slumming it and having a bit of a giggle."

"That's exactly what he said."

"It's sort of fetching, his sensitivity, the way you describe it. Macho man one minute, hurt and emotional the next. Very human."

"Very uncontrolled; he's like a horse without a rider."

"Same thing."

"Two nuns in a jungle, and one of them screws a gorilla . . ." I began.

2 2

In the dream that began recurring at about this time, the three of us—Daisy, Thirst, and I—are stuck in cement. It has encased our ankles, and we are about to fall. The thought of our ankles snapping, leaving us writhing on our backs in agony on the cement (jagged bones poking through flesh), makes me frantic. I see that the other two are also frantic.

Overhead, a city such as does not exist on earth soars upward in thousand-story buildings under a lurid sky. We seem to be in a wasteland at the dead center of the city, a concrete area of disused cars, tangled pieces of metal, tires, half-constructed reinforced-concrete apartment blocks with the steel reinforcement sticking out like half-fleshed skeletons. Despite myself, I begin to lean toward Daisy. She is not far away. Were it not for the cement, I could take one step toward her and touch her.

Immediately she begins to lean toward Thirst, who begins to lean toward me. In a matter of seconds we will all three topple over. Just as we do so, the city begins to spin as if seen through a spinning fish-eye lens.

The scene changes. We're in a squalid bedroom. Daisy has the cynical face of a whore, her teeth blackened, her body half naked; Thirst has amputated forearms. With one stump he points at me and laughs. "Look at you."

I wake up screaming.

"What's the matter?" Daisy is saying.

"How embarrassing," I said the first time it happened. "I just had a classic Freudian nightmare. I dreamed that I was castrated and Oliver was mutilated." I left out the other details.

It was not difficult to work out the origin of the dreams. Nothing traps us more effectively than the need to prove that we are reasonable, honest, and compassionate. Such a need forced me, in the end, to relent. After all, Thirst had fulfilled the condition I had set. He was straining every nerve to change his ways. How could I admit that in so doing he had ceased to be pathetic and become, instead, frightening?

For Daisy the new friendship with Thirst was an anticlimax.

"He doesn't even fancy me," she said after we had been to meet him together. "He's a typical working-class male: women only exist for one thing. He hung on every word you said and didn't even notice when I was talking."

"Is it a condition of helping him with his A levels that he fall in love with you?"

"That's not what I'm talking about."

We lay in bed on the evening before Daisy's mother's fifty-second birthday. Daisy lit up a joint. She rolled and smoked them with the pride of an old hand, as if it were a job at which she excelled after long practice. Sometimes the look on her face made me think of a cynical baby such as one sees in certain joke birthday cards: child in pram surreptitiously smoking a cigarette, with a balloon from its mouth saying something obscene and adult. There were times, I admit, when I wondered why I loved her.

"Bet I know what it is," she mused as the acrid smoke filled the room.

"What what is?"

I had my arm around her shoulder. With a finger I traced the dimple where her breastbone connected. I turned and with the other hand began to caress her breasts. It was curious how, occasionally, she could retract all sensation from them, as when she rode off on some inner speculative adventure fueled by dope.

"This castration complex about Oliver."

"Oh, that."

"I once did an interesting course with one of my classes about male sexuality in the English novel—you know, how with people like Hardy and Lawrence, even Dickens, it's working-class, possibly criminal, man who has true phallic power. The middle classes and the aristocracy are practically castrated—like in Lady Chatterley. There's not really any correlation in the States. Sometimes I think you people are more screwed up than we are."

I slipped my hand between her thighs, but there, too, all responses had been frozen. She was fascinated by the workings inside her skull. Which, by the look on her face, had given her a superior insight into the human condition.

"So?"

She took a deep drag and coughed as she spoke. "Well, it's the working-class boy in you—the hot street kid—who does the screwing. Not the middle-class barrister. You wouldn't be threatened sexually by any of your colleagues, because to you they're not sexual beings at all. On the other hand, you must be afraid that the more cerebral and middle class you become, the less potent you'll be. So when someone like Oliver comes on the scene—a real wild man from the streets—you're afraid he'll take over from you. . . . Stop it, I'm not in the mood."

I turned over. I must have dozed off. I'd had a difficult day in court, defending a girl on a manslaughter charge. In a postnatal depression, she had thrown her baby against a wall and killed it. A plain girl, not very bright, she hadn't understood much of the case against her. Everyone hoped she would never have another child, but we all knew that she would. Sex was all she had.

I awoke to a hand gently caressing my face. "Jimmy, are you in a mood because of what I was saying?"

"No."

"What do you think of it?"

"I think it's a load of rubbish. But then I'd have to say that, wouldn't I, or condemn myself to a life of increasing impotence?"

"Do you want to make love now?"

"No. The street urchin in me is fast asleep, and as you pointed out, the barrister doesn't know how."

She giggled. "Do you think I'm crazy?"

"Yes, it's part of your charm. Go to sleep. Your phallic hero is coming at twelve, remember?"

"Do you think he'll turn up?"

"Oh yes, he wouldn't miss it for the world. But don't throw a tantrum if he takes no notice of you. You know what wild men from the street think about spoilt little girls."

23

When the doorbell rang the next day I was as curious as Daisy. After the interlude in the brothel, I had a sadistic interest in how Thirst would handle simple social events. As usual, I was underestimating his resources.

He arrived in a battered Ford Cortina that, like Eleanor, must have been young in the sixties, to judge from the fading floral patterns in orange and mauve that crawled over most of its paint-work. I was standing at the front door, while Daisy remained up-stairs, packing presents. My smile broadened as I did a double take of him and the Cortina. His grin was infectious. I shook my head, started to laugh.

"Fuck!" I said.

"What d'you reckon?"

"To you or the car?"

"We're together."

He was wearing a double-breasted tuxedo with black bow tie,

frilly dress shirt, jeans, cowboy boots. It was exactly the costume that David Bowie had worn in a recent television appearance.

"Wonderful."

"Me or the car?"

"Both."

I shouted for Daisy.

"Fuck!" Daisy said when she came down.

Thirst rubbed his jaw. "Look, no offense, but you two masters of the English language are kind of monosyllabic before lunch. I mean, the main reason I'm here is to improve myself. Right?"

"You're terrific," Daisy said, kissing him on the cheek. "So's the car."

"Think the old lady'll like us?"

"She'll love both of you."

Daisy went upstairs again. Thirst beckoned me to follow him to the boot of the Cortina. After the initial impact, the car made me nervous.

"It's all right," Thirst said. "Honest."

"Are you totally sure?"

"Look, I know how you feel. I'm making an effort here. If it was hot, I wouldn't bring it within a mile of you. I swear. I borrowed it from a friend. A straight friend."

"I didn't know you had any except me."

"That was last month. I've got more upward thrust than a Boeing. Trust me." He opened the boot. "It's up to you, James. I mean, I thought it might be a bit of a laugh, add some color, but if you say no, then it's no. I'll just leave it in the boot. At least no one'll think I pinched *that*."

I peered into the boot to ascertain what he was talking about, stared, stepped back. I turned to sit on the bumper, my face in my hands.

"No, eh?" Thirst said. "Well, you know, they're all the rage with the punks, and you did say Daisy's mum likes a bit of a giggle. What's up? You laughing or crying?"

I wiped the tears from my face, put a hand on his shoulder to pull myself up, pointed at the boot, and had to sit on the bumper again. I tried to stop shaking.

"What's its name?"

"Lord Denning. After the judge."

"You don't say. Look, personally I think it's hilarious, but you'd better play it by ear."

Thirst nodded, closed the boot, grinned. "Tell Daisy not to bother bringing champagne. I've got enough to sink a battleship."

"I don't think she was intending to bring any. And thanks." I tried not to think about how he had come by the champagne.

Thirst drove, I sat in the front passenger seat, Daisy sat in the back. I saw her eyes studying us in the rearview mirror.

"Something going on with you boys?"

I bit my lip.

"Know what 'fulguration' means?" Thirst said.

I checked Daisy's eyes in the mirror. "No."

"What about 'fuliginous'?"

Daisy shook her head. "No."

"You should know that one, 'fuliginous.' "

"You're on *F*?" I said.

"Yeah. *Concise Oxford Dictionary.*"

"Everything up to *F*?" Daisy was incredulous.

"Most of it. Try me."

"What does 'fulminate' mean?"

"Easy. Express violently. Same root as the other two. From the Latin word for lightning, see?" Thirst explained.

We drove up through Hampstead Village, then down past Golders Hill Park to Hampstead Garden Suburb. Daisy had not warned her mother, so Thirst and I waited downstairs. I heard Daisy say, "Come on, Mom, I just wanted to show you something in the street," then Mrs. Hawkley appeared and we all burst out with "Happy birthday to you." My tone-deaf droning served as a foil to Thirst's fairly convincing baritone.

I kissed Mrs. Hawkley on the cheek.

"This is the man I've been talking about all the time," Daisy said. "Oliver, meet Doris."

"Ooh, such a handsome man," Mrs. Hawkley said, offering Thirst a cheek to kiss. "Are you my escort? Such a wonderful surprise. So big and strong. Ooh, and what a lovely tuxedo. A handsome man is the best therapy for a girl like me. Can I get you on the National Health?"

"Don't flirt, Mom," Daisy said.

"Why not? It's my birthday." She smiled at me, turned to Thirst. "You don't mind, do you, love?"

Thirst gave a broad grin. "Love? You South London?"

Mrs. Hawkley touched her hair. "Well, Essex, actually. But you mean I'm not stuck up. No, I'm not. I gave up pretending when I left America."

Thirst hugged her as he led her to the Cortina. He made her sit next to him, while Daisy and I sat in the back. He drove slowly, with seamless gear shifts, down Kingsley Way, turned right, then right again, until we were passing the stupendously wealthy mansions of Bishop's Avenue.

"This is the only part of London that reminds me of California," Daisy said. "People with so much money they get stranded in their own fantasies."

Thirst nodded. "Yeah. Look at that."

We stared at an Islamic ten-bedroom citadel in blue and white, adorned with domes and crescent moons.

"Lovely," Mrs. Hawkley murmured. "I love a bit of color. Don't you, Oliver?"

He looked at her, grinned. "Like the car, you mean?"

"Oh yes, I love it. Don't take any notice of Daisy; she's a socialist. They want everything small and gray so that no one stands out from the crowd."

"Mom, please," Daisy said.

"Well, it's true. One thing I did like about America was the way everything was so big. Big houses, big meals, big dominant men."

Daisy groaned.

Bishop's Avenue emerged into Hampstead Lane. We turned left, then crossed into the parking area of Kenwood. I took Daisy's bag of presents and food, while Thirst brought the champagne from the boot. It was a bright day but cool, with fast clouds and unsettling slants of dazzling light. As I remember it, my three companions spent the day emerging out of shadow into spotlight and back again. When we sat down under a huge oak tree, Daisy took off her down jacket to put over her mother's shoulders, leaving herself with a thick sweater that was not enough insulation. She was sensitive to cold, and this may have contributed to her poor humor. I was chilly, too, in my own sweater. I couldn't understand how Thirst was managing in nothing but a dinner jacket and shirt, but he seemed impervious to the cold, as to many other things. The fact was that none of us had a home fit to hold even a tiny birthday party. Only Mrs. Hawkley, in Daisy's thick jacket, was snug.

I watched Thirst carefully take four champagne glasses out of an old nylon shopping bag, give one to each of us, then start to open the champagne. I wondered if he'd studied a sommelier on television, the way he meticulously unwound the cage, then gently screwed off the cork so that it made only a faint pop. He looked at me to say that he knew I'd expected him to let the cork shoot out like a bullet.

The temptation to gulp the champagne and forget the cold was irresistible. Daisy and I finished our first glasses in a few minutes, but we couldn't compete with Mrs. Hawkley, who was on her third while we were still on our first. Her rising mood reached a plateau, and she lay back against the tree, smiling at each of us in turn.

"What a wonderful, wonderful birthday. Thank you all so much. Especially my darling Daisy, who arranged it all, I'm sure." Daisy beamed, went over to kiss her. "And very special thanks to Oliver, my gorgeous escort, who provided the car and the champagne."

We all drank to that. I passed around smoked salmon sandwiches, while Daisy gave her mother the presents we'd bought for her. We watched her open them: a pair of leather gloves, a Seiko watch, a particularly stylish corkscrew that we laughed about, a ceramic vase that we'd bought at Camden Lock.

"Time for some music," Thirst said. He delved into the bag again, to take out a small cassette player.

"Strauss!" Mrs Hawkley said as "The Blue Danube" started to leak out of the tiny speakers. "Oliver, how did you know? Did Daisy tell you?"

"I never said a thing," Daisy said.

"I guessed," Thirst said. "May I have the pleasure?"

I admired his guts. It wasn't quite a waltz, and it was obvious that Mrs. Hawkley had known more practiced partners, but he had a natural rhythm, and she adapted easily to his steps.

"Where the hell did you learn to dance?" I asked. I hadn't intended the tone, bordering on outrage, which seemed to imply that convicts shouldn't know how to waltz.

He gave me a triumphant glance as he glided past with Daisy's mother on his arm. "School. Music, dance, art, and math were my subjects. I was a natural. Picked them up like a sponge. Not so good on the English, though. No one in my house ever talked, that was the thing."

"You have wings on your feet, Oliver," Mrs. Hawkley said. "You could have won championships if you'd pursued it. Still could—you're young and vigorous."

As she spoke she pressed her hand against his iron biceps and sighed. Daisy noticed and gave me a look. I checked the bottles. We'd finished three. Mrs. Hawkley had consumed nearly a bottle on her own. She gave no sign of drunkenness, except that her appreciation of Thirst's body wasn't the same joke it had been an hour before.

"Such wonderful presents, and you're the best of all," she told Thirst as they spun together under the oak. The expression on his face was taut, almost professional. It was as if he'd determined to produce a flawless performance, just to prove to himself that he could.

After the dance Thirst set Mrs. Hawkley down under the oak and went back to the car. When he returned, he asked Daisy to dance.

"I don't dance," Daisy said. "I have clods for feet."

Thirst pulled her up anyway, just a little roughly. She looked at me for a moment, but there wasn't enough aggression in the action to merit a scene. His attitude, though, had none of the kindness he'd shown to her mother.

He held her close, with his right hand pressed firmly against the small of her back. Suddenly she screamed, pulled away, screamed again. She pointed at Thirst's dinner jacket, in the area of the left breast. The blood had drained from her face, and her jaw hung open. Mrs. Hawkley and I both stared at the large lump moving under the black cloth. Daisy backed away, stammering incoherently.

"What?" Thirst said.

A wicked grin spread over Mrs. Hawkley's face.

"Oliver, you bad boy," she said, and glanced at Daisy.

Thirst undid the top few buttons of his shirt. Lord Denning's whiskers and nose appeared in restless animation, followed by two small pink eyes, a humped white back, and a stringy tail, longer than his body.

"Oh, *gross!*" Daisy yelled, her hands to her face. She stood behind me.

"*Rattus norvegicus.* Albino," Thirst said, holding it so that it continually ran over one forearm after the other, as if on a treadmill. "Meet Lord Denning, my best friend."

"What a beautiful rat," Mrs. Hawkley said. "Can I hold him?"

Behind me, Daisy was standing close enough for me to feel the shaking in her knees.

"Don't mind Daisy. She has a problem with rats. Have a drink, dear, you'll feel better." Mrs. Hawkley looked up at Oliver while she fondled the rodent. "She's really an American, you see, through and through. They don't have the same attitudes and traditions as us."

"That's not it, Mom, and you know it," Daisy said.

"Well, her father was a bit of a disciplinarian and shut her up in the boiler room when she was a child. Apparently there were rats in there. She's got a bit of a phobia."

Thirst looked at me.

"I didn't know that," I said. "About the rats, I mean."

Daisy was calming herself little by little. She sat next to me, her face distorted with revulsion, while her mother played with Lord Denning.

"Phobia's right," Daisy said. "It's the weirdest thing. Totally irrational. That small creature is perceived by my subconscious as a monster the size of a lion."

"Rodents can't grow that big," Thirst said. "Although they did once. A fossil rat in Uruguay was the size of a small bull."

Daisy shuddered.

"How did you know that?" I said.

"Rodents are the most successful mammals. Fifty percent of mammals are rodents. Did you know there's one rat in America for every person? Over two hundred million."

"You've made a study of this?"

"How interesting," Mrs. Hawkley said. "When Daisy went into higher education, I hoped she'd be full of interesting facts, but she came out smoking drugs and talking about sex." She beamed at Thirst.

"You've got to admire them, rats," Thirst continued. "They're like miniature gangsters. They've developed a whole lifestyle predating on human beings. They eat anything we eat. Then when they've had enough of us, they hit us with plague. Knocked out twenty-five million people in the Black Death. They make Hitler look like an amateur." He looked up from his musings, caught my eye. "*Encyclopaedia Britannica*. Got hold of a complete set quite cheap the other week."

"How cheap?"

He winked.

"In the early years of the war," Mrs. Hawkley said, "I used to visit an army camp near where we were living in Dagenham. Sometimes the boys would play the old ferret-in-the-trouser game. They'd tie up the legs of their trousers with string and put a live ferret down the top. Whoever kept it there longest won. Of course, the secret was to keep still so the ferret didn't get too terrified and do some real damage." She covered her mouth.

"You're getting drunk, Mom," Daisy said.

Mrs. Hawkley giggled. "I daresay, my love." She gave her best smile, which seemed to express unlimited tolerance for human foibles worldwide.

"You game, James?" Thirst said. At first I didn't understand what he meant. He took the rat back from Mrs. Hawkley. "Anyone got a watch?"

"James, don't," Daisy said.

"Ooh, yes, I've got one." Mrs. Hawkley showed us her wristwatch.

I looked at the four perpetually gnawing incisors below the twitching nose of the rodent. Thirst undid the button at the top of his jeans and pulled the zipper down an inch. He thrust the rat in headfirst. Immediately he started jumping from foot to foot and yelling. Mrs. Hawkley began a guffaw with a spray of champagne. Even Daisy laughed, a hand over her mouth.

"How long?" Thirst yelled.

"One minute forty seconds."

He danced around under the tree for another minute, then pulled the rat out by the tail. He held it up for me to take. It seemed in a state of shock. Its whiskers were quivering in an unusual way, and I noticed that its body was contorting.

"I think there's an advantage to going first," I said.

"James, if you, I mean, damage yourself . . ." Daisy smirked at her mother.

Mrs. Hawkley smiled. "Faint heart never won fair lady, James," she said.

I was wearing a fairly loose-fitting pair of corduroy trousers. As soon as the animal was inside, I started doing exactly what Thirst had done, jumping from one foot to the other, yelling "Ah!" "Oo!" "Eee!" while Lord Denning conducted a tour of my genital area. Luckily the rat found its way down my left leg and out into the open, where Thirst scooped it up with a practiced hand.

"Oliver won," Mrs. Hawkley said between guffaws.

Daisy was rolling on the ground, shaking uncontrollably, her phobia and the cold suddenly forgotten. She had passed beyond laughter into a helpless gurgling that might have been life-threatening, to judge from the desperate intakes of breath.

"What a wonderful day," Mrs. Hawkley said.

"Oliver's a magician," Daisy gasped when she could talk again. She looked at him from the ground. "You turned this into a real party."

Thirst looked at me. His eyes said it: not such a social cripple after all, eh?

I smiled at him, then looked away. It had been a long while since I'd seen Daisy laugh like that.

24

Despite the mutual teasing and intermittent flashes of the old humor, I had to admit, sadly, that the texture of the relationship between Daisy and me had changed. She dedicated more time to her women's group, was less dependent on me for company. We no longer argued about news items, because she stopped sharing her political views with me.

A new member, named Mick, had joined the group, bearing greetings from a sister church in Sausalito, near San Francisco. Since I never met this person, the picture I have of her in my mind is almost entirely my own creation. I decided she was shorter than Daisy, attractive, with a habit of pulling up her sleeves when she spoke, as if about to fight.

There was a hunger for challenging leadership that Mick was happy to supply, and so she became the de facto leader. Daisy was fascinated by Mick's pilgrimage through the West Coast therapy ashrams: Primal Scream, Transcendental Meditation, Transactional

Analysis, Gestalt, a guru called Maharishi something who made microwave ovens precipitate out of the ether ("I swear I actually *saw* one of these things falling out of the sky"), and of course Mick's very own personal reclusive Master, called simply Kroom, who happened to be in England at the time.

"But make no mistake, sisters," Mick said in her cute-gravel voice (I imagined her to have a cute-gravel voice), "there's only one therapy that really works, and that's hands-on sex therapy."

Kroom apparently was a Master of Tantric Sex as well as a psychotherapist.

During the washing up one Saturday, Daisy said, "D'you know it's been more than a year since you licked my cunt?"

I had finished the last mug and was pulling off my rubber gloves.

"Really? That long? It seems only yesterday—"

"Don't mock. You're so damned English, the way you can only talk about sex in a mocking way. I'm making a significant point here. Cunnilingus is a very important way to please and satisfy a woman."

"Got it."

I threw the gloves into the cupboard under the sink. I hated washing dishes and would have preferred that feminist dogma not decree that I do it.

"I mean, I'm a much more generous lover than you are. Look how many times I suck you."

I cursed inwardly. I had missed a mug that Daisy had left on a high bookshelf, no doubt when she was stoned. How long had it been up there? Mildew left a scum. I fetched it.

"How can you compare?" I said, putting the gloves on again. "Fellatio for you is a displacement activity. You do it when you're bored with your book, or you've run out of dope. It's very hard for a man to have the same relationship with a vagina or a clitoris." Did one have relationships with vaginas and clitori? Was clitori the plural? Curious how seldom one needed the plural form. There was nothing for it, I would have to use a scour. I rummaged under the sink.

"Why? Will you stop doing the goddamn dishes for one minute so we can deal with this?"

I scratched my head and left off looking for the scour. The mug on the shelf reminded me to look under the bed. Despite my regular remonstrations, it was still a hiding place for cups, glasses, electricity bills, important letters from her employers. I found a dish with the remains of granola set like concrete. I stood up again, about to complain, thought better of it. Her sleeves were rolled up, hands on hips.

"Are you serious?" I said.

"You bet I'm serious. What's the big difference between cunnilingus and fellatio?"

I gazed into the treasure chest of facetious answers, resolutely closed it again. I was in a generous mood. My trial at the Bailey was going well.

"Must we discuss it like this, yelling across the room? Why can't we talk about it in bed tonight, while we're making love? This is so . . . I don't know . . . clinical."

Daisy nodded. "I'm just targeting one of your hang-ups. It's probably a *sansara* from a previous lifetime."

"A what?"

"Never mind. Will you answer my question, please?"

"Daisy, why are you doing this? We have the best sex life of anyone I know. You love it and I love it. Even our worst arguments can't shake it. And now you come out with this. D'you think it's a sensitive way of doing things, to lecture me into licking you?"

"Lecture! Look who's talking, the lecture king of North London. I try to make one little point, try to communicate a personal need, and he accuses me of lecturing. *Will you stop doing the washing up!*"

"All right, I've stopped." I took the gloves off, threw them on the draining board, faced her. Better, anyway, for the mug to soak. "I can't believe you're actually complaining about our sex life."

"Well, I am. It's time you realized how complacent you're getting. You're becoming a very self-satisfied man."

"Complacent? Just because I don't like that?"

"Ah!"

"I mean, I have liked it, I will again, I suppose." Why was I blushing? "But it's a very private thing, somehow; so much depends on . . ."

"On what?"

I hesitated. We discussed just about every aspect of copulation except that. It had remained locked away in some libidinous vault carefully protected from corrosion by words.

"I just can't talk about it."

"Ah! So you *are* hung up about it."

"Daisy, *this is so destructive.* Why are you letting them do this to us?"

"Who? What are you talking about?"

"Mick. The women's group."

"So now you're saying I haven't got a mind of my own?"

I sat down on the bed, bewildered, while she maintained her warlike posture. Outside, it was a pleasant day, one of the first of spring. On such spring days, when my father wasn't working, he used to take my mother for a stroll by the canal, pick daisies for her, ask her to recite something from Tennyson while he listened, enraptured. They held hands but let go if they saw anyone coming.

Suddenly a cushion came flying across the room in my direction. Then another. When the third hit me on the head, I remained immobile.

Daisy stood next to the bed, put a hand in my hair.

"Poor Jimmy, he's embarrassed."

"Get stuffed."

"Tch, tch. Never mind, it's part of your learning curve."

"Pompous bitch."

"It's what you say to me—all the time."

I looked up. It was true.

She crawled over the bed to lie behind me, her back against the wall. She started to tickle me with her toes.

"Jimmy."

"What?"

"Let's go to sex therapy."

"You really think we need to?"

"It's what people do when there's a blockage. You have this English wall of privacy. It really does frustrate the hell out of me sometimes. It won't hurt. It's not like going to the dentist."

"It is. That's exactly what it's going to be like for me."

During the journey from Belsize Park to Mick's place, Daisy was comforting and even confessed to wondering if it was really such a good idea. I felt nauseous. Did it really solve problems to share one's sex life with strangers? Where did it end? Were taboos necessarily wrong? Did a sense of the sacred not enhance a relationship? Could anyone genuinely love Mick, whose vagina was apparently as public as a subway?

"We don't even know this guy," I said.

"I know, but Mick says he's just amazing, and he has all these qualifications. He spent five years studying names."

"Names?"

"Yes, names people use for each other."

"Like James and Daisy? For five years?"

"Don't take the piss out of him, Jimmy; you always do that when you can't control something. This isn't going to work if you try to control it."

"Well, I'm not going to lick you in front of him, even if he did study names for five years."

I had rather expected Kroom to be a diminutive Indian with terminal enigmatism. Daisy was disappointed that he was a North American. A New Yorker who had spent much of his adult life in California, he now lived most of the time in Sausalito. He and Mick shared a houseboat when they were home.

He was a giant, six feet seven at least, with a long body and short legs. His receding gray hair was tied back in a ponytail. Around his neck he wore the kind of leather boot-lace tie that cowboys used to wear in B movies. He and Mick were living in a quiet North London suburb that had not yet been gentrified. Stooping, he filled the doorway of a small prewar semi smelling of sandalwood and mold growth. I discounted the foolish smile on his face; he was a psychotherapist, and therefore the foolishness of his smile must have a purpose. Daisy stayed close to me. I sensed she was uncomfortable with his being so tall.

We sat down on a sofa in the tiny front sitting room. He sat in a chair, wrapping his arms around his knees, perhaps to try to make himself as small as we were. Daisy smiled sweetly at him, raised her hands as if to say, "Well, here we are." Kroom, apparently much impressed by this semaphore, smiled back in a way that told Daisy she was delightful. I decided to smile, too. He nodded sagely. So far no one had spoken. Daisy finally said, "Ah ha!" apropos of nothing.

"What is your question?" Kroom said.

He wore thick spectacles. The myopia was clearly worse in the left eye, magnified by the lens to Cyclopean proportions. I found myself addressing his left eye.

"What is your real name?" I said.

Daisy dug me painfully in the ribs. "It's English humor," she said. "Don't worry about it."

"There are no real names," Kroom said. The left eye blinked with peculiar slowness.

"Well," Daisy said, "we're interested in sex therapy. Mick told us about you."

"Mick is very advanced."

The left eye dilated when he looked at Daisy and contracted when he looked at me.

"The therapy usually works one on one. That means I would work with Daisy for an hour, and then I would work with James, maybe tomorrow. Sometimes we work dyads, though."

"Dyads?"

"From the Greek *duads,*" I said. "Two."

"That is correct."

"I think we'd like a dyad." Daisy pressed my hand.

"For dyadic therapy we charge seventy-five percent of the double fee. Fifteen pounds per hour."

He took us into a large upstairs room full of sofas with stuffed Disney toys sitting on them. I had the impression that the curtains were permanently drawn.

"Sex is a game from infancy."

The odor of sandalwood was stronger. In one corner there was a plastic bucket, apparently to catch water from a leak. In the center of the room, two upright chairs faced one another. One was red, the other white.

"The red one is the hot seat. With dyads, one half of the dyad watches and listens while the other half is in the hot seat. I think James wants to go first."

I sat in the red chair, Kroom in the white. Daisy sat in a sofa and hugged Mickey Mouse.

"During the session you may wish to take off some of your clothes. Feel free to do so. There are only myself, whom you should regard as a mirror, and the other half of your dyad in the room with you."

I looked pleadingly at Daisy, who looked down into the stuffed toy. I undid the top button of my shirt. Kroom turned down the lights until it was almost dark.

"How frequently do you masturbate?"

"Rarely."

"Once a week, month, year?"

"Month, if that."

"As a dyad or alone?"

"Alone."

"And who is the focus of your fantasies at such times?"

"Daisy." I looked across at her. She looked down.

"Is Daisy submissive in your fantasies, or dominant?"

"Submissive usually. Sometimes dominant."

"Apart from regular intercourse, what acts does Daisy perform in your fantasies?"

"I just like to fantasize about her doing the things she always does anyway. Sometimes, you know, I think about her and get aroused, and it's somehow easier to fantasize than to seduce her. Not that she ever says no—I mean, not usually. Well, almost never, really."

"What are these things she always does?"

I tried to question Daisy with my eyes, but she would not look up. I answered vaguely at first, then in detail. I suddenly broke off. I hated Daisy and wanted to kill Kroom.

"I'm not going to answer any more of your questions—it's puerile. I think you're a prick," I said.

"James is not ready for the next stage," Kroom said. "I think it's time for Daisy to occupy the hot seat. If James wants to leave the house now to recenter himself, he may."

"No way," I said.

I sat in one of the sofas, held on to Donald Duck.

"I'm going to undo my shirt," Daisy said. "I'm not wearing a bra."

"I'm a mirror, and the only other person here is the other half of your dyad."

She undid her shirt.

"How often do you masturbate?"

She slipped a hand inside her open shirt to fondle one of her breasts. "Every day."

"If you wish to pull open your shirt, you may," Kroom said. Daisy slumped in her seat, bared her breasts, held one of them, and half closed her eyes.

"Of whom do you fantasize?"

"Oh, it used to be lots of people; you know, maybe someone I saw in a shop or on the bus. Never movie stars, only real people."

"Exclusively men?"

"Yes. Well, there was a very beautiful girl once in one of my classes I used to think about now and then—but usually men."

"Is there a root?"

"A root?"

"Often there's a seed, somewhere way back in our pasts, that seemed to first trigger our libidos."

"Oh yes. Definitely."

"Tell."

"Jay Katzo, a rapist. He never hurt me, but he trapped me in a padded cell in a hospital and took his clothes off and exposed himself to me. Jimmy knows about it."

"Tell more."

"Well, he had this massive erection. The nurses took him away before he could do anything. I was seventeen, a kid. I had nightmares afterward, but not for very long. A month maybe. Then, oh, say, six, nine months afterward, I started to dream about him in a different way."

"Please explain."

"I'd wake up from the dream so hot for him. I really did start to wish I'd gone down on my knees to him, impaled myself on him—you know, sacrificed myself like in some pagan ritual? When I thought of him I'd just burn—there's no other word for it."

"How long did this go on for?"

"Years. Till I met James. At first we used to make love so much I stopped fantasizing."

"But it's started again?"

"Yes."

Kroom coughed. "Do you ever include James in your fantasies?"

"Oh yes, quite often."

"And what has changed recently?"

"Pardon?"

"You said it used to be lots of people."

"Yes, well, we had this weird weekend at a country vicarage a while ago and James introduced me to this criminal who's become a friend and now I just can't get him out of my mind—my fantasies, I mean. Every time I think about sex, he's there."

"Does he resemble Jay Katzo in any way?"

"Yes."

"In what way?"

"Pure male power."

"When you have sex with James, is this other person there?"

"Oh yes, every time."

"It's this other person, this criminal, who is making love to you?"

"In my imagination, definitely."

"When you have sex with James, do you close your eyes more than you used to?"

"Yes, now you mention it."

"And when you close your eyes he's there, this criminal?"

"Yes."

"Is his presence necessary for your orgasm?"

"Seems to be."

"Let's go back to your fantasies. Is there something you can do to get in the mood so that we can share their flavor?"

Daisy undid her jeans, slipped a hand down between her thighs.

"How do your fantasies begin?"

She let her head fall back farther and spoke in clear, slow tones.

"Well, actually there are lots, but the most frequent starts off in a great mansion. I'm the lady of the mansion, and the master, my husband, is very old. We have a very strong, handsome man-servant."

"Who is?"

"He's this criminal, Oliver."

"And what happens?"

"When my husband is away he comes into my bedroom. I allow him to tie me up on the bed—it's a four-poster. He has me like that over and over again, maybe thirty or forty times."

"And after?"

"After that I'm his slave—his creature. He does what he likes with me. He dominates me totally with his erect penis—he uses it to sort of make me swoon. He does some fairly extreme things with me."

"Such as?"

"Stop!" I stood up, walked over to the rheostat, and turned up the light. Daisy took her hand out of her jeans.

"We're going," I said. Daisy started to straighten her clothes.

Kroom stood up, towering over me.

"Get out of my way."

He shot a look at Daisy, then stepped aside. I grabbed one of her hands and pulled her so hard she stumbled.

"No violence," Kroom said.

"Fuck off."

I slapped Daisy across the mouth, hard. She flinched, put a hand to her mouth. I pulled her out the door.

"James!"

"Shut up."

"There's no need to hold my wrist so hard—I'm not going to run away."

I let go her wrist. She followed me down the stairs, out of the house. We avoided each other's eyes while waiting for a cab. Inside the cab, on the back seat, we sat as far from each other as possible. My hands were shaking badly. Her mouth was slightly swollen. She kept licking her lip.

"You really hurt me, you know." She was looking out of the cab window.

"Good. You really hurt me." I looked out of the window on my side as I spoke.

"I'm sorry," she said.

"What?"

"I'm sorry—there. It was just a game for me, and I'm sorry you took it seriously and got upset." She turned to me as she spoke, licked her lip. The possibility that I might have hit her harder, done real damage, was frightening.

She slipped across the seat. "Look, your hands are shaking."

"I could have killed him—and you."

"I know. It was amazing."

"Amazing—another sensation to add to your collection? My feelings are just consumer items to you. You got a buzz out of seeing me care enough to hit you, to do my nut, make a fool of myself. To kill for you if necessary."

"Don't, James. I've said I'm sorry."

"I think your problem is that life doesn't really reach you. You're stuck in some fantasy world, and what you really want is enough pain and suffering to wake you up. Only I'm the one who cops it—so much for liberation."

"I said don't."

She tried to take my hand, but it was too unsteady. I watched her own hand vibrate as she tried to hold mine. I bit my lip.

She sat very still. After a while I felt a trembling next to me. I ignored it.

"I know I shouldn't be laughing," she said, "but it really was quite funny the way you scared the shit out of that big creep."

She cupped her hands over her face. The trembling increased. I tried to resist, but it was infectious.

"So you thought he was a creep, too?"

"Definitely. But I wanted to go through with it—it just seemed so wimpish not to."

"My guts were falling out all over Donald Duck, and you were worried about being a wimp?"

"I did enjoy it a bit—it was quite liberating. You didn't think so?"

I shook my head. The trouble was, in the cold light of day it did seem like a game. Nothing to be quite so upset about.

"I'm sorry I hit you."

"It's all right, you big brute. Is my face swollen?"

"A bit, around the mouth. You liked me hitting you?"

"No. Well, it's quite thrilling in retrospect, but don't ever do it again."

In the room, Daisy studied her face in a mirror. I held her mouth to curl back her upper lip. There was a slight nick where a tooth had cut, a little blood on her teeth.

"I'm sorry." I kissed her eyelids.

"Apart from sorry, how do you feel?"

"Weird. I should be really jealous, but I've known that you were fantasizing for ages. It's a bit of a relief to have it out."

"I've always fantasized a bit. Maybe I'm just one of life's masturbators, Jimmy."

"But does it have to be him?"

"I can't help it. Anyway, it's not really him, it's a fantasy of him. If you hadn't totally blown your top, Kroom would have told you that some people just need something exotic and mysterious for their libidos to work. We all need to escape from the humdrum, from mental control. Even you."

"That's exactly why I didn't want to see Kroom—I didn't want to lose the mystery by sharing it with a stranger. Anyway, *you're* my escape from the humdrum, you're the exotic, the wonderful. You certainly elude all control. I don't need any fantasies."

She smiled.

"Take this situation right now," I said. "I've hit you, I've dragged you across a room, in theory I've humiliated you, but you've been the more powerful one, really—because I worship you."

She shook her head. "Don't overstate your case, Mr. Knight— I saw a definite twinkle of mastery in you today. And I think you actually feel good."

"Perhaps I do."

"Masterful?"

"Well, he was so big, it did feel good knowing that I could beat him. I really could have killed him."

I drew the curtains, turned off the light, put a chair in the middle of the room.

"Okay, then, now let's have the rest—but I want to star in all of them."

I was familiar with most of her fantasies from her conversations with her mother and from our "talking dirty" sessions, but I'd no idea how baroque the details had become.

2 5

Daisy and I finally accumulated enough combined income to rent a real apartment instead of a bed-sit. We chose one not far from where we were living and looked forward to the day when we would move in, having stayed at the bed-sit during the two weeks' notice period. Thirst was proud to be asked to help us move.

He arrived promptly at eight-thirty on the appointed morning, with a van of uncertain provenance and his mate Chaz. Chaz came equipped with a deafening cassette player, but the air was full of the champagne of early June. It was the kind of morning we English identify with salvation and quaff greedily like desert plants in the rain. Thirst wore a T-shirt cut away to reveal his collection of tattoos.

Moving was a great opportunity for brawn and sweat, a chance for Thirst to show how effete we were, Daisy and I. He gave orders. He would not permit Daisy or me to lift anything capable of making his tattoos ripple if he lifted it himself.

His mate Chaz, a skinny tube-like form in identical blue jeans and cut-away T-shirt but with no tattoos and almost no biceps, had eyes that listened to rock music wherever they looked. He never spoke to Daisy or me but asked Oliver questions when he needed instructions, in a cockney dialect that Daisy found unintelligible.

We must have made about ten visits to the new apartment to resolve arguments about dimensions, color coordination. The four-story house was old, but the conversion into separate flats was brand-new. The landlady, who liked the idea of renting to a barrister, had let us have the entire second floor.

"Our first unfurnished place."

"Everything in it will be an expression of us," Daisy said. "Of our relationship."

"Or bank balance. There's a lot to buy—everything, in fact. Carpets, gas stove, telephone, soft furnishings."

"Can we afford a sofa? I love sofas."

"Who's going to have the fitted wardrobe?"

"You can."

"No—you."

When we arrived that day, a roll of hard-wearing wall-to-wall carpet had already been delivered. We'd saved ten percent by not paying for the fitting. Thirst brought Chaz up the stairs carrying his cassette player and a knife with a retractable blade.

Chaz set the player up on the windowsill nearest him and pulled the roll of carpet over onto the floor to lay it out.

"Owserrun?" he said.

"Which way you want it laid?" Thirst said.

"How do you mean?"

Thirst twitched. "How do you mean, Chaz?"

Chaz frowned, grappling with an intractable problem.

"Swayordat?" he finally said, making signs with his hands too fast to follow, before retreating to the windowsill and the cassette player.

"The join," Thirst said. "Lengthways or across?"

"Lengthwise," I said.

"Across," said Daisy.

Thirst started to pace.

"Across," I said.

"Lengthways," Daisy said.

"Let's leave it up to Chaz."

Chaz grunted, returned to the center of the room, and stood on the carpet. He maneuvered the carpet into position until it curled up the walls at the corners of the room, took out his knife, and without taking measurements began cutting the carpet that had taken up a large chunk of my overdraft. Daisy and I exchanged glances, but within minutes Chaz was dealing with another corner. The area where he'd been working fit perfectly, neatly negotiating two central heating pipes and some electrical cables.

"Very handy," Thirst said. "Best leave him to it. How long you going to be, Chaz?"

"'Our."

We stepped out of the house into the morning, leaving Chaz and electronic wails of Jimmy Hendrix behind us.

"Chaz seems very professional," Daisy said.

"Learnt it in the Scrubs," Thirst said. "He did crafts, I did O levels."

"How are the studies going?" I said.

"Oliver's very into Shakespeare," Daisy said.

"Are you?" I said, surprised.

"*Macbeff*'s okay. The sonnets are just groveling, though. Was he a bit of a cocksucker, Shakes?"

"You mean was he gay? Probably," Daisy said.

A question I had wanted to ask for some time came to mind. "Why are you doing English?"

"Because you told me I couldn't talk," he said.

I scratched my head. "I certainly got that wrong."

Thirst looked at me. I looked at Daisy. She was looking at him. A cruel grin spread across his face, and he slapped his thigh. "What about Chaz, then? Talk about can't talk! Inside, they used to say the only reason he went down was because he didn't know how to say 'not guilty.'"

"Exactly," Daisy said. She was clearly in the mood to talk literature, but Thirst went off on another tack.

"See all this," he said, spreading his hands to take in the sunlit street. "It was all under ice once."

"When you were a kid?" Daisy asked.

"No. Pleistocene period. Ten thousand years ago. Did you know the last ice age only finished in 1750, by which time there were more glaciers on earth than at any time since Pleistocene?"

Daisy and I exchanged a glance. We resumed walking until we reached the café just around the corner from our new house.

The café was one of those affairs to be found all over London that manage to combine the worst features of similar cafés in other countries. The coffee and food were expensive but of poor quality, the decor modern but third-rate, the service abrupt without being punctual, and the owner inclined to short-change his customers.

"You come to these sorts of places, I mean, a lot?" Thirst was looking incredulously at the price list.

"Almost never," I said. "I don't like them."

"Why not?"

I'd grown used to these questions, along with his remarkable gift for absorbing data and adjusting his course accordingly.

"The decor is high schlock, the waiter's a rude bastard, the food comes out of a can—and sometimes they don't even heat it properly—and the coffee's instant and the owner's a crook."

He studied the café with new eyes. "What was that word you just used?"

"Schlock. It's American. I got it from Daisy."

"What's it mean, then, Daize?"

"It's Jewish New York—maybe Yiddish. It means, oh, semi-expensive junk. You know, something someone who's got money but no taste would buy."

He narrowed his eyes. "Someone up from the gutter like me, you mean?"

Daisy fumbled. "No, don't take it that way. I didn't ..."

He grinned at me. "These Yanks—they miss the joke sometimes. It's all right, Daisy. I was only taking the piss."

Daisy looked from one to the other of us, puffed out her cheeks. "You guys! I don't know. Don't you ever stop mocking people?"

"Us guys? You mean the English?" Thirst said. "Nah, don't believe we do. We're always taking the piss. Best way. You miss the States, then, Daize?"

"Sometimes."

"What's it like, really? Skyscrapers and cowboys, gunfights, that sort of thing?"

"It's real. People do what they have to do. It isn't all a chick-enshit game. You know the most used English word? 'Sorry.' Jesus Christ, sometimes I wonder if the men here have any balls at all. All this politeness is just a cover-up for no guts. Sorry, sorry, sorry—it's all you hear."

Thirst winked at me. "Not polite in America, then, Daize?"

"Are you kidding? It's 'ouda fuckin' way schmuck 'fo' I break yo' face.'" She looked at us. "Okay, it's aggressive, uncouth, possibly even homicidal. But it cuts the crap. You have this word 'wanker': it means compulsive masturbator, right? You people use it all the time. This is a nation of wankers. Maybe mockery is the only thing you have left."

There was fire in her eyes. I noted a flicker of interest in his, before he turned to me and winked again. "Owner's a crook, you say? What's the betting we don't have to pay a penny? Tell you what, order anything you like. It's all on me."

"Oliver," I said.

He raised a hand. "I promise you won't be compromised. Daisy, what about a bolognese?"

She looked at me, shrugged. She ordered lasagne, I ordered a cappuccino, Thirst ordered steak and chips. He ate three quarters of his meal before calling the waiter.

"I wonder if you wouldn't mind letting me have a word with the proprietor," Thirst said in a soft, deferential tone.

"Something wrong?" The waiter was medium height, stocky, with a grim mouth.

"I'd prefer to speak to the proprietor," Thirst said.

"He's not here."

Thirst stared into the man's eyes, raised his eyebrows, smiled. "I think he is. And I think he'll be very cross with you if I do what I'm professionally required to do without giving him a chance to make good."

The waiter seemed less mystified than I was. He nodded, disappeared into the kitchen area. A few minutes later a tall, heavyset man in his mid-forties appeared. Small eyes looked out from a hard face.

"Well, you wanted to see me?"

"Sorry to spoil your day, sir," Thirst said, "but do the names *Rattus norvegicus* or *Rattus rattus* mean anything to you?"

The man reddened. "There are no rats here. This is a clean restaurant. I don't know who you are, but—"

Thirst raised a placating hand. "I can see the names *do* mean something to you. You have my sympathy; you've been infested before. I understand how you feel, and let me tell you it gives me no pleasure to point it out to you, but look."

He pointed to the skirting board that led into the kitchen. "You see that mark about three quarters of an inch thick running parallel to the horizontal?"

The owner peered, turned a shade of purple. "What are you insinuating?"

"Oh, *Rattus rattus* and *Rattus norvegicus* are cunning, no doubt about it, hard to detect, but their natural caution, you see, makes them brush by the sides of walls, leaving their telltale scum."

The owner stared again, then gave a hollow laugh. "Nice try, sunshine, but it won't work. That mark is caused by the rubber lining along the bottom of the door. Look."

He went to the kitchen door, which had a kind of rubberized flap at the bottom, opened it until it hit the wall. A ridge at the top of the flap matched the mark on the wall.

Thirst smiled indulgently. He stood up, startling the owner. "I wasn't talking about that mark, and please don't call me 'sunshine'—I always prefer to keep these things civilized. I was talking about *that* mark."

It was true that under the mark made by the door was another faint smudge.

"Could be anything."

"I don't think so. Not if you see how it is replicated elsewhere in your establishment." He pointed to similar smudges along the skirting around the café. Daisy swallowed.

The owner was finding it hard to speak. "Who the hell are you? Those are scuff marks from shoes."

Thirst shook his head. "I don't think so, sir. Let's look a little closer, shall we?" He knelt down by the skirting near the kitchen, scratched with a fingernail at the join with the floor.

"Are you a health inspector?" the man demanded.

"Now, I think it very much in your interests if you don't ask that question, don't you? I mean, we don't want this to turn into an *official* inspection, do we?"

"Scuff marks," the owner said again, in a small voice.

"I wish they were, sir," Thirst said, "but how do you explain this?"

He stood up, opened his hand. Half a dozen coarse white hairs lay across the palm.

"*Rattus norvegicus,* or I'm a Dutchman. Of the albino variety. If you catch enough, you could sell them to laboratories. Set a few nonlethal traps in the kitchen, might make a few quid before they close you down. Of course, if you don't believe me, we could call the local environmental health officer to take these samples away and have them analyzed?"

The owner wiped his face with a handkerchief. "You're bent, I know you are. What d'you want?"

"It so happens that my brother-in-law runs a small but efficient extermination service. . . ."

Relief spread through the owner's facial muscles.

"Just give me his number. If he's competitive—"

"Oh, look, if you can find someone cheaper, use them with my blessing. My only interest is that you exterminate the vermin." Thirst wrote a number on a paper napkin, paused, looked at the remains of his meal. "I must say I'm a bit put off the food, though."

The owner waved a hand. "Forget it. Just get out of here."

"Rat hairs," Thirst said to Daisy when we were outside. "Never leave home without them."

"You've got steel balls," Daisy said, shaking her head.

He stopped in the street under a tree, avoided my eyes as he spoke. "No, see, that's the mistake people make. Thieving, yes, it's mostly just a question of balls, but a good con needs some of this." He tapped his head. "It might have looked very simple just now, but it had a classic structure. The best way to work a con is to get the mark to think he's conning you. He was in a hurry to get us out of his café because he had no intention of phoning that number I gave him. He thought not charging us for the food was a small sacrifice." He searched Daisy's eyes as if inspecting the progress of a slow student. "Got it?"

"Got it," Daisy said.

26

The next morning was even sunnier. Thirst returned with the van, Chaz, and a refrigerator which Daisy had bought from the two of them, strictly without my consent. I insisted she use her own money and refused to have anything to do with the transaction.

I watched nervously in the street while Thirst lifted the fridge out of the back of the van. He managed to do this single-handedly, and in a display of heroics staggered across the pavement to the steps of the house. He set it down, wiped the sweat from his brow with the back of his hand, and grinned. "Used to be able to pick up the back end of a Mini."

"Did you do weight training?"

"No. Don't believe in it; got all my exercise running away from the Old Bill." He grinned again. "Here, do you bet me I couldn't carry this fridge as far as that lamppost?"

He saw I was anxious about the origin of the fridge.

"No. I'm not betting. Please get it in the house. I'll help you."

He grinned. "I'll do it anyway. Need the exercise."

Spitting on both hands, he crouched down to pick up the refrigerator. It was barely within even his strength, and for a moment I thought he would drop it. He staggered out of the gate. When he reached the lamppost he set it down, gave a great yell, and laughed.

"Thought I'd ruptured myself. Well, I bet you I could take it to the lamppost—I never said I could carry it back again."

"I'll help you."

"Why don't *you* carry it back?" His eyes glittered. I was the same height as him but much slimmer and probably about half as strong. Perhaps if it had not been June and Daisy was not upstairs helping Chaz with some furniture, I would have been more sensible.

"How much do you bet me?"

"Fifty quid." He folded his tattooed arms, leaned against a wall, and whistled. Quite suddenly he seemed to have lost all humor and become ruthless. It was obvious that he was not going to lay a hand on the fridge, which sat surreally under the lamppost. To my mind it gleamed like an exhibit in a burglary trial.

I crouched down to put my hands—they were the soft hands of a paper-pusher—under the refrigerator. I found that by exerting all my strength I could lift it but that it had a tendency to topple forward because I could not control its bulk. My hands were already cut. Thirst roused himself.

"Fuck off," I said.

He looked surprised. I tried again, this time stretching my arms as far as they would go and arching my back dangerously. I could feel the pressure in my lumbar region, the protest of muscles long unused. Slowly the refrigerator came up. I staggered to keep balance. Somehow I managed to set it down at the steps of the house.

As soon as I released it I felt a stabbing pain in my back. Daisy's feet had appeared at the top of the steps.

"Jimmy, what happened?"

"Working-class machismo," I said. "We were playing dares. You owe me fifty pounds," I said. My hands were bleeding.

"Right," Thirst said. Daisy took in the situation. The steps gave her a natural platform. "You've probably slipped a disk, you dickhead. Don't men ever grow up? You're like a couple of troglodytes. All I did was turn my back. Why don't you take your bows and arrows and go hunting saber-toothed tigers? Just don't ask me to nurse you if you've slipped a disk."

She turned on her heel and went back inside the house.

"What's a troglodyte?" he said. "I haven't got to *T* yet. What was she on about? I know she's your missus, James, but sometimes I think she does too much dope—know what I mean? What was all that about bows and arrows and saber-toothed tigers? If it was me, I'd slap her around the chops."

"I think at the moment in a straight fight she'd beat the shit out of me." I was holding the small of my back with the palms of both hands.

"Best to lie down flat." He took my arm, and putting it around his neck, he lifted me gently and laid me on the little patch of garden in front of the house. I could not help admiring his immense physical strength and the superior vitality that seemed to consume him. By any criteria he had won what Daisy would call our ego battle, but when, briefly, he caught my eye, I was reminded of that fleeting moment on Waterloo Bridge: something limpid behind the pupil; a sorrow, maybe, or even when all was said and done a fatal compassion, together with the perception that escape was impossible. Then he left me to go into the house.

I lay on my back and found that the new green leaves of a plane tree cut out irregular patches of blue. Or was it the blue that cut out the shape of the leaves? The knowledge that Daisy was in the flat with Thirst and that I was lying temporarily crippled, as if a prophecy or fear fantasy had come true, put me in a strange state of mind. I found that I could alter my mood by focusing either on some primitive suspicion or on that fleeting look in Thirst's eyes. It was ridiculous that I had never until then considered the possibility that his experience of life was identical to my own. I suspect that my mind began to close in the dead center of that morning while Chaz's cassette player pumped out Eric Clapton. I woke up a few minutes later to find Daisy's face over mine.

"Sorry, Jimmy, for being such a bitch. Are you really hurt?"

"It seems much better now that I've lain down flat. Help me up?"

*   *   *

Chaz and Thirst drove off as soon as we had emptied their van. A couple of hours later, another van arrived to deliver a pine table and chairs. That was as much moving as I could take for the weekend.

I lay on my aching back on the new carpet while Daisy wandered light-headedly from one room to another.

"I can't believe all this space just for us!"

Propped up against the wall and using pillows for cushions, we drank wine.

"Isn't it great?" Daisy said.

"I just hope we can keep up with the rent."

"But you're working so hard now—all those briefs coming in."

"There's a credit squeeze, so solicitors take even longer to pay than ever. Do you know I was only paid last week for Thirst's appeal?"

"Have some more wine, cheer up; we'll manage. I'll do some evening classes if you like."

I drank. "Do you know what? I've just started looking at myself in a new way. Daisy, darling, I have to admit, I think you've been right all along."

"How's that, dear boy?"

"All my struggling, all that fighting for money and status—my endless searching for a state of arrival, of having arrived. It really is a stupid male game. Arriving is now, living is now."

"Of course it is. The mystic now. There's nothing else."

"Man is a time-fragmented animal."

"Quite."

"Where has it got me? I'll be thirty before too long, and all I've got is a rented flat with furniture I can barely afford. And if I do even better over the next few years, what will it mean—a little house somewhere in the suburbs with a massive mortgage repayment to meet every month."

"Exactly."

"Do you know what? I've made a resolution—no more commitments. No more waiting to arrive."

Daisy clapped her hands, switched to one of her New York accents. "Far out, dah kid's a bum after all."

Happily tipsy from the wine, she turned me over on my front to massage my lumbar region. Her small hands caressed me with special care, then she turned me over and kissed me and slowly undid my jeans. When I reached for her she pushed my hands away. She continued to kiss my face and neck, then took her top off to hold her nipples up for me to kiss. I reached up and held her breasts in my hands.

Suddenly she was vulnerable, bruised. "Jimmy, now that we've got all this space, do you want me to go off the pill?"

What happened next was entirely wordless. I disengaged her eyes and looked away for less than a second, as I had been doing now for many months whenever she posed this question in its various forms. When I looked back, her face was ravaged with disappointment.

"I thought space was the problem," she said, fighting tears.

"You know it's not just that. Ever since I left university I've been working my balls off. The only way I can handle it is by believing that one day I'll be financially free. I just can't stand the burden of a kid right now. It's for life, right? I don't want to spend the next twenty years feeling as though I'm buried alive. And how much time would I get to spend with a kid anyway? I'm really sorry."

Her face was horribly twisted, and she found it hard to speak. "I want a baby, James. Badly."

"Why?"

She wiped her eyes with the back of her hand, got up and spoke with her back to me. "Think about what you just said. You labor for years and find in the end you've given birth to a bank account. I want to have produced something living. For life."

27

Daisy continued to help Thirst with his A levels. He was able to obtain an educational maintenance grant from his local authority that enabled him to work incessantly throughout the spring of that year. He only raised his head from his studies to ask increasingly pertinent and academic questions.

He had not, in the end, gone to the college where Daisy had taught, as I had suggested that day on Waterloo Bridge. He found one more to his liking near the Elephant and Castle; but he consulted her on such topics as the function of puns in Shakespearean dialogue, the use of pathos in the nineteenth-century novel, and the impact of the 1914 Education Act on modern English Literature. This last stemmed from his study of sociology, in which subject he was developing a passionate interest.

We met up with him from time to time, ostensibly to keep in touch but in reality because we were the only friends upon whom he could practice his new vocabulary. This was full of words like "agency" (the police was an agency used primarily for the protection of vested interests under the pretext of maintaining law and order) and "presents as" (Chaz, his favorite guinea pig, "presented as" a moron chiefly because of a deficiency in communication skills, which agencies responsible for his education had neglected to assist him to develop).

In the right mood his natural bravado enabled him to say such things without a blush. I was with him once when he said in his thick cockney, without stammer or pause, that "incarcerated persons experience a controlled violence applied chiefly through the medium of time which is equal and opposite to the violence that society inspired in that person before he was incarcerated."

It was one of his best. We slapped hands.

"Hot shit!" he said.

I knew, though, that his new persona was perforated with doubt. In front of Daisy he would always cover his fumbles with an ironic grin, but sometimes when he was alone with me he allowed his confusion to show.

I had the eerie sensation that we were presiding over a Frankensteinian experiment that had gone badly out of control. It was not a sensation that Daisy shared.

As he grew thinner and more serious, as his eyes blazed painfully in a combination of intellectual strain and dissolving identity, as the evolving power of disciplined thought was applied, inevitably, to his past life so that he now saw the seductive poetry of his crimes as no more than the reflexes of a monkey in a Skinner box—in short, as the great delusion of a secondary education (that there's an expert somewhere who knows) made him ever more self-conscious—Daisy began to find him compelling.

I realized that I had been quite mistaken in my earlier crises of jealousy. So long as he was no more than a muscular and aspiring young man, he had been merely an instrument to tease me with— or an object of fantasy. It was the disintegration of his soul that she now found so attractive.

At the same time I was so intimately connected to her, so dependent upon her for my emotional life, that I experienced her lust for him as if it were my own. I could have been the one with the yearning thighs, the wetness between my legs. I understood him better than she ever would and wanted to warn her.

Yet Thirst showed no interest. Even when her eyes turned limpid in the chaotic blaze of his presence and I, many times, almost got up to leave, he still showed an indifference to those charms that most other men found irresistible. It was as if an unexpected purity of vision enabled him to see her in a way denied to others—as a woman corrupt and unwholesome. She was, after all, some years older than he, and he despised drugs.

The occasions when Daisy and Thirst were alone together were few. Even when Thirst came over with his books, which he did from time to time, he and she would work together for an hour or so, usually with all of us in the same room, and then he would leave, often with a suggestion that he and I meet up for a drink together when I had the time.

The only exception to this general rule that I can remember occurred one weekday afternoon when Daisy and I were sitting alone together. The trial in which I was involved had been adjourned early so that counsel could prepare speeches. I was working on the summing-up to the jury that I had to make the following morning; Daisy was experimenting with her latest fad, a new set of watercolors. The phone rang. Daisy answered.

"That was Oliver. He's at Swiss Cottage library. Seems to have convinced himself that he's going to fail his entire English A level because he can't understand a poem by John Donne." She touched my cheek. "Do you mind? He sounds in a bit of a state. You know how fanatical he's getting—he has a sort of identity crisis if there's something he doesn't understand."

I reminded myself that I was a civilized, enlightened middle-class man, and in any event it was doubtful that any infidelity would occur with Thirst feeling the way he did about Daisy.

"No, of course—Daisy Smith's intellectual ambulance to the rescue."

She smiled and kissed me. "I won't be long."

About two hours later she returned. Her face was white and drawn, her hands were shaking.

At first she avoided my gaze.

"What happened?"

She walked over to me. "Hold me—just hold me for a moment."

"What happened? Did he hurt you? Did he make a pass at you?"

"No, no—nothing like that."

"Did you make a pass at him?"

"Nobody made a pass at anyone. Stop being so jealous and just hold me."

I held her while the energy seeped out of her.

"I'm exhausted—I'm going to bed."

She got into bed with most of her clothes on. I tried to return to my work, which was urgent. My client had contradicted himself about five times under cross-examination, but they were minor points. Did I tell the jury frankly that he was a bit of a liar but that didn't make him necessarily guilty, or did I try to paper over the cracks? By a prodigious effort I was able to concentrate for another couple of hours.

I went back to Daisy in the bedroom, sat on the bed. She was not asleep.

"Daisy, don't you think you should tell me? If nobody made a pass and nobody hurt anybody, what's it all about?"

"I don't want to talk about it. It's too embarrassing."

After the trial the next day (my client was convicted of burglary and given two years), I was half relieved to find a telephone message from Thirst. I phoned the number my clerk had taken. Thirst wanted to meet for a chat "about your missus." I was still nervous being seen with him anywhere near the Temple, so we arranged to meet in a café in Piccadilly.

It was about five in the afternoon; already a punk was lying propped against a wall near the underground ticket office. It was more than an ordinary case of narcotic poisoning; he looked dead. Police and ambulance men came as I took the escalator. I bought an evening paper while waiting in the café.

Thirst wore a sheepskin flying jacket, clean jeans, new running shoes. He obviously had a modest source of income; it didn't do to ask. I was in my new beige Burberry. I noted a posture of grim responsibility, which increased as he developed his account of the previous afternoon.

When I returned to the flat, Daisy said, "He told you, didn't he?"

"Yes. So can we talk about it now?"

"Oh God, I've been thinking about it all day. Why am I so pathetic? All I wanted to do was make him a present. And it was a good book, too, the best criticism of John Donne to emerge for a decade. Only I didn't have the cash on me. I don't do it much anymore—hardly at all since that time in college—but when I do I'm bloody good. I swear nobody in that shop could have seen me. Especially not the store detective. I can spot them a mile off. Oliver was waiting outside the shop—it was uncanny how he knew, as if he could smell it. I've never had such a dressing-down in my life. He wasn't going to do time for some little tart still wet behind the ears, a rank amateur, et cetera—and he made me throw the book away. All day I've been shuddering with embarrassment at least once every half hour. He was scary, though. Man, that was a real blue-collar talking-to he gave me! I see what you mean about potentially homicidal. . . . Could you please not look at me like that?"

I left her to go into my study. I was looking at a book, trying to concentrate, when she came in. It was unusual for her not to make physical contact. She sat in a spare chair, a yard or so away from me.

"I suppose Oliver was pretty disdainful. What did he say about me?"

A reservoir of resentment made it easy to tell the truth.

"He said quite a lot of things, actually, but the basic message is that he thinks you're ridiculously immature. The way he puts it is that you hide behind your good looks—a plainer girl would never get away with what you get away with. Eleanor's right about his being perceptive—he asked if you have any close women friends. I had to tell him that you haven't."

"Meaning?"

"That only men will tolerate you. Your narcissism."

"English women hate me, James," she said quietly. "We both know that. It's not news."

2 8

And so for one reason or another it was I who received the bulk of Thirst's attention, or whatever remained after his fanatical studying. He would emerge from the libraries where he worked with the look of someone suffering from shell shock. I suppose I did not wait for him more than twice outside a public library, yet so vivid is the image of him pushing, exhausted, through the dull brown doors—blinking distractedly in the alien light, a look of anger on his face, his clothes going slack on him, a certain yellowness around the gills—that this picture has remained in my memory ever since.

"'Lo, James."

"Oliver. What was it today—*Macbeth,* or Jones and Metford on teenage criminality?"

"Fucking Jones and Metford. Pricks. I tell you, they haven't got a clue. How many motors did *they* pinch at fifteen?"

I had expected him, by then, to have adopted some pliant sociologist as a mentor, one of London's many tired-faced young men with well-practiced explanations of what's wrong with society and only too eager to drink beer in pubs with reformed criminals. Instead he chose whenever we met to let me know his latest thoughts in a half-mad gush and then ransack my face with suspicious, earnest eyes.

"Well, am I right? I must be! Christ, James, we're living in a sewer, everyone shitting on everyone else and nobody admitting it. Nobody." He checked my face. "I wouldn't tell anyone else this, but I don't always find it easy to walk into those seminars. The lectures are all right, but the seminars—four or five seventeen-year-old kids sitting about when *I* walk in, big hairy ex-con. I scare the fuck out of them, especially the teacher. Same age as me. To tell the truth, I have to force myself all the way."

On several occasions he took me back to his little room in Camden Town. As he crossed the threshold his mood would change. Not sure how hosts were supposed to behave, he would become awkward, and at the same time he would be nonchalant, because it was, after all, his home. The bed-sit was of the kind that had suffered from a certain amount of pride the landlord had taken in it. A large and lurid picture of a brown girl on a tropical island (Thirst called it "The Tart") hung over the bed. Frilly curtains were bunched like petticoats at either side of the windows. When you used the communal lavatory, a printed sign ordered you to clean up afterward and not to run a bath after eleven o'clock at night. It was a relief to see Lord Denning pacing restlessly in his cage in the corner of the bed-sit. Above him two shelves held a battered set of the *Encyclopaedia Britannica*. Next to the last volume was the latest edition of *The Guinness Book of Records* and a copy of *The Concise Oxford Dictionary*.

Thirst was eager to discuss his own process of rehabilitation.

"Most people know nothing about changing themselves."

"Most people never really change," I said. "Their programming is fixed early on; they just respond when the buttons are pressed."

"You know what it's really like?"

"What?"

"Being in the nick, except the nick is in your own head, and you're the screw as well as the con. One day I'll write a book explaining that rehabilitation is just an internalization of the prison system."

"Good word, internalization."

"Stinks, though—life. You never get free. Never."

He did not keep alcohol on the premises, or any other medium of hospitality, and so we would often buy a pack of canned beer to drink with crisps while we talked. When drunk, he sometimes claimed to have killed a man, but it was impossible to tell if the alcohol had unleashed a true confession or merely inspired an extravagant development in his personal mythology. The story, though, was always the same: "I knew he had a shiv, see, left me no choice. Quick one in the balls, then straight fingers to the throat—all the way, as if you're sticking them in mud."

In a confidential mood, I would sometimes talk about my mother, her courage, how much I owed her. The importance of mothers. He would listen quietly with a queer look on his face, almost as if he disbelieved me. Once he said, "I wouldn't know, James; I was a Saturday-night bunk-up."

He was not always morose. When his studies were going well, he would show off his line in unnerving insights.

"You know what I was thinking the other day? I was thinking about you and Daisy. Know what she is to you?"

"Tell me."

"She's your trophy. She's what you use to prove to yourself that it's all worth it. I've been watching you. You don't care that much about money and status, not like she thinks you do. She gets you confused with her old man. You worship her, I mean in the book sense—she's your icon. Wouldn't be surprised if you didn't really know anything about her as a person; probably you don't care. You took everything that makes life worth living for you and put it into a myth so you can carry on. A myth called Smith."

He grinned, proud of the rhyme.

"Thanks for telling me that, Oliver."

"No, but I'm right, aren't I? See, there's a difference between you and me. I've gone further than you. I haven't got any myths; I can't use crutches. I have to go on pushing shit uphill every day without kidding myself that there's a payoff. You couldn't do what

I do. You couldn't shovel the shit if Daisy wasn't there—the myth of Daisy, I mean." He sipped some beer. "Tell you what, though— if I was to choose an icon, I'd choose a Yank, too."

"You would? I didn't know you admired the States."

"Didn't know anything about it till I started on this sociology course. There was a bit about the psychology of Europeans who emigrated—what's that island they had to pass through?"

"Ellis Island?"

"Yeah. This book goes on about the psychological revolution, the optimism, the smiles on people's faces, knowing they'd escaped . . ." He waved a hand to include The Tart, the frilly curtains, London. "All this. Course, I'd have to be a different person. There's no way I'm going to shack up with a woman, not even a Yank."

"Never been in love, Oliver?"

"Me? Leave off. All my life I've been in the nick or on the run. Tarts I know wouldn't want any of that love crap. It's always been a quick one up against the wall after the pub so she can have a good wash before she goes home to her old man. That's the way they want it, nice and sordid. Turns them on. I'm a wild man to them, a hot cock and a bit of S and M—guaranteed not to leave bruises for the other bloke to see. I don't reckon Daisy's that different, really; you just don't see it. I don't reckon you know much about women, James, frankly."

"You do?"

"Yeah, as a matter of fact."

"From all those quick ones up against the wall?"

"What're you getting so pissed off for? What did I say?"

"I'm not getting pissed off. I just don't think you know so much about women."

"'Cause I'm an ex-con? You think I'm queer?"

"No, Oliver, I don't think you're queer. No more than the next man, anyway."

He sniffed. "Animals, women. In pretty packets. Just tarted-up bundles of animal cravings. Easily manipulated."

"Bullshit. Women are the only thing that saves us from self-annihilation."

His laugh was a sneer. "You got it bad, old son. An' after what she did the other day in that bookshop. Could've been very embarrassing for you as well as me."

"I know."

"Better get her under control, mate, before she does some real damage."

"How do you suggest I do that?"

"Teach her a lesson."

"You mean slap her about? Tie her to the bed and gang-rape her?"

He feigned shock. "That's very uncivilized, James. And very unsubtle, especially from a man of your standing." He smiled. "I did have an idea the other night, though."

I had to admit it was ingenious, if a little cruel.

Later that week Daisy and I met him in the garden of a pub in Belsize Park. An unexpected improvement in the weather had brought out crowds of people, mostly in their twenties and early thirties. Daisy wore a V-neck cashmere sweater with no bra and a short skirt.

On returning from a visit to the lavatory, Thirst beckoned us to lean forward while he whispered.

"Look what I found just outside the gents."

He showed us a set of car keys with the letters VW on the ring tag.

"Oliver!" Daisy said.

"Don't worry, I'm not going to do anything. Tempting, though."

"But it could be any number of Volkswagens."

We all looked through the iron fence of the pub garden at the street on the other side. As far as I could see, there was only one Volkswagen, an old "Beetle" in poor condition.

"What's the betting it's that one?" Thirst said.

"Bet it's not," I said.

"Why not?" Daisy said.

"The keys are from a microbus, not a Beetle."

"You're wrong," Thirst said. "It's the Beetle."

"Bet?"

"Fiver."

"So how are we going to find out?"

Thirst and I looked at Daisy.

"Well, I can't risk it, with my record," Thirst said.

"Me neither, for opposite reasons," I said.

Daisy looked at me. "Are you suggesting . . . ?"

"Not at all."

"Can't do any harm, though, just to try the keys in the lock," Thirst said.

"After that heavy-duty lecture you gave me last week?" Daisy said.

Thirst shrugged. "Maybe I was a bit hard on you. You do seem a bit of a pro when it comes to nicking things."

Daisy looked at me again.

"If you try the keys in the lock with no intention of taking the car, no offense will have been committed."

Daisy smirked. Without another word she stood up. We watched while she walked out of the gate and leaned back against the car with her hands behind her. She returned grinning.

"Oliver won. It *is* that car."

I took five pounds out of my pocket, gave the note to Oliver. We drank our beer in silence.

"That was pretty professional, Daize, the way you checked out that car," Thirst said.

"Thank you, Oliver."

"What did you think, James?"

"Too professional."

"No, you can't be too professional. You know what, there aren't many people I would trust on a TDA these days, but with Daize here, I might be tempted."

"What's TDA?" Daisy said.

"Taking and driving away," I said. "It's an offense. Punishable on conviction with a fine or imprisonment."

Thirst leaned forward. "See how they allocate resources, Daize? Costs them millions to stop a little harmless TDA, meanwhile in the City, upper-class con merchants are bleeding the country white. It's not justice, it's repression of one class by another. That's why I'd be tempted."

"The owner would see you," I said.

Thirst looked around. "Doubt it. Everyone's too busy drinking and ear bashing."

He had a point. The rare warmth of the evening combined with large quantities of alcohol had made even Londoners loquacious.

"It's an offense," I repeated.

"But Oliver's right," Daisy said. "Think of the money they spend policing the working class, while the rich get away with murder."

"I forbid you to steal that car," I said.

Her face flushed. "What did you say?"

"I said that I forbid it. You'd be risking my career."

"Forbid? You forbid? Take back that word or I *will* steal the fucking car."

"I repeat, I forbid you."

Daisy turned her enraged face to Thirst, who was grinning.

"Don't worry, James, she ain't gonna steal it. Takes nerve to pinch a car, not like a little shoplifting." Daisy stared at him. "But if you were serious, I wouldn't mind a bit of a joyride myself."

Daisy turned to me. "I'm giving you one last chance. Take back what you said."

"I forbid it," I said, frowning. "It's time you started to understand, Daisy, that there are times when it's right for a man to say to a woman, 'No, these are the rules; you are forbidden to step over the line.' "

Daisy stood up. "Are you coming, Oliver?"

Thirst laughed. "Wait, wait, sit down a minute. Look, I'll come, but I don't want to be seen leaving the pub with you. Too many people know me. I'll meet you up the road. Take the car and give me ten minutes. I'll see you on Willoughby Road and we'll have a little fling."

When Daisy stood up, Thirst beckoned her to lean over him while he whispered. "When you approach the car have the key in your right hand so you don't have to fumble. It's an old car, so treat it with a bit of contempt—swing the door open a bit rough, act like you've had it for years. And make sure you don't spin the tires when you move off. Only amateurs do that, from bad nerves."

Daisy nodded, stared at me contemptuously for a moment, then left the pub. She tried to obey Thirst's instructions, but she was white with fear when she opened the car door. After we had watched her drive away, Thirst telephoned the police.

By the time we reached Willoughby Road, two police cars had already arrived. Daisy was shaking badly. She looked frail and naked in that skimpy skirt and thin sweater. I could see she'd been crying and was on the verge of hysteria. I waited in the shadows while Thirst went up to the police to explain that there had been a mistake. He'd bought the car a week before. He happened to have the registration documents in his pocket to prove it. Daisy was his friend, and she had his full authority to drive it. He didn't know who had called the police.

"Why didn't you say that?" one of the policemen snapped at her, after examining the papers.

"You probably never gave her a chance. You blokes scare the shit out of little girls like her," Thirst said. "Intimidation, it's called. You all right, luv?" he asked Daisy.

She nodded, apparently unable to speak.

It was days before she would talk to me again.

"I suppose you got a big kick out of making an asshole out of me?"

"Can't you take a joke?"

"Can't you see what he's doing?"

"He just wanted to teach you a lesson."

"If you believe that, you really have got your head in the clouds. Can't you see he's driving a wedge between us?"

"Because he wants you?" I sneered.

"I didn't say it was me he wanted."

29

When Thirst finally finished his A level exams, he threw a party to celebrate.

Hogg was there, and so were Eleanor (minus her husband) and other people from the parole board, a social worker who knew Thirst well, a policeman whom I had once cross-examined, some students from the college where Thirst had been studying, and a lot of people I'd never met.

He had persuaded the college to allow him to use one of its halls for the night, a smallish affair with gray linoleum and, at one end, a stage covered by a curtain. There was beer or cheap wine to drink, served in polystyrene cups by an ex-convict behind a folding table. The ex-convict had taken the alternative route to rehabilitation. His hair was long, he wore an earring in a pierced ear, and he spoke in a phony American accent. "Wine, man?" he asked Daisy.

Neither Thirst nor Chaz was visible for the first part of the evening, which meant that people who hardly knew each other could open conversations with the question, "Where's Oliver?"

"He said he would be a little late," I told a girl with orange hair.

"Ooh! You must be one of the toffs," she said.

There was a stark division between people from Thirst's murky past, who were better dressed and spoke in thick cockney accents, and the rest of us. I was immediately ill at ease, which set up a tension between Daisy and me.

"You're getting into one of your moods," she said.

"No I'm not."

"I can feel it, I can feel the paranoia freezing up your guts."

I caught sight of Eleanor and James Hogg across the room.

"Nonsense. You know I love parties—especially this sort."

"Try to enjoy it, Jimmy, for me. You know how important it is to Oliver."

Daisy often chided me on social occasions for my lack of interest, but when people like the policeman I had once cross-examined came up to speak to me, a look of envy would cross her face.

"Nice to see you again," the policeman said.

"That's an even bigger lie than the ones you were telling in the box," I said. He laughed.

"Who was that?" Daisy said.

"Just another bent cop."

"Oh God, you're so important these days—everybody knows you." While she spoke, her eyes searched the room.

I sensed her restlessness and rebelled inwardly at being identified as a burden to her. I put it down to her American origins that for her a party, any party, was an event of great importance, something like a holiday for which one spends the rest of one's life waiting. She always seemed to be on her best behavior on such occasions, like a young girl anxious to please. It was hard to explain to her my view that such affairs required an enormous expenditure of wasted energy. No conclusions were reached, no decisions made, no problems solved, no money was earned. One simply woke up the next morning with a hangover and a feeling of guilt for having once again caused unnecessary damage to one's health. I knew that in expressing this unhip view I would merely confirm her worst fears that I was an old fogy before my time. I looked around the bleak hall with a feeling of dread at the hard work that would be involved in finding enough people to talk to and enough small talk to fill the next four hours. Daisy, I knew, would not want to leave before midnight.

"Daisy, if I get really bored, would you mind very much if I left early?"

"Yes, I would."

"But you don't need me. I spoil it for you."

"I am *with* you, understand?"

Anxious to escape from the heavy judgment she was forming at my expense, I encouraged her to join a group of young people I saw sharing a joint. As usual, she seemed reluctant to leave my side. But as the unmistakable smell of her favorite drug wafted over, she found it in her heart to abandon me to the cold interstices between social groups that were my natural habitat.

I watched her say something cute and fetching to one of the young men in the group to gain acceptance and a share of the joint. She smoked it expertly through cupped hands. I thought, not for the first time, that there was something dirty about the way she smoked grass.

The young man she had first spoken to watched with approval.

"Not bad," Daisy said. "Reminds me of Afghan black."

"Exactly right."

"Nineteen seventy-one, from the southern end of the slope." She smirked. I watched his eyes light up.

I consoled myself with a few polystyrene cups of red wine before indulging a prurient curiosity I felt about Hogg, who was standing in a corner talking to Eleanor. The hall was filling up fast. I shouldered my way between two men standing back-to-back and felt cruel packs of muscle squeezing me. Both men turned to stare as I passed. "So he copped five in Dartmoor," one of them said to his group, resuming the conversation.

"The Tories are all fascists," a girl in jeans and sweater was saying to the next group through which I had to pass. "It really really surprises me that people don't see that—I mean, why does *anybody* vote for them? That's what I really can't relate to."

"People are deceived."

"It's a conspiracy, I mean, d'you think the CIA are behind it?"

"Definitely, I mean, they control the media, right?"

Passing Daisy's group, I noticed that the policeman had joined them and was at that minute about to smoke the joint. He caught my eye and winked, which affected me oddly. I was sure Daisy was studying me.

"There goes God," the policeman said as I passed. Some of the group turned.

"You could say that," Daisy said.

I was finally close enough to manage a wave at Eleanor and Hogg. He held up a fist in a kind of greeting to me over the heads of the crowd. She'd said he had suffered a nervous breakdown, but peering at him between bodies, I thought Hogg had the appearance of a man who had suffered not so much a breakdown as a thoroughly liberating change of identity. His hair was cut short, in a style favored by many gay men; he wore a gold ring in one pierced ear. Instead of embarrassment, there was pride in the power of that wrestler's body.

Eleanor and Hogg stopped talking as I approached and watched me without smiling. Eleanor was dressed in tight jeans, which had the effect of emphasizing her belly, but it was the change in Hogg that unnerved me. Eleanor was giggling, presumably at something he had said.

"Having a good time?" he asked, then exchanged a look with Eleanor as if the question were a great joke. "Doesn't James Knight look as though he just loves parties?" he said. Eleanor seemed to be trying to swallow a smile. I felt suddenly disoriented, as if I were surrounded by people who only resembled those I had known.

"Oh yes, I love parties," I replied, undecided, at the moment of speaking, whether to sound ironic or not. This left my words sounding merely polite. Hogg and Eleanor burst out laughing, and Eleanor put an arm around my shoulders.

"Poor James! There's a whole hemisphere of human life he's never even tapped." Her voice sounded half malicious, half kindly. The curious use of the word "hemisphere" stuck in my mind like a thorn.

By now I was feeling strange, and it occurred to me, with a sudden lurch of panic, that the wine had been laced with something. I was about to ask if they thought so, too, when there was a deafening twang of an electric guitar, and the curtains across the stage parted, to reveal Thirst and Chaz dressed in the kind of striped pajamas prisoners were supposed to wear at Alcatraz. A fluorescent sign proclaimed them to be a group called The Underground. There was stunned silence for a moment, then laughter. Eleanor said, "How superb!" and Hogg stared openmouthed at Thirst, whose pajama top was cut away to show off his tattoos.

"My God, he's beautiful," Hogg said.

"Evening, everybody," Thirst said into a microphone. His voice, much distorted by the cheap equipment, had a quality I had never noticed before: commanding, metallic, inhuman.

"I hope you enjoy the Prisoners' Ball. We're going to do a few little numbers for you. Before we do, I think you all should know that the agency primarily responsible for law enforcement in this country is represented here tonight in its most benevolent form. In other words, he's as bent as a two-bob watch."

I looked across at the policeman and was astounded when he merely smirked. Somebody cheered.

"Yeah, let's hear it for the bent cop," Thirst said. There was a small hooray. I tried to find a face that was as shocked as I was. Everyone seemed merely amused.

They played a few songs—with Thirst singing not very well and Chaz playing a huge guitar that dwarfed him—then came off the stage to mix with us. Chaz made a few adjustments to the electrics; recorded rock music began to play, and somebody switched on ultraviolet strobe lights. For the whole of the rest of the evening, the lights flicked on and off, picking out certain colors like white and blue in people's clothes and making the owners look dazzling for a few seconds. Hogg was wearing a pair of white trousers so tight that his crotch was emphasized whenever the light picked it up.

Thirst, whose uniform proclaimed him to be Prisoner 666, made his way through the hall like a conquering king, his features radiant with confidence and magnanimity. He looked every bit the man who had finally got the world where he wanted it—and indeed it seemed as if everyone in the hall wanted to be his friend. By now I was convinced that the wine had been laced, probably with lysergic acid or some similar drug.

As he approached the group Daisy had joined, I winced to see her put her arms around his neck and kiss him full on the mouth.

"You're gorgeous," I thought I heard her say.

The policeman also embraced him, in the ingratiating manner of an obsequious courtier, whose tribute Thirst accepted condescendingly. I wished to annihilate the repugnance I was feeling and went back across the hall to the Formica table for some more wine—which, I noticed, was being ladled out of a tub rather than poured from a bottle. In a self-destructive impulse I swallowed a cupful and stood by the door, watching Thirst's progress.

I heard people saying things like "I feel really weird," although many appeared unaffected by whatever was in the wine. To my annoyance, Daisy's group was slowly moving toward me. Its members, who had not been drinking very much, appeared quite normal, which is to say their behavior was typical of people who have been smoking marijuana. Someone would make a joke, which would not strike me as funny. The joke would hang in the air for a long moment, then two or more members of the group would get it at the same time and there would be loud incredulous guffaws that stopped abruptly. They would eye each other affectionately, then suddenly break eye contact, look at the floor, and retreat into smug grins. Daisy had managed to make herself leader of this group.

"I was so stoned," she was saying, "I put all their essays in the bath and started to run the hot water. That's how I got the sack that time."

The whole group cracked up.

I watched her from my solitary position at the door and did not immediately realize the extent to which the drug intensified familiar fears. The suspicion (which increased as I watched to an unshakable conviction) that her narcissism left no room for love and that my passion for her was based on a delusion, or some kind of spell that she cast over me, caused me to break out in a cold sweat just as if I was staring at the incontrovertible evidence of her treachery.

Paranoia gaped like a void at my feet. I was staring into an internal abyss when Hogg came up to join me, a look of triumph on his face. When he spoke, he might have been reading my thoughts.

"You look as if you're just seeing women for the first time. Aren't they hideous?"

I had been looking only at Daisy, but now I looked and listened and found that the other women in the room all seemed to be vain, powerful, manipulative. For a moment they struck me as creatures formed from an identical pattern, a perception that did not increase my anxiety but made me laugh. This startled Hogg.

"Aren't you leaving something out?" I said.

"What's that?"

"Well, look at the men."

I was thinking particularly of Thirst—who had not hesitated to drug us all, I was now convinced, in his lust for power and revenge.

"But the men are beautiful," Hogg said.

The word "beautiful" immediately made me think of Daisy, who at that moment caught my eye and made a wry face. I had teased her many times about her ego trips when she got into a group she could dominate. Her expression seemed to say, "Yes, I'm getting a cheap thrill and making silly jokes that everybody laughs at." My sense of revulsion was immediately replaced by a feeling of boundless love that was rapidly extended to the other women in the room and then to the men.

"It's a puzzle," I said, as if Hogg had been part of my inner dialogue. I then had the startling idea that my abrupt changes of perception were much more rapid than I had supposed and followed the rhythm of the strobe lights: on / off, black / white. The awesome thought that human life amounted to no more than this, a mindless alternation between binary opposites (wasn't that the way computers were supposed to work?), frightened me so much that I held on to Hogg's arm, causing him to look uncomfortable.

The moment passed. I experienced a state of total calm, remembering the panic of the moment before as if it were a vortex which I had traveled through and miraculously survived. I was now entirely possessed by the drug, but the state of inner calm enabled me to think about my condition in a disinterested way.

I tilted my head back so that I was looking up at a corner of the ceiling. I remembered doing that when I was ill in bed as a child. There on the ceiling I saw Thirst again in his prison costume, with the sleeves cut away. He was pushing a huge boulder uphill, hands worn to stumps with the effort, and bleeding. In the hallucination, he was about to reach the top of the hill, which ended (though he could not know it) in a precipitous cliff. I stretched my neck back still farther, until I was looking at the ceiling directly above me. There he was again, with his rock, about to reach the precipitous edge. Farther back still, he reappeared and so on wherever I looked. Why was he persisting with his rock?

The vision intrigued me, as if it might provide an answer to some perpetual conundrum of mine, and I tried to sustain it, but it disappeared in a flash.

I felt another panic attack coming on. I turned to Hogg and saw that by now he, too, was possessed by the drug. Rapture illuminated his face. I sensed that I did not want to know what he was staring at, but I seemed powerless to keep my eyes from following the direction of his.

"Look at them," he muttered, apparently in a religious ecstasy, "the king and the queen."

I finally turned to see Thirst and Daisy walking toward us, hand in hand. They were, indeed, a handsome couple. Hogg's rapture proved highly suggestive. Knowing that if I did not escape immediately I would do or say something terrible, I rudely tore myself away from Hogg as they approached. I caught a worried, disappointed look on Daisy's face as I fairly rushed across the room, bumping into people like some panic-stricken animal, trying to escape them.

I found Eleanor standing near the stage, holding a polystyrene cup of wine, staring into space. She blinked when she saw me, smiled stupidly.

"Hello, James Knight," she said slowly, as if in a dream. But she extended her hand to hold me tightly by the arm. "He's poisoned us, hasn't he? The filthy little crook."

Her words reached my consciousness out of sequence, so that I had laboriously to arrange them into a sentence. My attention fixed itself upon the word "poison."

"Poison? Yes, I think he has."

"It's LSD, isn't it? Why has he done it?"

I searched around for an answer, then beamed. "He's tired of being a slave in our kingdom—he thinks it's time that we were slaves in his."

She smiled dreamily. "You understand him so much better than the rest of us."

"Yes."

"It seems that he's the one with Daisy tonight, is that right?"

"Yes."

She stared again into space.

"Nevertheless, it's a remarkable experience. Do you know that just a few minutes ago I started thinking about my son Michael and was immediately transported to the night he died? I'm sure only a mother could follow her child into death like that. Only mothers love that much."

I remembered that words were also experiences and that by entertaining the word "death" we also invited the experience. I held her arm as I began to shake with terror.

She was oblivious to me. Large tears formed at the corners of her eyes and spilled down her cheeks.

"Damn Thirst for doing this to us. Who the hell does he think he is?"

"Eleanor, I think I'm dying."

"Will you excuse me. I don't think I could face them right now." She left me abruptly. I sensed rather than saw the reason for her sudden departure and felt like a small cornered animal.

"We came to see if you were all right," Daisy said.

I wished fervently that she was not there. I saw that they were still holding hands, like lovers, and began to shake violently. They seemed solicitous after my welfare—a trick, I felt sure.

"You put acid in the wine," I said. The enormous concentration required to utter this simple sentence left me exhausted. I felt small and hunched, an old man spitting venom. "Why?" I asked him.

"Everyone here tonight has been carefully selected," he said. "We want to see what each one of you is really made of. I want to know how well you handle yourself when your structures are all gone."

I stared and shook.

A word that seemed to have been hovering on the threshold of consciousness for some time, perhaps forever, erupted in my mind like something both sinister and man-made—a nuclear submarine surfacing in a clear blue sea: schizophrenia. As soon as it emerged into full consciousness, I became convinced that I was suffering from that very disease and that perhaps because of it I was unworthy of Daisy. I was a rat scuttling across a crowded floor, evoking shrieks of revulsion from the godlike humans standing there.

The detritus of the party lay strewn all over the ceiling. Then the ceiling swung round and became the floor. There was a smell of vomit, possibly my own. The aftereffects of the drug made me feel disoriented in all my senses, while my mind seemed to function with icy clarity. What terrible damage had I done to myself? I found that I was lying with my head against a wall. I groaned for the sake of demonstrating to myself my own existence.

"Jimmy?"

Daisy's voice floated across the floor of the hall, bounced off walls.

"Jimmy, I've been so worried. I wanted to phone for an ambulance, but the others wouldn't let me. They said it would ruin your career—but they were just scared for themselves. That schmuck of a cop thought it was hilarious. Then they all got paranoid and fucked off. Even Oliver left. Oh, baby! I've been feeling so guilty, sitting here praying for you. Tell me you're not crazy anymore. I've never seen anyone react like that to drugs."

"What happened?"

"You were yelling and talking to people who weren't there and everyone was watching and you crawled across the floor like a baby. Then you puked. It was horrible. Oh, Jimmy, I shouldn't have left you—can you ever forgive me? Tell me you're all right."

I reached out and held her for so long that she became uncomfortable and had to apologize for moving her body.

As we left the hall I remembered that I had to catch a train to Sheffield in a few hours' time.

30

I recognized George Holmes immediately from the train window as he walked briskly down the platform, although it was the first time that I had set eyes on his companion, Vincent Purves. George wore brown baggy trousers and brogues. The pipe clenched between his teeth made it look as if he were grinning with menace.

I had learned a lot about him since the Crook Street trial. His choice of dress aside, he belonged to a category of policeman whose day had come. Not for him the indulgent smile for young or female transgressers, the avuncular warning, the "Good night all," the measured plod home. He seemed hardly to notice petty crime; his eyes were fixed on the exploits of heavy gangsters. Those of us in the business of defending them felt uncomfortable around him— George was a man with a mission.

"Someone's got to clean this city up," I heard him say once in court. Barristers who worked with him testified to an amazing energy, an attention to detail, a refusal to mind his own business. He told younger counsel how to cross-examine and deserved his reputation as one of the most skilled interrogators in the Metropolitan Police—those reassuring old English clothes camouflaged a ferocious ambition. It was ambition that moved him to sit in the same compartment as me on that ride to Sheffield, although he made it look like coincidence. Vincent Purves left early to buy a cup of tea and did not return until we drew into Sheffield three hours later.

"Is this seat taken?"

When he was settled, he asked me with an inflection of his eyebrows if I minded his pipe. He poked around in it and lit up.

"You're on this fraud thing, of course, in Sheffield?"

I nodded.

"On the wrong side, as usual?"

I managed a weak smile. Most of the effects of the drug had now worn off, except for occasional disturbing flashbacks. But I must have looked awful. Daisy—haggard with worry, drugs, and alcohol—had helped me home and bathed me like a child. Most terrifying of all for me was the total loss of concentration. I found that my mind wandered like a hyperactive child's, the intellectual discipline of a lifetime shattered. For the first time that I could remember, I was deprived of the power to think. I could not have provided George with a more malleable audience for what he wanted to say.

"How did you like the party last night?" he murmured, so low that I had to ask him to repeat the question.

My paranoia must have been painfully obvious. "How did you know?"

"We've been watching Mr. Oliver Thirst for some time—and that bent copper he keeps as a friend. Don't you think it's a little unwise, being so close to someone like Thirst? A man in your position?"

George would sometimes spend days thinking up the right first question to ask, but he could not have predicted the effect this one would have on someone suffering from the aftereffects of induced psychosis. I felt a paralysis of will; his presence oppressed me like that of an overweening father.

"You all right? That bastard didn't slip anything in your drink last night, did he? You know he'll do anything to compromise you."

"I drank rather a lot, I'm afraid."

He grunted. There was a pause while he pulled on his pipe.

"You must have seen enough bent men to know better than to try reforming them."

"He's trying to change. I've never seen anyone try so hard."

George shook his head. "At the moment. It's pathetic; it's like watching an animal in a trap. Do-gooders just make the trap bigger, add a few options, a new treadmill, a tunnel that leads to another part of the trap. They do it to make themselves feel better; they don't like the idea that their good fortune depends upon squashing people like Oliver Thirst. That's what they pay me for, to do the squashing. Makes me sick. If I had my way, people like Thirst would be tattooed on their foreheads, whipped in public. Society hasn't changed since the days when those kinds of things were done, you know; people have just got very squeamish. Instead of shackles and torturers we have Librium and psychiatrists. In the end it comes to the same thing, because what Thirst wants is to be like you and me, but he can't; he has a disease that sets him apart."

"Disease?"

"Criminality. It's like leprosy, a slow-moving disease that makes people crumble from the inside, inch by inch. All you have to do is restrain them till the disease has done its work and they've collapsed. You can let them out for their harmless last gasps. The best you can hope for is a burnt-out case. That's what the prison system is for—to exhaust them, make them old and useless before their time, institutionalize them. Break them."

"Thirst isn't broken."

"More's the pity. They let him out too early—it happens a lot. We nail him again and again. As often as it takes, till he's broken. Kinder to break them from the start—slit their noses, cut their lips off—but we're too squeamish for that, so we use time. For a man in gaol, time is like a pile of rocks on his chest. Each new gaol term adds another rock, till he can hardly breathe. It's the cruelest method of all, but we use it because you can't see time. The BBC can't film it in a documentary, the *Guardian* can't describe the suffering it causes—it's invisible. Keeps the liberals quiet. Thirst knows that."

"Yes, I believe he does. But he's fighting. He says he'd rather die than go back to gaol."

George raised his shoulders, opened his hands. "Let him die!"

"But someone's given him hope."

"Do-gooders. People who never grow up, never see the world as it is. They wish the world was a kind of padded playpen with no serious consequences. But you know better than that. I've been on the receiving end of your cross-examination. You're a killer."

"There's no salvation in your system?"

"Salvation is just a safe toy in the playpen. Maybe you're not quite old enough to agree; you still have a bit of the liberal about you. But not for long, I reckon. You're not really the playpen type."

The effects of the drug had completely worn off by the time we drew into Sheffield, leaving that unusual clarity of mind that sometimes occurs when the body's resources are spent.

It was wet and appreciably colder as we walked, the three of us, down the platform. Since we were staying in different hotels, we said goodbye at the taxi stand. It was Vincent Purves who turned at the last minute to make some ambiguous but significant gesture, something between a handshake and a wave. George simply got into the taxi and stared straight ahead, as if I was not there at all. It's up to you now, the back of his head seemed to say.

It's curious how foreign different parts of England can seem. The Yorkshire accent struck me as perverse; there was something stunted about the land, and darker. A peculiar density crept into my mind and sat there. I had a feeling that something would go terribly wrong—and that there were no precautions I could take to save myself. I thought about Daisy all the time.

Beaufort was already installed and drunk when I arrived at the hotel. We both had suites, but his was the one we worked from. The sitting area was a chaos of files and lawbooks, every available surface covered with documents. The bedroom part of the suite gave off the smell of an aging bachelor's decaying ego.

His inner crumbling was almost tangible. The man who, even drunk, had never left a sentence unfinished, or missed a syntactical nicety, had begun to lose concentration. Often he forgot what he was saying and stared at me, waiting for me to find some tactful way of reminding him. I was not especially fond of Beaufort, but this decline depressed me. Fraud cases consist of a mass of factual detail, usually contained in dozens of box files. Beaufort had the ability to master this detail. It was not simply that his memory was photographic; he could retrieve information and turn it into aggressive cross-examination questions in a seamless performance under the glare of the court. I didn't have his memory or his polish, but if he deteriorated further I would have to carry the whole case.

His cries for help were accompanied by the use of my Christian name.

"I'm getting a bit old for this game, James."

"You'll manage."

"James, I've been thinking, you might have to represent us at the prosecution's opening on Monday. I'm not quite up to it."

"On the first day? But you're leading counsel."

"There's never much to do, James. Old Thomas will just put the boot in a bit—you know how to rattle him by now. I'll be better once the thing's under way."

This was blackmail. Barristers do not abandon trials any more than physicians abandon dying patients. If he collapsed I would have to take over. The alternative—of simply deserting our client— was too shameful to contemplate.

And then, on Sunday morning, before the first day of the trial, when I stopped by his room, I found that he had finally snapped. He sat in a chair half-dressed, tears rolling down his cheeks. His eyes, when he looked at me, were pleading. "I've lost it," they said, "and I'm too old to start again." I had twenty-four hours to take over.

It was the same day that Daisy's mother killed herself.

The phone rang in the middle of that night, destroying the sleep to which I had finally surrendered after an exhausting day with the files, trying to make sense of Beaufort's margin notes. At first I thought it was a crank call, there was such a strange sound on the other end of the line. The sound repeated itself several times, and I would have hung up were it not for the note of familiarity I sensed even in that inarticulate gurgle. The third or fourth time, I realized the sound was a sob.

"Oh God, Jimmy!"

I was immediately alert. The possibility that Daisy had somehow been hurt caused a cataract of primeval emotions.

"She's . . . oh God—oh God!"

"What?"

"Mommy. It's Mommy. She was the only one, Jimmy, the only one."

"What?"

"The only one who loved me totally."

"Is she dead?"

"She . . . oh Christ, she killed herself. I'm at the hospital. Oh Jimmy, it's all horribly real. You've got to come now, I can't wait, I'm going out of my mind. You've got to come now, Jimmy."

"Listen, darling, Daisy—"

"No, Jimmy, I can't listen, that's the thing, I can't even think. Nothing like this has ever happened—how could she do this to me? Jimmy, I'm desperate, I don't know what I'm going to do, I'm totally crazy. Listen, this is the address of the hospital."

With agonizing slowness she read out an address. Each word seemed to require an effort of concentration, after which her mind would wander for moments until she could muster the strength to articulate the next word.

"I've got to go."

The phone clicked, leaving me stranded with a racing brain. Half an hour later she telephoned again, dramatically calmer. She even sounded listless.

"They gave me a tranquilizer at the hospital; apparently I'm in shock. I need you. This stuff makes me feel like a zombie, but I know when it wears off I'm going to be screaming. Don't let me down, Jimmy."

"I won't, darling, but you've got to give me a day."

"A *day?*"

"Please listen. Beaufort is having some kind of breakdown, and I'm the only one on the case at the moment. We start tomorrow. The judge—"

There was another click.

I spent the rest of the night telephoning the hospital and our flat. At the hospital they told me that Daisy had been helped, after a while, by a young man who came in. The matron could only remember that he was wearing jeans.

"Did he have a strong cockney accent?"

"Half the people here have cockney accents."

No one answered the phone at our flat.

I did not sleep again that night. At about eight the next morning I telephoned my opponent on the case to request an adjournment. He was of the gentlemanly school. "But what are you going to tell the judge?"

"That my girlfriend's mother is dead."

"You'll have to say wife, old boy, if you want your adjournment."

I said wife and got the adjournment. As it happened, the judge had finished another long trial only the week before and was glad of the respite. Only George Holmes was irritated.

In London, there was no sign that she had been back to the flat after the hospital. It was obvious that she'd left in a rush. With my heart in my mouth, I telephoned Thirst's flat, but there was no answer. She was not at her mother's, either. I thought about phoning her father in the United States, Professor Sebastian J. F. Hawkley at Yale, but even in my despair knew that she would not have contacted him. As far as she was concerned, he was dead, too. I had helped her kill him.

I toyed with the idea of calling the police. But I knew I'd be told that people go missing all the time; she would be merely one more name on a list. I also knew she was not really missing.

Wearily I got on a train back to Sheffield, where it was still raining.

For the next few days, dialing the number of our flat was a neurotic tick that overcame me every couple of hours. She never answered. In the end I did phone the police, who dutifully put her

on the list of missing persons. The skepticism in the desk sergeant's
voice was predictable. He didn't know Daisy or me from Adam;
he just knew she had gone off with another man.

Then, after a weekend during which I was glad to be occupied with helping Beaufort's ex-wife collect him and take him
back to the matrimonial home he thought he'd escaped, a letter
arrived.

> Jimmy—you let me down. I needed you so badly but
> your fucking career came first, as usual. I needed com-
> fort, Jimmy—I still do. When I'm out of shock I'll
> call you. I'm with Oliver. Daisy.

Shock. It's funny how it can take you. And sometimes nothing
makes us go into shock more effectively than when the long feared
and suspected comes to pass. I held the letter, and my brain went
into a tailspin. Specific, very vivid images of Daisy and me from
our years together—little cameos, extracts of life—exploded in
my head. For a moment the past seemed infinitely more real than
the present. It was only a few hours later that the pain really
began.

I had left with her, for safe custody, the most vulnerable part
of my self. It seemed to me that she had chosen to torture it, like
a mad surgeon who in the middle of an operation starts to eat his
patient's liver.

"Why are you doing this?" I said it aloud, not always when I
was alone. I experienced cycles of anguish that sent me spinning
out of control, followed by a strange peace that disintegrated when
the next onslaught gathered momentum.

At the same time I kept working, was even capable of inspi-
ration. My intellect seemed liberated from all restraint. It was a
piece of computer software that had been switched on and now
had to run its furious program to the end, independently of me.
My colleague on the other side of the case found me disturbing—
whether due to forensic ferocity or because I was on the point of
a nervous breakdown, I never knew.

Alone in my room, I found it impossible to make the different parts of my self work in unison. I loved Daisy. I hated Daisy. I would beg her to come back. I would never speak to her again. It was all my fault. I was blameless. The world was black, the world was white.

3 1

For what happened next I have no excuse or explanation, only
a howl.

There were many letters, some long and explanatory, others
short and desperate. Once or twice she tried to strike a humorous
note. I replied to none of them.

> Jimmy, it was a terrible thing I did, I know how I
> must have hurt you. I know this is so hard for you
> to understand, but now that I'm out of it I love you
> even more. My mind is clear at last—I've been such
> a stupid self-indulgent bitch. Love is the only thing
> worth living for, whatever the price. Suddenly I see
> you for what you are—you're a true hero, darling,
> you've struggled more than anyone I know. I feel so
> ashamed. Why do we need to have such ghastly jolts
> to make us grow up?

I understand why you won't talk to me over the phone. These things take time to heal. Perhaps in a week or two, or in a month, you'll let me come and see you in Sheffield. I would like that. But you know what—maybe it's too soon for you to see it, but this is really good what has happened, because now I know you're the only man I can ever really love. Please, please try to find it in your heart to forgive me. I know how busy you are with your case, with Beaufort gone and it all being on your wonderful shoulders, but if only for the memory of our love, please take an hour out of the day to read this letter and think about it.

Jimmy, how stupid of me, I write a long rambling letter and completely forget to reassure you. For me it is so obvious, you see, but for you up in Sheffield it's probably not so clear. Darling, I haven't seen Oliver since the week my mother died. When he phones I hang up. I've now written to him explaining everything; I'm enclosing a copy of my letter to him. So you see, it was just a panic reaction by a dumb woman desperate for comfort.

Dear Oliver,

This is a difficult letter to write and I feel very stupid having to write it, but it has to be done.

It was very kind of you to pick me up from the hospital that night and I have to take full responsibility for what happened. I don't think it's quite fair for you to say that I seduced you, but I do admit I was in shock and in need of comfort. And as you so shrewdly pointed out over the phone, I was basically getting back at Jimmy. I'm sorry my selfishness has had this effect on you, but you know, Oliver, a couple of nights with someone isn't a marriage. Whatever you are feeling now will pass in a month. It will have to, because I'm not going to see you again. And let's be totally frank here, Oliver: I had no idea that you were dreaming of one day starting a new life in the States. Doesn't your attraction to me have just a little bit of self-interest in it? I have to tell you, forget it. With your record you'll never get a green card. You probably won't even get a visa to visit. Think again.

I wish you a long straight happy life—without me. Daisy.

Jimmy, I've been following the reports of your case in the newspaper. There seems to be something about it every day. I was so proud when I read about the judge saying that your client had not suffered any detriment by losing Beaufort (meaning that you were brilliant, of course). Your client does sound like a character, though. It's just like a movie, a Rolls-Royce and all that clever skulduggery. You must be so talented to follow all that stuff about holding companies and off-shore companies and subsidiaries.

What you used to say is so true, that it was my father problem that prevented me from taking an interest in your work. It really is so glamorous, isn't it?

Slowly, slowly, I'm getting used to the idea of Mom being gone. I hope in time you'll understand what a blow it was. She had to give me the love of two parents, you see, and losing her was like losing mother, father, grandmother, brother, sister, all at once. Please understand. I know that she was weak and foolish and probably never really grew up, but she saved my soul with her love. Do you know, I've even gone a little bit religious. I pray for you—for us—every night, and last Sunday I went to a church. I'm always going to be here for you, Jimmy. Daisy.

Dear Brick Wall,

Are you ever going to crack, Brick Wall? My words are graffiti scratched on you with bleeding fin-gernails, Brick Wall. You think it's easy, writing these

letters, Brick Wall? Well, it isn't. Every letter makes
my fingers bleed. I scratch and scratch until my nails
are all broken and the blood runs down my hands
and I think that this time I must have left a mark,
but I haven't, have I? Just a lot of messy female blood,
which you'll wipe off by morning. D.

Okay, schmuck, this is an American letter. Better, this
is a New York letter. I'm sick of this chickenshit British courtesy game. I'm telling you, you need me. Want
to know why? Because after you cut out your heart
so it wouldn't get in the way of your goddamn upward mobility, I'm all you've got to pump your blood
around. I'm your subconscious, asshole. I'm the only
life you've got. Law isn't life, it's death. So I hurt you,
big deal. I never said I was totally straight. I never
concealed from you that I had a fucked-up side. And
you love me for it, Jimmy, oh yeah! Like it or not,
it's the wild in me, the sociopath if you want to use
that word, that's kept you going all these years, while
your heart's been on ice. D.

You bastard—can't you see what you're doing? THIS
IS EXACTLY THE WAY MY FATHER WOULD
HAVE ACTED.

It's been three months now. I know from the news
that your case will finish soon. You must be preparing
for your summing up to the jury. I remember how
tense you used to get. I ought to be feeling optimistic
because you'll be coming back to London, but I'm not.
During this past month, when I haven't written so
many letters to you, it's finally begun to sink in that
we might not be together again. Oh, James! This is
something I never thought would happen, even in
my blackest moments. I thought you would punish
me and punish me until you had decided that I had
suffered enough, but I never really believed it was

the end. Even you must realize by now that I've suffered, too, whether as much as you or not, who can ever say?

I didn't tell you this before, because you might have misunderstood (I can guess how raw that nerve still is), but somehow it doesn't seem to matter anymore, so I can tell you that two weeks ago I saw Oliver (once—in public). He was lurking around a corner, obviously waiting for me, and begged me to go to a café with him, so I did. He told me he thought that everything good in his life had disintegrated, and I said it was the same for me.

He asked if I'd seen you, and I said we wrote a lot (I didn't want to raise his hopes by telling him that you've not spoken or written a single word to me since the night my mother died). Then he suddenly blurted out that he loved me. He said he couldn't love in some anemic bourgeois way, so he just had to tell me that he adored me and that he would die for me. Then he burst into tears. And you know, all the time I was thinking, if only it were you. If only it were you, Jimmy, I wouldn't even demand that you adore me. If you would just let go and cry, to put yourself in touch with yourself again, I'm sure (see how conceited I am!) that you would find your love for me again in the depths of your heart. D.

Dear James,

So your trial has ended and you're back in London and I'm having to write to your chambers because I don't know where you're staying. I ought to be congratulating you on your victory (well done! another crook back on the streets!), but I find for the first time a certain bitterness has crept into my heart. If I don't find love again I will lose all generosity. I think I'm losing my soul. I really thought that you had no more weapons to hurt me with. But you found one, didn't you?

Even as I write, I can hardly believe it, that you would be here in London and still inaccessible to me. Have you found another flat? Are you staying with friends? I waited for three days running outside your chambers, but you didn't appear and your clerks were embarrassed to talk to me. All they would say was that you preferred to take cases out of town at the moment.

Can you really just write off all those years like that? You loved me, more deeply than most men ever love; perhaps that's what hurts so much, but you can't deny it. Not before God. Not even in front of a mirror. D.

Dear James,

I went for a walk on the Heath yesterday, to those places we used to visit together. It was cold and windy, and even though it's supposed to be summer, there were lots of leaves on the ground and many of the ones on the trees were curling up and turning brown. I stood on a hill and felt that I was no more than a body, an empty body with the wind blowing through it. I don't think I shall write to you again. D.

And where were you, James Knight, when she was pouring out her heart? Were you kneeling with your ear to the keyhole, grinning maniacally? Were you?

In part, yes. A devil with my face was feeding off her suffering. I struggled against him, but he was stronger than I. I could not get out of my head the thought that she had in some way planned it— that her mother's death had merely provided an excuse. Nor could I forget the vicious slash ending that first letter: "I'm with Oliver. Daisy."

I knew perfectly well that what was required was forgiveness. Not the word but the phenomenon. I discovered that one can no more command the power to forgive than a sunny day. I knew myself to be in essence a fragmented man; I had depended upon her to give me wholeness. It was wholeness that was lost forever. And the fragmented man does not forgive. He loathes with a vengeance the one who stole the missing piece.

3 2

On a cold dead day in the dead of winter (or so it seemed to me), Daisy Smith changed her name again. On a cold dead day in the dead of winter, she became Daisy Thirst. Two thieves bore witness to the event.

It was raining, George Holmes told me. He had arranged for me to be briefed by the Director of Public Prosecutions, a great honor. George came to the conference and took me for a cup of tea afterward to tell me about the wedding.

"That's the way these villains are—they worm their way into people's lives specifically in order to betray and destroy. They can't help it, they're carriers of a disease. If I had my way, I'd have both his hands chopped off like they do in Saudi Arabia. It's all done professionally, by a surgeon. They strap them down, give them a shot of local anesthetic, saw off the hand with a surgical saw, chuck it in the bin for the hospital dogs. I'd love to see the look on Thirst's face when they did that. Expect you would, too."

I started to see a lot of George after that. I became a prosecutor, known for the cold passion I brought to my new role. George Holmes had never had so many successful convictions. I was indirectly responsible for his rapid promotions, and Commander Holmes was not a man to forget a friend. He would have told me a lot about Daisy and Thirst if I had let him. But after the wedding I didn't want to know any more.

Like any twentieth-century mutant, I cast about for alternatives. For a short time I pretended to be gay. I went to bars where broken men like me mixed with painted queens, male whores, and aficionados of the low life. An aging regular who befriended me put it neatly: "Just because you're terrified of love doesn't mean you're gay."

I liked his shrewdness. While others were diagnosing homosexuality for anybody who sneezed, he maintained that the club was just the size it had always been.

"So what is a homosexual?"

"Simple. I have a lifelong obsession with other men's erections. It can be diverting or exciting or tender; sometimes I even find love. But turning gay can't heal you. You won't stop bleeding even if you force yourself to screw one of these poor boys."

In a few months I found that was true of many things: Buddhism, alcohol, scuba diving, a package holiday in Crete for singles, yoga, three afternoons with a Catholic priest, some cocaine from a friend in the BBC, a string of sexual contacts from which emotion was excluded by agreement in advance. I tried parachuting, tried to love my career, wondered what it would be like to be a single-parent father and how one would go about it. I found that I could fixate on anything and sustain nothing. I could be frantic that someone didn't phone, then instantly bored when she did. I loathed television and watched it every night. London disgusted me, and I developed a phobia about leaving it. I woke up every morning at about three, arguing with Daisy. Sleeping alone was unbearable; so was the presence of another in the bed.

Little by little I began to recognize my disease in others, though I cannot say what it was. Life can fail anytime. The personality that was working so well for you yesterday can disappear overnight. Reach for it in the morning, it's been eaten away by the latest dystrophy. The man in the mirror has become a cipher, victim of some new ailment unheard of even twenty years ago. It can befall anyone. Parenthood is no prophylactic, nor is money or youth or sex appeal.

I acknowledged a gnawing hunger. It had been there all the time, and now that there was no chance of assuaging it, I knew the hunger for what it was. I didn't want Daisy back; I wanted back the person I had been with her.

PART

THREE

33

When George Holmes came to arrest Daisy that Tuesday morning, the two constables he brought with him knew who I was and called me "sir" more often than was necessary. By way of counterbalance, they were rude to Daisy. I don't know what story George had told them, something of the banality of a banner headline, no doubt: FEMME FATALE COMPROMISES EMINENT BARRISTER; or LOVESICK BARRISTER SEDUCED INTO HARBORING MURDERESS.

Daisy didn't seem to notice their rudeness. Before George had finished ("Mrs. Daisy Thirst née Hawkley and also using the surname Smith, you are hereby charged with the murder of your husband, Oliver Harry Thirst, on the . . . day of . . . 1986, at the intersection of . . . Street and . . . Street, by means of a shot fired from a small-caliber pistol at point-blank range sometime between the hours of one and five A.M."), Daisy had fainted. Over her prostrate body I hissed at George that he would pay for this with his career. He mumbled something that sounded almost like an apology.

When she came to, it was clear that Daisy had forgotten why she had fainted. George had to repeat the charge, adding this time that she was not obliged to say anything but that anything she did say would be taken down and might be used in evidence against her.

Comprehension broke in her eyes. She saw in a blink the shattering of our sixteen-day dream, her entrapment in the sadistic maze of the law, the long tedious months of depression that would inevitably follow, whatever the outcome.

George wanted to take her to the police station in the car they had brought.

"I'll take her," I told him.

I drove Daisy to Hampstead police station, which was really within walking distance, and had to let her out while I parked the car.

"Don't go inside without me," I said, and she was waiting, obedient and bewildered, when I returned. Suddenly a half-dozen press photographers appeared from out of nowhere and took pictures. The evening paper that day carried a front-page picture of a bewildered Daisy about to walk into the station. There was a picture of me, too, pinch-faced and furious. The headline, of course, read: GIRLFRIEND OF EMINENT BARRISTER CHARGED WITH MURDER. The story gave plenty of details of Thirst's past and ensured through innuendo that I would never, now, become a Queen's Counsel.

Apart from the presence of the press, that day was largely occupied with formalities. George showed none of his usual ferocity when dealing with suspects. He had no objection to bail and did not even attempt to question Daisy without a solicitor present. We went home after her fingerprints had been taken, promising to return with one the next day. I spent the afternoon discussing with my old pal Roland Denson which solicitor out of a short list of six we should use. We spent several minutes arguing about one in particular. Cyril Feinberg was probably the most ruthless criminal solicitor in London. A good part of my career had been spent dismantling the intricate alibis he had coached his clients into learning until they were word-perfect. He gave the impression of hating everything about his profession—the police, the clients, the barristers, the judges, the other solicitors. Roland Denson was convinced that I would never choose him.

I looked across at Daisy. We were downstairs in my study. She sat in an almost catatonic state, waiting while the men decided her fate. These were men's rules; daughter, wife, defendant, murderess—male definitions, male traps.

I made my decision. "It's Feinberg, Roland. He's our man."

Not for the last time in the case of the *Queen* v. *Daisy Thirst,* Roland Denson puckered his brow. He knew very well that I intended him to be junior counsel.

I nerved myself to phone Feinberg, whose personal secretary was almost as hostile to clients as he was.

"Mr. Feinberg is very busy—"

"Tell him it's James Knight."

"I'm afraid he's in a meeting at the moment—"

"Interrupt the meeting and tell him it's James Knight, with a case for him."

He would not yet have read the evening papers, but his contacts in the police were too good for him not to have known about Daisy's arrest—probably before she did. I knew he would find the publicity surrounding the case irresistible. Feinberg came on the line in seconds. He spoke in a rapid, impatient staccato.

"It's about your girlfriend. Murder charge. You wish to instruct me. I accept. When does Holmes want to question her?"

"Tomorrow."

"When?"

"Sometime in the afternoon."

"When exactly?"

Already Feinberg was furious.

"Anytime we like to stroll in. Holmes is going to be in Hampstead police station all day."

"He said that?"

"Yes."

A short pause. "Weirdest thing I ever heard. Is this a murder trial or an exhibition match at Lords?"

"He's being gentlemanly. I don't know why."

"Don't like it. Bring her to my office tomorrow morning at eight-thirty. I have a meeting at nine-thirty, but I'm free in the afternoon. We'll do the cop-shop bit then."

He put the phone down without waiting for confirmation. The next morning at eight-thirty exactly (Feinberg had been known to refuse to see people who were ten minutes late), I took Daisy to see him. I was glad that she found the spirit to wear her Sunday-morning hat and her best dress, in case the press surprised us again.

Although he maintained a branch near the Bailey, Feinberg's main office was in the West End, a piece of slick, tinted-glass modernity carved out of the ground floor of one of Mayfair's Georgian structures. A caricature receptionist (platinum blond, slim, tight black sweater, long legs in fishnet stockings) showed us into his inner sanctum, where his real secretary sat outside his door like a guard dog. She eschewed glamour to the same extent that her colleague cultivated it: old-fashioned spectacles, a shapeless but expensive suit, a shrewd appraising glance. I had heard that she adored Feinberg with animal loyalty and shrugged at his transient affairs with his front-window receptionists. Without saying a word to either of us, she clicked an intercom switch.

"Mr. Knight is here."

"Mrs. Thirst and Mr. Knight are here," I said.

Daisy put a hand on my arm. "It's all right—I got used to being invisible a long time ago."

The secretary showed us in without apologizing. Feinberg stood up from behind a vast desk and walked around to meet us. He was short, not even five feet five, wore black-framed spectacles, and had a shock of curly gray hair. His head was large for his body, and his face and thick lips were a nest of insect twitches that stopped only when he talked, or when he was concentrating. As with many gifted people, when he concentrated he seemed to dwell in a different state of consciousness, from which he emerged angrily into the present. I could sense his attraction to Daisy, which might be useful.

"I made inquiries," he said the moment we sat down. "We'll do the background later. This is what you'll have to explain. Convincingly. And in detail."

He took a photograph out of his drawer and flung it in front of Daisy. It was the one George Holmes had shown me that Sunday. Daisy in earmuffs at a firing range.

The blood drained from her cheeks. "Oh God, oh God, oh God."

"That's exactly the reaction that will cost you ten years in Holloway," Feinberg snapped.

"Who took it? Where did they get it?" Daisy was shaking.

Feinberg shrugged. "Who knows? Some Special Branch caper, no doubt." He looked at me. "Naive, isn't she?" He slouched back in his chair, stared at Daisy. "This is England, dear. They don't necessarily stop you breaking the law, but they always know. And they use it against you when it suits them."

Daisy clawed slowly at her face. "Special Branch? I thought they caught terrorists."

He leered, leaned forward to stab at the photograph. "And what d'you think you look like to them?" He drummed his fingers on his desk. "That's all I have to say this morning. Except to tell you about my fee structure. Take that picture. Study it. Live with it. Learn to love it. The way you react to it in the box is what this case is going to be about. We'll sort out the story later."

He spent the next few minutes telling us about his fees, when he wanted them paid, and how lazy he would become if they were not. I told him that I wanted Roland Denson as junior counsel.

"So long as I get to choose the leader," he said.

I did not need to guess who he wanted. There was only one Queen's Counsel at the English bar with enough ferocity to please Feinberg.

"You want Sir Simon Carlford?"

"I get Simon Carlford." His thick lips broke into an ugly smile. "When I want him."

"It's time we talked," Daisy said in a taxi on the way home.

Later that day we went together to my study and I unwrapped a new floppy disk that I put into my personal computer. We looked at each other grimly.

"In law it's the details that count," I said.

34

To prepare a case properly for trial is a work of art. This is doubly so when the preparation involves the concealment of a fundamental lie. And yet, if you pause to think about it, it must be so. Any human calling higher than bricklaying is about the manipulation of human perception, and if the perception you set out to manipulate is not naive, but canny and expert (that of a judge or prosecutor, say), then the sleight-of-hand must not falter, the magic must be seamless, the will that underlies the act so strong that even the impresario believes, for the instant that counts, that the pantomime horse can win the derby. All of which necessitates an intellectual and emotional discipline to which a lifetime of drugs and slogans had left Daisy unaccustomed.

"We're going to make a man of you," Feinberg told her with a leer.

In a way, he did. She made the mistake, one day, of saying that doing time in Holloway would be preferable to another day with

Feinberg and me, which gave Feinberg the excuse he needed. He arranged a visit to the prison, which left her pale and very frightened. Few people have any idea how low in the mental slum it is possible to sink. When Daisy came back, her mouth was set. Feinberg had finally whipped her awake.

"I'm not going to gaol, James," she said. "Believe me."

After that she learned her lines so well that we ran up against a new problem.

"She's too perfect," Feinberg said. "There isn't a convincing hesitation left in her."

"Fuck you," Daisy said.

Feinberg looked at her curiously. "Listen, dear, there's one question I've never asked and I'm not going to. I couldn't give a carrot if you did him in or not. What bothers me is that you don't have an alibi. George Holmes doesn't like losing—if all you can say is that you were at home all night playing with yourself, you're going to go down. There's only one sure way of winning any criminal trial, and that's to lie so well they couldn't convict you even if they wanted to. Right?"

The last word was directed at me. I had spent most of my career avoiding becoming the kind of lawyer Feinberg was. Even now, with Daisy's freedom at stake, I found it difficult. I looked away without replying, which enraged Feinberg.

"I want to talk to you," he said. "You can go," he told Daisy.

We sat for a moment in his office, looking at each other across his desk. He seemed to be even more angry than usual. The twitches in his face were at war with each other, and his thick lips were chewed almost to the point of bleeding. Finally he held up two fingers.

"Two surprises. Two very strange, very interesting surprises. The police statements arrived yesterday. Not exactly crammed with evidence, but enough, just enough, to put her away for the last years of her youth. To ensure she'll be senile in mind if not in body by the time she comes out."

"So what's the first surprise?"

"This. This pathetic excuse for an eyewitness account."

He took a single sheet of paper off the top of a stack of documents on his desk. The stack all bore the insignia of the Metropolitan Police. The sheet of paper he gave me was a witness statement in standard form. At the top it bore the name of the witness, the name of the police officer who had taken the statement, the time and date, place and address, age and occupation of the witness. At the bottom of the paper there was a place for the witness to sign, proof that nothing had been added after the statement was taken. Normally the sheets in a witness statement are carefully numbered, but in this instance there was only one sheet.

It was, as Feinberg said, a pathetic excuse for an eyewitness account. A ten-year-old boy awakened by his parents' drunken row had slipped out of his house at about 3:00 A.M.. As he turned a corner, he saw, some three hundred yards away, the silhouette of two people cast by a streetlamp. One seemed to be pleading with the other, who walked in front. The one who was pleading knelt down; the other turned and aimed a gun at him. There was a shot, and the kneeling figure collapsed. The other walked to a car parked about one hundred yards away, which is to say four hundred yards from the boy, and drove off in the opposite direction. To the crucial questions "Was the assailant tall or short, a man or a woman?" the boy could give no answer. He was mildly shortsighted and in that light saw no more than silhouettes—a shadow play against a desolate London street. It was not even possible, at that distance, to have any sense of the height or weight of the two people. They could have been dwarfs or giants. True, the boy had assumed, thanks to the kind of social programming Daisy deplored, that the assailant was a man. Under carefully biased questioning, the boy agreed that this was an assumption based on prejudice rather than perception. I put the statement down. Somehow I knew that the boy would not be called as a witness.

"Very interesting, don't you think?"

I shrugged. "A useless statement; it proves nothing."

Feinberg stared at me. I looked away.

"What was the other surprise? You said there were two."

"They've retained Nigel Monkson."

I examined Feinberg's face to see if he was engaging in some sadistic joke.

"Monkson?"

His lips broke into a grin. "I phoned his clerk this morning. It's kosher."

I smiled back. Nigel Monkson, Q.C., was the buffoon of the English bar, a harmless fool more concerned with male fashion than with legal practice. His connection with backwoods aristocracy and a conservative Lord Chancellor had enabled him, somewhat late in life, to become Queen's Counsel, but he was not taken seriously by solicitors or judges. Apparently incapable of grasping legal complexities, he had been known to have juries in stitches with his unaffected naïveté. "My Lord, if I've understood him aright, my learned friend is accusing my client of telling fibs," was one of his famously indignant lines. "Oh, I seem to have got that wrong," was another. To make matters worse, when excited he pronounced the letter *r* as if it were a *w,* a comic effect much appreciated by English juries.

"So maybe you would like to tell me exactly what George Holmes is up to," Feinberg said, his eyebrows raised and the insects in his face twitching again.

"I really don't know, Cyril," I said. He hated being called Cyril.

3 5

For reasons which he kept to himself, although I was able to guess at them, George Holmes dragged his feet so much that Daisy was seven months pregnant by the first day of her trial.

The judge treated her with the tenderness of an old man who had spent his life observing some chivalric code, and Nigel Monkson could be heard complaining in the robing room that in his very first murder prosecution the defendant was "pwegnant."

No one doubted that the pregnancy was calculated, or that it was a calculation of dramatic cunning, or that George Holmes had badly slipped up on his timing. Number One Court at the Old Bailey, reserved for murders and rapes, is large, intimidating, and austere. Everyone in the business saw the theatrical possibilities of Daisy on the elevated island that is the witness stand—lonely, female, and fecund, a figure of primal innocence in the shadow of all that cruel used oak, of men in gray wigs and black gowns and behind them the infinitely black prospect of prison. It was, people said without thinking, one of Feinberg's most brilliant ploys.

George sat behind the solicitor from the office of the Director of Public Prosecutions who was instructing Monkson and his junior for the prosecution. I sat behind Feinberg and stared across at George. Daisy stood in the iron cage reserved for defendants. Every morning I made a point of irritating George by taking out a sheaf of papers, nodding at him, and returning them, carefully folded in three, back in my jacket pocket. I made sure that Daisy kept the disk from which they were printed.

Nigel Monkson surprised all of us by showing an exemplary grasp of the law and the facts. Neither was difficult, but the effort showed on his face. The many emblems of his vanity (a gold bracelet on his left wrist, a fob watch, a large crimson silk handkerchief to wipe his brow, a crystal wineglass for his drinking water) seemed somehow forsaken in the grim intellectual struggle he was bringing to his first murder trial. Sir Simon Carlford, Daisy's ruthless Q.C., decided on a policy of seductive sweetness. He called Monkson "Nigel dear" and used phrases like "we silks." Monkson beamed in gratitude. I overheard him tell Carlford that "one does not weally become a man at the bar until one has pwosecuted a murder at the Bailey," a confidence Carlford rewarded with a discreet grasp of Monkson's forearm.

After the usual preliminaries, the jury were sworn in. The defense has the right to object without cause to a total of two jurors. Roland Denson, Carlford, and I had spent some time discussing whether or not we would make objections. It is generally known that middle-aged housewives are the most lenient jurors, but then, the average defendant tends to be young and male. After much debate, we decided the juror we did not want was the young misogynist—men of the intense angry type who have been hurt or enraged by feminists. The jury we ended with comprised seven women and five men. This pleased Carlford, who thought he would be able to dress up his natural aggression and make it look like a passionate defense of womanhood.

Monkson opened with a speech that was overlong and emotional. He talked about cold blood and malice aforethought and could not say the word "murder" without investing it with Dickensian melodrama. The jury was not to know that Monkson looked upon his first murder trial the way some men look upon a new car—as a source of pride to be polished and petted now and then. Every time he said "murder," Daisy shuddered.

There was the usual progression of forensic experts establishing the approximate time, cause, and place of death. Thirst had died between 3:00 and 5:00 A.M.. in a London street when a small-caliber bullet fired at close range penetrated the frontal lobe of his brain. The bullet came out at the lower back of his head, about a centimeter above the top of the spinal column, tearing away an irregular piece of flesh roughly the size of a marble. The hole drilled in his forehead was as small and neat as the red marriage spot Indian women wear. The assailant, therefore, had been standing above him. Two unsavory-looking business associates—with perfect alibis—were called to tell the court when they last saw him alive. Then Nigel Monkson called the only witness in the trial who did not seem to be a timeless player in the eternal drama of wife-husband-lover.

She was an inch, or maybe two, under six feet and walked with head lowered, as if about to charge. She wore dungarees in court, which had the effect of concealing what must have been a full figure. In another personality her body might still have been sexy— a suggestion, I felt, which one was likely to pay for with one's life. She spoke in short, staccato sentences, each of which carried a political message. Her hair was cut short at the back and sides, and her forehead clenched whenever she talked to men.

It was clear that she had access to an unlimited reservoir of loathing and had mistaken Nigel Monkson for a self-appointed persecutor of womanhood. In a series of leading questions to which Carlford made no objection, Monkson established that she owned a small area of farming land in Suffolk she had turned into a retreat at which the threatened, the beaten, the paranoid of her sex (whom she referred to as wimmin) could seek refuge and develop self-defense skills. Having herself reached killer level in every martial art from karate to Thai kick-boxing, she proudly told the court of her many successful rescues of damsels in distress from male bullies. The judge said something about a Don Quixotrix: Carlford laughed loudly and Monkson beamed, unsure at that stage whose side the judge was on. Now Monkson came to what he invariably called "the gravamen" of the evidence.

"And it is right, is it not, that in addition to unarmed combat you teach other martial skills?"

"The female human body tends to be smaller and weaker than the male body. I always encourage the wimmin to develop physical strengths and skills in unarmed combat."

"But some of the wimmin, as you put it—"

"My friend is cross-examining his own witness," Carlford put in. He had no real objection. Having lulled Monkson into a false feeling of comradeship, he now proceeded to betray him.

Monkson gave him a hurt glance. "Sorry. In addition to un-armed combat—"

"I allow some of the more harassed wimmin to use small arms."

"Including firearms?"

"Leading question," Carlford said.

Monkson reddened. He seemed bewildered. Carlford, after all, had allowed a whole succession of similar leading questions without objection, as is the custom with noncontentious evidence.

"M'Lord, I knew not that this part of the evidence was con-tentious," Monkson said.

"I didn't say it was contentious," Carlford said, standing as he spoke. "I simply said it was a leading question. There's no entitle-ment to ask leading questions in examination-in-chief, as my friend ought to know. I've shown exemplary patience up to now, but I cannot be expected to tolerate such conduct indefinitely. However, if he undertakes not to do it again, I'll withdraw the objection."

The judge nodded. Monkson turned scarlet, stranded in a crisis of embarrassment. To make matters worse, from now on he would struggle with the discipline of asking neutral questions to elicit the evidence he needed.

"Those wimmin who are especially vulnerable may bring fire-arms to practice on my firing range," the witness said, in response to Monkson's last question.

"And with regard to those women who bring guns—we're talking about handguns, are we not?—are they or are they not legally entitled to own such weapons?"

"Less than one percent of gun licenses in this country are owned by wimmin. Men dominate the right to violence, just as they dominate the right to wealth. Wimmin are only attempting to defend themselves. Wimmin do not start wars. Men do—"

"We appear to have strayed from the point—not for the first time, Mr. Monkson," the judge said.

Embattled, Monkson stared at the judge. Then he nodded, bowed his head, read from his notes. "And do you see in this courtroom any wimmin, as you put it, whom you allowed to bring a handgun onto your property to practice on your firing range?"

The Don Quixotrix gazed at Daisy and nodded.

"Whom do you indicate?"

"The defendant, Ms. Thirst." Her voice had softened.

"And do you recognize the person in this photograph?" Monkson held out the photograph for a clerk to pass to the witness.

"Yes. It's the defendant practicing on my firing range."

Monkson explained to the judge and jury, with Carlford nodding his consent, that it was an agreed fact that the photograph had been taken by Special Branch during a routine investigation of all activities involving firearms as part of an ongoing antiterrorism exercise. Of course there was no suggestion that Daisy was a terrorist; it was her bad luck to have been caught by the concealed camera. Special Branch had not closed down the illegal firing range because they hoped it would attract and lead to the identification of real terrorists. Daisy blinked every time Monkson used the word "terrorist."

The photograph was passed to the jury. I could see each of them—seven women and five men, solid, good-natured Londoners who had never seen bloodshed or handled guns—look at Daisy in a new light. This was the worst point of the trial for her, the moment that Monkson, for all his foolishness, had quite skillfully arranged. It was close to lunchtime, but Carlford wanted, at all costs, for something else to be in the jury's mind over lunch. For the jury to know that Daisy practiced at a firing range was one thing. The damage done by the visual impact of her grimly holding a gun and shooting it was quite another. He had already rattled

Monkson; now was the time to create a diversion by thoroughly unnerving him.

Sir Simon Carlford was tall, stooped, and beaked, with a large bald patch on his crown where the hair had been worn away by his wig, leaving the rest to fly wildly around his ears. He generally waited like an impatient vulture to cross-examine, then went at it with a horrible and remorseless pecking. But when he stood up that day, he asked perhaps the most extravagantly irrelevant question of his career.

"Madam, is it correct to say that you are a homosexual—or a bull dyke, as I believe it is known in the vernacular?"

The public gallery tittered, the jury gasped, the judge looked perplexed, and Monkson jumped up. Carlford sat down to permit Monkson's objection. There was a puzzling moment of silence while Monkson turned purple as he wrestled with this blatant provocation from Carlford.

"You have an objection to make, Mr. Monkson?" the judge asked helpfully.

Still Monkson seemed capable only of jaw movements unaccompanied by sound. Finally his anger exploded in a cataract.

"Never in all my caweer at the bar—"

"Does my friend wish to give evidence about his career?" Carlford asked. "I'm sure it's been fascinating and illustrious."

Monkson pressed his upper arms to his sides and moved his fists up and down in a mime of intense frustration. "I know not what twick, what demonically cunning subterfuge, my fwend thinks he's pursuing—"

"If my friend is accusing me of professional misconduct, this is neither the time nor the place," Carlford said, standing again.

The judge turned to Carlford and began to discuss Monkson as if he were in another room. "I agree, Sir Simon Carlford. I thought at first he wanted to object to your last cross-examination question."

"I *do*," Monkson pleaded, "want to object, most vigorously, most vigorously, My Lord. When I was a pupil at the bar of England and Wales, it was instilled into us that we are guardians of the English language—"

Monkson stopped when the judge hit the bench in exasperation. Carlford, who had sat down again, was busying himself with his papers. In the intervening moment of silence there was a loud cough from the witness stand.

"I'm very proud to be a lesbian," the witness began. "I—"

The judge silenced her with a strained smile. "Your evidence is most valuable to us, madam. Unfortunately, just at the moment prosecuting counsel seems to have—"

"Got his knickers in a twist," she interrupted.

There was a guffaw, immediately stifled, from the gallery. Anger flashed across the judge's face as he turned from the witness to Monkson. "Mr. Monkson, I do not propose to allow this trial to degenerate into a circus—"

"Iwelevant," Monkson said, subdued. "The question was iwelevant."

"Ah!" the judge said. "Sir Simon Carlford?"

Carlford nodded as if he were considering a difficult forensic point. "In what manner, exactly? It would be most helpful if my friend would specify which category of irrelevance he has in mind."

The judge gave Carlford a stern look. "I think that will do, Sir Simon Carlford. Do you acknowledge the irrelevance of the question, now that you have had time to consider it, or not?"

Carlford looked at the ceiling for a long moment, then down at his watch. "Possibly. In any event, in the interests of expedition I withdraw the question. Would Your Lordship consider this a suitable moment to break for lunch?"

36

Carlford's ploy could not have been more successful. When they had done with giggling at the comic diversion provided by Monkson's distress, the jury would spend the lunch break pondering the mysteries of lesbianism and discussing the outrageous choice of words by the very eminent Sir Simon Carlford. The first shock of seeing that photograph of Daisy would have been softened, perhaps even eclipsed. The effect would be reinforced when they saw the headlines of the evening newspaper they were not supposed to see but always did: EMINENT Q.C. ACCUSES WITNESS OF BEING BULL DYKE. The evidence of this witness would be forever tainted in their minds not because of her homosexuality but because she had been laughed at. Still more important, their faith in the competence of the prosecution was now permanently damaged.

As people filed out of the court, I signaled to someone in the public gallery who had caught my eye. He waited for me by the exit to the Old Bailey.

James Hogg's face and figure had collapsed into middle age. His smooth, heavy jowls were androgynous in their obesity, his once powerful body now enormous and walrus-like in the folds that filled his shirt. He was wearing a Roman collar.

"I half expected you," I told him.

"I was undecided whether to come or not. What decisions can a court of law make about matters of the soul?"

"So you've found God again?"

"Not again. Before, I had a religious posture merely. Oliver Thirst was one of God's instruments who made me see how wretched I was. In the end my lusts destroyed my pride, such are the mysterious ways of the spirit."

"And now?"

"Now I'm a fat and sexless spectator, as you see. But on my good days I walk with my God."

The streets were so crowded with people searching for lunch that our discussion was sometimes conducted over the heads of men and women who pushed between us. A woman turned and searched Hogg's face on overhearing him pronounce the word "God," then shrugged and turned away when she saw it was a clergyman.

He walked heavily, as if the gravitational pull on his immense bulk was almost beyond his powers to resist.

"I decided to come because I had a dream last night," he said. "Oliver was in it. In the dream he possessed exceptional beauty, like an angel. He was with a group of people like himself, who all seemed to be enjoying themselves. Then he turned from the group to speak to me. There was a small red hole in his forehead. He started to say something about Daisy, but I woke up."

We walked to a crowded sandwich bar. The urgency of people clamoring for lunch made a sharp contrast to the sedate progress of Daisy's trial. In the courtroom I had loathed every minute of the slow march of law, but now I found a passing nostalgia for it. The truth was that my nerves were jangled and I was in that state of mind in which one perpetually wishes to be elsewhere. In court I had felt hungry and in need of replenishing the nervous energy I was expending; now I could hardly bring myself to take two bites out of a small ham roll. Hogg, on the other hand, ordered a "super sandwich" with the confidence of a connoisseur. It consisted of two large slices of whole-meal bread that captured between them an inch and a half of ham, shredded chicken, avocado, lettuce, tomato, and mayonnaise. He had to open his mouth to the point of unhinging his jaw in order to take a bite. After each mouthful he pulled a fresh paper napkin from a holder to wipe the folds of his face. Even so, a tear-shaped blob of mayonnaise suddenly appeared on his black vestment.

"I envy Daisy for being on trial," he told me. "We all participated in his destruction in one form or another. I would have been honored if God had chosen me as the scapegoat."

"Leaving God aside, the law requires that you actually pull the trigger." My words were hard little bullets. "Participation—you need to participate in order to be honored by a trial for murder."

"Ah yes, your anger—I remember it now. You've always despised me; that was a help. But what about you? Have you still not come to doubt the basis of your righteousness? You must be nearly forty, after all."

He spoke between huge mouthfuls, so that his shrewd words formed a curious juxtaposition to the impression of stupefying gluttony. But where had he found the power to unlock in me all that cold anger?

We pushed our way out onto the busy street. The effort had made him pale.

"I shan't come back to court," he said. "I cannot be of any help there."

So it was to me alone that he had come to deliver his message. As we parted, he said, "By the way, in the dream it was clear, somehow, that Daisy was innocent."

37

After lunch, Carlford found that he had no questions at all for the Don Quixotrix. Since it was the end of the prosecution case, Carlford called his first witness.

It was the first time in my life that I had ever given evidence in a criminal trial, the first time I experienced firsthand the unutterable loneliness of standing in the witness box under the examining eye of a skeptical judge and a packed courtroom. The costumes, the heraldry, the swearing on the Bible, all these symbols have a magical affect on a psyche made vulnerable through isolation. The effect is a thousand times stronger when the story one has to tell is a fabrication from beginning to end.

I understood the importance of Feinberg's relentless drilling when I found that my response to Carlford's questions was automatic. The lie had become more real than the truth. I said that Daisy and I had been together all night on the night Thirst died. We had, of course, added details to make the whole thing credible (we had resumed our relationship a few months before, met secretly once a week, had spent a couple of weekends together in the country).

I could see Monkson conferring hurriedly with George Holmes just before he stood up. I felt an inexpressible relief that it was Monkson and not someone more competent who would cross-examine me.

"Mr. Knight, you are aware, are you not, that your conversation with Commander Holmes at your house that day was recorded by police technicians waiting in an unmarked van near your house?"

"Yes."

"Will it be necessary to recall Commander Holmes to produce the tape and testify as to its accuracy?"

"No."

"But, Mr. Knight, the account you gave to Commander Holmes, and which we find recorded for posterity, differs to a radical degree from the account you have only minutes ago given to this honorable court."

"I know."

"And out of these two conflicting accounts, which one do you select?"

"The one I've just given to the court."

"In other words, you claim to have lied to Commander Holmes?"

"Yes."

The obvious next question, the one old-fashioned schoolmasters always used to ask, was "If you lied then, why should we believe you now?" A more sophisticated barrister would have avoided it.

"But, Mr. Knight, if you, a member of the bar, admit to telling lies to Commander Holmes, why should this honorable court accord cwedence to your evidence now?"

The judge half closed his eyes as if in pain, but the jury were on the edge of their seats. It is not often that a barrister is cross-examined in a murder trial by another barrister.

I paused, as Feinberg had recommended, as if the question were difficult to answer. I began in a voice so quiet that the judge (wearily) asked me to speak up. I said it again, still fairly quietly but loud enough for the jury to hear.

"I didn't catch the answer to that question," Carlford complained on cue.

"Would you repeat the answer, please," the judge said. Unlike his exchanges with the other witnesses, he never used any polite form of address with me. In his eyes I had betrayed the glorious club of the bar, I was a traitor to the mess. In my case the war was no longer elsewhere. I suppose it never really had been.

"When Commander Holmes came to see me that day, I didn't know that Mrs. Thirst's freedom was at stake. Now I know it is."

Monkson saw the tempting cheese in the trap Feinberg and Carlford had set months before.

"Therefore, do you tell the court that at first you told untruths in order to protect your career and to hide the fact that you had recently been associated with the wife of a notorious criminal?"

"Yes."

I caught the gleam in Monkson's eye. "And now you say that your conscience has got the better of you and like Sir Galahad you have come forward to save Mrs. Thirst?"

"I've come forward to tell the truth."

"But you are in love with Mrs. Thirst, are you not?"

"Yes."

"Have been for over a decade?"

"Perhaps."

"And you will do anything to save her—anything at all?"

"No."

"Even lie in order to give her an alibi."

"No."

"Throw away your career, your integrity, your very character, to save her skin, so infatuated are you with her."

"No."

When I came down from the witness box I felt sick, but Feinberg sent a note to congratulate me. The first part of his plan had operated perfectly. Probably there was not a member of the jury who actually believed the alibi that I had given Daisy. But I had given the very best reason twelve goodhearted people could ever have for pretending to believe it. I was the lovesick saint, the archetypal good guy who is always around when the lady really needs him. The unexotic, unphallic, solid yeoman. Not a lot of fun but a good man to have children with. Now it was up to Daisy.

Feinberg made sure that before she mounted the witness stand she paraded her pregnancy in front of the jury. We had done what we could to ensure that the jury members were fathers and mothers themselves.

She was able to walk and stand with some, at least, of her former elegance. Pregnancy, too, had had a wonderful effect on her skin. She glowed like a young virgin. She had also reached the stage where her energy and attention were all on the baby, the world of men a matter of serene indifference. Everything about her bespoke a faith that providence could not possibly be so cruel as to send her to jail and separate her from her newborn child. Some of the jury were dewy-eyed before she spoke.

The judge, naturally, was anxious that she sit down. Carlford immediately pointed out that the stool in the witness stand did not have a back. The purpose of his stratagem arose from the curious fact that unlike any other court in the country, the witness at Number One Court at the Old Bailey stands or sits with her back to the jury, facing the judge. By persuading the judge to let Daisy come down from the witness stand as soon as she was sworn in—and sit in a chair in the well of the court at an angle so that both judge and jury could see her face—Carlford ensured that the glow of motherhood was never out of the jury's sight.

Anxious ushers brought her water. The subtleties of Carlford's maneuvers were all lost on Monkson, who was working furiously on his notes for cross-examination. He was the kind of barrister who would scribble, "If witness says (a) below then ask question (i); if witness says (b) then ask question (ii)."

Carlford took her quickly through her early relationship with me, the first meetings with Thirst, the death of her mother, our estrangement, which led to her marriage to Thirst. As Feinberg had coached her to tell it, this was not so much a marriage on the rebound as a giving in to the relentless pressure from the lovesick Thirst. She had known, of course, of his criminal record, but one had to remember that he presented—Carlford's word—at that stage as a reformed character. Thirst's image from those days floated in front of my mind as she spoke: confused, book-haunted, and frighteningly earnest.

"Those of us who spend their careers in the field of criminal law come to look, let us say, skeptically upon claims by hardened criminals that they have reformed," Carlford said. "Was there any particular reason for you to suppose that Oliver Thirst, whom you knew to have been a criminal since childhood, had genuinely changed his ways?"

Daisy first looked down at the floor with a frown. It seemed almost as if she would not answer the question, or perhaps had not heard it. Finally she raised her head and said with a shrug, "Love."

There was a hush over the courtroom while we waited for her to carry on. Even the judge leaned forward. When it was clear she did not intend to elaborate, Carlford said, "Yes, I think I understand, but perhaps for the sake of clarity you would expand your answer a little."

Now Daisy looked across the jury with a sweep of her eyes, glanced at Carlford, and settled on the judge.

"It's very hard to talk about, isn't it? I loved him. And he was a soul who lived in hell. Sooner or later you have to at least try. I mean, if you love, if you feel love, you have to believe it has the power to save someone, even if you're not a Christian. Otherwise what's the purpose of living?"

Carlford waited for this answer to sink in. "I see. You felt that your love was a kind of insurance against your husband's recidivism?"

"If you must put it like that." She glared at his slightly cynical choice of words. "I was determined to be a good wife. I was faithful, caring. I put a lot into it, our marriage. I put everything into it. I was sure at the time that I was strong enough to change him."

"But it's right to say, isn't it, that from the start there was a shadow over your marriage?"

"Yes."

"And that shadow took what form?"

"James Knight."

Thirst, it appeared, was obsessed with me. Sometimes she wondered if he had only married her as a perverse way of reaching me. He constantly demanded her reassurance that he was a better lover. But there were whole areas of aspiration in which I had ten years on him. He frequently talked about me and at each difficult turn of the road asked her what I would have done. There was a mystery in his obsession with me that she never penetrated or understood.

"But not to put too fine a point on it, Mrs. Thirst, yours would not have been the first marriage in which one of the partners had a history unpalatable to the other. Was there anything else that, with hindsight, might have doomed the relationship from the outset?"

"He was bent!" Her voice was unexpectedly loud and cracked. She stared at the jury, ticking them off one by one with her eyes. "Nobody knows what that word means until they've lived with it. Everything he did, every thought he had, every word, every relationship, was bent, twisted, perverse. Even when it was in his own interests, he couldn't be straight. He couldn't even fill in a form for council housing without trying to be clever, lying. I found out. When someone's psyche is twisted, it twists everything around it. My husband couldn't be straight to save his life."

Carlford nodded. "Nevertheless, your life together continued for some years?"

I winced at the description of their life which emerged. They drank cheap cider and made love all the time. She was still broken and vulnerable from her mother's death and her breakup from me, and sought solace in sex. Her strange, American psychology, which at first he had found exotic, was confusing and infuriating to him. As she turned to him once in postcoital gratification, she found that he was staring at her with cold curiosity.

"Christ, you make me sick sometimes, Yankee."

It was an early indication of the extremes of violence which raged within him.

Carlford wanted to dwell further on Thirst's character and history. Through Daisy's lips he painted a portrait of Thirst that anyone could believe. He took us through Thirst's early aspirations, triggered by me. A career in law was obviously out of the question, but he was not prepared for the doors of other professions to be shut in his face as soon as his past began to be revealed. Whoever the liberals were, they did not seem to be running the country after all. Daisy, with genuine sorrow, described his depressing journey from courageous optimism to despair and from there to the fury that lies beyond despair—to the animal at bay. Out of more than five hundred applications for jobs (they ranged from trainee social worker to publisher's assistant to transport coordinator for a firm of minicabs to editor of a monthly journal for ex-convicts), he was called for interview twice and on both occasions was paralyzed with nerves.

He held fast for two years, at the end of which he began to disappear at odd hours and have more money in his pockets. The maudlin note of despair that had begun to dominate his mood was replaced by a new tension that exploded whenever he drank too much—which was often.

"And what effect did this transformation have on you?" Carlford's voice was tender and respectful.

"At first I welcomed it," Daisy said. "I thought that even if he was doing something dishonest, he was at least doing *something* again. And he had found his anger at least. He wasn't just passive and bleeding anymore."

"And did you continue to welcome this new mood?"

Daisy paused before answering. "Not when he started to beat me up—no, I didn't."

This was a matter that Carlford went into at length. Violence and the fear of it formed an obvious motive in the eyes of the prosecution, and it was standard practice for defense counsel to steal the prosecutor's thunder by bringing out in evidence-in-chief what might otherwise emerge in a more damaging form under cross-examination. But Carlford went much further. He seemed to be possessed by a reptilian fascination with Thirst's sadism.

I had noticed the judge sending increasingly irritated glances toward Monkson while he continued to scribble his cross-examination points. Then all of a sudden Monkson seemed to wake up. He threw Carlford a suspicious look, grew red in the face as he realized he needed to make another objection. He stood up slowly this time, his confusion under control. Carlford sat down.

"My Lord, I do not pretend to understand the gravamen of this portion of my friend's examination-in-chief. He appears to be establishing a motive for murder on the part of his own client."

"It is puzzling, I agree," the judge said. The ice in his voice suggested that he was anything but puzzled.

"My Lord," Monkson continued, "I hesitate to criticize any of

Her Majesty's counsel with the experience and reputation of my learned friend, but . . ."

I heard the gallery hold their breath in anticipation of another blunder. I felt a professional compassion for him. Carlford was scrupulously obeying the rules, but with the ethics of a fox. It was not an easy objection to formulate, and poor Monkson was not the man to carry it off.

". . . but . . ."

"Yes?" the judge said.

"I mean, why is he doing this?"

The judge shook his head at Monkson as if at a disappointing child. He shot a cold glance at Carlford, who was standing up again.

"Well, Sir Simon Carlford, why are you doing this?"

Carlford looked up at the judge with undisguised contempt. "The categories of permissible objections are well known to Your Lordship. Nothing my friend has said can be made to fit, even with the best will in the world, into any of them. As to Your Lordship's question, why, I am using the best of my professional endeavors to present my client's case. I take it Your Lordship has no objection to that? This is a jury trial after all, and the jury will be required to judge the facts for themselves without any interference from the bench."

This time there was a sharp gasp from the gallery. The judge, though, an old pro, knew that Carlford had won. He could not be seen to favor the prosecution case, even if it was presented by an incompetent.

"Very well, Sir Simon Carlford, pray continue." The judge slouched in his high-back chair, his fingers steepled, his mouth pinched.

Carlford nodded once as if acknowledging an inevitable concession from an inferior player, and turned back to Daisy.

Feinberg had drilled her well; her performance was immaculate. With dignity and a minimum of adjectives, she described the last year of their life together. Her narrative style had been rather different the first time Feinberg forced her to remember those horrors.

It had been soon after she had been charged with the murder.

Feinberg made it clear that she would have to describe Thirst's cruelties in detail, but with restraint—above all she must not crack at the trial and look like a crazed killer, something that could easily happen if she was reliving those experiences for the first time in the witness box.

"So let's have it," Feinberg had said.

We were sitting across from him on the clients' side of his desk. I looked at Daisy. She seemed confused. After a short silence Feinberg, with a curl of his lips, said, "Looks like I'll have to help you. Let's start with the buggery—most heavy criminals are compulsive sodomites. Hurt, did it? Make you bleed?"

Daisy whitened, stared at him for a few seconds, then jumped up. She ran out of his office.

"You cunt, Feinberg," I said, before running after her. I grabbed her arm as she was opening the glass door to the street. She stared at me.

"We'll get you a drink," I said.

"Sorry," she said after she'd finished the brandy I'd bought her. "I just wasn't ready for that this morning."

"Of course you weren't. He's a very crude man, and a twisted one. But he does have his methods. He's basically right."

"I know. But I can't just sit there looking at all those sadistic twitches and tell him things—things I haven't even told you."

"Then why not start by telling me?"

She looked at me for a moment.

"It'll be easier to show you. Somehow I just can't face trying to describe it with you looking at me. We'll get a taxi. If we take your car they'll just smash it up."

"Take a taxi where?"

38

The address she gave to the driver was in Hackney. "Chaucer House in the Sunningdale Estate."

A vast vertical dormitory, an instant slum where a dehumanized workforce could sleep and copulate, the Sunningdale development was one of many such, built in a hurry in the sixties. Most of the buildings were empty now. The construction had been so cheap, the quality of the concrete so poor, that even by Hackney's standards the place had become largely uninhabitable. In a lift smelling of urine, she took me to the twenty-fifth floor of Chaucer House.

"How d'you know we'll be able to get in?"

"Someone will have broken in, the lock will be smashed," she said. Then, when we had walked the few paces down the corridor: "Told you." The front door of 25-D was hanging off its hinges. I followed her into the main hall of the empty flat.

"Welcome to my bed of nails."

"I suppose it was not quite so bad with furniture," I said.

"What furniture? We couldn't afford any, except a mattress on the floor I had to turn every day because it rotted and stank. He never did a thing. Nor did I in the end—just watched the mushrooms grow. We were desperately poor. He was too jealous and possessive to let me work, and he'd only just started to deal drugs. Look." She pointed to a large purple fungus emerging from a crack in the wall. "You see, you have entered a different country. Everything has a different meaning in this place. Take doors, for example—"

"Daisy, I don't think this is good for you—"

"Don't interrupt. Take doors. To someone like you, I expect doors are for entering and leaving a room. You let women go first, make sure small children don't get their little fingers trapped. But you're wrong. Suppose, like now, you are following someone you love, someone you're trying to get close to, a few paces behind— yes, like that. Well, this is what doors are for."

She kicked the door behind her with her heel. I just had time to raise my hands to stop it hitting me in the face.

"More of doors later. Let's go to the kitchen, so I can show you what hot plates are for. You've guessed. Not necessarily to burn a person's flesh, you understand, more to exploit the possibilities of menace they offer. It's done like this. You'll have to pretend I'm ten times stronger than you."

She grabbed some hair at the back of my head. I allowed her to force my head down so that my face was close to the hot plate.

"Imagine it's red hot and you can smell your hair starting to burn."

She let go. She was pale again and starting to shake.

"Daisy, this—"

"No. We have to go through it all, just as the wise Mr. Feinberg says. Bathrooms are next. You think that bathrooms are for washing and relaxing? Perhaps to have fun in with lovers from time to time? Wrong, my friend. This is what baths are for. You fill the bath, d'you see, then you make your wife kneel on the floor and you force her head down into the water. There's a peculiar gratification, apparently, in fucking your wife from behind while she's half drowning. And buggering her, of course—as Mr. Feinberg so as-tutely points out."

"Daisy, you're shaking so badly. I think—"

"We can't stop now; suppose I get like this at trial? Where was I? Ah yes, back to doors. Such useful things. First you open it, like so, then you force a person's fingers into the gap like this, then you close it again, quite slowly—am I hurting you yet? Quite slowly, till all the fingers break, one by one if possible, unless two or three snap at the same time. At the more advanced stage you trap your wife's fingers in the door and you put your foot behind it like this so it can't open, then you grab her by the hair and with your spare hand you do what you've been looking forward to doing for years. You hit her in the face with your big hard fist over and over again because her face is delicate and beautiful and beautiful things must be mutilated. . . ."

In the taxi home, Daisy had finally allowed herself to burst into tears. She held me close.

"It was when I'd been crying. I said, 'D'you know why I cry, Oliver? I cry because James hit me once and that little slap hurt him so much I was the one who apologized, and now I'm married to a man who can torture me and actually enjoy it.' That's when he smashed my face in. . . . Of course, by then I already knew I could never let myself have his child. It would have been a monster, like him. So you see, I didn't get what I wanted at all. Not at all."

39

"And now, Mrs. Thirst," Carlford was saying, "happily, thanks to the surgeon's skill, nothing remains of those horrific injuries but some well-healed scars?"

In a masterstroke of theater, Carlford made her waddle past the jury with her chin up to show them the hairline scars under the jawbone. I would guess that there was not a member of the jury who did not see those old scars inflicted by a man now dead as a threat to the unborn child.

"Finally, Mrs. Thirst, please tell the court what his last words to you were, on the day that you left him for good."

"He said that he would find me, and when he found me he would kill me."

After that her alibi was hardly more than an afterthought. He took her through it with perfunctory speed, as if it were a kind of wink at the jury—this is the vehicle we have provided for you

to set her free. The lady foreman nodded conscientiously as Daisy trotted out the Feinberg fabrication. It was, even for Carlford, a masterpiece. There was probably not a member of the jury who believed her to be innocent of the charge of murder. Nor was there anyone in court who did not feel in his heart that the homicide was justified. With a craft that was almost seamless, Carlford had created in the minds of the jury exactly the claustrophobic, sadistic, and insufferable domestic situation in which so many ordinary people, especially women, can imagine themselves committing murder. Behind Monkson's back, and before the helpless glare of the judge, Carlford had played the English vice of fairness for all it was worth.

He ended with the small matter of the gun. It had been carefully taped, and therefore no fingerprints had been found on it. But to be frank, it did look very much like the gun she was holding in that photograph.

"It probably *is* the same gun," Daisy said, a little wearily. "It was his gun that I used to take to the firing range. He kept it locked in a drawer. I used to steal the key, use the gun, then put it back. I don't think he ever knew."

"And what was your purpose in developing the martial arts and shooting small arms?"

"I wasn't going to let him beat me up again. Never."

Carlford sat down. Monkson rose to his feet in order to walk into our final trap.

"Even if that meant killing him, Mrs. Thirst?"

"I believe I have a right to live in peace, Mr. Monkson."

Carlford and Monkson made their final speeches to the jury, the judge summed up. For all his chivalry, I knew he had seen through us, and his last words to the jury sent a shiver down my spine.

"In just a very few moments you will retire from this court to the jury room, where you will remain until you have reached your verdict. In so doing, it is your duty to cast ruthlessly out of your minds all thought of sympathy, all natural tenderness normal people feel for a woman in the defendant's condition." Here he leaned forward toward the jury. "Still more importantly, you must cast out of your minds any compassion for the defendant arising from the history of domestic violence she apparently endured at the hands of the deceased. You must, instead, weigh the facts in your mind and decide, quite simply: did she kill her husband or not?"

40

Daisy's bail had been renewed daily, so that she had been able to come home with me every night, not that this had made intimacy possible between us. All our energies, all our thoughts, were sucked into the terrible psychic vortex of the trial. Not only had we stopped making love; Daisy avoided eye contact. But there is not a judge in the world, of course, who will grant bail to a defendant while the jury is considering its verdict in a murder trial. And so two women officers of the Prison Service took her away. She gave me one long look before she went.

I found myself fingering the thick sheaf of papers in my jacket pocket and was tempted to give them immediately to George Holmes and be done with the whole thing. Holmes saw me fingering the papers, and out of the corner of my eye I caught Feinberg staring at Holmes staring at me. Feinberg suspected at least one person in this trial of being more devious than himself and wanted badly to know who it was. I stood up jerkily—all my movements for the next few days would be involuntary, as if caused by an accumulation of energy in joints such as knees and elbows that could make a limb spring irrelevantly to life—and walked out into the dirty London street.

I was restless and needed to exercise, even if it meant missing the verdict. In fact, I experienced a temptation to simply run and keep running. As it was, I walked everywhere at lightning speed, propelled by the adrenaline that was flooding my bloodstream.

I passed a billboard for the evening newspaper that said VERDICT IN BARRISTER MURDER TRIAL TODAY. Because my mind was incapable of focusing on anything except Daisy in her cell, I did automatically things I had been doing in that part of London for half a lifetime. I went to a tiny café where you could buy espresso if you were prepared to sit on a stool with your nose almost touching the wall. I reread the papers in my pocket, despite the fact that I knew every word of them by heart. There were in fact two sets of papers: a letter addressed to George Holmes, with a copy to Nigel Monkson, Esq., Q.C., Barrister at Law. One way or another, Daisy was going to be free before nightfall. "Important trial on today, Mr. Knight?" The Italian proprietor of the café, who had a cockney accent, liked to know all the court gossip. Perhaps he had not read the papers. Perhaps he was merely being discreet.

"Oh yes, quite important."

The proprietor eyed me strangely when I was leaving. It was only a few days later that I remembered with a twinge of shame that I had forgotten to pay for my coffee. If honesty is a form of social conditioning, then by and large the system succeeded in my case.

On London Bridge, I found myself looking east toward the Tower, where it had all started. Except that it was no longer a glorious morning full of promise. It was late afternoon and beginning to drizzle. Was it me, or was there something about London that makes us tired of life? A bizarre emotion to have in the circumstances. My sudden fury was not with Thirst or Holmes or Daisy or even myself but with the whole city. Many people said it in different ways: to live in London is to live in a heavier element, as if under water. Each movement, each flexing of the muscles, requires an extra effort for which the human frame was not designed. In the end it exhausts us, and we join the other empty shadows who flit hurriedly past in the street, out of the underground and into the office, with the shadow's shyness of the light. In the distance, Big Ben struck the three-quarter hour.

Carlford paced the corridor outside Number One Court. Feinberg seethed. Both looked ready to murder me. Only George Holmes, further down the corridor, gave me a sheepish nod. No one had expected the jury to be out that long, least of all George. Then out of nowhere Monkson appeared, with all his comic repertoire of narcissistic gestures, his anger with Carlford quite forgotten, and in spite of it all I found myself smiling. Being, like Daisy, a sucker for kindness, he walked toward me.

"I just wanted to tell you that I hope you feel that I've pwosecuted this twial fairly and that there are no hard feelings."

"None, Nigel," I said. "I think you've done a fine job."

He broke into a reckless smile before remembering that he was an eminent Q.C. and decided to confer with his junior. Then, all of a sudden, the usher called us back into court. This time I sat next to Feinberg as the jury trooped in. Daisy was brought back from the cells. All the women and some of the men looked her harshly in the eye as they took their seats.

"They've been punishing her," Feinberg whispered triumphantly. "They took this long just to punish her."

"Has the jury reached a verdict?" the chief usher asked loudly. The woman foreman said that it had.

"And what is your verdict?"

"Not guilty."

"And is that a verdict of you all?"

"It is."

As she said it she gave Daisy a severe glance.

It is a feature of the legal system in democratic countries that the defendant must be set free the moment a verdict of not guilty is delivered, for there is no longer any constitutional power to hold her against her will. The prison officers opened the gate to the barred box where she was held, and she walked away in a state of shock. The judge walked out. Ignoring Daisy, I made a bolt for the door, aware of George Holmes's heavy tread behind me.

He followed me down to the barristers' changing room, where an attendant greeted me—thinking I was involved in some case of my own, no doubt. George was still lumbering breathlessly behind me.

"I'm sorry, sir," the attendant said. "No police officers are allowed in here—only members of the bar." George barged past him.

I was standing by the sink, setting fire to the sheaf of papers I'd been carrying with a small gas lighter I had bought for that purpose. The sheets turned into hot flames for a moment, then into frail wisps, then, finally, into a squalid mess of black water when I turned on the tap. George stood watching.

"They were the only copies, George. You have my word."

"Still, I would have liked to read them first." He looked at me. Old age and exhaustion had crumpled his features. "It's all over, then."

"Oh yes, George. All of it."

41

Daisy had refused to look at my letter to George until the trial was over. She'd said she would never be able to go through with it if she knew what had really happened. On the other hand, she was entitled to some measure of security. I had hit upon the idea of letting her keep the disk whose secret bytes contained the text of my account. She took out the disk in the taxi on the way home and looked at it.

"How do you feel?" I said.

"Terrified. Terrified by what might have gone wrong, terrified by what I'm going to find out. I never thought I would be crazy enough to go through all that for a man. Everyone on that jury thinks I'm a murderess."

She seemed not so much terrified as angry, like someone who is conscious of having given too much. I touched her hand. She turned her head away from me, watching the dull wet streets go by. "I hope you're satisfied."

As soon as we reached home I locked and bolted the front door, then for double measure locked the door to my study behind us. Daisy gave me back the disk, which I inserted in the computer. A quick manipulation of the keys threw up the first words on the screen.

Dear George,

This is the confession you hoped never to receive. As you will see from the last page, I have given a copy to Nigel Monkson, who is probably reading it at the same time as you. I know he will ensure that Daisy is set free as soon as possible and that I'm charged with Thirst's murder. George, my purpose here is not to tell you that I killed him; you've known that from the start. My purpose is to set down such a mass of incriminating detail that no one will doubt that I did it.

Poor George, you are so far gone you imagine that everyone in the world must be bent. You really did think that I would let Daisy go down in my stead. Worse than that, when you came to see me that Sunday, you expected me to welcome your mad ploy as a way of exacting revenge for what she did eleven years ago. You're mad, George, quite mad. Of all the unsettling truths which Thirst turned up in his passage across our lives, your madness is the strangest and most frightening.

You manipulated him, George. He was your greatest betrayal, the man you loathed and loved. You bent him in your own image.

You knew I was the one who killed him because you had been tapping his telephone, illegally and probably for more than a decade. There was nothing in his life that you didn't know, and you guessed that he told me all about you on the night that he died. When I pretended, on the Sunday, to confess, you knew exactly what I was saying: charge me and I will tell all. What a twist that you thought you would be

doing me a favor by charging Daisy. And then, in a
panic, to see that Nigel Monkson was briefed in the
hope that he would lose the case. I would be curious
to know exactly when it dawned on you that I had
found something more important to me than my own
skin, that I would not let Daisy go down for me.

I showed Daisy how to manipulate the keys of the computer to
shift the text up and down the screen and left her to read on. What
could she possibly make of it? I realized now that the letter pre-
supposed a wealth of knowledge on the part of the reader. Only
George could really understand it.

I crossed the room to the window, half expecting to find George
with his trilby and pipe standing in the front garden, staring in.
But the garden and the street were empty. The drizzle had turned
into a steady rain, which had cleared the pavements of people. It
must have been the release of tension after Daisy's acquittal that
allowed a long-suppressed image to float, or rather jerk, to the top
of my mind. In my first sober hallucination, I saw Thirst lying in
the street across from my house, a small black hole in his head.
The hallucination was particularly realistic because his clothes were
soaked from the rain—as they had not been on the night I killed
him. I closed my eyes tight, and when I opened them again he was
gone. I shuddered.

I knew what was wrong with my account, the account that
Daisy was reading with such close attention. If I could, I would
have produced a narrative that conveyed the texture of all that led
up to his death. I would have begun by telling her about the telephone calls.

The first took place a good twelve months before he died. Of
course I had heard of him from time to time over the years, as had
most people involved in the criminal law. After a long period of
poverty, when he was attempting to go straight, he eventually became one of those villains who appear in every generation and are
able to charm the decadent of high society. He was the purveyor
of fine drugs whom every cocaine-sniffing debutante boasted of
knowing. Magazines for the glitterati sometimes carried a picture

of him in tuxedo at a party for wealthy rock stars and young aristocracy.

For a period he was styled as a famous pop star's business manager, but everyone knew what that meant. It was sometimes said that he was mountainously rich. It was also said that he was permanently broke. He loved expensive cars—Jaguars were his favorite—and seemed always to be losing his license for speeding around Knightsbridge and Kensington late at night. In many of the drug prosecutions that I undertook for George, Thirst's name was somewhere in the background, a shadow behind the scenes.

If I thought about him in a personal context at all, I suppose it was to assume that he wore a triumphant grin at my expense. In his own terms he had won. He was wealthier, flashier, more glamorous, drove more expensive cars. What's more, he had got the girl. My one small consolation was that in order to succeed he had become a cliché of English society—the handsome working-class crook selling drugs and sex to fallen Brahmins.

And then, out of the blue, he telephoned.

It was, inevitably, in the early hours of the morning, and I assumed, at first, that it was a solicitor with some frantic message about a trial due to start the following day. What baffled me for at least five minutes was the voice. There was a queer flatness to it, such as is said to occur when people try to change their accents. I realized that even during his scholarly phase I had enjoyed his cockney vowels. The voice on the end of the line that night was a bloodless ghost of its former self. To my own surprise, when I finally realized who it was, I found that I was pleased to hear from him.

I forgot for a moment my resentment and welcomed the exotic promise that he always managed to convey. My life had been very dull of late. And then, of all the people who might have called me, in his case there was the unusual luxury of my owing him nothing—not even courtesy. I drew my legs up under the covers and listened. It was obvious that he was under the influence of some drug; in addition to being flat, the voice had a slightly eerie quality.

"Just thought I'd phone. Surprised, huh? Yeah, well, a lot's happened. You know she left? Must be over four years ago. Can't really blame her—I was a bastard. I was never cut out for marriage anyway. I suppose I only wanted her because you had her. She was the only thing of yours I could pinch that you would have cared about—your trophy. There, I've said it. You must have guessed it anyway. Always ten jumps ahead. Christ, I wish I was like you. I'd like to swap places with you for a week. If you knew what it was like to be me, you wouldn't hate me—you'd pity me. I'd give up ten years just to be you for one year, but I'm finished, James—totally finito. He's in trouble and can't afford to cover for me this time, so he's going to let me go down. But I'm not going to. I'm not going back to jail, James; I'd rather do myself in."

The voice continued in that vein for some minutes, then abruptly stopped as the receiver was replaced.

I mused dreamily on the strange mutations thrown up by each turn of the wheel, then dozed off into a light sleep full of the most pleasant dreams that I had dreamed for years. They possessed a quality of weightlessness, a feeling of total release from the prison of gravity. It was when I was shaving the next day—something to do with seeing the no longer young face in the mirror—that I remembered the call in a state of normal consciousness. There was the mysterious "he," whose identity was not so difficult to figure out, though the implications were awesome.

Then the night call was driven away by the remorseless business of the day. A female bank clerk had succumbed to the temptation of embezzlement, a small sum but a clever scam. She did it out of boredom and to prove she was not as unintelligent as her boss seemed to think. It was not until I was sitting in my car in a traffic jam on the Victoria Embankment about a hundred yards from Waterloo Bridge that Thirst came back to mind. It was already evening; under streetlights, people hurried to the tube. I resigned myself to a long wait while police in riding boots and helmets dealt with the traffic. My memory opened up, and I heard the voice again in my ear: "I suppose I only wanted her because you had her. . . . There, I've said it." It was not only the content, it was also the tone that was so surprising. I searched for an adjective. Impotent, I decided. The voice, against all expectations, had lost virility.

"Daisy," I said, "you poor sucker." I smiled into the rearview mirror.

About a week later I was again awakened in the middle of the night. The voice was much the same, though on this occasion it possessed the harshness of sobriety.

"Did I phone you the other night? I seem to remember doing something like that. I was stoned, of course, probably came out with a load of crap."

"I'm sure you're going to deny all of it."

There was a pause.

"No. It was probably true, just not worth saying. You're going to think I'm a cunt until the day I die."

I endorsed this comment with silence.

"I'm not asking for help, but I'm in trouble this time. I'm going to be sacrificed. Someone very big in the Old Bill has noticed that everyone seems to get done except me. He says I'll have to go down just to make it look better. Reckons he can make it easy—say, four years in the library at the Scrubs. But I'm not going to. I'm never going back to gaol, James—never. Did I ever tell you that before?"

It took me a moment to realize the question was a form of cockney irony and that the "he" was not the same as the "someone very big." By that time Thirst had hung up.

Those two calls established a rhythm that continued for a few months. He would telephone in a state of advanced narcotic poisoning, as the forensic scientists put it, and blurt out his heart. A week or so later he would remember the call and phone me again, this time to try to find out what he had told me when intoxicated. The theme of his being in trouble featured in each call. I never encouraged or discouraged him from calling; the mysterious monologues in the dead of night added a fresh dimension to the dreary pattern of my bachelor life.

Looking back, I'm struck that we were like two exceptionally coy dancers growing closer only by the tiniest increments. It was four or five months before we actually met. Again it was late at night, and he arrived on my doorstep almost incoherent from whatever drugs he was using. I have no rational explanation for the fact that I let him in without argument. Except perhaps to say that I had come to identify with the tense, incorporeal voice of the night.

His entrance into my house was something of an anticlimax. I must have expected him to be impressed. He seemed disappointed. My furnishings, apparently, were not up to the standard to which he'd grown accustomed. Such silver and crystal as I possessed were, it seemed, substandard. And he disliked even expensive reproductions. In the midst of his ramblings—a mixture of remorse, braggadocio, and terror—he claimed to have known a man who had briefly owned the original *Sunflowers* by van Gogh. Four or five personalities fought for possession of his body—fatter than eleven years before but still impressive. At least one of them was a snob of the nouveau riche variety. Another claimed, as he was leaving, that I was the only person in the world he'd ever really loved.

"I bet you say that to all the boys," I said on the doorstep. He broke into a broad cockney chuckle and hugged me sentimentally for a moment before walking away to his car, an unexpectedly modest Mini. I wondered if he'd stolen it.

His visit to my house must have signified a high point in our *dance macabre,* for it was at least two months before I heard from him again. During that time I picked up with a girl who was to be the last of my transient lovers. Ironically, she might have come closer than any of the others to sharing the rest of my life, were it not for the undisguised desperation with which she longed to start a family.

She was in her mid-thirties and had begun to describe her single state as the consequence of too much feminism in her youth. With startling honesty she explained that a long hard look at the daunting wasteland of freedom had eventually sent her scuttling in search of a position of economic slavery from which to reproduce in peace and security. She amused me with her frankness, and we discussed at length the process by which unbeknownst to myself I had passed from the category of politically unacceptable to eligible bachelor.

Like scientific field-workers, we compared notes on some of the

less-charted aspects of promiscuity. It was a way, we agreed, of
making friends. There was something not quite trustworthy about
someone you had never been to bed with. For a moment in time I
found myself looking forward to a compromise state of sex and
friendship, where the old, foolish idea of passion was mentioned
ironically in the context of an emotional toy long since outgrown.

Then Thirst telephoned and inadvertently caused the argument
that led to our final parting. Again the phone rang in the middle
of the night, and she answered before I could reach the receiver.
He had already hung up by the time I was ready to take the call.

"You should have let me take it," I said.

"Why? Who's Daisy? Whoever it was seemed to think I was
Daisy and hung up. It was a man—friend of the family?"

It was not her passing jealousy that caused the end of the affair.
It was everything the name Daisy evoked. Like a superior magic,
the mere name was able to dispel, in an instant, the enthusiasm I
had tried to muster for the girl next to me in the bed. The incident
furnished dramatic proof, too, of what he had already told me: that
Daisy and he were no longer together. Hope reawakened within
me like a wound.

I had grown skillful in the art of rejection and contrived,
somehow, never to see the girl again. For that reason I was alone,
once more, the next time he phoned. On this occasion he sounded
more drunk than stoned.

"That was Daisy, wasn't it, the other night?"

"Well, yes," I said, though her voice possessed virtually no re-
semblance to Daisy's. No doubt his deranged state was responsible
for his mistake.

There was a long pause. "I told her that if she went back to
you ever, I'd kill her. And you."

"Aren't you a little old, Oliver, for that kind of talk?"

Another pause. "Yeah, you could be right, old son. Can't say it
doesn't hurt, though. Silly, isn't it? I don't really want her, but I
can't stand for you to have her. The thought of you two living
happily ever after, talking about poor Oliver, stupid Oliver, fetching
and carrying in the Scrubs, being rogered by buck niggers and thick
Irishmen—it makes me want to puke. No, I'm lying. I'll tell you
what it makes me want to do. It makes me want to die."

Now it was my turn to say nothing. After a while he hung up, but the call was a signal that communication had been resumed. He continued to telephone about once a week, sometimes drunk or stoned, sometimes edgily sober. In addition to the previous themes of being in trouble and thinking a lot of me, there was the new concern about Daisy and me. I made no attempt to put him out of his misery.

When I saw him again it was the night of his death.

I glanced back at Daisy, who was staring intensely at the computer screen. I was embarrassed about the way I had written my confession; it was so full of "George this" and "George that," it struck me now as mawkish. What was she thinking? Would Thirst come between us in death as he had in life? It is impossible to murder someone in the late twentieth century, I can report, without wondering what lifelong price one may have to pay. It is not a question of guilt so much as a question of having committed an act that stands outside the pale of contemporary experience.

I crossed to the other side of the room and stood behind her. The last few paragraphs of my letter were glowing in the screen. I began to read them with her, but they described his last night with less detail than it deserved. Memory supplied the color. I dropped my eyes from the screen while she stared, transfixed.

He had awakened me again, and for the last time, in the early hours of the morning. I opened the door, knowing that it was unlikely to be anyone other than him—and stood back a step. He had lost weight over the past months and in the darkness cast a younger silhouette. I even fancied that he grinned in the old way—the street-urchin grin that said he, at least, knew where the open window by the drainpipe could be found. In his hand he held a gun.

It was a small-caliber pistol, and he was pointing it at me.

"You're pointing a gun at me, Oliver."

He looked down curiously at it, as if it had appeared there by accident a moment before.

"Yeah. I think of it as Daisy's gun. She used to pinch it from time to time and go on shooting practice with a bunch of dykes somewhere in Suffolk. She thought I didn't know. Used to make me laugh."

Now that he had spoken a full sentence I could tell that he was drugged again. Or if not drugged, then in some strange somnambulant state.

He looked thoughtful. "I want us to go for a ride—in your car. I hear you've got a nice new Jag."

"I'm not dressed, Oliver," I said, touching my dressing gown.

"Ah, right. Better get dressed, then. I'll watch."

He followed me into the house and up the stairs to my bedroom. I was suddenly conscious, of all things, of my small bookcase with the glass doors that held my mother's books. The thought that I might never see it again gave it a surreal glow, as if my fear had made it luminescent.

He must have had an uncanny perception of what was going on in my mind, for he walked over to the bookcase to touch it. He then proceeded to open its small glass doors and take out the book that was dearest to me: *The Golden Treasury of English Verse*. I felt sure that he was about to commit some sort of malicious dismantling of my identity prior to the destruction of my body. Instead he caressed it.

"This is you, isn't it?" He set the book down on the case. "I always wondered why I never really reached you, what kept you together. It was this. A silly little book. You got stuck somewhere in a romantic teenage fantasy—about women, about the world. And you fed the fantasy with books of poems. But poems can't stop a bullet, old son. Get dressed."

"Are you really going to stand there and watch?"

"Yeah."

He stared at me as I slipped off my dressing gown and bent over for some underpants.

"Stop. Freeze. That's just the position, Jimmy, just the position. In prison—you know, when they're going to roger you—they make you bend over. Just like that. They use soap or Vaseline. And a couple of blokes on either side to hold you down. They're experts, Jimmy, experts."

He spoke slowly, in a hallucinatory drawl.

"Can I get dressed now?" I said.

"Yeah. Don't fancy you after all. Too skinny, except for that rotten little potbelly. You look better in a suit."

I dragged on some trousers. My hands were shaking wildly. When I was dressed, he gestured with the gun that I should go first down the stairs. He seemed to know where my lock-up garage was and waited while I pulled up the horizontal swing door. I got into the driver's seat. I wished I could drive off—possibly crushing him against the wall—and cursed myself for my squeamishness.

He got in beside me and looked around with a connoisseur's eye.

"Nice motor. Always did like this model. Got class, James— like you."

"Where are we going?"

"Anywhere. Don't mind, really. Where's the best street to die in around here?"

I shuddered. "You're not really going to kill me, are you?" Terror was doing nothing for my repartee.

He looked at me curiously. "Scared, huh? Green balls running down your trouser legs? Been like that for over a year, me. I'm not scared now, though. Matter of fact, I feel wonderfully relaxed. Wonderfully."

"That's because you're holding the gun."

He smiled. "Yeah—at last. Old Oliver is finally holding the gun. Not much of one—a peashooter. Have to get you between the eyes at point-blank range. Even then you'll probably get off with a headache. Trust my luck—when I finally do get to hold the gun, it's shrunk to the size of a peashooter. If I'd have been smart like you, I would have gone for those big invisible guns—the unde-tectable guns you men at law always carry around with you, the ones you've been pointing at me all my life. You know?"

"Yes, Oliver—I know."

I reversed out of the garage and drove aimlessly down the deserted streets. The Jag gave a smooth ride, which soothed me a little. As I drove, he began to talk about George Holmes. I en-couraged him. *One Thousand and One Nights.*

"Embarrassing, when I finally discovered what all those words mean that the shrinks and probation officers use—very embarrassing. It's like being a thalidomide cripple—everyone's heard of it and everyone wants to look. I needed a surrogate father, didn't I? And there he was, Detective Sergeant George Holmes, waiting for me on an old bomb site when I was twelve years old, burning alive with lust and ambition. Dear old father Holmes, more bent than any man I ever met—inside or out. Of course, no one's ever taken *his* psychological profile. And he made me in his own image, James. Oh Christ, I can't believe this."

I assumed "this" was the tears sliding down his cheeks. He wiped them away with the back of the hand that held the gun.

"You know what's really amazing? Really amazing is that I loved him, that I still do. Can you believe that? Most of it I did for him, right from the start. Can you believe that?"

He talked at length about his relationship with Holmes. He had been mesmerized from the start by the policeman's compulsive duplicity. His love of sheer cunning was boundless, his secrecy impenetrable. His only weakness was to boast to his male lovers about the cleverness with which he was able to lead two lives. He liked them to know that he'd beaten the system, that he, in his words, was one snake that did crawl out of the pit. And who could deny it? He was at one and the same time the most successful criminal and policeman in London. The young Thirst had been overawed.

"He loved telling me about the way he used you, James—he couldn't believe how naive you were, prosecuting all those drug barons while the biggest of the lot was sitting behind you in court. He thought it was hilarious the way he got you to prosecute by hyping it up about the evil of criminals, me in particular. Of course I never told him that I'd known you in another lifetime, so to speak."

With a slow, delicate gesture, he put the gun down on the low shelf in front of the gearstick.

"I wanted you to save me from him. I wanted you to be my escape—you and Daisy—but you failed. And now you'll have to do your duty, because I'm not going back to prison—no way."

I grabbed the gun and transferred it to my right hand. He put his head back on the headrest and smiled.

"Now all I have to do is make you kill me."

"Why should I?"

"Because I'm the part of you you've been keeping in the deep freeze all these years—ever since your mum died, remember?"

"I'm not responsible for you, I never have been. Thinking that I am, or anyone is—that's part of your problem."

He raised a weary hand. "Don't. I know that catechism in words of ten syllables. Let's just say I'm a mess. Before I met you I was a very ordinary mess. Now, because of you and Daisy and Eleanor and Hogg, I'm a very weird mess. I can tell you everything that's wrong with me in the vocabulary of every social science. I'm very aware, very. And it doesn't help—it just makes the pain worse. I'm an embarrassment to myself—'Oh no, there he goes again, fucking up his life for the ten thousandth time.' That's not what *they* say about me, it's what *I* say about me. I suppose I've learned one thing that almost nobody else ever finds out—I've broken my balls for something that doesn't exist. My own identity. And that's what you've done for me. You and Daisy and the rest. Only you're different, James, there's something about you that won't let you walk away. We're connected, you and me. Just as you had to answer the phone and open the door so you'll have to do the deed tonight. But . . . Did Daisy ever tell you her theory about us being queer together?"

"Oh yes. There's hardly a dysfunction, especially sexual, that Daisy didn't accuse me of at one time or another. I think she fantasized about our having a homosexual affair—I think it turned her on."

"But you never told her the truth?"

"The truth?"

He looked at me incredulously.

"No, I never told her the truth."

He sighed. "No, me neither. I never told anyone we were mates as kids. I couldn't believe my eyes when you turned up that day at Tower Bridge and turned out to be my barrister. You—of all people in the world."

"There was nothing to say. There was a glass wall between us—what could I have done?"

"It was pride with me. I know it was a long time ago, but I have a terrible memory for these things. You cut me off, James—

all of a sudden. You were my first experience of treachery, know that? You were the wildest of all of us, you taught me how to pinch motor scooters. Remember that night when there was just you and me—I was a nipper, but you must have been in your early teens? You showed me how to bump-start a Vespa and we went joyriding all round Camberwell. Then that day on Waterloo Bridge you had the brass balls to act like you'd never seen me in your life before. That was a very weird way to carry on in the circumstances. Thought you'd gone psycho."

I broke out into a cold sweat. My hands were trembling on the wheel, especially the one that also held the gun, and I felt a great inner shuddering as two parts of my mind that had been sealed off from each other for decades came violently together. It was not that I had forgotten my early friendship with Thirst. I had simply never talked about it with anyone, not even him, so that it had had an independent existence for me, like a fantasy.

"Perhaps I *was* psycho, Oliver—I really meant it, you know, what I said. As if I really was another person, with no history."

"You amputated me—the whole gang of us looked up to you. You were Jack the Lad, James—a born villain. Everyone said so. In the street they said you drove your mum to an early death. I could write a case study on you. Talk about guilt-driven. You cut out and left me to inherit your mantle. I've lived the life you were supposed to have. You got away with it—at a price."

"I'm sorry," I said.

"Just tell me one thing. What was it made you turn like that? Your mother's death, that's all?"

I gave a loud involuntary groan. "Not really. I was addicted to pinching motorbikes. One night I took a Norton 750—you remember them? Massive things. It was too big for me. I skidded round a corner, hit a kid, made a dash for it. The next day it was in all the papers. Ten-year-old girl with multiple fractures. Legs, arms, skull, the lot."

Thirst grunted. "But you didn't kill her? Maim her for life?"

"No. She lived. She was none the worse after the bones healed."

"Hm," Thirst said. "You must have been more squeamish than you let on." He pondered for a moment, frowning. "Hey, just a minute—" He peered at me through the gloom. "Oh, James! Oh, Jimmy old son! I've just tumbled to what you're so coyly trying to say. I remember it now. It was in all the local papers. 'Child's Body Smashed by Brute on Motorbike'—that sort of thing. There were pictures of a kid done up in bandages from head to foot. Yeah, I remember, Norton 750. But, James, Fred Snark went down for that! He was one of us, only a good bit older and not very bright. He was just turned seventeen, so he got prison instead of borstal. He was like a brother to you, James. After all that publicity they threw the book at him. Grievous bodily harm, reckless driving, theft, driving without a license. With his record, they gave him some consecutive sentences. The kid was all recovered in four months, but he got five years. Fred know you did it?"

I swallowed. "No. He never knew. I stood outside Camberwell Green police station every day, willing myself to go in and confess, but I couldn't. Just never had the guts. I was pretty young, really. Just over fourteen. In the end I told my mum. She told my dad. I was sure he'd make me go and confess. That's what I wanted him to do, I suppose. Instead he got a relation of his who was a prison warden to give me a talking to. It was a graphic description of life in gaol. Male rape, syphilis, enforced fellatio, murder, beatings, calculated humiliation and degradation, the lot. This guy didn't pull any punches. When he'd finished, my dad made a speech to me in front of him. It was the only time I ever heard my old man get eloquent. He said something like: 'If you let your best friend rot in gaol for a crime you committed, you're the lowest form of human life, no better than scum, not fit to lick the boots of an honest man.' Then he paused. I'll never forget. It was the most brilliant rhetorical trick I ever witnessed. 'But if you confess, they'll be so pissed off with you for making fools of them, they'll throw the book at you. They'll have your number. You'll spend the rest of your life in and out of prisons. You'll destroy your mother's life, my life, and your own. So: you're in such a fucking hurry to grow up, now you've got yourself a man-size dilemma. It's a choice we all have to make in the end. Be a bastard or be a sucker.'"

Thirst grunted again. "Fred Snark thought the world of you. You know what? You made the right choice for *you*, but me, I'm the sucker sort. If it'd been my best mate, I would have confessed. No wonder you've always stuck with women. Male love scares you. You betray it."

Confession has its own momentum. I hurried to finish. "A few days later my old man came home with a pile of books and an exam syllabus. Told me that since I'd decided to be a bastard I might as well become a lawyer, and if I didn't get my head down and work my arse off, he was going to confess for me. I suppose I should thank him. I became very driven, knowing I was a shit for life."

"So it was nothing to do with your mother's death?"

"It was one of those weird twists of fate. My mother didn't give a damn about Fred Snark. As far as she was concerned, he was just another born loser who would have done time one way or another, whatever happened. She was just relieved her son was going straight at last. I'd never seen her so happy. Then she got one of those viruses that attack the central nervous system, died in four days. Of course, when you're young you feel guilty anyway. And my father always blamed me for her death, told everyone it was my fault, which didn't help."

Thirst was quiet for a long moment. He twisted in his seat, spoke in a whisper. "Daisy said that to survive, you put one whole part of yourself on ice. Overcontrolled, that was her favorite phrase for you. She said my agony was a relief compared to the vacuum inside of you. She said we were like two halves of the same person. I had the bits that in you weren't functioning."

"But she didn't stay with your half, either."

An empty laugh. "No. In the end she needed to be idolized. Only you could do that. Programming from her daddy, I suppose. I always knew she was an idle, horny little bitch. She was never going to be my virgin princess. Are you ready now?"

"I'm not going to kill you, Oliver."

"Don't worry—I'll make it easy for you."

He was complacent about his power to make me kill him. I was afraid that he might be right. I wanted, above all, to escape from that confined space.

"I'm leaving the keys in the car," I said. "You can drive it away, steal it, go home, go to prison. Drive it off a cliff—I don't care, just get out of my life. Just get out of my fucking life for good."

I stepped out into the deserted street, a dull, squalid London street. I had driven blindly and now did not know where I was. I started walking. It was impossible, somehow, to leave the gun in the car, or anywhere else for that matter. I held it in my right hand and hardly noticed it. Then I heard his footsteps behind me.

"Stick like shit, don't I?"

I didn't answer but kept walking.

"There's one thing you've left out, James—one thing that can reach you. She was great that night when her mother died. So soft and seductive. Did everything I wanted, and believe me, I made her do things you'd never dared to ask her to do. Of course it was even better when we were married. She loved being my slave. Even if she didn't love it, I made her do it anyway. I remember once at a party I made her go down—like this, James—on her knees, in front of all the blokes, and I took out my cock—"

He was kneeling in the street some five yards behind me. I turned on my heel and took the few steps back. With as much malice aforethought as is possible to cram into a split second, I aimed the gun. My index finger whitened on the trigger. I felt no compunction about killing him, but after a couple of seconds my finger relaxed. I let my hand drop.

"You're probably lying," I said. "Anyway, I just don't hate you that much."

He lowered his eyes. "So do it for love, old son," he said gruffly.

In what seems to me when I think of it (as I still do every waking hour) to have been a casual reflex, I raised my hand again and this time pulled the trigger. He fell back instantly. At his feet I dropped the gun that he'd thoughtfully taped to protect me.

The last few paragraphs were now showing on the screen.

> You're a wicked man, George. In biblical times they would have said that you were unclean. You have had congress with evil. You must have sweated blood when Thirst was killed.
>
> You knew right away that it was me, for the same

reason that Feinberg now knows and Carlford knows, even if you hadn't guessed from tapping his phone. That young boy saw my car. He couldn't read the number, and he was too far away to see if I was a man or a woman, but he was just the right age to recognize and remember the latest Jag. You needed at all costs to close the file on Thirst before you retired. You could not afford to have some ambitious young detective ferreting out unexplainable coincidences.

Above all you could not risk a prosecution against Thirst's murderer, especially not after your visit to my house that Sunday. I guess a part of you must have relished that visit. The Someone Big must have been watching you carefully for you to go to the length of wiring yourself up and using that radio van so that detection could be seen to be done. That pathetic old van with its two bored operators trapped inside was probably the only joke we've shared, you and I. There you were—interviewing the man you knew to be guilty, anxious that I not confess—and there I was threatening to tell all on tape if you pressed me too hard, and poor Vincent as usual not quite knowing what was going on.

When I let you know that Thirst had told me all about you, you hit upon the idea of prosecuting Daisy. And then when it finally dawned on you that I would confess rather than let Daisy go to prison, you hit upon one of the cleverest, maddest ideas of your career—a prosecution against Daisy which would fail, but fail in such a way that the world and Scotland Yard would believe her guilty and close the file on Thirst, so you could enjoy your retirement in peace. That's why you briefed Nigel Monkson. Why you wouldn't allow that boy to give evidence. Why you delayed the trial so that Daisy was seven months pregnant when it started. But it didn't work, George. I'm guilty. I can prove it.

Daisy looked up. I stepped over to the computer and pressed some keys. The legend DELETED flashed up on the screen. I knelt beside her chair, took her hand, kissed it.

"I really was going to confess, if they'd convicted you. You know that, don't you? I made sure George knew that; that's why I kept waving those papers at him. He knew exactly what I meant."

She waited a long moment before speaking. "Well, it worked, didn't it? His crazy stratagem? You wrote the letter in case it failed, but it worked, like all his other schemes. I honestly don't think a woman would ever be so demonically cunning. How does he live with himself? How does he sleep?"

"According to Thirst, he's a connoisseur of fine drugs. Very disciplined about it—administers to himself exactly the dose he needs for the effect he requires. Sleep isn't a problem. Never touches the hallucinogens, of course. Favors cocaine."

She shuddered. "And the world really is run by men like him?"

I left the room to fetch a large glass of Armagnac to steady my nerves. When I returned I patted her large belly. "Well, we came through, didn't we?"

She didn't respond.

"I think relationships are very weird," she said after a while. "You know why I did all that—went through that trial and so on? You know what kept me going all these months?"

"Guilt. Love, I hope. That sort of thing."

"Not really. Love doesn't keep you going—it disappears when things get tough, I now realize. This is the first day for months I've been able even to think about loving you. During the trial I simply hated you. Mostly what kept me going was machismo. We've been dumb to think that only men have machismo—women have it, too, right? It's the only way anyone keeps going. A kind of grim bravado, the quiet satisfaction of doing something real, of playing for real stakes. I didn't really think I had to gain your forgiveness for sleeping with Oliver that time; that was just a game you made me play. It was the most natural thing in the world for me to seek comfort from a friend the night my mother died; you were an asshole for making such a fuss about it. I went down on my knees to you not because I was wrong but because I wanted you back. I was doing it for love, I mean Love with a capital *L,* not for the sake of your little ego. You weren't big enough for love, so I married Oliver. But what stayed in my mind, all through the years, was your mockery of me. The way you would always say that I never had the grit to really make anything happen, I was all hot air. I suppose deep down I thought you had a point. I got sick of my own wimpishness. I thought being married to Oliver would cure me of all that, but actually Oliver was pretty pathetic—he spent more or less the whole of his life feeling sorry for himself. Self-pity helped him justify everything, even beating me up.

"I wanted to have my name carved on a rock somewhere, somewhere secret maybe, but somewhere hard. I'm not smart like you, but what I've got, when it comes down to it, is nerve. That was the side to Oliver that I liked. You thought I married him out of revenge while I really loved you all the time. Partly true, but I also loved the amazing audacity that emerged when he wasn't feeling too sorry for himself. You know who I was being all through that trial? I was being Oliver, and I was doing it better than he would have because I didn't let self-pity get in the way and I didn't blow it all by showing off as a man probably would have done. I learned something, too. It's possible that breaking the law in a big way is the only real thing left to do in this country full of wankers. Well, it worked—I got my man off a murder rap so he can be a father to this child."

She looked at me and laughed.

She seemed happy but distant, as if she did not want to be contaminated by me.

42

We went through a bad patch soon after the child was born. We were married by then, and my practice had gone to pieces. More or less overnight, the bar decided that I was a spent force with dangerous connections. It was not just the trial itself; I suspected someone of gossiping. Perhaps Feinberg, more likely Carlford. They both knew I had killed Thirst, and Carlford was too eminent, rich, and old to care if he hurt me. I think the whole case had amused him and provided him with a source of stories at dinner parties. Whatever the reason, solicitors stopped sending me work.

It was not the loss of income that shook me, so much as the collapse of identity. I grew increasingly nervous and moody. By the time Oliver was born, I was in a bad way. But it was the change in Daisy that caused my final breakdown.

Nothing had prepared me for the appalling banality of motherhood. My last great dream of love drowned in a tepid baby bath.

Daisy gave her soul to Oliver—he crawled around with it while she watched him with dumb adoration. I'd reluctantly agreed to the name out of a reflex of guilt, as if the life I'd put an end to could be continued through a word, but the magic worked against me in a way I could never have foreseen: he seduced her.

Daisy lost her edge, did not make a good joke for months. Forgot all about the heroism of crime. Her conversation became meticulously mediocre, as if any sharpness might hurt the child. She even smiled sweetly at the small army of nurses, social workers, and doctors apparently necessary for modern motherhood. She professed, all of a sudden, not to be able to understand the wickedness in the world. She read carefully the ingredients list on the outside of food packets, was concerned about the environment, used only prescribed drugs. Quite often she watched children's television in the afternoon, even though Oliver was too young to follow it. She would smile happily at jokes intended for five-year-olds.

Oliver manipulated her. His mewling could call her out of the deepest sleep. And she didn't really like me to hold him. She would wince to see him in the arms of a murderer.

I felt no wish to bond with him; he had taken Daisy away from me more effectively than his namesake ever had. If Daisy suspected that black thoughts tempted me when I was alone with him, she was right.

But I resigned myself to fate. Our son would be brought up by an empty mother and a disappointed father, just like all the other kids. Of all the punishments, that seemed to me to be the least endurable.

I have no idea when it was that Daisy finally realized what I was up to at night. I imagine she had some trouble crediting her own worst fears. The first automobile I pinched was an old Morris Minor. I vomited in the street afterward, but it did me good. I knew then that it was going to become a habit. I assumed, without really thinking about it, that sooner or later Daisy would find out and turn me in. I was amazed the other night when she said that she was coming with me.

It was a Porsche, a red one. I took her to see it a couple of times before I stole it. I wouldn't let her hang around with me at the heist itself, just in case I got caught. The drive off is the dangerous moment. I had her wait in a side street near South Kensington underground station.

We had a lovely ride. She has nerves of steel, Daisy. Afterward, we made love for the first time in months. I know in my bones that our new game is going to bring us together again. I could tell by the shine in her eyes and the wicked jokes she thought up on the way home.